Rachel Dove is a writer and teacher, living in West Yorkshire with her husband, their two sons and their animals. In July 2015 she won the *Prima* magazine and Mills & Boon 'Flirty Fiction' competition. She is also the winner of the Writers Bureau Writer of the Year Award in 2016. She has had work published in the UK and overseas in various magazines and newspaper publications.

Born and raised just outside Toronto, Ontario, **Amy Ruttan** fled the big city to settle down with the country boy of her dreams. After the birth of her second child, Amy was lucky enough to realise her lifelong dream of becoming a romance author. When she's not furiously typing away at her computer, she's mum to three wonderful children, who use her as a personal taxi and chef.

Also by Rachel Dove

A Midwife, Her Best Friend, Their Family
How to Resist Your Rival
A Baby to Change Their Lives
Faking It with the Firefighter

Also by Amy Ruttan

Nurse's Pregnancy Surprise
Reunited with Her Off-Limits Surgeon
Tempted by the Single Dad Next Door
Rebel Doctor's Boston Reunion

Discover more at millsandboon.co.uk.

ONE NIGHT TO TWIN SURPRISE

RACHEL DOVE

SNOWBOUND WITH THE SINGLE MUM

AMY RUTTAN

MILLS & BOON

First published in Great Britain 2025
by Mills & Boon, an imprint of HarperCollins*Publishers* Ltd,
1 London Bridge Street, London, SE1 9GF

www.harpercollins.co.uk

HarperCollins*Publishers* Macken House, 39/40 Mayor Street Upper,
Dublin 1, D01 C9W8, Ireland

ISBN: 978-0-263-32522-5

10/25

FSC www.fsc.org MIX Paper | Supporting responsible forestry FSC™ C007454

This book contains FSC™ certified paper
and other controlled sources to ensure responsible forest management.

For more information visit www.harpercollins.co.uk/green.

Printed and Bound in the UK using 100% Renewable Electricity
at CPI Group (UK) Ltd, Croydon, CR0 4YY

ONE NIGHT TO TWIN SURPRISE

RACHEL DOVE

MILLS & BOON

For Alyssa, Milly and Toby

Love, Auntie Rach

CHAPTER ONE

THE BLAST FROM the past had never looked hotter when he walked right into the middle of her divorce party. Time had been kind to her, but it had worshipped the holy heck out of him. The man was fine, chiselled, muscled. He had an air about him that she hadn't noticed before, a determined stance. His presence took her breath away, and it wasn't the first time she'd almost hyperventilated around him—which was a good thing, because it meant she was adept at hiding her reaction. Her friends, who were both quite well-lubricated by now, were looking at him with open mouths.

'Hi,' he said, and she was right back there to the time when she'd first heard those silky tones. His eyes lasered on hers as he added, 'Can I buy you a drink?'

Liv and Bron were wide eyed on her periphery, but she was stuck, staring at Colton.

'Er, yes. Ladies, this is…'

She'd been about to introduce him, wondering how much to divulge of their history, when he cut in.

'The guy who really wants to buy you a drink.' He turned that easy smile on the other two women at the table. 'Sorry for cutting into your evening, ladies.'

'No! No,' Bronwyn jumped up from the table, half-dragging Liv out of hers. 'That's fine, because we were just going to dance, weren't we, Liv?'

Liv was trying to stay on her heels, looking at Neve as if she wanted to say something. All she managed was an, 'Oof!' when Bronwyn jabbed an elbow into her ribs before pulling her to the small dance floor, leaving the two of them alone.

'So.' He smirked. 'What would you like to drink?' He picked up one of the shot glasses, sniffing. 'Tequila?'

'Oh, no. Just a vodka tonic, please.'

'No problem. Wait there, okay?'

He headed to the bar, and she looked at the girls, who were dancing but obviously watching proceedings. Liv mouthed, 'What the hell?' at her, and Bronwyn gave her a thumbs-up. When he came back, drinks in hand, he took the seat next to her, bringing his knees in close, till they brushed against hers.

'Thanks for the drink, stranger.' She meant it as a joke, but he didn't even flinch.

'You're welcome, stranger. Looks like you're having a good night. I thought I might just be able to make it better.'

'Oh, yeah?' She tried to act normal, but her blush gave her away. 'How?'

'How? Well, I guess that's up to you. All I know is I saw the most beautiful woman I've ever seen and wanted to come and talk to her.' His full lips parted. 'Tell me something…'

She looked into his eyes and thought back to her chat with the girls, and the fact she was at her divorce party and he was here. She'd thought of him often over the years, wondered what he was up to, but she'd always shut those wonderings down pretty quickly because of who they were to each other. Tonight, she felt different—wilder, freer than before. He'd taken her playful talk in his stride, as if he knew she didn't want to talk about the past. Tonight, she wanted to live in the present, be that carefree woman, just for once.

'How about we don't?' she breathed, leaning closer, the slight buzz from the tequila buoying her confidence. 'Just for tonight, why don't we just be two strangers, enjoying each other's company?'

For a long moment, he didn't speak. He watched her, as he used to, before lifting the glass of whisky to his lips and draining it in one long swallow, then he got to his feet. Neve's gut plummeted, then his lips were at her ear.

'I have my bike with me. If you want to enjoy my company a little more, I'll wait outside for you. No talking about anything you don't want to. Just us, together. If you're not there in fifteen minutes, I'll understand.'

His lips brushed against her cheek, making her shiver, and then he was gone. Ten minutes later, she'd waved goodbye to her friends, who were by now inebriated enough to believe the fib she'd told them about a waiting taxi, and then she was pushing through the doors.

He was leaning against his motorcycle, a bike helmet in his hands. His eyes lit up when he saw her standing there. The warm night air did nothing to deter the goosebumps from pebbling across her skin. She wanted this—tonight. She wanted one night. One night when she didn't think about the opinions of others, of what they might think. When she did what she wanted, for once. To start living the new life she had fought so hard to put back together after Brett had left. When she met Colton at the bike, he stood tall.

'Hello, sweetheart,' he murmured, running his thumb along her cheek. 'Where do you want to go?'

'My place,' she told him, taking the helmet from his grasp as his eyes hooded before her. 'I'll show you the way.'

CHAPTER TWO

SHE BARELY HEARD the bike at first. She'd stopped listening for it in the two months since she'd last heard its throaty rumble. She was too busy leaning against the countertop in the bathroom, trying to pull herself together for work. The low thrum from outside didn't even register till she heard the gravel chips on her drive, and then she couldn't hear anything else.

Not now. Seriously? This cannot be happening. Slamming the bathroom door behind her, she skidded across the wooden floor on her socked feet and hid behind the curtain of the window that looked out. Heavy boots mirrored her thudding heart as they ascended her stairs, and then the doorbell went.

With a shaky hand, she pulled aside the curtain, just enough to peek out one eye. Dr Colton Anderson was standing on her front doorstep, looking like a snack in his bike leathers. He appeared as casual as they came, hand on one hip while the other raked through his bike-helmet hair. He had no right to look that good, standing there as if he was ready to go for round two if she let him. Which would not be happening. Not now, or ever.

'Leave, please,' she muttered under her breath, and his head cocked. as if he'd heard her. His eyes fell right on her at her peeking spot. She let go of the curtain like it was a hot potato and froze rigid, listening: nothing; no movement from her porch. She prayed she'd hear the bike depart any minute, that he'd think she'd already left for work.

Billy had dropped her off last night, after she'd taken her clunky old car to his garage the night before. She'd been planning to get a car to work, not wanting to put the girls out by swinging by to pick her up. Something to thank her lucky stars for now, because the explaining she'd have had to do, having a helicopter medic on her doorstep, would have been greater than her reluctance to ask her friends for help. She'd take the usual ribbing from them later with relish, after the full-blown panic attack her morning had been so far.

Her stomach roiled again, and she rubbed at her tummy, willing herself not to projectile-vomit again and give up her hiding spot. Her phone rang on the counter, and she groaned inwardly as her ring tone sang out her favourite song—the one she'd put on her phone after the divorce to cheer herself up. It was all female rage and, unfortunately, it was on loud.

'I hear your phone in there, curtain twitcher. You going to open the door, or not?'

'Rats,' she breathed, uncurling herself from her wall-hugging spot and reaching for the door handle. His amused smirk was the first thing she saw, closely followed by the phone in his hand lit up with her name on the screen. He ended the call and pocketed it, taking a step closer but not moving a toe over the threshold.

'What are you doing here, Colton?'

His brows narrowed for half a second, before he righted himself. 'Well, I bumped into Billy from the garage last night, and he mentioned your car was in the shop. Thought you might need a ride.' Stooping down, he picked up a cardboard container, taking one of the coffees and holding the other out to her. 'I brought coffee too, since I thought you might have this reaction.'

Oh no. Her nemesis, holding out her current kryptonite. It had been the damn coffee that had tipped her off about her…situation in the first place, and now she was trying not to gag at the smell. Especially when he was looking right at her, as though daring her to make the next move. What was she going to do—slam the door in his face? *I mean, I could, but…*

'So, can I come in? I can wait for you to finish getting ready on the doorstep, if you don't mind the neighbours gawking.'

He tilted his head in a boyish way she couldn't help but find cute—which annoyed her even more. It reminded her of their night together, the way he'd let her lead the night. Till they'd got to her bedroom: he'd taken the reins then, taking her apart in his arms. Oh, his arms…thick, strong, protective.

Stop it. She couldn't have him here, especially not now. The urge to stick her head in the toilet bowl and then ring in sick was strong, and that was bad enough. She never cried off work. Even through the worst days of Brett and her, she'd still been at work on time, giving one hundred percent, even when her heart had felt as if it was flatlining in her chest.

She replayed the remark about her neighbours Colton

had made and started. Mrs Chivers was a bit of a lookyloo, and she was a friend of Brett's mum to boot. Poking her head past Colton to see if the older woman was suddenly out pruning her already well-maintained bushes, she was hit with the smell of the coffee again and his cologne, and her stomach gave up the pretence of being nonchalant.

'Oh no…!' She lurched, thrusting the coffee at Colton and dashing for the bathroom. Thank God for ground-floor bathrooms. 'I'm going to throw up again!'

'Again? Neve, are you sick, sweetheart?'

She answered with a slam of the bathroom door, dropping to her knees and wrenching up the rest of the water she'd managed to get down earlier.

Sweetheart? Another memory flashed through her mind. Him murmuring the same word in her ear as he pushed into her. *You're so perfect, sweetheart. You feel so good.* She retched again, throwing her hand over the bowl to steady herself.

'Neve? Are you okay?'

'Yes!' she managed to squeak, wiping at her mouth and dropping her clammy forehead back on her forearm. She felt so drained, shaky. 'I'm fine. I'll get a taxi to work, I don't need…'

He opened the door and strode right in. *Fan-blinking-tastic.* He'd rocked her world a few short weeks ago, and now he probably smelled her puke. If that didn't get him off her doorstep and out of her life, nothing much else would.

'You're not getting a taxi, Neve. You're sick. What can I do for you?'

What can you do for me? Hmm. I think you've done enough. Job done.

'Nothing.' She lifted her head high enough to shake it. 'I'm okay. It's just a little bug, that's all.'

'Yeah?' His sceptical tone wasn't lost on her. She went to reach by the sink for a fresh wash cloth, but he beat her to it. 'You don't look well. It came on a bit sudden for a bug.'

He flicked on the hot tap, wetting the cloth, and she watched the moment his eyes fell on the counter. Her heart sank into her chest as she saw him blink twice at the pregnancy test she'd left sitting there—the one with two pink lines sitting pretty in the result window. His hands stilled for a beat, and then it was as if he'd rebooted himself. *Had he not seen it?* She couldn't look at him as he turned off the tap and squeezed out the cloth before sinking to his knees next to her.

'Here,' he rumbled, his voice so soft she barely heard it. When she didn't do anything but stare at his cheek, his fingers moved. Lifting her chin so she met his eye, he ran the cloth over her forehead, wiping at her brow before moving down her face. Once her eyes locked with his, she couldn't do anything. He'd rebooted and she'd glitched. She searched his face for something, anything; the only thing she could decipher was concern. 'That better?'

Pushing her frazzled brain to move, she nodded once and, taking the cloth, wiped at her mouth.

'Er...yeah. Thanks.'

He pressed his lips together as his eyes dropped to her mouth and roved lower down her uniform-clad body. The space contracted to nothing around them as they sat there. They'd been closer than this, but she'd never felt so scrutinised, so naked, before him: *vulnerable.* She hated it with every fibre of her being. She looked after people, not the other way round. It made her bristle even through the panic she was trying her best to hold at bay.

'I'll be fine. Thanks for the coffee, and the offer of a ride, but—'

'What made you sick just now—the smell of the coffee or me?'

The random question threw her for a loop, and the truth came flying out of her mouth. 'The coffee.'

He nodded, standing up and leaving the room.

What? Was that it? She scrabbled to her feet, waiting for the inevitable sound of her front door closing. It didn't come. He was in the kitchen when she stepped out, pouring both coffees down the sink and swilling out the cups.

He nodded to the cabinets when he saw her watching. 'Got any crackers in?'

Padding across to him, she pulled out a packet from a cupboard behind him and started to nibble on one. As soon as she tasted the salt, she sighed in relief.

'Better?' He delved in her fridge now, pulling out a bottle of water and sliding it across the counter towards her.

'A little,' she agreed, feeling as though she was being handled but letting it slide. Her stomach had been responsive to these crackers for the past few days, so she'd stocked up. Any minute now, he'd leave. Looking at the clock, she noted that would give her a good hour to die of shame, pull herself together and get to work on time.

He can't have seen the pregnancy test. She didn't know how to feel about that. Right now, she didn't have a clue how to feel about anything. One part of her was thrilled, but the logical part, the realist portion of her, was fast recognising that this was going to be tough—life-changing tough—and that was without the complication of the man standing in her kitchen.

Don't panic, she told herself, wanting to hold it together, if only long enough to not be under the scrutinous gaze of Colton. She needed to act normal, get to work and figure things out when she could hold a coherent thought. If she could get through her shift without vomiting, she'd consider that a win for today.

'The crackers help.' She shot him a half-smile, trying to dislodge the look of concern from his features.

'Good, drink the water too.' He made no move to leave.

She frowned but threw him a nod. 'I will. I'm good now, honestly. You can go.' His reply to that was to pull out two stools from the breakfast bar and nod to one as he lowered his bulky form to the other. 'Colton, seriously…'

'Would you have told me, if I hadn't come back to town?'

She almost choked on her cracker. Swallowing it down, she took a deep breath. 'You saw the test.'

'I saw the test. What I'm wondering is whether you would have told me. You gave me your number, but didn't take mine. I called, you never answered. My messages went unread. Would you have made me a part of this?'

'Colton, I haven't thought that far. I just found out half a second before you showed up. I've never been regular; I've missed periods before so I didn't question it. I was tired, sure—but work has been busy. I figured I was just a little run down.'

She had felt tired, but that was after the divorce and moving house, all while maintaining her job. She'd thought, *hey, this is 40.* Missing a period wasn't unusual at all; she'd figured it was just another sign she wasn't going to be a mother. Not that she could tell him that, especially not in light of this morning's revelation.

Keep it simple, Neve. This is complicated enough.

'I had symptoms, I guess, but I didn't want to believe it. Couldn't believe it.' Even in the store the night before, she'd laughed at herself for buying the test in the first place, telling herself it was more likely to be the menopause starting than a baby. 'I never thought that this would happen.'

He didn't say anything, but she saw the clouded look in his eyes. Realising she hadn't answered what he'd asked, she bit her lip. 'Yes, I would have told you. I don't know how or when, but I would have told you. It's only fair.'

She hadn't expected him to drop by the second she'd peed on the stick, that was for sure. She hadn't even thought he was anywhere near Swallow Falls. He was a doctor but, rather than staying in one place, he chose to be a helicopter medic. His home was in the skies, not in bricks and mortar. She wanted to ask him why he was back in town, but after what he'd just found out she held her tongue. Carrying his child didn't give her access to his life any more than him to hers. She was the one who'd caused this, throwing caution to the wind and living out a night of fantasy she'd never imagined realising.

Well, it's realised now, Neve. 'I'm still in a bit of shock, to be honest.'

She didn't miss the slight drop in his shoulders when she spoke, but didn't stop to think what that meant. None of this meant anything, right? It was just some big laugh the universe was having at her expense. She still felt as if she owed him an explanation, though. He hadn't asked for this either.

What a mess. The one time she'd veered off the track, and she'd fallen right off a darn cliff into another world. 'It's yours, by the way. I haven't been with anyone else. I don't make a habit of doing that. The night in the bar? That was a first for me.'

His eyes darkened. 'I never questioned that, Neve; and I know it's mine.' He looked away for the first time, and she felt she could finally breathe again. 'Are you...keeping it?'

Awkward. The man had come to give her a ride, and she was derailing his whole blessed life. But she knew the answer. It was the only thing she was sure of. Before she'd even bought the test, she knew what she would do if it was positive. Regardless of how complicated it was, having a baby was something she'd always yearned for. Hell, it had been a major factor in her divorce, and she'd never stopped wanting it.

'Yes. I'm sorry, Colt; I am. But I want you to know

that I don't expect anything from you. This is my fault. I honestly didn't think I could get pregnant; I should have taken you up on the protection when you offered. It's down to me, and I accept that. I'll accept it if you want to leave and not be part of this. I won't even tell people who the father is—'

'No,' he practically growled. 'It's mine, Neve. I don't expect you to hide that, and I don't run away from my responsibilities either. I don't know what you want in this, but I know I want to be there, for everything, if you'll let me.'

'Colt, you can't know that—you just found out!'

'So did you,' he countered. Moving off his stool, he came to kneel in front of her and, Lord save her, it was a sight she didn't need in her head. Her brain automatically replayed him on his knees before her that night, a lot more naked and a lot less…tense.

'You know you want to have my baby; why shouldn't I feel the same?'

'Oh.' She pushed at his shoulders, trying to gain some kind of equilibrium. Her lady parts weren't quite as panicked as the rest of her. 'I don't know; the fact that you're Brett's friend, the fact that it was a mistake or that I'm practically a stranger? We were playing strangers that night and now look what happened! I don't know—take your pick!'

He hadn't moved a muscle, despite her attempts. He stood tall, leaning over her so close she could smell him again, smell his cologne. *Yep, it was definitely the coffee.* Her horny, pregnant body was definitely not rejecting the scent of her baby daddy.

'Sleeping with you was not a mistake, Neve, so I don't want to hear that come out of your mouth again. I'm shocked about this, sure, but I'm not unhappy about it. And as for Brett? I haven't spoken to the guy in years, and I don't plan to.' Something flashed across his face and his jaw flexed. 'Do you still love him? Is that it?'

'No!' she practically screamed at him. The thought of still loving Brett made her want to retch all over again. 'I don't care about Brett; I haven't in a long time.' The fight left her in that moment, and she deflated on her stool. 'I just don't know what to think, Colton. I only recently got divorced; I was celebrating it that night. I was still finding my feet being single. We're not exactly friends, and you didn't even seem to like me when I was with Brett. To be honest, I was pretty shocked you even approached me at the bar.'

Well, that made him flinch. His chest jumped as though her words were knife blades. His jaw was so tight now she was amazed he managed to bite out, 'I liked you well enough, sweetheart, and I'm here for this, for whatever you want me to do.'

His eyes narrowed to slits. 'I knew what you needed that night, and I was more than willing to play along. As for your ex? Brett is not part of our child, he's in the past.' He ran his thumb along her bottom lip, and she practically shuddered at the contact. This kind of chemistry was going to be hard to hide from people as her pregnancy progressed. If she acted like this now, how was she going to keep it together when he was around her as her pregnancy developed?

It wouldn't stay a secret for long. Being discreet at the Outback Bar had worked, but they'd soon find out in this small town. Bronwyn and the rest of the girls would sniff it out like a pig did truffles in ten minutes flat. They would put two and two together in a heartbeat even if she didn't tell the truth. They'd seen him in the bar that night. The first thing they were going to ask was why they weren't together; why she was having a baby with a man who she wasn't involved with. One who wouldn't live in Swallow Falls with them.

Colton was a wanderer. He moved from contract to contract, never staying in the same place for too long. He'd done so ever since they'd parted ways after they'd all qualified, before she'd got married to Brett. She didn't even know where Colton worked now. He would leave, just as he always did, and she would be fodder for the town's gossips once again. Poor, barren Neve—knocked up by a fly-by-night helicopter medic and left holding the baby she hadn't been able to give her husband. She could practically see the headlines.

Colton snapped her out of it, his hand cupping her jaw to lift her face to those stupidly mesmerising eyes again. Eyes that years ago had scowled at her across the room many times, when she'd first been with Brett. They looked so different now, as though they were wide open and saw every infinitesimal part of her.

'Tell me what's going on in that head of yours, sweetheart.' His brows lowered, as if something new and distasteful had occurred to him. 'Do you not want me to be part of this? Not want to tell people?' His grip tightened just a fraction but he didn't look as if he was quite in control or even aware of it. 'I'm not ashamed you're pregnant, Neve. The question is, are you?'

Jackpot. The million-dollar question. She didn't want to feel like this but, since those two lines had confirmed what her nurse brain already suspected, she hadn't had a second to process anything. And now she never would, because he knew—and he was saying all the things she should want to hear, right? She didn't have much experience in this situation but having a man who'd given her the best night of her life say he was there to help with the resulting child was a good thing, wasn't it?

Except she knew Colton's type, or thought she did. He had done a pretty good job of surprising her since she'd set eyes on him in that bar. She just…hadn't had this on this year's bingo card, that was all—none of this. She'd wanted an adventure and, well, she'd got one. One that would take up the next eighteen years of her life, and beyond.

'Neve, answer me, please. I have no idea what's churning around in that pretty head of yours.'

'I… I just need a minute.' He didn't stop her when she clambered off the stool. The loss of his hand on her face left her feeling oddly cold, and she wrapped her arms tightly around herself as she looked at the clock on the wall. 'Shoot, I'm going to be late for work.'

'Screw work.' Colton rebuffed her. 'Tell them you're sick. We'll be an hour or two later, that's all.'

'No, I can't do that. We're short-handed as it is, and a medic down.' She walked over to the door, pulling it open for him. She couldn't bring herself to say the words she needed to get him to go. 'I'll see you later, okay?'

'Nope.' He shrugged, throwing her a defiant look as he passed her. 'I brought my spare helmet; I'll still take you to work. I'll drop you off on the damn corner if you're bothered about people seeing us together. Get your stuff; I'll be out front.'

His body was practically vibrating with tension but, just when he reached the door, he spun on one foot, grabbing a few packets of crackers out of her cupboard before striding off to his bike. From the doorway she watched him stash them in his bag. As he slung one leg over the bike, he saw her standing there. 'It's safe, Neve. I wouldn't do anything to put you in danger.' His lips pressed together. 'I won't ruin your life more than I already have, trust me. For what it's worth, I've got you, sweetheart.' He put on his helmet, stopping their conversation short with a snap of his visor as he shielded himself from her.

As she got ready and locked up her house, she played those words over and over in her head. He sounded upset, angry with himself. But he'd said he wasn't unhappy about the baby, so what was the truth? She thought back to the possessive way he'd held her jaw, the way he'd searched her eyes for answers she didn't have yet. This whole thing was a huge mess, and as she headed to the bike, and Colton, she couldn't help but think that somehow she was missing the complete puzzle. All she had was a few pieces, rattling around in the box.

The second she reached him, he got off the bike. His arms were around her waist before she could let out a yelp, and he placed her on the seat. He showed her the pins where her feet should go, holding out the helmet for her. It looked brand-new, a purple stripe running along the edges, matching his older looking one. The one he'd given her to wear the night he'd got her pregnant. She couldn't help but side-eye him.

'Bought it this morning,' he muttered, not meeting her eye. 'For you.' She didn't say anything, the odd relief of knowing no other woman had worn it before her adding another piece of the puzzle to the box. She held her breath as he slid onto the seat in front of her, reaching for her arms and wrapping them around his torso.

'Hold on tight, sweetheart. I'll take it slow.'

Words to kill a horny pregnant woman, if ever she'd heard them. Being back on this bike, clinging to his taut body, had her queasy stomach replaced by a soaring libido. Something about this man made her feel seen, bold.

Brett hadn't been the one to make her heart beat faster for a long time. Trying for a baby together unsuccessfully had broken them, but more than that, it had knocked her confidence. Knowing that he'd given up on them when it had become apparent that it was her who couldn't start their family had hurt but, more than that, it had made her realise that she'd wasted time on a man who hadn't been right for her; the type of man who wouldn't fight for her, for them. She hadn't been enough for him without the ability to give him a child.

A child she was now going to have, and hadn't planned for. Her forties were to have been her time to rediscover herself, and she hadn't wanted to waste a second of her new life. The night with Colton was supposed to have been the first part of that. She'd wanted a night with a man who she could trust not to hurt her but to make her feel passion, want and need. A man who would give her what she wanted and needed, and want nothing more from her when the sun broke through the clouds the following morning.

When he'd walked into that bar and spoken to her, she'd seen the desire in his eyes, and one thought had rung out in her head louder than the doubts about him not liking her, about his connection to Brett and about the fact that she'd never gone to a bed with a man for just one night. That thought was that she wanted him.

She loved the way he hadn't taken his eyes off her, how he'd come home with her and how he'd treated the whole night as though it were his last night on earth. He'd not only rocked her world but had made her feel more like herself than ever before. The haughty, aloof man she'd known before was amplified—intense, brooding but caring too. He'd just taken everything in his stride and taken care of her without blinking.

A lot of men would have seen that positive pregnancy test and run for the hills. But Colton was still here. For now, at least. In the back of her mind, she knew that she needed to remember that. She was in shock, her hormones were raging and any stupid steps now would only make things worse in the long run. One man she'd thought she knew well had left her because she couldn't give him a baby. There was no reason to think that giving Colton a baby he'd never signed up for would be any different an outcome.

Don't confuse him being kind for caring more than he does. She had to think about how he felt, being ambushed like that. He'd never even said why he was here. She felt awkward about asking now. Did he want to talk to her about something? Had he felt more since the night they'd spent together? She certainly had. He'd been on her mind for weeks, even before she'd started to suspect that he'd left her with more than a flutter in her heart.

It didn't change anything, though. The fact was, she wouldn't have contacted him if not for the baby. It was too complicated, and she wasn't looking for complications. *Hadn't been,* she corrected herself. Turned out her forties were going to be different from anything she could have imagined.

She clung to him the whole way there. She wondered to herself whether the Neve from a year ago would recognise this new woman, being driven to work on the back of a motorbike. And, more to the point, would she have been as oddly thrilled as today's Neve, even with everything her morning had entailed?

Neve clung tighter to Colton, needing the contact and deciding to have it, just this once. He would never know; she could blame the ride. Once she got to work, and had a minute to think away from him, she could figure out her next move. For the moment, she just held on tightly. All this, coming from one night when she'd decided to throw caution to the wind.

CHAPTER THREE

'BUSY ONE TODAY on the house calls.' Dr Ferry eyed the trio of nurses over his clipboard. 'Full schedule, so our new flying doctor has requested a nurse to accompany him—show him the ropes. Neve, that okay? As senior nurse, I think you would be best suited to show him our regulars. He's an experienced pilot and fully qualified doctor, so we're lucky to get him, actually. With his experience, he's usually further afield and booked solid.'

What? No, it couldn't be Colton…could it? He would have said, surely? He'd only left her at work half an hour ago. *Yeah, right after he came to my house and I dropped a baby on him.* She hadn't even had to give him directions to work, but that didn't mean it was him, right? He knew where she worked. He was a pilot, too. If he could navigate the air, then he could certainly find the medical centre in a small town without any trouble. He also knew where she and Brett had moved to. It could just be a coincidence. Still, the more she considered the idea, the quicker her heart thumped in her chest.

'Where is he? Do you have a name?' Dr Ferry, bless him, wasn't the best with names. He regularly triple-checked his patient files before he worked on any patients, and she could tell by his face he didn't know. She saved him from looking it up. 'Doesn't matter.' I'll get my supplies.'

Dr Ferry threw her a look of relief. 'He's waiting at the office.'

Bron and Liv, fellow nurses as well as friends, helped her get her stuff together, both eyeing her and flashing each other odd looks.

'What? I know you want to say something.'

'No, we want to know what's wrong with you,' Bron replied, Liv nodding in agreement. 'You've been acting flustered since you walked in.'

'The guy from the divorce party showed up at my house this morning.'

Both women gasped, before speaking at once.

'So romantic!'

'What a creep!'

They rounded on each other, one talking over the other.

'Liv, it's creepy! He spent the night and then left, and that was weeks ago. Months! Why now? Screams "stalker" to me!'

'Bron, you've been watching too much true crime. It's obvious, isn't it? He couldn't stay away; he's been pining for her and decided to come back! Must have been one hell of a night, Neve!'

'Still…' Liv puffed out her cheeks. 'He called her, and she ignored him. Stalker!' She sang the last word, making Neve laugh despite the adrenaline she felt.

'It's neither,' Neve chuckled, her earlier panic melting away as the friends she adored bickered. Might as well rip off the plaster, at least halfway. 'I know him. I've known him a long time.'

They were both united in confusion.

'Eh? Why did you hide that?' Liv asked. 'Why did he?'

'I don't know. When he came to offer to buy me a drink, I called him "stranger", and he played along. I think I was feeling bold that night.'

Bron smirked. 'I knew you wouldn't just take a random stranger home.'

'Why? Cos I'm so boring?' Neve teased. They both rolled their eyes at her.

'No,' Liv retorted. 'It's just not your style. You're a planner, that's all. Nothing wrong with that. So, what did he want?'

'Er…' *Whoops.* She'd walked right into that one. What could she say? She wasn't ready to tell them everything, not yet. She needed a minute to process things, and something Dr Ferry had said still lingered. 'I have to go, ladies; the new doctor's waiting.'

She didn't give them time to protest. She just slung the supplies bag over her shoulder and headed off to the helipad area. At the back of the medical centre, was another office. This one was next to the helipad and hangar. Their service had a helicopter and two small aeroplanes, all kitted out with emergency kit and medical supplies.

Living on the outskirts was beautiful, but dangerous. Tourists came through Swallow Falls on their travels, backpacking around Australia, and many of them were naïve and inexperienced when it came to the rigours of travelling in the more challenging areas. So, in addition to a flying medical service, where their doctors and nurses travelled to homes and businesses to provide medical check-ups and help with emergent situations, they also attended a lot of emergencies. They took back to the clinic whatever they could deal with there, but often they were transport for the hospital in Melbourne too.

They were far more than a GP service to the local residents; they were the medical hub of the community. They did more than serve their residents: they assisted with medical emergencies, providing a vital link between the city and the surrounding areas. Every day was different, from the clinics they offered and the house calls, to the more serious situations. Less than an hour outside of Melbourne, it was another world, and they kept people safe and healthy.

It made work exciting and varied, something that she hadn't experienced as much when doing her training in Sydney. Life working in a hospital wasn't for her. Here, they really had the time to get to know the patients and give them top quality care and attention. They got to see babies grow whom they had helped bring into the world and be there for their cut knees and illnesses. It was home, and she was never bored of the quiet place that was Swallow Falls.

She loved flying too. What better adventure was there then seeing her country from the sky, enjoying the landscape and saving lives? Swallow Falls was beautiful. Even in the cooler temperatures, tourists came to hike the trails and connect with nature. Whenever she'd lived away from the Falls, she'd missed the peace of her home town. She could picture herself at home with the baby: going to the park; sunbathing in the garden; BBQs in her neat, enclosed back yard; taking her child and showing it the sights of the beautiful corner of Australia it would be raised in.

What was unclear in any of those dreams was whether the father would be there as well. Something about the description about the new flying doctor had definitely set her on edge. It couldn't be him, could it?

As she neared the hangar, she got her answer. Colton Anderson was waiting for her by the helicopter passenger door, and his flying jacket bore the medical centre's logo. Her feet barely managed to keep her upright as she approached him.

'Colton, you took the job? When?'

He stepped forward, taking the bag from her shoulder and offering a hand. She didn't take it, which made him huff. He didn't drop it, his eyes narrowing on hers.

'I came to tell you this morning… I got sidetracked.'

'So you knew when you dropped me off at work you were starting today?'

'Yep, but in my defence, I thought Dr Ferry would already have told you. I took the job a while ago. It's why I was in town that night. I'd been to see him then, to discuss the temporary job.'

'So you're here,' she said dumbly, more to herself than him. 'For what, a year?'

'Roundabout. That's the contract.'

'You should have told me!'

‘I tried, Neve—that night. You told me that you didn’t want to talk about anything personal, remember? The whole “strangers in the night” thing?’

‘You went along with that.’

‘I was giving you the chance to turn down my drink without having to tell your friends I used to be friends with your ex; I was trying to be considerate. You kept up the “strangers meeting” thing, and when we got to talking and I tried to bring up the past you shut me down.’ He ran his tongue over his teeth, his gaze darkening. ‘Then you asked me to come back to yours, and I forgot all about the job.’

Neve blushed. ‘Yeah, well, it seemed hot at the time, with the surprise of seeing you there, and the tequila. I thought you were just passing through. I never thought I’d see you again. It’s not like we usually cross paths. More of a “girl in every port” kind of thing.’

The clench of his jaw told her she’d said the wrong thing.

‘I don’t do ports, let alone have women waiting on me. Do you remember seeing me with any women?’

‘Well, no, but…’

‘Let me guess—Brett told you I was that type of guy. He’d know, wouldn’t he?’

She didn’t bother replying. Talking about Brett with Colt felt too weird when she was carrying Colt’s baby. It made her head spin, trying to reconcile the Colton she’d thought she knew back then with the guy standing in front of her now, the man who’d given her an unforgettable night. It was the reason she’d not taken the offer of his phone number in the first place—because some lonely night, she would have remembered how she'd felt in his arms and called him.

She needed to remind herself that, whilst she'd always found him attractive, and had enjoyed the limited chats they'd had back then, it had still only been a one-night thing. He'd taken a temporary job in her town, and they had a lot of grown-up decisions to make. After her divorce, she was more than a little battle-scarred, and it wasn't just herself she had to consider now. The little miracle inside her could still go away, and that was enough to deal with without falling out with Colton too.

'I'm sorry, I just thought it was a flying visit. Pardon the pun,' she quipped.

He didn't laugh. 'Not this time. I'm going to be here for a while. So, if you were planning to keep me as a dirty little secret, the cat might be out of the bag, I'm afraid.'

'It wasn't like that, Colt.' She used the name she'd called him back then.

'No?' He almost looked hopeful, stepping closer. 'So, what was it, then? I've been wondering myself ever since that night.'

'I... I...don't know. I never expected it to happen.'

His jaw clenched.

'That it? Just the result of the tequila, eh? Because I don't get into drunk women's beds, Neve. We were both there, present in the moment. It was a mutual decision to spend the night together.'

'I didn't say it wasn't.' She blanched at the hurt she saw under the anger clouding his features. 'I did—do—

fancy you, Colton. I always thought you were attractive, but you were Brett's friend. It's not like we were close back then. When we were all studying together, we hung out, but never together. We had chats, sure, but nothing like this.'

Though she had thought about him. She was only human, and they had got on when they had talked. He'd just seemed to drop away, into the background, and things had developed with Brett. Which was normal, right? When people fell in love, friends came and went. They had their own lives to live.

'But you wanted me that night.' He was crowding her into the doorway now, her bag already on board. 'Enough to take me home.' He leaned further, and she felt his warm breath on her ear. 'There's nothing in our way now, Neve. Why didn't you take my number when I offered it the morning after? I wanted you to.'

So did I, she wanted to say. The truth was, when she'd woken up that morning with Colton Anderson in her bed, she'd felt too many things: a need to ask him to take her again; panic at who he was to her in the past; a stark confirmation of what she'd pushed down for a while. Because when Brett had first introduced them, she'd noticed him, well and truly. She could still remember the hot, flushed feeling that had come over her when she'd held out her hand to his in greeting, and he'd looked at it and pulled her into a hug. Whenever they were in the same room, her eyes always seemed to find his, and he'd look her way with a detached, cool expression on his face.

But he was Brett's friend. Brett was the one she'd

been falling for, the man with whom she'd spoken about settling down. Colton was the one who'd made her nerve endings sing. Made her feel as if life could be exciting, sexy. He was forbidden fruit, the bad boy. Men like Colton Anderson didn't look twice at safe, organised women like her. He was the opposite of Brett, and she'd wanted that settled life. Work provided the excitement, the adrenaline. That was enough. She needed a partner who would be there to pay the gas bill and change the nappies, not one who wanted to run off and climb some mountain at the drop of a hat.

She knew from Brett that Colton was a different type of man—a solo wanderer who wanted to travel the world and chase thrills. He would never have looked at her twice anyway, the girl from Swallow Falls who wanted to save lives and settle down with family and friends. Her adventures didn't match his. No, it had been a stupid crush, which she'd squashed pretty quickly.

Colton had been around less and less and then, before the wedding, he'd dropped out altogether after he and Brett had had some kind of fallout which had left Brett with a black eye and a tight lip about the details, and she'd been secretly relieved, glad that he wouldn't be standing next to the groom on her wedding day. And then she and Brett had started their lives together, moving back to Swallow Falls and buying their first home. She hadn't remembered the pull of Colton till that night, when he'd appeared at the Outback Bar, and she'd chosen to play out the fantasy of having him.

Because a woman like her didn't get to keep men like Colt—no-one did.

The woman in the bar that night had taken the bull by the horns. It had bolstered her confidence to go for what she wanted, but it looked as if she'd annoyed him in the process. She needed to shut this down before it turned into animosity. She'd blindsided him with the pregnancy test this morning, and he was reacting. He was entitled to his feelings. She certainly had them. They'd both made this situation happen, but she needed to take charge now and navigate the aftermath. Swallow Falls was a small place, especially in terms of people knowing each other's business. Her child didn't deserve to be brought into a world where they would be talked about. The woman in the bar needed to let Nurse Truby take over and regain some control.

'I did want you, but it was just one night, Colton. I didn't think I would see you again, so I didn't take the number. You have a life very different to mine. I didn't expect to get pregnant or have to work with you after.' He was so close, she had trouble getting her words out. 'I just want us to be on the same page with this. I don't want to deal with any more unpredictable chaos. This is not how I expected my new life to start. You being here this morning…it's just a lot to take in.'

He blinked, pulling back. She resisted the urge to tug him back closer. *Head over heart.* She needed to get a grip on that. Knowing he was the father of her baby had somehow made her feral for him. It had to be hormones. *Or the way he held you, made you feel like you were the only woman in the world while he made you come.* She ignored that voice, folding her arms across her chest and stuffing her hands under her arms.

'You feel trapped.' His low voice came out sounding defeated.

'No. If anything, I'm feeling like I trapped you. I said I didn't need contraception, Colton. You trusted me enough not to use a condom and look what happened. I believed you when you said you were clean, but I still should have said yes to you using one. I'm a nurse, for God's sake; I should have known better, but in the moment I just got carried away.'

I wanted nothing between us. Nothing and no-one. 'I never thought I'd be able to conceive. That's on me, and I'm sorry. You might have asked for my number, but you didn't ask for this. And now we work together. I think it's for the best if we keep everything as professional as possible. Dr Barnes will come home in a year's time, and you'll leave. I think working together is going to be awkward enough, without you feeling like you owe me anything.'

'I don't,' he refuted. 'I asked for your number because I wanted it, but when you didn't want mine I—'

'I just didn't want to get into a no-strings thing, that's all. I'm not the type, as hypocritical as that sounds.'

Sighing out a breath, she turned to get into the helicopter when Dr Ferry's voice came over the radio. Colton stilled her by putting his hands on her waist, lifting her onto the seat with ease before shutting her door. When he slid into the pilot's seat next to her, she placed a hand on his thigh.

'I'm sorry for this. It's such a mess.'

His throat worked. 'I chose to come and work here, Neve. I don't regret that night, and I don't feel trapped. Do you want me to be in your life or not?'

She wanted to say yes. *Be in my life! Raise our baby with me! Give me more orgasms!* Of course, she didn't, because the fantasy portion of their relationship had well and truly ended. Reality was screaming at her to get a grip. He was Brett's old friend, they'd be worked together temporarily and then he would leave. Sexy and perfect as he was, he wasn't hers to keep, but he had given her something she had never thought would be possible, so she would focus on that. Her child, and the new chapter of her life that it would bring.

'If you want to be involved with the baby, then of course I want that too. I would like my child to know his or her father. I just think we need to set some boundaries and, now we work together, we'll have to maintain them. This job means the world to me, and I have to be professional.'

'I wouldn't want anything less for you, sweetheart,' he murmured, before leaning over to strap her in. She tried and failed to ignore the combined rush of desire and feelings of safety that rippled through her. He was so protective of her, as if she was incredibly precious cargo. *It's his child he's bothered about, stupid. Down, woman.* 'I'll let you do this your way.'

He strapped himself in, pulling on his headset helmet, and began speaking into the radio to the clinic. For the rest of the shift, he was nothing but professional. It was what she'd asked for but, when she got home that night, she couldn't help but feel sad about it.

She was finally here, close to him again, but everything was so screwed up. As they got out of the helicopter to head to the farmhouse where their final patient waited, he was crawling out of his own skin. He'd been with her all day, watching her deal with their regular patients and greet each one as if they were old friends. Which of course, most of them were. He could see the love she showed them, the way she listened to everything they had to say and laughed with them. He was in awe of her, but the guarded looks she gave him cut into his already battered heart every time.

'Mr Endoy next. You know him?' he asked.

'Yeah. He's a frequent flyer with our service these days. His type-one diabetes has got a lot worse since his wife passed last year. She used to take care of his diet, make sure his insulin levels were monitored. He finds it hard to get to the clinic so we've been monitoring him once a week, and Dr Ferry or one of the nurses also calls him during the week to check on him.'

'No other family?' Colton asked, looking round at the dilapidated farmhouse. It had definitely seen better days, with most of the pens around the property lying empty. 'It doesn't look like a working farm.'

'It's not. They retired three years ago, but didn't want to leave. Joanna loved this place. It would break her heart to see it like this. I know it upsets Alfred, but we tried to talk to him about going into assisted living, and he refused. Because he is of sound mind, there's not a lot we can do, and they never had children, so he's on his own out here. It's getting to the point where the system might need to step in, but we're doing what we can to keep him in his own home. I've been talking with some services about getting him some daily help.'

'But, with his location, it's difficult, right?'

She shot him a sad smile. 'Definitely. It's the down side to living this quiet life, I suppose.' She fell silent as they got to the porch, and he couldn't help it. He brushed his hand against hers just once.

'No-one should be alone. Let's see what we can do today for him.'

That earned him a smile, and he stored it for later.

Knocking, she called out his name. 'Alfred, it's Neve! I'm here with Dr Anderson. Are we okay to come in?'

Nothing. Colton tilted his head towards the door, listening for any signs of movement. Seeing Neve bite her lip, he took charge, knocking again. Still nothing, so he tried the handle and walked in. Neve came round him, heading straight for a room off the hallway. Alfred was sitting slumped in an armchair, the television blaring.

'Alf!' She ran to him, grabbing her kit and checking his pulse. 'It's weak, thready! Alfred, it's Neve, honey! We've come to check on you. Can you hear me?'

All attempts to wake him up failed, and they moved into action. Colton got to work with some fluids in an IV while Neve pricked his finger. The machine beeped with what they already knew: he was dangerously low on insulin, his blood-sugar level sky high.

'Administering insulin now,' she called out, stabbing

the insulin pen into him and checking his vitals again. Colton reached for his radio, alerting the hospital.

'This is Swallow 1-9, we have an incoming patient. Type-one diabetes.' He rattled off the stats for their patient as Neve ran to a medical box in the corner of the room, tutting when she saw the doses of insulin sitting there. 'Will call with an ETA once in the air. Patient is currently unresponsive, insulin and fluids administered.'

'Copy, Swallow 1-9. ETA expected. Hospital aware and ready.'

'He hasn't had his insulin for three days,' Neve told him, her expression grave. 'Administering next dose now.'

She stabbed the pen into his body, and by the time Colton ran back with the equipment needed for transporting him to the chopper Alfred was starting to come round. Old grey eyes gazed back at him as Neve placed an oxygen mask over his face.

'His oxygen stats are in the low eighties.'

Colton nodded, updating the hospital as Neve readied him for transport.

'Hello Mr Endoy, Dr Anderson here. Neve and I are going to take you to hospital now, get you better. You ready?'

The old man nodded, but his hand reached out towards the dresser on the far wall. 'You need something, Alfred?'

Neve followed his line of sight, snapping off her gloves and taking something from one of the shelves. 'Joanna.'

She showed Colton the frame of a happy-looking

couple, standing outside the very building they now stood in. It looked like a different world, and Colton couldn't help the sadness that filled him as they locked up and dashed with Alfred to the helicopter. He didn't want to be like Alfred, sitting alone with his memories, waiting till life was done with him.

As he watched Neve strap herself into the back, he slid into the cockpit and took to the skies. If he was going to end up alone, it wouldn't be from lack of trying. He wanted memories, a lifetime of them, with the woman who was holding Alfred's hand as he clutched the photo frame to his chest. It was Neve or nothing, and he wasn't going down without a fight. Knowing that the night together had created the life growing inside her only strengthened his resolve that he was finally on the right path. That all the years of being aloof and not bothering with a relationship with someone who would never stack up to his best friend's wife would finally be worth it.

'Hang on in there, Alfred,' he murmured as he did his final checks and got the bird up in the air. 'My girl's got you.'

A week later, things hadn't changed much. Working with Colton was a maelstrom of emotions, and Neve felt out of sorts, grumpy in more ways than one. She was tired; the morning sickness was getting easier to handle, but she still felt queasy a lot of the time, and hiding things from the girls was taking its toll. She usually told them everything, but now she was hiding so much she felt she couldn't relax around them.

The heat was getting to her at night. Her little house was cosy but the air conditioning wasn't great. She kept waking up, desperate for a drink and some respite from the heat. She needed to sort something out before she got bigger. Searching online for fans that wouldn't keep her up with the noise at least gave her an excuse not to make small talk with her inquisitive driver. Which was a strategy she'd been employed since the awkward day they'd worked together in the helicopter.

Since then, she'd tried to stay in the clinic as much as possible, keeping herself busy whenever Colton came near. Everyone really liked him at the medical centre, which was weird too. He'd slotted into her life so easily; he got on with her friends and family. It was a double-edged sword, seeing how things could have been in another life. *This is temporary,* she had to keep reminding herself. *The baby isn't. Focus on that.* Today was going to be hard enough. She was having her first extra sonogram, and her out-of-control feelings were riding high.

'How are you feeling? You were pretty quiet in the car. I've barely spoken to you all week. I thought you got over the working together thing,' Colton said.

'I did.' She pouted. 'It's just been busy, and with the morning sickness I pretty much work, sleep and eat.'

She had got over it, for the most part. Of course, if she'd known he was going to swoop in with his big size twelves and take the job covering for Brian, the night at the Outback Bar might have gone a little differently. But it hadn't. She'd been the one who'd insisted on no small talk that night. She'd assumed he was happy with that arrangement; he'd seemed okay with it at the time.

Now, all he seemed to want to do was talk. It was unnerving. She couldn't help but be snarky, to push him away. She wasn't some young twenty-something up for playing games, but around him she couldn't stop the flip-flop of her emotions. Add to that the pregnancy hormones, and the fact she couldn't ignore his presence after knowing what he felt like in her bed, and she was a hot mess.

'That everything?' he pressed. 'Because I sense tension in you when I'm around.'

'It's not you.' She patted him on the arm. It felt so fake, so unlike what she felt. 'I am glad you're here. It was nice of you to drive us. I just have a lot on my mind.'

Colton had insisted on driving her car over to the hospital in Melbourne. She could have done it at the clinic, but she'd be having the baby at the hospital. Women over forty had the glamorous accolade of being classed as geriatric pregnancies, and she knew she'd possibly need extra monitoring as well as the extra scans they'd already scheduled. She wanted a natural birth, but if a C-section was necessary then she wanted the doctors to know everything about her pregnancy when she went under the knife.

The joy of being a skilled nurse who had delivered many Outback babies was knowing how to prepare for any eventuality. If things went bad, she didn't want her friends to be the ones caring for her. Family and friends didn't operate on each other for a reason, and she needed to keep that distance during this process. Plus, she hadn't even fessed up to her colleagues yet, wanting to wait till she got her head straight, and wanting to make sure everything was okay with the baby at the scan. She was still reeling from the fact she'd been able to get pregnant in the first place. Everything that could still go wrong played in her head like a horror reel. As weird as the situation was, she couldn't bear to think that anything bad would happen now. She wanted the little scrap of life growing inside her to be okay. She wanted to be able to keep it safe and healthy.

'Sweetheart, are you listening?'

'Sorry.' She adjusted herself on the plastic chair. Whatever he'd just said, she hadn't heard a word of it. She was sweating in the mid-morning heat, and even the air conditioning in the obstetrics waiting room wasn't cooling her down. 'I'm okay.'

'Tell me how you really feel.' His hand almost closed over hers on her lap, but when a nurse passed she clasped them together. 'Listen, I know that this is a lot to handle.'

'It really is. I'm…pretty scared, to be honest.'

'Of…?'

'Everything. If the pregnancy is going well, if the baby is okay… I mean, I didn't even know that I could get pregnant in the first place, and now, at my age…'

'You keep saying that, but I don't get it. What made you think you couldn't get pregnant?'

Oh. Awkward. The elephant they were avoiding suddenly bounded into the room.

'Brett and I tried, for a very long time. Years.' She

didn't look at him, not wanting to see his face. 'He went for tests and came back fine. I was about to get tested myself but things just…they didn't work any more. If I'm honest, they weren't quite right before that. Then we split up, so I didn't see the point in going, but I guess I just assumed it was me with the fertility issues.'

Colton's brow quirked up. 'What?'

'I didn't say anything.'

'You didn't need to; I saw the look.'

He motioned around them, where a number of pregnant women were filing in or waiting for their appointments. 'Fine. I just don't think you ever had an issue. One night with me and…'

'Okay.' She blushed. 'Keep your voice down.'

His lip-curl developed into a full smirk. 'Sorry. I'm only speaking the truth, though. As for the other stuff, let's not worry until there's something to worry about. We've got this between us.'

'Easy for you to say—you don't have stretch marks, gas and heartburn to look forward to. And that's without factoring in work, time off, baby stuff, childcare…'

A warm hand covered her clasped ones, silencing her. 'Slow down there, sweetheart. Let's just have the scan. As unexpected as this baby was for us both, I really want to enjoy this too. I want this to be a happy time for you, not a stressful event. I'll do whatever you need to feel comfortable. I want to be there for you as much as you will allow me to be a part of this with you.

'You're not alone, Neve. This is something we can experience together; I really want to go through this with you. I mean, I can't have the stretch marks, sure—

but I can empathise, buy you cream. Hell, I'll even rub your belly if you want me to! We both have the day off; we can deal with some of the other stuff later, if you like? We have time.'

'Oh yeah? You're up for a bit of baby shopping? I don't think they make bike helmets small enough for newborns, Colt. I think it will be a while before you can pick the baby up on your hog.' She knew she'd gone too far when his smile dropped. 'Sorry, I didn't mean that. I'm just stressed out.'

'No problem.' He squeezed her hand. 'Actually, I was thinking of getting a—'

'Neve Truby?'

Neve smiled at the ultrasound technician calling her name, and stood to follow, Colton close by her side. He dropped his hand from hers the second her name was called. It was what she wanted, of course. She didn't want people speculating any more than they already did. They hadn't even talked about the logistics of all this, without all the touching and him being so attentive. It was strange, and nice…too nice. She didn't want to get used to him being around. That would only lead to trouble.

One thing she'd learned in her forty years on the planet was that, when things got tough, that was right about the time when people pulled the rip cord. Having a baby with an adventure-seeking, no-ties flying doctor wasn't exactly a recipe for longevity. It made her all the more aware that, really, she was in this alone. He was here now, sure—till the job ended. Then what? Would he just fly in whenever he could to see the baby? What if he met someone and decided to start a real family with them?

When they entered the room, she walked over to the bed, lying down while the ultrasound tech got the equipment ready. She'd focus on the baby first. Everything else was too messy to contemplate on top of her anxiety about her unborn child.

'So,' the cheery tech started. 'I'm Penny, your ultrasound technician. First ultrasound today?'

'Yes, that's right. I think I'm coming up around the eleven-week mark.'

'Fantastic. I know you're a nurse so, rather than giving you the usual spiel, do you have any questions?' She turned to Colt. 'Or your husband?'

'Oh, he's not my husband.' She blushed. 'He's... my...'

Colton hadn't piped up. What did she call him? 'Father of the baby' sounded a little clinical. 'Baby daddy' sounded like something from a bad rap song. 'Temporary work colleague' sounded like something from a daytime soap opera.

'I'm her partner,' he supplied smoothly, reaching for the hand gripping the bed guard and slipping his fingers through hers.

Partner?

'I'm also a doctor, so we're good, Penny. We're just excited to see our child.'

Penny grinned at him. 'Ah, well, you both know what's what, then. I will just check the measurements first, and then you can have a look and listen. Now, as you know, it's not always possible to tell the sex at this age, but if there is something to see, do you want to know?'

'We've never talked about that,' Colton said, leaning in close from his chair at the side of her bed. 'Do you want to know, when we can?'

'I'd honestly not even thought that far ahead. I'll go with whatever you want.' Right now, she couldn't think about the gender; she was too busy trying to stay calm as she lifted her top up and got ready for the jelly to be put on her stomach.

'Okay.' Colton gave her a long look before turning to Penny. Whatever he'd seen in her expression made him squeeze her hand. 'We kind of have a thing with surprises, so we'll just find out when the little one arrives, I think.'

Neve snorted a laugh, catching Colton's eye. His whole face lit up at her amusement, and she felt herself relax. 'Yeah, I think we should wait. Be something to look forward to when I'm in labour.'

'Sounds good, sweetheart. Whatever you want to do, I'm here for it.'

'Great.' Penny smiled, turning the screen away from them both. 'Ready for the cold jelly?'

Neve nodded, watching as Penny gelled her up and started to run the probe over her skin. She could hear her taking still photos, the click of the keys as she typed. The more seconds that ticked by, the faster her anxiety rocketed. All kinds of things ran through her head, things she'd watched patients go through and never wanted to live first hand. The clock on the wall seemed to take longer to tick the harder she stared at it. Fear was not the word for what she felt right then. Terror was a better description. She had never wanted anything more.

In this moment, she didn't care how complicated things between Colton and her were. If he flew out of Swallow Creek and never looked back, she'd survive. She'd be hurt, of course. Being around him and feeling such an intense attraction was all-encompassing at times, but if he left her to do this alone she would carry on. She'd get through it. She'd pulled herself together after her divorce. What she wanted more than anything was to hear that baby's heartbeat and know in her bones that everything was going to be okay; that the little surprise making her vomit every morning was thriving and growing.

She ventured a look at Penny. She was frowning, leaning in close to the monitor. The look on her face turned Neve's insides to water. She grasped Colton's hand tightly. 'Colton…' she whimpered as Penny turned to face them with a professional smile on her face. A professional smile was something all medics mastered early on. It was a calm smile to put people at ease before they gave bad news.

'Everything's fine.' Penny grinned. 'You were correct; your pregnancy is twelve weeks this week. 11 weeks plus 4, by my estimates.'

'What's wrong?' Neve demanded. 'I know that face; I do that face myself. What's the problem with my baby?'

Colton caged her hands between his. 'Neve, it's okay.'

'No, it's not.' Neve didn't take her eyes from Penny. 'You're not telling us something. Please, tell me.'

Penny turned the screen to face them. 'Miss Truby,

everything is fine. Measurements are on track; healthy heartbeat. One-sixty-one from rump to crown. I did detect something, but it's nothing to worry about. We can't tell the sex yet, but Baby A and Baby B are perfectly healthy.'

It took a moment or two for Neve to process Penny's words. Colton had turned to stone. When he spoke, his voice was husky. 'Sorry, Baby A and Baby what now?'

'T-twins,' Neve stuttered, dilated pupils zeroing in on the screen. 'I'm having two babies?' There they were, up on the screen: two separate amniotic sacs, each one holding a tiny little foetus. Two. She was having dizygotic twins. 'There's two babies in there?'

Penny looked a little less comfortable now. 'Sorry, I didn't mean to worry you. I just needed to double check the measurements; it took a little longer.' Colton was sitting open-mouthed at the side of her, and Penny noticed. 'I'll give you two a moment, okay? We can listen to the heartbeats when I come back. I'm happy to answer any questions.'

When the door closed behind her, Neve sat up. 'Colton?'

His blue eyes flashed to hers. 'Yeah?'

'You're freaking out too, right?'

He shook his head as if he was trying to snap himself out of a stupor. 'Sorry, I…er… I wasn't expecting to hear that.'

'I know. Me neither.' She looked back at the screen. 'I have no twins in the family; you?'

'Nope, this is a first in the Anderson clan.' He leaned in closer to the screen. 'Twins. I can't believe it.'

'*You* can't? They're not going to be playing football with your bladder. I mean, two? I just got my head around one. Two is…a lot.'

'Non-identical twins—two eggs.'

'Yeah,' she drawled, the shock wearing off. 'Two eggs, two sperm.' A giggle bubbled out of her. 'When we…hooked up, we really didn't do things by halves, eh?'

He chuckled, dropping a kiss on the side of her temple.

'It's definitely becoming a pattern—all in.' He looked back at the screen and she saw his expression soften. 'They are healthy though; you're obviously looking after them.'

'Don't be cute right now, Colton. We are having two babies!'

'I know,' he said softly. 'I just want you to be happy, that's all. Stress is not good for any of you.'

Something in her stomach flipped and it wasn't the babies. 'I'm not unhappy about it.' Tears welled in her eyes. 'Actually, it's more than I've ever hoped for. If I don't think about the logistics of it and freak out.' *He hasn't run from the room. He's still here, comforting you.* 'How do you feel?'

He looked surprised by her question. 'I'm not unhappy about this either, Neve. Two babies are a lot of work, sure, but I'll be here, and we can work out a schedule; we have time to get organised.'

And there it was, the panic again, the sense of being out of control. She tried to fight against it, but her heart was beating so fast she felt sick.

'But you're going to be leaving, Colton. These babies are only going be, what…?' she did the maths in her head. '…four or five months when your contract is up. Twin pregnancies rarely go to term, Colt. They won't exactly be independent then.' She had an image in her mind of trying to get two babies ready before a long shift at work, and her gut clenched. 'I don't even know where you'll be, and there's all the time off work…'

The soft smile had dropped from his face the longer she spoke. 'Where do you think I will be, exactly? The job might end, but it's not like I'm going to jet off somewhere.'

'Colton, that's exactly what you'll do; it's what you've always done because that's your life.'

A defeated sigh broke free from deep within. She didn't want to discuss this right now. She was still reeling from the news that the baby was healthy…well, babies. It seemed as though when one hurdle was jumped, the next one was right there, waiting to be conquered.

'You never asked for any of this, Colt, and you've been great, but we know what this is. I don't want your whole life derailed because of one night. We're both adults, and your life is not here. You live for being free, full of adventures and experiences. I can't ask you to sacrifice that to stick around Swallow Falls and change dirty nappies with me.'

'You didn't ask. You've kept me at a distance, if anything.' He dropped her hand, his eyes focused intently on the screen. 'You talk about changing my life, but what about how I came in and wrecked yours? You wanted an adventure, a night of passion. I heard you that night, you know, and I wanted more than anything to give that to you. I didn't foresee this. If anything, I changed yours, Neve. You had your new life starting and I derailed it.'

Her brain stuttered now, a reel of the night of the divorce party screaming at her.

'What do you mean, you heard me?' Something about that night clicked into her memory: outside, talking with Bronwyn about Brett, and how their love had felt more like puppy love than passion. How she wanted something different, something unexpected and exciting—an adventure with someone new.

Oh, God. He'd heard that? She blushed at the thought. No wonder he'd came straight over. He'd known she wanted to throw caution to the wind. She could be a night of meaningless sex with a woman he knew didn't usually sleep around, one he wasn't interested in beyond the physical. He'd proved that attitude over the time she'd dated Brett—he'd never bothered to get to know any women in any depth. She'd known from Brett that he dated, but she'd never seen him with anyone. What more had he heard? It can't have been about Brett, as when she'd mentioned him that night Colton had shut it down quick. But still, he'd come to see her and had taken her home, and the morning after he had taken her number and offered her his. It didn't scream 'player' to her.

Which version in my head is the truth? At forty-three, he'd never been married, but she had, and it hadn't worked out. Had she just assumed he was the type to sleep around? Trying to understand this man was giving her whiplash, just like his babies were giving her morning sickness. These Andersons were keeping her on her toes, that was for sure.

She steeled herself for the answer to her question. 'You heard me outside?' she repeated.

'Yes, I did. I know you were looking for some fun, and I decided I wanted to be the man for the job.' He cringed. 'Well, that sounded terrible. I didn't mean that like it just came out. I meant to say…' He ran a hand over his scruff. 'I like you, Neve. I heard some of what you said, but that's not why I came over to you. It just gave me a little hope that you'd speak to me for a while, maybe. I never expected what happened or planned it.'

He huffed out an exacerbated breath. 'I'm messing this up.' His blue eyes caught hers and held them captive. 'The truth was, I wanted to see you again. I obviously didn't mean things to go like this, but I don't plan on leaving.' He pointed to the screen without looking. 'I want to be a father to those babies and support you in any way you will let me. Trust me to make it work, for all of us. It would be nice if you just gave me a chance to prove that.'

He looked so sincere, his blue eyes blazing with emotion that pinned her to the spot. Her heart fought against the walls her mind was busy putting up brick by brick. She was still trying to work him out, and now time seemed against them. They weren't in their twenties any more; this wasn't some horny hook-up. It might have been like that the night they'd spent together, but he hadn't exactly been in a rush to go the following morning. She'd got rid of him pretty quickly; she'd brushed him off when he'd wanted her number.

He was here, saying all the right things, doing all the right things; asking her to trust him.

Had she really read him so wrong? She only really seen him being aloof when she'd seen him with Brett, and heard what her ex-husband had told her about Colton not being interested in being tied down. She'd changed, so maybe he had too. Gosh, her mind was on the fritz right now. Perhaps the baby brain had already kicked in.

A sensation of warmth brought her out of her head. His hand was back in hers again, her fingers instinctively linking with his as he ran his thumb along her skin.

'I know you're out of your comfort zone right now, sweetheart.'

'You do?'

'Yeah.' He shot her a knowing smile, which made her heart melt and her stomach do that flipping thing again. 'I understand you better than you think. You're pretty easy to read, you know. You need to have everything planned, and…well…none of this is on brand for you. I get it, but not knowing all the answers right now is okay.'

She wanted to rebut his comment, and she would have, but he could read her like a blessed book and she knew it. She didn't always like it, being the snarky independent woman she was, but he had a way of getting round her. Maybe it was the way he looked at her with a smouldering look; maybe it was his dimples. Who knew? It appeared the man was a wizard when it came to her.

'Fine, I don't like knowing everything. I can't help it.' She looked down at her stomach, imagining the little mini-Coltons hanging out together. 'I do feel better knowing that the babies are healthy.'

'Me too.' He kissed the back of her hand and she resisted the shiver that ran through her. 'Listen, we have the rest of the day, so let's…'

Penny knocked on the door, coming back into the room and cutting him off. 'So, are we ready to listen to the heartbeats?'

CHAPTER FOUR

COLTON SAT ON his couch, poring over the photos of his unborn children. The second he'd heard those little heartbeats—before, even—he'd been a goner for them. They couldn't tell the sex of either yet, but he didn't care whether they had sons or daughters. He knew that they'd probably be blonde. *I hope they have green eyes, like their mother.*

He loved her almond eyes. They were so open, but wary when looking his way. That uncertain look he caught her sporting slayed him every time. He just wanted to chase it away, get her looking at him the way she had that night—with trust and lust, something that would settle his worry and confirm that she believed in him. And fancied him—because he felt the pull of her more than ever before, knowing that she was carrying his family. He wanted to take her home and never leave, wrap her up in cotton wool for the next few months, wait on her hand and foot and show her how much she deserved to be worshipped. One night together and they'd created life—two tiny beating hearts that were half her and half him. It was like a dream in so many ways, as though fate had anchored them together.

She doesn't want you, Colt. You'll never know if she would have chosen you for yourself. You messed up again, not speaking up that night and just declaring what you wanted. He didn't know what to do for the best. She was fragile, and this soft approach was alien to him. He wanted to spill his guts, claim her and his children and tell her that he was right there with her, in every way she wanted and more. But she wasn't just Neve now, she was an expectant mother. She was scared and excited. Her life had changed along with his, and he only wished that they had been on a surer footing before the pregnancy.

He knew it would have been different even if they'd just been dating a month. He would have had the chance to show her everything he was, felt and wanted. When he'd walked into the Outback Bar that night and asked her if she wanted a drink, he'd half-expected her to tell him where to get off. He'd never been the most receptive when they'd all hung out together, but he'd always been aware of her.

When Brett had first told him he was dating a nurse from Swallow Falls, he'd thought nothing of it. Brett was a businessman; his life was in Sydney and chasing that big dream of success. Colton hadn't seen it sticking. They'd seemed too different. She'd been working there in the hospital as part of her training. The nurses from the smaller towns often worked in the larger hospitals for the experience, undertaking placements in different areas to broaden their knowledge, but he'd known that she was a home-town kind of girl. It was something he'd always really liked about her. He was someone who'd never really had a stable home growing up and the fact that he'd never grown roots was something he'd always found lacking in himself. Sure, it made him more open to seeing the world, but he'd also spent a lot of his life being alone.

Brett was different—a city boy through and through, passionate about climbing that corporate ladder. Colton had figured that she'd go back home and it would fizzle out between Brett and her. He knew his friend, and how he worked, and he was happy as long as his friend was. Till the night they'd all gone out for drinks, and Neve had walked in on Brett's arm. He'd thought she was breathtaking; bubbly and friendly. Her smile had lit up the room, and everyone around her seemed to brighten in her presence. He hadn't believed this was the girl of whom Brett had spoken, and she was a nurse to boot. He'd seen it in her—the way she moved around the room, caring for people, being attentive to Brett and his friends.

He'd watched her the rest of the night, devouring her with his eyes, feasting on her smile and her mannerisms; the way she laughed, free and joyously. It had become his new favourite sound, and he'd wanted to be the one on the receiving end of her joy.

Something had clicked in him that night, certain and stark in its reality. He'd felt as if he'd been punched in the gut. From the moment he'd set eyes on Neve Truby, he'd hated his best friend for having had the fine luck of meeting her first. He hadn't been the dating type, usually because he'd been too busy chasing his doctorate and laying the foundations for his life, but Neve had changed all that. He hadn't been able to stop looking at her, so he had done the right thing.

He'd kept his distance. It hadn't helped. Whenever they had spoken, they'd got on—well. The first time he'd made her laugh, it had almost knocked him off his feet. He'd kept searching for some red flag, other than the one emblazoned with the words *she's not your girl.* But Neve Truby was a walking green flag, and he'd just found it harder to be around her and act as if she was nothing to him. Whenever they'd been in the same room, even in a crowd of people, he'd found himself watching her. She'd caught him a few times too. He'd even convinced himself that she might feel a tiny bit of what he did.

But Brett was keen on her, and he hadn't wanted to upset his friend, so he'd backed away from hanging out with them as a couple. He'd satisfied himself with hearing snippets about how she was from his friend.

Time had moved on, and he'd thought his attraction to her would fade. It hadn't, and he'd had to sit on the sidelines as they'd got more serious. When they were due to get married, and Brett had asked him to be his best man, he'd crumbled. They'd had a huge fight, and something Brett had said had triggered a rage in Colton that he'd never felt before. Fire in his veins, he'd spilled his guts about Neve and punched him.

Friendship that he didn't want to even try to mend in tatters, he'd cut ties with Brett. He'd gone to work further afield; tried to forget Neve and convince himself that she was happy and with the right man. He'd kept tabs, though, and checked on her from time to time. He'd focused on his career. He'd dated a bit, never finding another woman with a laugh that made him feel that way. So he'd worked some more and seen the world. He'd saved a lot of lives, and over time he'd made peace with the fact that his own life would have enough meaning through his work. Not everyone got that fairy-tale dream of a personal life and a family.

When years later he'd found out she was single, he had done a little Internet sleuthing. When he'd seen chatter on her social media between her friends and her about the divorce party, he hadn't been able to help himself. He'd heard there might be some work coming up in that area, a chance to use his pilot skills in the Outback. It seemed meant to be and, when he'd walked up to her and asked if he could buy her a drink, he'd wanted much more. It was a shame he'd inadvertently spent years painting himself as an aloof asshole. She'd bought it a little too well.

And now he was looking at the result of their night together. The woman he'd been in love with for years was pregnant with his babies, and she wanted nothing from him. He'd wanted to be in her new life, not change it completely or stress her out and give her worry. He was thrilled they were having twins together, but not like this. If he'd had his way, then they would have been together in every sense before they started a family.

Every time he thought that they'd taken a step forward, something happened to shoot them right back to the start. He'd thought she was starting to let him in after her freak-out about the news of their twin babies. He'd been about to ask her to spend the rest of the day with him when Penny had come back. After that, she'd scuttled right back into her hard shell, and he had no idea how to coax her out of it without scaring her off for good. She'd been quiet on the way back from the hospital, only speaking to ask him to take her straight home. He'd managed to get her to agree to meet him later, but he was half-expecting her to cancel. He'd thrust a piece of paper with his number into her hands at her front door. He knew she had his number from before, but he wasn't taking any chances.

His phone sat next to him on the couch, and every little beep made him jump, thinking it was her cancelling on him. He wanted to claim his family, and nothing would make him happier than to tell her how he felt, but something she'd said had spooked him. She was right: he had lived that loner life for a very long time. He'd never even had a pet to be home for. He was used to focusing on work and hiking or biking on his days off.

Would he be a good father? He'd never held a baby outside of work. He'd helped birth a few in his time and had rescued a few from some tricky situations, but feeding, nappies, and night feeds—what did he know about any of that stuff? No wonder she was so willing to go it alone. Neve was accomplished, independent, organised, and caring. She'd be the best mother. He already knew that their babies would adore her as much as he did.

All he wanted was to see it, be part of it. He'd seen plenty of his buddies be part-time dads over the years: weekend visits to the zoo, watching some other man live under the same roof as his kids, raising them. The thought killed him. He wanted those twins to be Andersons, proud of their mother and father and settled in the stable family home he'd never had the fortune of growing up in.

Having some other guy answer the door when he came to see his kids… 'Not on my watch,' he grumbled to himself, checking his watch. He still had a couple of hours before he was due to pick Neve up. Sure, he didn't know everything, but there were things he could do right now to play to his own strengths. Neve was organised, but he could go all out when he wanted something. If he needed something in place, he didn't wait. He made it happen. He corrected the course at the first sight of trouble.

Well, apart from that one time when you let her slip through your stupid fingers in the first place, buddy. And look how that turned out. She stayed with Brett, and you pined for years like a pure chump. You're here now—fix it.

He had just enough time to prove to her that he wasn't afraid of this adventure. It was one he very much wanted to take with her. He'd rather be scared and fail with Neve Truby than do anything without her in his life. He had caused this whole thing, uprooted her new life, but she wanted the babies. He knew that deep in his gut. He'd seen the love she had for them when she couldn't stop poring over the ultrasound photos on the way home.

Penny had been great, answering their questions and spelling out the extra care that would be needed. Neve being an older woman, the pregnancy was riskier and, given it was twins, it put her firmly in the high-risk category. She'd need low stress and extra rest—not easy when she was freaking out about everything and holding down a full-time job. If there was ever a time to prove to the woman who'd haunted his daydreams that she wasn't just some fun one-night stand to him, it was now.

'Where's the bike?' Neve asked him the second she got into his car.

He nodded to the back seat. 'My babies aren't riding on the hog. Dealer told me that this has an excellent safety record for families. Plenty of room for car seats and buggies.' He shrugged as he drove off very slowly, like a grandpa in Sunday traffic. 'Besides, I figured they could ride their own hogs when they turn eighteen.' He winked when she threw him a shocked look. 'Kidding, sweetheart. Keep calm, no stress—remember what Penny said.'

'And you thought bringing me to a baby store would destress me?'

Wait, what? Was she serious? All morning she'd been worried about being ready. Now the babies were confirmed to be healthy, surely planning for them would be the way to go? What did she want from him here?

When they arrived, Colton pulled into one of the spaces at the front of the store. Trying to keep his irritation at her contrariness in check, he focused on the objective. 'Wait here.'

He came to open her door, holding out his hand. When she practically scowled at it, something in his chest broke loose and stabbed him in the ribs. He just wanted to be close to her, and she didn't trust him. He knew she was still picturing raising these babies alone, but the thought of that killed him as much as it did her. The game he was playing, trying not to pressure her into falling for him madly, was backfiring—badly.

'I can open my own door, you know,' she said shortly.

He stilled for a moment, biting his lip. 'You know what, Neve? You could be nicer to me.'

'What?' She visibly blanched at his bleak tone, but he was done being the puppy she kicked.

'You heard me. We're not total strangers, sweetheart. We've known each other for a long time. I don't know what kind of man you think I am. I'm guessing Brett told you a few unflattering things about me, but I doubt there was any truth in them. I'm not some fly-by-night guy, despite what people assume about me.'

'I never thought—'

'Yes, you did. A lot of women think that way. I'm the guy who's only good for a fun night or two. It's why you didn't take my number, right? You never expected me to call you. But I did, and you didn't pick up. So I came for you, didn't I? I haven't left, haven't panicked. I'm here for the whole thing, but you can't see it, can you?'

He ran a hand through his hair when a blond lock fell forward. 'I can't do this—be here for you—if you won't let me in. Let me look after you.'

'Colt, I didn't have a very supportive family unit growing up. I grew up independent, trusting nobody except for myself. Looking after myself. Then I got married, I finally let someone in and it ended badly. I struggle with relying on people. Always have.'

'Yeah, don't I know it? Brett let you look after him like a damn mother hen, and that's not me.' He shook his head, his other hand clenching into a fist. 'And I just brought up Brett again, which was the last thing I wanted to do. I don't want him anywhere near us like some spectre.'

'I don't want that either.'

Colton nodded, but it was tight. 'Good. We agree on something. Progress.' He couldn't keep the determination from the look he gave her. In fact, he let it show. *See me, sweetheart. I'm right here, just look at me. Open those pretty green eyes and see me.* 'Now, will you let me help you out of the car and stop being so stubborn?'

Well, holy ovaries. After that little display, hers were in overdrive, screaming to him, *impregnate me again!* She'd well and truly set him off, and she felt guilty and horny at the same time. *I came here for you,* he'd said with a blaze in his eyes she'd never seen before in anyone but him. She didn't dare take a minute till the throb between her thighs settled down so she took his hand. He helped her out of the car, tucking her tightly into his side as he locked it up.

As they headed to the large glass doors of the baby store, she had the sudden urge to laugh. Damn her hormones. Lately she went from down to up to horny at the drop of a hat, and at least some of it was due to being in Colton's presence. Right now, she was trying not to giggle while the father of her babies was livid. *Get it together, Neve.*

'What?' He frowned down at her, his mood still brooding.

'Nothing.' She couldn't hold in her laugh, which earned her a curious scowl. 'I shouldn't say it.'

He raised a brow. 'Neve, seriously.'

'Okay, okay. I'm sorry. I am trying.'

'Okay. Say more.'

'It's just...you know, you're pretty hot when you're all mad like that.'

She could have sworn that she felt his step falter, but it was so quick she dismissed it.

'Yeah?' he asked gruffly, those gorgeous blue eyes of his caressing her face. 'Is it your hormones or me?'

You. 'Hormones,' she lied. 'Definitely hormones.'

'Good to know,' he said drily, holding open the door for her. 'You been here before?'

Baby Heaven in Melbourne was the best baby store for miles. They had the basics in Swallow Falls, but this place was like a department store compared to that. Aisle after aisle of parenting aids confronted them both, and Neve gasped.

'I've bought a few baby shower gifts for friends over the years.' She came to a stop when they reached the baby section. 'Geez, I don't remember this much stuff, though. Maybe it's still a little early for all this. I mean, where do we start?'

Colton stepped closer and she turned into him automatically. 'You said "we". Maybe I should get mad more often.'

Neve laughed and, before she could over-think it, she reached for his hand and placed it on her stomach, under hers. She watched as his pupils dilated and felt the tension drain out of him.

'You're so beautiful, Neve. I can't wait to see you be a mother.'

'Yeah?' She felt the tears behind her eyes, threatening to spill over. 'I still can't quite believe it's happening.'

'Oh, it's happening all right. You are going to be so big and gorgeous, carrying our babies.'

Neve raised a brow, trying not either to dissolve into happy tears or ravish the man in front of her. 'Is that a nice way of saying I'm going to be huge?'

His soft laugh was everything. She wanted to bottle it up to listen to later.

'Well, it is twins…' She went to swat his arm, but he was quicker. His arms were around her waist before she could blink. 'And, just so you know, I think it's not just your hormones that react to me.'

Her hands were on his chest, and she couldn't help but flex her fingers against his shirt. 'Oh, really?'

He leaned closer, his eyes dropping to her mouth and his own raising into that boyish smile she found so disarming.

'Really, Neve.' He dropped his head, and his lips almost brushed hers.

Outside, there was a scream, followed by a screech of wheels and a loud bang. The customers in the shop all turned to the noise, shock and worry marring their features. Neve and Colton barely noticed. One second they were staring into each other's eyes, the next they were off and running through the front doors.

Colton cursed when they saw the scene. 'Neve, call it in!'

Neve scrabbled for her phone in the bag slung around her middle. Dialling the emergency services, she relayed the scene. 'Yes, just outside Baby Heaven. RTA. Off-duty nurse and doctor on scene. Ambulance required, possibly fire engine too.'

Once they confirmed help was on the way, she zipped her phone away and ran towards Colton. The car, a small hatchback, was smoking from the engine in front. The lamppost it had hit had crumpled the front fender like a drinking straw. Under the front right wheel, there was a crumpled bicycle. Colton was giving CPR to a woman on the ground. Her leg was turned at an unnatural angle, blood on the floor behind her head. The dark-red liquid flowed onto the road like a hellish halo.

'Colt?' At the sound of his name, he looked up, his arms not stopping as he pumped her chest. She could tell by his face that the cyclist was in a bad way. He gave a tiny shake of his head, aware that the crowd around him were all crying and praying for her to make it.

'Get the driver, he's conscious.'

Neve took off towards the car, managing to pull open the passenger door.

'What's happening…?' The man groaned. He couldn't be more than twenty years old. 'Did I hit her? Is she okay?' Pulling on his seatbelt, he let out a scream.

'Don't move, okay? What's your name?'

'Sean,' he mumbled, trying again with his right hand to unclip his belt. 'I need to get out. Is she okay? I think I hurt her. She came out of nowhere.'

'Sean.' Neve covered his hand gently, leaning over him to get him to look her in the eye. 'Sean, I need you to sit still. You're hurt, and I need to check you over.'

'It's just my arm.' He winced, trying to lift it. 'I think I hit it when I crashed.' A tear ran down his cheek, mixing with the blood from the cuts on his face. 'I tried to avoid her, I really did. I wasn't even going fast.'

'I know, but my partner is with her now. He's a doctor, and help is on the way.'

'He's a doctor? Can he help her?'

Neve closed off the part of her that knew he was going to be scarred by this day. The girl that Colton was working on wasn't wearing a helmet. The blood on the ground wasn't a good sign.

'He's going to try, but we need to focus on you now. I'm Neve, Sean, and I'm a nurse. Can I check your pupils?'

He turned his head towards her, and she stopped him by holding his head. 'Try not to make any more moves till we clear you. There is a chance you could have sustained other damage, so we need to take this a step at a time. I can check you from here.' He was responsive, alert, if a little in shock. His pupils dilated when she shone her camera torch in his face. These were all good signs. She sent up a little prayer to the heavens for that.

'Good, that's really good, Sean. How old are you?'

'Twenty-one. I just had my birthday.'

'Oh, well, happy birthday! Twenty-one, eh? I remember that. A long time ago,' she joked. Sean smiled. *That's it, Sean, keep smiling. Stay with me.* 'When you crashed, Sean, did you pass out at all? Hit your head?'

'No, no. I saw her and swerved. Next thing I know, there was a loud bang. I was thrown into the door. The glass shattered around me. My mum's going to be so worried. She's always telling me to drive safe.' He looked down at his arm, his lip trembling. The wrist was swollen, already bruising, obviously broken. It looked like both the radius and ulna, from the amount of swelling and the way it hung limply. Taking off her cardigan, she buttoned it up and leaned close.

'Sean, I'm going to strap that arm up, so please stay as still as you can. It's a safe bet that it's broken, so it's going to be painful till we can get some pain meds. I need you to not flinch when I do this. Keep that head against the headrest, if you can. Try not to turn your neck at all, just until the ambulance comes and we can get a head collar on.'

'Okay.' He shuddered. 'Can you ask your friend if she's okay?'

Neve glanced through the windshield. Colton's mouth was covering the cyclist's, and she watched as he turned his ear to her chest, watching for signs of life. The minutes were ticking by. The cyclist hadn't moved, and even from here Neve could see the look of helplessness on Colton's face. Her heart clenched for him, and she moved her gaze back to Sean, to where she could do something. One life was already too many to lose.

She wanted to be able to go back to Colton and tell

him that them being there had been worth something. She was pretty sure that before they'd heard the car crash he'd been about to kiss her right there in the store—and she had been about to let him. She tuned out the noise in her head. Sean was her priority right now. Somewhere out there, he had a mother who loved him. Neve had the power to help him return home to her—a gift from one mother to another.

'She's getting help, Sean—I promise that we are doing everything we can for you both. Now, without moving too much, tell me—can you wriggle your toes?'

Resting the body of the cardigan under his arm, she tied the sleeves around his neck and pulled it tight slowly, so that the arm was strapped to his chest and elevated. Leaning down towards the gears, she looked at his trainers. She could see his footwear and the slight movement as he flexed his toes. She'd never been so happy to see a foot move. *Good.*

'That's great, Sean. Now, I'm going to touch your legs. Tell me when you feel something, and where.'

Slowly, carefully, she lifted the denim hem of his jean leg and ran a pen from her bag over the skin, first one side, then the other. Moving up slowly, she released a breath every time Sean told her he could feel it. Sirens came, louder and louder, and she reached for Sean's hand, checking his pulse and watching the breaths in his chest. He was stressed and pale but otherwise lucky. He could feel his legs and, other than his arm and a few cuts and bruises, he was uninjured. She scanned for Colton through the windshield, but the fire engine had pulled up in front of them.

'Help is here now, Sean. They are going to get you out and take you to the hospital. Get that arm sorted.'

'Can they call my mum? I don't know where my phone is; it was in the jack but I can't see it.'

Neve looked around the car floor. His phone was sitting on the mat, the screen smashed. *Great.* 'Don't worry about your phone right now. The fire service will deal with that, and they will call your mother when you get to the hospital.'

'Okay, okay. Yeah, thank you. I was supposed to be at hers later. She'll worry.'

Neve took his uninjured hand again, giving him a gentle squeeze. 'That's what mothers do, Sean, but she will be fine when she sees you. She'll just be glad you're all right.'

A paramedic appeared at her window, a neck collar in his hand. Neve took it and began strapping it onto her patient as she gave the first responder the patient update. 'Nurse Truby, Swallow Falls Medical Centre. This is Sean; he's twenty-one. Alert and responsive, no loss of consciousness on impact. Broken left arm and superficial cuts and bruising from the glass of the broken windows. Normal sensation response in both legs and back.'

'Understood.' The paramedic nodded. 'Sean, how's your pain?'

She squeezed Sean's hand. 'I'm going to check on things outside; you good now?'

Sean's eyes slid to hers. 'Yeah. Thank you, just help her out there, please. Tell her I'm sorry. Tell her I didn't see her, and I tried to stop.'

'I will,' she said, flashing him a warm smile before stepping out of the car to let the others get in to assess how best to get him out. 'Try not to worry. We've got you.'

She watched as the paramedic got to work, preparing a syringe with the pain medication he would need to make his extraction easier. The door was crumpled due to the impact, the car a write-off. And he was the lucky one.

Rounding the fire engine, she nodded to a couple of the crew she recognised from work and searched for Colton. She found him sitting on the pavement, holding the hand of the evidently dead girl on the road. A paramedic came over and covered her face with a blanket, but Colton never dropped her hand.

'Oh, Colt.' She sank down to her knees beside him. The crowd was being pushed back behind a cordon by the local police, but she still saw their upset faces when she scanned their surroundings. 'Are you okay?'

'That's my line,' he tried to joke, but there was no trace of humour in his words.

'I'm fine. Do you want to get up, or sit here for a while?'

He didn't say anything for a moment, finally releasing the girl's hand with a slow nod and placing it gently under the blanket. Neve stood, reaching for his hand without thinking. He took it, pulling her with him over to the kerb in front of the baby store. He went to sit down and, as she followed him, his hands shot around her hips and she sank down onto his lap. It was only then that she saw they were both covered in blood. Colton's shirt was red, half-plastered to him where he'd tried to save the girl, and her hands were tinged with the blood from his.

'Sorry, I...'

He went to pull back, but she shushed him. He needed her right now.

'We'll clean up in a minute. Just take a breath.'

'I...don't know why it got to me. She didn't even wake up. No helmet; can you believe that? If she'd worn one, she might have made it. She was pretty much gone by the time I worked on her.'

'I thought so,' Neve murmured. 'I'm so sorry, Colt. Sean, the guy in the car, he's going to be fine.'

'No, he won't.' Colton's expression was bleak, his eyes hazy. 'He'll blame himself. If she'd just worn a helmet... Her legs were broken, but it was the head injury. Her pupils were blown when I got to her. She'd crashed, and I just couldn't get her back.' He leaned his forehead against her side. 'Probably for the best. Even if I could have got her heart beating again, the deficits would have been too great. Her skull was fractured.'

Greg, one of the paramedics she knew well from her hospital drop-offs, came over with bottles of water and a couple of blankets.

'Just checking on you guys. It's a good thing you were here. How come you were so close? The call came through in seconds.'

'We were at the baby store,' Neve said without thinking. Colton stilled beneath her, and she felt his eyes on her, waiting for her to cover up what she'd said or take it back. She couldn't do that, not now. She'd just seen him try to save a life, spring into action and be her team mate. She was proud of him. She couldn't spill their life story, but she could do this.

'Colton, this is Greg. Greg, this is Colton—my partner.' She reckoned using the term he'd coined for them would please him.

Greg smiled, reaching out to shake Colton's hand but stopping when he saw the blood. 'Good to meet you.' He smirked at Neve. 'Glad to see you happy. We can take it from here, if you need to take off and get changed.'

'Does Sean know? About the cyclist?'

Greg's easy smile sobered. 'No, not yet. He's in a bit of shock. Reckoned it could wait.'

'Was it his fault?' Colton asked.

Greg shook his head. 'Nah; police said traffic cameras saw the whole thing. You beat them to the call for help. She was on her phone, if you can believe that, not looking at the traffic. He was under the speed limit and tried to avoid her.'

She felt Colton's nod, his defeated sigh.

'Stupid,' he muttered, looking back at the covered body on the floor. 'So stupid. Such a pointless waste of life.'

Greg shrugged, turning to leave. 'It's life, man; people think it's going to last for ever. Thanks for the help, guys.'

'Well, that was blunt,' Colt commented when Greg was out of earshot.

Neve knew Greg well. She'd worked with him a lot over the years. They'd both seen some horrible things, injuries and deaths that never left them. She understood his dismissal for what it was: a shield against letting everything in. Working in emergency medicine was like rowing a boat: if too much water was let in, it started to sink pretty quickly. It didn't mean they didn't feel the losses, it was more a case of managing them well enough to keep doing the job to the best of their ability.

'He cares,' she told him. 'He just blocks a lot of it out, you know?'

Colt's lips thinned. 'Yeah, I see that.' He looked back at the body under the blanket. 'She was so young—nineteen, if that. She had textbooks in her bag. They were scattered around her.'

'I know. Come on; let's get off the street and get cleaned up, okay?'

They were passing the doors of the baby store when a woman came out with a few packs of baby wipes. Neve smiled, seeing her name tag.

'Thank you, Sheila.'

'Oh no.' She waved them off. 'Least we could do. I saw you two run straight out there.' She held out a flyer for the store. 'Just so you know, we do delivery too, if you order online.' She looked down at their dishevelled clothing. 'I put my email address on there. I would be more than happy to help you, if you still need to shop.' She held out a carrier bag for their used wipes.

'Thanks.' Neve's now clean hands came to rest on her stomach. 'We do need a bit of help.'

'First time parents?'

'Yep.' Neve grinned. 'We need everything.'

'Well, have a look on the website, and if you have

any questions, I'm here.' She looked from Colton back to her. 'And, just for the record, you make such a nice couple. Seriously, your baby is very lucky to have two superheroes like you in their corner.'

Neve didn't protest when he went to open the car door for her this time. His gaze was on hers when he slid into the driver's seat. Whatever he saw on her face had his brows knitting together.

'Are you okay?' he asked softly.

'She called us superheroes. I don't feel like one.'

'Me neither, but we helped save a life today. We tried everything to make sure everyone got to go home, but sometimes these things are beyond our control, no matter what we do.'

'I know.' She sighed, feeling the loss of seeing that poor girl on the pavement and thinking of the man who would never get over the events of the day. 'It's just so sad. It reminds you of how precious life is. I'm sorry for being a pain lately.'

'You haven't.'

She raised her brows, making him chuckle. 'I have, and I'm sorry. I realise now how silly it was, in the store. We were freaking out about having two cute little babies, but we didn't think about running into a car accident. We are being a bit wussy, in the grand scheme of things.'

He winked at her, his lips curving into a slight smile. 'We?'

'Yes, we! You went as white as a sheet when Penny said it was twins.' She made her voice all deep and growly. 'Baby A and Baby what now?' she parroted. 'I swear, I thought you were going to hurl or pass out.'

'Hey! You freaked out too! Your voice goes all pitchy and high, dead giveaway.'

She tutted through her laughter, playfully swatting his arm. The sadness shifted into something else as they fought to remind themselves that they still had things to look forward to. That life was happening and, as cruel as it often was, it still went on. In their line of work, they knew that more than most. 'Whatever you tell yourself, Robin. Wait till I have two tiny humans coming out of me. We'll see who's sweating then.'

'No problem,' he said, his voice low and growly as he leaned closer. 'But I'm Batman, baby.' The laughter between them receded quickly when they recognised how close they'd moved to the other. Her legs were facing towards him, her whole body leaning towards his. Their mouths were a hair's breadth away from the other.

'We should get home,' she prompted, looking down at the blood on their clothing. 'Get cleaned up.

The drive home was quiet, but comfortable, as though they didn't need to talk and that just being with each other was a comfort. When she invited him in for a shower, he didn't question it. Afterwards he found her in the kitchen, striding over to her in clothes he'd retrieved from his boot. He looked handsome with still-wet hair as he came to stand next to her, taking the cup of hot coffee she offered.

'You were great today, you know?' he said. 'We work well as a team. The other day, working with you on the house calls, I saw how good you are. You knew what Alfred needed in his moment of fear, and he was better cared for with you by his side. You put people at ease. I knew while I worked on that girl that you had the driver. It helped me to focus, knowing you were there.'

'Well, it's the job.'

His gaze dropped to her lips, and she ran her tongue along them, a silent invitation she couldn't help but extend. 'It's not just the job, sweetheart. You have a way about you; it makes people glad to be in your orbit.'

'Back at you, Colton. We do make a good team, you and I. Seeing you stay calm helped me do the same. I knew you were right there with me, too. It helped.'

'I will always be there, Neve. You have to know that I would do anything for you.'

She kissed him. Well, that wasn't an accurate description of how she practically moaned and grabbed him. Her hands were around the back of his neck in half a second, yanking his mouth to hers in desperation. His cologne was still there somehow. Maybe his scent was just indelible, unmistakably him, and it fuelled her libido like an injection in her fuel tank. Her teeth nibbled his bottom lip, her tongue running along the seam of his lips.

He didn't miss the memo. He RSVP'd with a few moves of his own. His arms went around her back, lifting her till she was resting on the kitchen island, her legs around his waist. She moaned at the sheer strength of his grip, the feel of him at her core. His hands cupped her cheeks, turning her head so he could feast on her better. His tongue licked against hers as they made out like a couple of teenagers. It was all hot breath and grunts from him as she rocked against him, desperate to feel more friction against her centre.

'Neve…' He groaned when he broke away to nip at her neck with his teeth. 'You drive me crazy.'

'Back at you, Batman,' she breathed, tilting so he could reach lower to lick and bite more. His scruff felt like perfection against her skin. 'Need you.' She couldn't even get a full sentence out. 'Want you, Colton.' All she could think about was how good he felt, how turned on she was.

Her phone rang in her bag, breaking through the fevered sounds of them together. She sprang away from him, breathing heavily in his grasp as he stared up at her. He looked thoroughly kissed, all half-hooded eyes and mirrored surprise in his eyes.

'Sorry,' was all she could get out as she scrabbled to put some distance between them. Her underwear was soaked, and she didn't dare look at his crotch. She suspected she might have left a mark in more ways than one. Straightening herself up, she clocked his hands flexing together. The knuckles were white as he clenched them by his sides.

'It's okay,' he said, his voice so husky it made her core clench again. 'Believe me, that's nothing to be apologising to me for. Just answer me one question—hormones, or me?'

She didn't answer him. Barely able to draw breath, she willed herself to set the record straight. This was a bad idea. They weren't together, and they were about to become parents. She wasn't this person, had never been this person, but Colton Anderson had a habit of making her feel she could be. As if she could do anything and laugh her head off doing it. She was pregnant, forty and pretty sure that, if that phone call hadn't come through, she would have popped her 'have sex in the kitchen' cherry. *Yeah, and had a* lot *of fun to boot.*

'I…er…'

She clasped her hands around her waist for something to ground her and risked looking at him. *Geez.* Looking at him there, his blond hair raked through by her fingers, didn't help. His lips were utterly kiss swollen. It was a look she wouldn't forget any time soon. The man was *hot* and, after the night when he'd well and truly rocked her world, she knew just what he could bring to the table. She was about to tell him when he got there first.

'You can't look at me like that right now, sweetheart. After that, I'm finding it pretty hard not to show you it's definitely me.'

She whimpered, actually whimpered, out loud. His eyes darkened, and when he leaned in to kiss her again she didn't stop him. She didn't want to. She was ready to be devoured all over again, but his kiss was soft, a brush of his lips as he pressed his forehead to hers.

'That little noise you just made, Neve Truby, was not hormones.' Breathing her in, he dropped a kiss to her forehead again and lifted her down. 'Come on.' He smiled. 'We need to eat, and we have some online shopping to do. Maybe you could show me the spare room, and we can see how things could work as a nursery for the little ones.'

'Sounds good—after food. I'm starving.'

It had been a while since lunch, and the adrenaline of the last couple of hours had burned off some energy.

'At your service, sweetheart. Let's get you fed.'

CHAPTER FIVE

WORKING ALONGSIDE NEVE TRUBY was both a dream come true and an unbearable curse.

He ordered enough Chinese food to feed a small army. Which, in a way, they were—their little army. They put some medical drama on the television and gone through Baby Heaven's website together. It was nice, but the tension between them was still there. She was all business with the shopping, writing down the list of baby things they needed and ticking them off. They argued about who would pay, till he insisted that he was in this all the way. Eventually, she let him pay, but had insisted on sending half to his bank account.

He returned the payment the second he got home, so over the next few days they played a game of 'pass the deposit'. It was annoyingly cute on her part but still made him bristle underneath it all. If she wasn't going to let him at least pay for things his babies would need, how was he ever going to get her to let him in? He didn't need the money. He was renting a small apartment in the Falls; he'd bought the car outright. He had money in the bank, and he knew her divorce couldn't have been easy. The house she lived in now was nice, but it wasn't as big as the one she'd bought with Brett.

He knew enough about Brett to realise that he wouldn't be hurting for money. Neve had done what she usually did, she'd taken care of herself and not asked for what she deserved. The relationship between Brett and her had always been a give and take one, favouring Brett. He'd seen them go halves on meals before, and he knew that it was Brett's way. Heck, the bloke would moan if he had to buy a round, and buying his girlfriend dinner…

When Colton had ordered the Chinese takeaway, he'd paid before Neve had even got out of the shower. When she'd offered half, he'd refused. He could feed his woman and look after her. Maybe it was old-fashioned, a little protective, caveman-adjacent, but it was what he wanted to do. Neve looked after everyone else; it was her turn to be pampered. If she would let him do it, he would make it his life's work. After all, he had a lot of time to make up for. It just made working alongside her all the harder. He was more than done with the whole 'aloof separation' thing.

Liv and Bronwyn knew he was the man from the bar that night, but they didn't know the rest. Neve wanted time to tell people and, given he was the fox in her henhouse, he had to go with it. Let her get her head around the babies and what that entailed. She'd called him her partner when she'd introduced him to Greg, but they worked together. 'Partner' was a vague word with medical colleagues. Greg had seemed to pick up that it was a personal attachment but, other than Bronwyn and Liv watching him like a prize fish in an aquarium when he was near Neve, nothing else had been said.

Dr Ferry would have to be told eventually. They weren't technically breaking any rules, given that they were not in a relationship, but time was ticking. He wasn't going to leave here at the end of his contract without her being his. Working with her, helping her to prepare for the babies, was his best shot at getting her really to see him. To want him to stick around once Dr Barnes came back. He'd have to work, but that wasn't his priority; not any more. He'd make it work somewhere close by, if he had to, but he needed her to trust that he was always going to come back to her.

She was more relaxed around him. She accepted his deliveries of crackers and ginger ale when he came to her house to check on her. She ate lunch with him, and the others sometimes, but it was surface level. There'd been no more kisses, no more heated make-out sessions. He'd caught her watching him, but she hadn't been on house calls with him since. It was always one of the other nurses, her two best buddies back at the clinic. She kept out of his reach. She seemed to be getting used to him being around, but it would never be enough. It was comfortable, in a way he liked, but he still couldn't help but feel gutted. It was as if he'd finally got a taste of her, but he'd messed everything up. He'd heard her that night at the bar, known what she wanted and would have done anything to give it to her. And he had, but he'd wanted so much more than she did.

That first morning at her house, he'd gone to play the dashing hero, giving her a lift to work on his bike. He'd planned to ask her out before the news of the job landed; beg her for a proper date. It had been the chance to show her the real him, not the commitment-phobic wanderer she'd assumed he was. Now, it was all skewed. Some of the pieces were there but not fitting into the right pattern—the one he'd had in his head for years as he watched her from afar.

He'd been delusional, coming here to Swallow Falls like this. As soon as he'd heard about her divorce, he'd felt the pull of her. He'd known that, if ever there was going to be a chance to get his woman, it was then… or never. A woman like her wouldn't have been alone for long, and she might have ended up carrying someone else's child, with her babies calling him Daddy.

Which was the other thing. She was carrying his children, and he wanted to shout it from the damn rooftops. He wanted to be there for every moment, but the space between them made him ache. He'd always pictured being a father at some point, loving his children and being there for everything from night feeds to taking them up in the air and showing them the world below. Neve was having his twins. Every time he looked at her, his whole body tingled with the urge to be close. To touch her stomach and picture the lives they had created within.

In short, he was a great, big, growly bear who wanted to roar and slash any threats away with a swipe of his paw, to protect his family. If only he'd had the chance to have that chat with her that morning. The irony was, he hadn't wanted to scare her off. It had seemed too much to tell her his intentions and reasons for coming to work near her when she'd given him the time of day in the bar, before she'd fallen pregnant. Now, he wished he'd not waited as long. He should have called her right after, but he'd wanted to make sure the job was his and that he had a place nearby. To get himself set up as the perfect man; show her that nothing would stop him from staying in Swallow Falls for a while; finally take his shot. Now, the end date on his contract was a barrier between them. He was caught in a game of 'softly softly catchee monkey'.

As he did his final checks on the helicopter and felt the pull of her once more, he realised that, if this didn't work out the way he wanted, he was in for more of the same: worshipping her from afar, wishing she were his. But it would be far worse then, because his babies would be with her, calling him Daddy and witnessing their dad be the weak-willed man who couldn't snag the only woman he'd ever wanted. All because he'd wanted to keep a friend who hadn't deserved her in the first place.

Neve stooped to pick up the clipboard she'd dropped, breathing in to stave off the wave of nausea that roiled through her. They were setting up for the day, before the patients started rolling in. They had their GP service there and the rest of the facility was for urgent patient care. With them being on the Outback skirt, they dealt with everything from snake bites to flu shots to the bigger emergencies. They had two fully operational operating rooms out back, but thankfully they were rarely used these days. The critical patients were usually helicoptered to the nearest city hospital, but Swallow Falls Medical Centre was geared up for anything. The people who lived here tended to want to stay out of the city if they could help it, preferring their quieter way of life. When she'd studied in Sydney, she'd loved the bustle of it all, but Swallow Falls was home. Luckily, Brett had been happy to commute, and as it turned out that had been a blessing.

'What's with you today? You're all thumbs,' Bronwyn commented.

'Nothing, I'm just tired.'

Bronwyn rolled her eyes. 'No, it's more than that. You've been skittish since Colton came. I know you had a thing, but you've been off your game lately—quiet, disappearing off to the toilet. Is there something we need to know?'

Neve checked around them. Liv wasn't in yet, but the receptionist Cara was within earshot.

'Come in here a minute.' She pulled Bronwyn into the supply room, leaning on a shelf as yet another wave of morning sickness rippled through her. Some days were better than others, and today she was definitely feeling pregnant. Her uniform was starting to feel a tad snug. The time for avoiding telling people was pretty much over.

'Okay, so it was more than a thing. It's more of an ongoing...thing.'

Bron's jaw dropped into an excited squeal. 'Oh my God, spill!'

'It's not like that. He's Brett's friend, Bron. They were best friends, back in the day. We used to hang out together, well, in a group. I've known him almost as long as I have Brett.'

Neve shushed her friend's audible gasp. 'Sorry.'

Bronwyn winced, furtively glancing towards the door before leaning closer. 'I thought it was weird. There seemed to be a lot of familiarity between you both.'

'We've known each other a long time, as I said. He had a fallout with Brett, but he would never speak about it.' And she'd never ask Colton. He'd already made it clear that he didn't want Brett to be involved in their conversations. 'We got on well; I liked talking to him. He just kind of melted away from our lives.'

'So, he always liked you, then?'

'What? No.' *Had he?* She'd started to suspect as much. He'd more or less hinted as much, but then why the silent, brooding looks back then when they'd been around each other? The closer she and Brett had become, Colton had been around less and less. And then there'd been the whole best man thing that had seemed to end their relationship altogether. Brett had always been tight-lipped about it, but she knew whatever had gone on between them was a bust up big enough to end their friendship and had made both men turn on each other.

'I don't know,' she finally admitted. The side she'd seen of Colton since his return definitely didn't add up. The intensity of their intimacy was nothing she'd ever felt before. Was it mere animal attraction or not? She didn't think so. She liked talking to him, being around him. *Hormones or him?* 'Honestly, mate, I don't really know. It's...complicated. I'm sort of losing my mind over this. That's why I've been so weird; it's a lot being around him at work.'

'I get the looks he shoots you now. I thought it was just lust, but I think he really likes you, Neve! That's kinda romantic, you know.' She was in full-on swoon mode now. 'Yearning is pretty hot.'

'Yeah, well, it's not really like that.'

'But you spent the night with him, right? Has he been wooing you this whole time or is it just pure sexual tension?'

Neve blushed, remembering the hot session in her kitchen, and all the little things he'd done for her since, which just made Bronwyn more excited. 'I knew it! You didn't fool me with the whole leaving separately thing that night. I just knew you were hot for the doctor. Jeez, I could see the heart eyes going on between you two. Liv sees it too.'

'Liv does? What did she say?'

'Well, she's still pretty salty after the last doctor left, so she's all down on love at the minute. She still noticed a weird energy with you two. You fancy him, don't you?'

'Yep,' Neve admitted, realising the jig was up. She should have known her friends would spot something between them a mile off; they were her ride or dies. Nothing went on without them telling each other… till now.

Sucking in a breath, she rectified the problem. 'There's more, B. I'm…pregnant.' Well, it was out there. She'd have to tell HR anyway, and her friends should know first—the whole truth. 'With his twins.'

Bronwyn's jaw dropped so low to the floor, she looked like a cartoon character. Neve gave her a minute, half-expecting her eyes to pop out of her head. She waited till she cracked. 'Say something, B. I'm freaking out here as it is.'

Her friend replied by pulling her into a rib-compressing hug.

'Oh, girl. Twins? I can't believe it! You're going to be a mum!'

Neve crumbled at her words. Choking on a sob, she hugged her back just as fiercely.

'I know, it's…'

'Amazing,' Bronwyn finished for her. 'I can't believe it! We've all wanted this for you so badly, and after Brett… Wait…' She pulled back, wiping at Neve's tears. Her own eyes were watery through her happy smile. 'Are you telling me that Dr Chopper got you pregnant on the first try?'

Neve laughed through her sobs. 'Well, first, second, third.'

'Wow! What a divorce party, eh? I bet that one will be hard to top.'

The two women laughed together till they cried, hugging each other before cracking up again.

'You're happy, right?' Bron checked, her brows knitting together. 'About the babies? You won't be alone, you know. Those babies have two of the best aunties a baby could wish for. We'll help.'

The door opened, and Liv's brow quirked up. 'Help with what?' Her expression turned murderous. 'What's happened? Who's upset you?' She glanced round the room, fists clenched against some unseen threat. Both women laughed even harder.

'Come here.' Neve grinned. 'Calm down, Livzilla. We're okay. I'm…pregnant.'

Olivia's jaw dropped. 'You're what? We're having a baby?'

'Babies.' Neve giggled. 'It's twins.'

Olivia was bouncing on the spot now, clapping like a cheerleader. 'Twins? We're having two babies! That's amazing, Neve!' She barrelled into the pair of them, and the three women hugged each other, jumping round in a tight circle as they embraced each other. 'Hey… wait.' Liv brought them to a stop. 'Who's the father?'

Neve didn't get chance to answer. There was a soft knock on the door before it swung open.

'Hey,' Colton said, causing them all to turn towards him. Bronwyn, to her credit, kept it together better than Olivia did. She took one look at Colton, saw the flush on Neve's face and gasped theatrically. Bronwyn, thankfully, took charge.

'Come on, Liv, we have work to do.'

Liv's protest was swiftly cut off by Bronwyn, who practically dragged her out of there. Behind Colton's back, Liv mouthed, 'He's the daddy?' just before Bron clamped a hand over her mouth, shutting the door behind them.

'We've had a call-out—persons in distress. I'm heading out, but the patients will be coming here. Possible leg fractures, probably dehydration and sun exposure.'

'Okay, we'll be ready.'

Colton nodded, turning to the door. One hand on the doorknob, he turned back. 'So, I'm guessing from the squeals you told the girls.'

'About the babies?' She smiled at the memory. She was glad to have the news out there. Her friends were more like sisters than mates. Her babies would have two aunties who would protect them like velociraptors would their young. Especially Liv—that girl was a firecracker when someone lit her fuse. They either had to defuse her or stand back and enjoy the show. Colton was in for a rough ride with those two as his children's aunties. 'Yeah, I told them. It was time, and they sensed something was up. They were pretty happy about it.'

'I could tell.' His blue eyes scanned hers. 'Did you tell them I was the father, or did they guess?'

'I *knew it*!' Liv's voice carried through to them, just before Bronwyn's chiding tone cut her off amidst the tell-tale noise of a scuffle.

'Ow!' Liv whined. 'You just hit me in the boob!'

'Yeah, yeah,' they heard Bron retort. 'Keep it moving, sister, before the whole of Swallow Falls hears you.'

Neve giggled as their bickering voices receded. 'Er, I told Bron. I'm guessing she just filled Liv in. Is that okay?'

He was in front of her in an instant, his hands on the rounds of her shoulders. 'It's more than okay, sweetheart. I want everyone to know. I think we should tell management—Dr Ferry. No more hiding.'

She looked down at her snug uniform. 'It's definitely time. I'm growing by the day.' His smile was so cute as his eyes fell to her little bump. 'People will have something to say, you know.'

'I don't care.' He lifted her chin with a firm hand. 'Do you?'

A few months ago, smarting from her divorce and the knowledge that everyone knew about the breakdown of her fifteen-year marriage, she would have said yes. Colton wasn't a rebound, but he was unexpected. She would have dated eventually. It was not as if she'd planned to spend the rest of her life on her own.

When Colton had first dropped back into her life, she hadn't seen a for-ever kind of ending. But with him working here, being so sure of everything, she didn't feel quite so alone. With the gift he'd given her, she would never be alone again, and in this moment, with her sisters in her corner, her heart felt full. Even more so, being so close to the comforting presence of Colton.

Not for the first time, she wondered why she'd never gravitated to him more before, when she'd been dating Brett in those early days. More than once she'd wondered to herself about that time. If she'd got to know him better first, would she still have had the same life path?

'Neve,' he pressed, patient as always as he waited for her head to clear, for her to come back to him. The air charged when she finally met his gaze. They were close together, the scent of him all around her. The way he said her name made her spine tingle. 'Neve, do you care that people will know I'm the father?'

She could see the vulnerability in his eyes, and she wanted to kiss it away, use her lips to turn off her brain and show him that, even with everything warring within her, she'd never be ashamed that he was the man who'd made her pregnant. 'No, I suppose I don't.' She gently pushed at his chest. 'You need to go.'

He nodded once. 'Come with me.'

'Really?'

'Yeah, I could use a hand. Dr Ferry sent me here to get one of you anyway. Will you—come with me?'

'You really want me to?'

'Sweetheart, I always want you with me.'

She grinned. Another adventure with Batman. She was here for it. 'I'll get my kit.' He gave her the 'not a chance' head tilt. 'Okay, you can get it.'

'Finally catching on, Robin. Let's get going.'

'They should be right past this ridge,' she told him as he expertly flew the helicopter into position. Mount Feathertop loomed ahead, the landscape both lush and dangerous. The sun was blazing high in the sky now, raising the heat in the bush below. She'd hiked this area many times over the years, but it wasn't the easiest place on earth to be. People getting hurt out here made rescues tricky. They'd sent the unique co-ordinates through to the emergency services.

Colton nodded, and she had to remind herself not to ogle him in his headset and flight uniform. Seeing him flying the helicopter was yet another side of Colton. Flying doctors deserved their own shelf in the bookstore, because that erotic fiction would fly off the shelves. *Focus, Neve. You are a medical professional. Down, hormones. Bad baby brain.*

As he flew over the next rise in the rock, Neve spotted them. A man was waving wildly, a white piece of material in his grasp. He started gesturing wildly to another person just behind him, lying on the ground at the bottom of a small grouping of rocks. 'Got them!'

Colton radioed in. 'Contact made, two persons on

scene. One male with no visible injuries. One female on the ground. Is she moving?' he asked Neve.

Looking again, she watched as the man made his way back to the woman on the ground, and she shoved him away. 'Yep, she's awake and moving her upper limbs.' She added, 'Looks like she's not happy with him, though.'

'I bet,' Colton murmured, scanning the landscape. There was a piece of flat ground just big enough to land on. 'I'll set her down. Looks like we'll need the gurney and back board.'

Colton fell quiet as he set the chopper down, killing the engine and springing to action. He met Neve at her door, kit already on his back by the time she scrambled out. She'd already donned her hiking boots and protective gear, but he still gave her a nervous once-over.

'What?' she asked.

'Nothing.' He bit his lip. 'Just, be careful. The ground's a little rocky here.'

'Aw, worried about me, Batman?'

'Always, Robin. I know you got this; just watch your step. I don't want to be carrying your fine behind back.' He laughed when she stuck out her tongue. 'Saucy. Come on, let's go.'

She took the lead, Colton following behind with the gurney. It was essentially a back board with straps and wheels on the bottom, to enable him to pull the patient back to safety. It would be a very bumpy ride, and she could feel the tension rolling through Colton as they got to the patient.

'Thank God…' The man breathed, his cheeks red-hot against his pale complexion. 'We've been out here a while; I had to hike to get a signal.'

'No satellite phone?' Colton tutted. 'It's pretty remote here.'

The woman, a leggy redhead, winced as she glowered at her companion. 'That's what I said, but oh no! Bear Grylls here said we'd be fine. I ran out of water a couple of hours ago. Lost my footing on the rocks.'

Neve put her kit bag on the ground, crouching down to assess her injuries.

'Did you hit your head?'

'No. Scraped my arm pretty badly, though.' She lifted her right arm and Neve could see the gash from her elbow to her mid-forearm. The blood flow had been minimised by the belt that was serving as a tourniquet above her elbow.

'Good thinking with the belt. I'm Neve; what's your name?'

'Helen, and this big doofus is Scott.'

'Hey, I'm Colton. Scott, let me check you over. Neve, you good there?'

'For now. We'll need to dress the wound before transport and it's going to need stitches.' Helen groaned. 'Let's take a look at that leg. Mind if I cut these leggings off?'

Helen whimpered when Neve's hands gently touched her leg. Her shoe was already off, and the ankle was definitely broken. It was already bruising, the skin turning purple and black.

'Please, it's so tight, but I couldn't move to get them off.'

Colton passed Scott a canteen of water, checking his observations off quickly.

'No problem. Hold still for me, okay?'

She gently cut away the material. Helen's leg was straight, no open fractures, but obviously broken. There was a large dent at the right-hand side just below the knee. This type of indentation was a telltale sign that the bones were broken and the muscles misaligned.

'Definitely broken, possibly tibia and fibula,' she said over her shoulder to Colton. 'We need the inflatable splint.'

'I told you, Scott! We should have gone to Sydney, like I said, but no, you had to damn well hike, didn't you?'

'Helen!' Scott whined. He looked a little better now with some water in his body. 'It was an adventure, okay? I didn't know that this was going to happen!'

'Yeah,' she spat, wincing as Neve readied her arm for some pain relief and a fluid drip. 'Well, adventures suck, you idiot! I never should have gone out with you in the first place.'

Neve glanced at Colton, who pulled a funny face at her.

'Accidents happen, even on adventures,' he murmured, and Neve felt the warmth flood her cheeks.

'Not always a bad thing, though,' she replied, and was rewarded by a panty-melting smile in return.

'No,' he agreed, his eyes burning through her. 'Sometimes it works out perfectly.'

Helen wasn't in on it, however, and she shot them both an incredulous look. 'Oh yeah,' she grumbled. 'This worked out so well! What are you two talking about?'

Neve administered the morphine and opened the saline drip, and passed the bag of fluid to Scott. 'Keep this above her head. Stay close when we move her. Helen, how's your pain now? Try to keep your leg as still as possible.' Colton carefully strapped her leg into the inflatable splint, adjusting the straps so that it would hold her firm but not cut off the circulation.

'How's that feel?'

'Good.' Helen pouted. Neve readied the gas and air, holding out the mask.

'Have you had gas and air before?'

Helen eyed the mask. 'No, but I was a birth partner for my sister. She got pretty loopy.'

'It's perfectly safe, and it will help with the pain whilst we get you into the helicopter.'

'We're going to take you straight to the hospital in Melbourne,' Colton added, readying the gurney. 'Scott, do you think you can help transport her?'

Neve narrowed her eyes at him. 'I can assist.'

Colton pursed his lips. 'You need to bring the tank and the kit.'

'Scott has the IV bag.' His look told her that he wasn't letting this drop, and she decided to let him win this one. He had a point, but the thought that this might be her last day out in the field for a while bothered her.

'Fine,' she agreed, getting to work to show Helen how to use the gas and air. In minutes, Helen was as happy as a clam. Colton carried most of Helen's weight, with Scott holding up the back of the gurney. Neve trailed behind with all the equipment, checking her vitals on the way.

'I love you, Scott.' Helen grinned at her boyfriend once they were all in the helicopter. 'I'm sorry I was such a pain.'

'No,' Scott murmured, kissing her free hand and pushing the mask back to her face. 'It was a bad idea coming here. I just wanted to be romantic, and you got hurt.'

'I really did.' She giggled, wincing as Neve cleaned her arm wound and applied a bandage. 'I think I might have a scar.'

'Just a little one,' Neve promised as Colton started the engine. 'A few stitches, and it will fade.'

'It will?'

'Of course, and your leg will heal. No open fractures, and blood flow is good. A few weeks in a cast and crutches, and you will be back on your feet.' She nodded to Scott. 'I prescribe lots of get-well flowers and waiting on her on hand and foot.'

Helen giggled again, reaching for Scott's hand.

'He'll look after me. He's pretty good that way.' Her brows knitted together, as though remembering something. 'Did you really hike to get me help?'

Scott kissed her fingers one at a time, straining against his seat belt to stay close to where she was strapped in. 'I would do anything for you, you know that.'

'I do love you, Scottikins.' He laughed, dropping a kiss on her forehead and resting his against hers. It reminded Neve of Colton, and when she looked towards the cockpit he was already looking back at her. Which set off another frisson of butterflies in her stomach.

'You strapped in, Neve?'

She gave him the thumbs-up, but he didn't look away till she showed him she was fully protected.

'Over-protective,' she mouthed at him. He just winked back, and then they were in the sky.

'What a day!' Neve groaned as Colton landed back at the clinic.

'I know; Scott and Helen were great in the end, though. It's good that she didn't need surgery on that leg.'

'She was lucky. A few months in a cast and a scar; it could have been a lot worse.'

'Did you hear him ask the nurse if they could have adjoining beds for the night?'

'I know, bless him. I felt a little sorry for him. If she hadn't got that pain relief, I think we could have had a full scale break-up on our hands.'

'Situations like that tend to break people down to their base feelings.'

'True.' She smiled. 'You were pretty protective out there, you know.'

He didn't look a bit sorry. 'And?'

'It was quite annoying.'

'But necessary. You can't be carrying patients, Neve. I was just keeping my partner safe.' He stepped out of the chopper, coming to her side. She waited for him to open the door, rolling her neck to try to stretch out the kinks in her back.

'There's that partner word again.' She sighed to herself, rubbing her slightly rounded tummy. Things were getting complicated. If the call-out hadn't come through, she would have kissed him again. She always wanted to kiss him. It was getting harder to know what the boundaries were—boundaries she needed to keep for her own sanity. She couldn't fall for Colton. He wasn't hers to keep.

He helped her out of the cockpit, and when she felt that familiar zing at his touch she knew what she needed to do.

'I think you're right; it's time to tell Dr Ferry.'

He took the kit out of her hands the second she picked it up. 'I agree.'

'You do?'

'Of course.' He shrugged. 'You are starting to show, and your duties will need to change soon. I know you don't like this, but I think going out in the field will have to be out till after you deliver. We need to get out in front of this—make plans for your leave.'

'We? You're going to come with me to tell Dr Ferry?'

He stopped walking. 'Neve, not this again.'

'Not what again?' When she faced him, his face was stony.

'This.' He motioned between them. 'I don't know whether I am coming or going with you. You call me your partner; let me in and then push me away; kiss me and then bail; agree with me, and then question whether I'm going to see things through. I never wanted to hide any of this from anyone.'

He sighed, a sad smile crossing his features. 'I'm in this. I told you then, I'm telling you now. I wish you could believe that, fully, trust me fully, like I have you from the start. I'm getting whiplash here, sweetheart. We are too old to play games with each other.'

Well, that was direct. And true.

'I'm not playing games with you, Colton.'

'Prove it,' he retorted, his voice full of challenge as he stalked closer to her. 'Tell me something.'

'Like what?'

He reached for her, dropping the bags and pulling her to him. 'Tell me what I am to you, because a partner means many things. I know you like me.'

'Of course I like you.' She tried to be light-hearted. 'That's why we're in this position in the first place.'

'I don't just mean in bed, Neve, and you know it. I know you find me attractive. I think we can agree we get on, but you keep putting a wall up between us. What do you want?'

'Colton, you can't ask me that.'

'To hell I can't. I came back after that night to see if you wanted to see me again. I didn't run when I found out you were pregnant. I don't plan to run. I've told you before, I am in this—for the babies, for you.'

'You say that now, but it's been what, a few weeks? This is not what it will be like. When we have two babies to look after, and real life sets in, that's when I can't have someone running out on me. I need to do this myself, stand on my own two feet. After my divorce, I told myself that I would live my life for me, put myself number one. I don't want to worry about anyone else. I won't have room for anything but these babies.'

'They come first, but what about you? Who's going to look after you?'

'I will,' she countered, feeling like the worst person in the world. She wanted nothing more than just to go with the flow, be with Colton and not worry about what came next. But life wasn't like that, and she wasn't built that way. She needed a plan, security. 'I'm not some bright-eyed twenty-something any more. I don't have the time or energy to get into something that might end badly, and we have children coming that will bind us for ever. I don't want that for them. My parents were never happy together. I was pretty much left to raise myself, while they barely tolerated each other till I was old enough to leave.'

'Why can't you get that I am not leaving? Just because the job has an expiration date doesn't mean we do. I want to date you, Neve. I know you feel what I do. I just wish you could trust me.'

'I do trust you, Colton.'

His expression lit up, and she hated herself.

'I trust you with being a good father, by being there for the babies, but we each have our own lives. We have a weird history, and I don't trust what I feel right now. I am tired, and a little scared. My body's changing; my hormones are all over the place. I'm newly divorced. I didn't expect to be in this situation. I thought my chance to be a mother was gone, and I just want to do things right.'

'That's all I want, but surely the best thing for our children is for their mother and father to be together?'

'In an ideal world, perhaps.' She forced down the feelings his words stirred up in her. 'But we had a one-night stand, not a relationship. If it doesn't work out, that will be too much for me.'

'I won't leave you, sweetheart. I want this.'

I want this too, she wanted to say. They were both in their forties, but their lives were so different. They got on, yes, but what if the thing pulling them together was just sexual attraction? If that faded then all he'd be left with was a very tired woman and two demanding babies. Life on the road would surely be a pull then. He'd be fine, but she would be left broken-hearted, with two constant reminders of him to raise. It was too much of a risk.

'I was with Brett for years, and he left when things got tough. I have to be careful with my decisions right now.'

Colton pulled away, scooping up the bags in a flourish. 'I am nothing like Brett. I thought you understood that.'

'I do, but I knew him for years. I can't be blindsided like that again. I just think it's best if we keep things simple, Colt: co-parenting colleagues.'

'That's really what you want?' His whole body was clenched, taut with tension. 'That's what you wanted when you were wrapped around me on your kitchen island? Because I feel a lot more than friendship for you, Neve. Co-parents; colleagues…? If you think that's all we are to each other, you're lying to yourself. Let me know when you're ready to go and see Dr Ferry.' His jaw clenched. 'I'd like to be there, if it's not too much trouble.'

'Colton, don't be like that.'

'I'm fine, Neve. You constantly think I'm leaving, but it's you that keeps running. I'll see you inside. I'll tell Dr Ferry we need a word.'

Tears stinging her eyes, she waited for him to walk away before following him in. It was nearing the end of her shift, and she was bone-tired. Luckily the staff was all busy when she entered the medical centre, and she managed to avoid small talk and awkward questions.

Colton was already in Dr Ferry's office when she knocked.

'Come in.' Abe Ferry smiled. As one of the founding doctors of the new medical centre, he was a good boss: fair; excellent with his patients and staff. But Neve still felt nervous as she smiled back at him. 'Take a seat. You both look tired.'

'Busy day,' Colton murmured. Taking a seat at his desk, Dr Ferry eyed them over the rim of his tortoise-shell glasses.

'I heard. So, what was it you wanted to talk about? Dr Anderson said you have something to inform me of?'

She glanced across at Colton, but he kept his eyes front.

'Well, I'm pregnant.'

Dr Ferry didn't flinch. 'And?'

What? 'And… Dr Anderson is the father.'

He pushed his glasses up his nose. 'I see.'

'It happened before he started the job, and it won't affect our working relationship.'

'Strictly business,' Colton added, his tone cold. 'We have agreed to co-parent, and I understand if you wish to look for another doctor to cover for Dr Barnes.'

Neve's heart clenched at the thought. She'd shut him down, but the thought of him leaving now didn't sit right at all.

'So, you're not in a relationship?'

'No,' Neve confirmed.

Abe turned to eye Colton. 'Do you agree?'

'I agreed to co-parent and work together, yes. I am a professional; I can separate the two. Our twins come first.'

That got Abe's attention. His eyebrows rose so quickly, his glasses did a little jump on the bridge of his nose.

'Twins?' He broke out into a huge smile, rising from his desk and coming to Neve. She rose to meet him as he held out his arms. 'Congratulations! I am very happy for you. I know how long you have wanted this. Let me know what you need.'

'She needs to be benched from the outreach care,' Colton supplied, standing but keeping his distance.

'Of course.' Dr Ferry held out his hand to him. 'Congratulations to you too, Dr Anderson. It seems we might have you around longer than we expected.'

Colton shook his hand. 'Thanks.' His eyes fell to Neve, intent evident in his expression. 'I'll be here as long as Neve wants me to be.'

'Good.' Dr Ferry smiled. 'Well, we are all adults here. Neither of you reports to the other so, if you are both happy to sign a disclosure that you have a personal relationship outside of work, then HR will be satisfied. Do either of you have anything to discuss in private?'

Colton was already walking towards the door. 'Not me. I have to finish my work in the hangar. Let me know when the paperwork is ready.'

When it was just the two of them left in the room,

Dr Ferry guided Neve into a chair. She hadn't even realised she'd wobbled a little on her feet.

'How are you feeling? Are your scans up to date? I am assuming you are under the care of Melbourne General?'

'Yes, we had the scan—non-identical twins.'

'I'm guessing you're around the sixteen-week mark.'

'Yeah…you can tell that?'

Dr Ferry blushed. The man had never blushed in the whole time she'd known him. 'It's a small town, not much to do around here. I can recognise morning sickness when I see it. My wife used to eat crackers too—something I noticed Dr Anderson always seemed to have on hand.'

'It's that obvious, huh?'

He waved her off. 'I'm an old soul, my dear. I am a fan of love.'

'It's not love. I don't think he's even speaking to me right now. This wasn't exactly the plan for my life post-divorce.'

Abe took the seat next to her, patting her hand. 'This must be daunting for you. You've always been the most organised nurse I've ever had. It's why you're such a good senior nurse. You always have things under control; you look after everyone around you.'

'That's half the problem. I don't know how to let someone look after me.'

'And Colton wants to?'

'I don't know what he wants. It's all so up in the air right now, and I just want to focus on what I can control.'

'That's not going to last once those babies arrive,

Neve. Raising children is not easy, and if you try to control everything you might just miss out on all the best things. If Colton wants to help you, let him.' He flashed her a trademark Abe smile. Her boss was as wise as he was kind. 'Without over-stepping, I've seen how you two are around each other. It doesn't take a genius to work out that you mean something to each other.'

'It's complicated, I'm afraid.'

'Life is complicated, my dear. Don't let the past dictate your future. It's nice to see you happy. Now, get yourself home and put those feet up. Swollen ankles are common with twins.'

'Now you tell me.' She laughed. 'Thanks Dr Ferry. We won't let the clinic be affected.'

'Never doubted you, Nurse Truby. You just look after those babies. It will be nice to have some little ones around the place.'

When Neve got to her car, she saw Colton's bike was gone.

'Well,' she muttered to herself. 'You got what you wanted, Neve. Well done.'

She headed home, showered, ate and headed to bed. Bron and Liv both called her, but she sent a message to the group chat telling them she was tired and would talk later. She turned off her phone and she was asleep as soon as her head hit the pillow.

CHAPTER SIX

For the next three months, Colton stewed. Working with Neve every day was easier, given the distance, but working in such close proximity to her was starting to get to him. She was getting bigger each week that passed, and her baby bump well and truly popped. It made him feel a certain way, seeing her swell with his children and not being able to be there with her. He left her lunch every day in the break room, and every night when he checked the fridge and found it gone it filled him with emotion. She was letting him take care of her in tiny ways, but not how he really wanted to.

The separation was too much. Bron and Liv had taken on the out-of-clinic duties, and they were careful not to mention her. Which was worse, because all he wanted to hear about was her. She had her next scan in a couple of days, and they both had the afternoon off to go. At least she'd let him know about that. She'd texted him the dates, and when he'd texted back to offer to drive them she'd agreed.

He couldn't wait to see his babies on the screen again and try once more to avoid being able to tell what gender they were. They'd said that they would wait for the surprise, but given their medical knowledge it was getting harder at each scan not to see something. He should check with Neve how they should handle it this time, which would mean another short burst of texts. Other than working together and talking about patients, that was the extent of their interaction and it was killing him. He had hoped that she'd miss him, but other than catching her looking his way occasionally she was nothing but professional.

News of her pregnancy was well and truly out there now, and everyone was thrilled to hear the news. But he was still out of the loop. It wasn't as if he expected her to tell everyone she was pregnant by the temporary doctor after a one-night stand, but to see everyone congratulate her and not be part of that was hard.

Every night after work, he pounded the weights at the gym. He rang his friends, who mostly worked, and sat in his apartment. He'd read two books on childcare, readying himself for what was to come, but he didn't know how much of it he'd be able to put into practice. Sooner or later, he'd need to put plans in place if he was going to stick around: look for a permanent place and see what work was available that would enable him to stay there.

Beyond that, he'd need to get used to the fact that Neve might meet someone. A woman like her, even as a single mum, would not be alone for ever. Then he would have to share his family with some other guy, all the while wishing it was him.

He was sitting on his couch, watching some programme he wasn't even following, when his phone buzzed.

Hi, are you busy?

Am I busy? she asks. Yeah, thinking about you.

No. You okay?

I'm fine, but I could use some help at the house if you're not doing anything.

He was off the couch before his reply pinged.

On my way.

She looked as cute as hell when she answered the door. She had a pair of oversized pyjamas on over her bump, her blonde hair up in a loose bun.

'Thanks for coming over.' She smiled, moving aside to let him pass. 'Sorry for bothering you.'

There was a ton of boxes in the hall, and she was brandishing a screwdriver.

'The baby stuff got delivered? Why didn't you tell me?'

She shifted from foot to foot, the guilt evident on her beautiful features.

'Hell, Neve. I thought you would have told me.'

'Are you mad?'

Colton folded his arms, leaning against the wall. 'Frustrated. Tell me, if you didn't get stuck would you have called for help?' She winced. 'Exactly. I'm about done with this. I'm playing things your way, but you are halfway through your pregnancy. You shouldn't be doing stuff like this on your own, and this equipment is for my babies too. You either want me in this or you don't, but no more half-measures.'

'I didn't send the money back today.'

That stopped him. 'You didn't?'

She shook her head. 'No. This stuff only got delivered today. I made a start, but then I realised that we should do it together.'

'Finally.' He looked closer at the boxes. Not one of them was open. 'So, you waited for me?'

Please say yes. I've waited for you for years.

'Yes. My neighbour took the boxes in, but I wasn't going to do it tonight. I just felt a bit overwhelmed when I came home.' She waved at the boxes all around them. 'This is a lot. My spare room is decorated but it's an empty shell. With the scan looming, I…panicked, I think.'

'There's no need to panic.'

'Have you not seen all the boxes?'

He took the screwdriver from her grasp, pulling out his phone. 'Pick a box; I'll ring for pizza.'

'Extra pepperoni?'

'Sure, whatever you want. Just pick a box, and we'll make a start.'

CHAPTER SEVEN

IT WAS LATE into the night, and they weren't even halfway through the boxes.

'The cots look great.' Colton smiled as he ran his hands along the twin white wooden cots.

Neve sat in the matching rocking chair, her feet up on the foot stool. She was dead tired now, her back hurting. Colton had let her open some of the smaller boxes, with nappies, teddies, clothes. He'd put the rocking chair together first, insisting she sat in it for the rest of the time and just read out the instructions. For once, she hadn't even argued. When the boxes had arrived, she'd taken one look at them filling her downstairs and her first instinct was to dial his number. 'It's a good job your spare room is big enough for two.'

She was about to answer when she felt it. 'Colton!' she squeaked, her hands going to her belly. 'Get over here. The babies are kicking again.'

He came to kneel in front of her, his hand outstretched. She took it, placing it over the spot where one of their children was kicking up a storm. They waited, Neve watching Colton's face. When the kick happened again, his face lit up from the inside. He was glowing as his hand was jolted by his little baby.

'Wow,' he breathed. 'We have a little soccer star on our hands, sweetheart.' His eyes were watery when they met hers. 'What does it feel like? Does it hurt?'

She shook her head. 'It feels weird, but a good weird, if you know what I mean. I'm pretty sure one of them gets the hiccups, too.'

Colton's laugh was loud and joyous. 'That's amazing.' He dipped his head close to her bump. 'Hey there,' he murmured, his hands cupping her stomach. 'It's your daddy here. Your mum and I are getting your room ready for you. You had better get used to the sound of my voice, because I can't wait till you get here and cause a little havoc.'

Neve chuckled. 'Not too much, I hope.'

He winked at her. 'Ignore your mum. She's all about the adventure too.' His lips kissed the spot where his hand had been. 'I love you.' He moved, kissing a spot on the other side. 'And I love you.' His hands moved around her waist, his head raising to look her in the eye. 'And your mum too, for having you.'

Neve's breath caught as she drank him in on his knees before her, proclaiming his feelings. Had he just said he loved her? Not in so many words, but she knew emotions were at play. It was hard to tell what there was about them as a couple and what was caused by their growing feelings for their impending family. He kissed her belly again then went to stand.

She grabbed his arm, stilling him. 'Colton, I—'

'Tell me,' he said, his voice hoarse. 'Tell me you feel this too, sweetheart. This pull between us.'

'I do, but I don't fully trust it.'

'Is this the "hormones or me" thing again?'

'I don't know.' She bit her lip, and watched his eyes darken as he tracked the movement. 'I've never really been with anyone but…'

'He who shall not be named?'

'You're going there, really?' They burst into laughter, which was swiftly cut off by a yawn. 'Sorry,' she said sleepily. 'Long day.'

'Hold still.' He wrapped his arms around her, lifting her as he stood. 'Time for bed, I think.' He walked into her bedroom and placed her on the edge of the bed, then knelt to take off her slippers. She winced as he brushed against her heel. 'Sore, huh?'

'I have cankles at this point.' She moaned as he started to knead her foot. 'Ooh, that's nice, but you don't have to.'

'Of course I do. Lie down properly; rest your legs.'

She didn't need to be told twice. Pulling the blanket over her, she switched on the bedside lamp and settled down against the pillows. He worked on one foot and then the other, his fingers like magic as he soothed her aches and pains.

'Thanks for today. It was nice tonight, putting the nursery together. I'm glad you're here.'

'Me too.' He came to lie with her, resting his head on the pillow. 'I'm glad you called. I like being here with you.'

'Stay the night.' It slipped out before she could process it. 'It's late.'

'You sure?'

'Yes. Stay. It's fine. Work know now, so it makes sense if we travel to work together in the morning.'

'Oh, so you only want me for a lift?'

Laughing, her hand slipped back into his. 'I need to save on petrol money; babies aren't cheap.'

He brought their hands over her bump, and she felt it again, that pull of him, stronger than before. He was back in her bed, but things had evolved since then. Just the memory of them together in her room made the flush creep across her cheeks. She could tell by his face that he sensed it as well.

'I could help with the hormones, you know.'

Her eyes locked with his. 'It's complicated enough already.'

'Doesn't have to be. I'm playing this your way, sweetheart, but taking care of you means taking care of every part. You just have to say the word.'

'It's not just the hormones, Colt. It is you too. That night we spent together was the best night I've ever had. I'm just scared of ruining this. You're not some one-night stand. I would never have done that if I didn't have some kind of attraction to you. I like you, but you're the father of my children, and that has to come first.'

'No matter what, we will work together to make sure they are happy and healthy.'

'And loved.'

'We already have that covered. I'm here for you too, Neve, not just the babies.'

She closed the distance between them and kissed him.

'Neve,' he muttered when they broke apart. 'Hormones, or me?'

'You,' she told him.

'Good to know,' he rumbled, pulling her close and sealing her mouth with his. He kissed her till she couldn't breathe, only breaking contact to kiss down her jawline, her neck and the tips of her collarbones. 'You're so beautiful, Neve. The bigger you get, the more gorgeous you look to me.' A devilish grin on his face, he came to kneel over her, straddling her legs without crushing her. 'Let me take care of you, sweet-heart.'

His hands slid down the waistband of her pyjama bottoms over her bump, his eyes searching her face in a silent request. She nodded, and he kissed her stomach twice before slowly lowering her bottoms. She was naked beneath, her breath rapid as she exposed herself to him.

'Perfect,' he mumbled, kissing the base of her belly. Lowering his body down the bed, he kissed the apex of her sex. 'So sexy, Neve.'

'I don't feel too sexy at the minute.' She blushed, but his gaze told her otherwise.

'Are you kidding? Baby, you're stunning. I've always thought you were beautiful, but every day, watching you grow our kids… I've been all over the world, and seen it from the skies, but you…'

He pressed his thumb to her centre and her whole body felt it. 'You're my favourite view, sweetheart.' He swirled his thumb in a circle, watching every tiny movement she made as his fingers made her nerve endings sing. 'That good, baby?'

'Yes,' she panted. 'More, Colt.' His grin was almost

wolfish as he lowered his head and pressed his mouth where his thumb had been, sucking, lapping and coaxing.

She whimpered as her orgasm began to build. 'Just like that,' she urged him on, her hips starting to buck as she reached forward and grasped tufts of his blond hair. He didn't let up, and when a finger pushed into her glistening sex she shuddered around it. He groaned, and she felt him everywhere, all around her, inside her. Her breaths were coming in rapid puffs and, when he crooked his finger and hit that sweet, sweet spot, it was game over. She came, hard. Still he didn't stop, using his fingers and mouth to wring every last tingle of release out of her as she crested, feeling as if her whole body were on fire.

As she came down, she became aware of his movements slowing and eventually coming to a stop just as the sensations were becoming too much for her to bear. Climbing back up the bed, he covered her with the blanket, dropping a kiss on her temple as he tucked her into his side.

'That was…'

'Sensational. Earth-shattering. Bat-tastic…?'

She burst into laughter. 'You're such a dork!'

He kissed her hair, tiny little kisses, as though he couldn't stop himself from touching his lips to hers. 'A hot dork, though, right?'

'Yeah, sure,' she teased, yawning as her post-orgasm glow lulled her to sleep. 'A modest, hot dork.'

'I'll take that, sweetheart. Now get some rest.'

She thought of what he'd just done to her, for her, and tilted her head up to him. 'What about you?'

'I'll be here.'

'No.' She blushed. How did this man still make her feel like a skittish teenager, even now? 'I mean, I could do something for you. To make you feel good.'

His lips curved into a satisfied smile. 'You already did that. Just being here with you does that for me.' He dipped his head, taking her mouth in a languid, unhurried kiss. 'I just want to fall asleep with you and wake up with you here.'

He squeezed her to him, and she felt his warmth envelop her, physical and emotional. She felt so comfortable, so cocooned, it was hard to keep her eyes open.

'I can do that.' She yawned, placing a hand on his chest. Minutes later, she was fast asleep.

CHAPTER EIGHT

'YOU KNOW, YOU really should try to get some help out there.'

Belinda Higgins laughed, wincing as Neve gently pulled another shard of glass out of her hand with a pair of tweezers.

'The boys are busy working. My daughters-in-law are all busy raising my grandbabies and working themselves. It was only some Christmas lights; I put them up in the same place every year.'

'Yeah, but this year you were seventy. I went to your party, remember? Maybe it's time to put the ladders away. Next time it might be more than your hand that gets hurt. Did you slip?'

Belinda, a stubborn woman who was a stalwart of the Falls, looked a little sheepish. 'Not quite. It was Dash.'

'Dash?' Neve didn't recall a family member of hers with that name.

'Yeah, my dumb rooster. I had just set the steps up under the eaves when the stupid thing tripped me. I went forward, put my hands out with the hammer in my hand and smashed my way straight through the window. Cut my hand up.'

Neve nodded, relieved that she wasn't dangling off the roof. Belinda's neighbour had driven her in, having heard her shouting, but hadn't known the details. Neve often worried about some of the more isolated members of Swallow Falls. Sometimes, when accidents happened, it was impossible for them to get help. Luckily, Belinda had two neighbours in earshot of her small farm.

'I swear, that rooster gets more irritating the older he gets. I told him I would make him into a pie when I got back, but he knows I'm all hot air.'

'So, what you are saying is, it was "fowl play" then?' Neve quipped. Belinda laughed that infectious little titter of hers, and Neve felt energised by the sound.

'I think at this point he just likes to keep me on my toes. The little featherbrain gets mad when I keep him from the hens. But I tell him, it's like all males—sometimes the women just need a break from all the annoying crowing he does.'

'Amen to that.' Neve grinned.

'Oh, I think you got a good one, though.' Belinda nodded towards the window, where the hangar lay beyond. 'The way he looks at you, I can just tell it's true love.'

Neve finished up, wrapping the remnants in blue roll to go for disposal. 'The way who looks at me?' she asked casually, keeping up the pretence that the whole town hadn't cottoned on to the fact that Colton was the man in question. They'd hadn't exactly made a secret of it over the last six weeks or so. He'd taken her out for dinner a few times at the local restaurant; he always pushed the trolley when they went food shopping together.

Belinda was having none of it. 'Dr Anderson, of course. Don't you play coy with me, now. We can all see it; how happy he makes you. It makes my heart glad to see it.' She leaned in closer, whispering conspiratorially. 'I never cared much for Brett.' She forked her fingers under her eyes. 'He always looked a little shifty in the eyes. But Dr Anderson…phew. When he points those gorgeous blue eyes your way, I can tell he isn't looking anywhere else. He's all for you, and you deserve that.'

Her smile broadened when she looked down at Neve's now very prominent baby bump. 'You too. I'm just so happy for you all.'

Neve finished up and bade her goodbye. Her comment about Brett was a little left field, and she wondered what Belinda had meant. Did other people here not like Brett? She'd never noticed, but she'd also seen how receptive they'd been to Colton when he'd come here. Everyone seemed to like him, and Belinda wasn't the first person who'd told her how happy they were for her. That they were glad she'd found a good man. She'd put it down to the babies, but perhaps it was more than that.

Brett had spent a lot of time away for work, and small-town life had been a struggle for him at times. She'd figured it would ease, and when their children came it would be different. When that never happened, Brett had started spending more and more time away. They would never have lasted; she knew that now. Having kids would just have kept them stuck together, he trapped here in the Falls. Maybe that was what Belinda had meant about Brett and him looking elsewhere. She'd seen that he'd had one foot out of the door throughout their marriage. After the first few years, they'd just settled into a rut; gone through the motions.

Neve didn't see that in Colton, but he was the wanderer, to Brett the city boy. How long would Colton stick around once the novelty of the impending babies wore off? Raising two children would be hard and they were in a kind of 'babymoon' bubble now. He lived for the moment, but what about when that moment passed? Would she be left holding the babies?

As if the babies could sense her scattered thoughts, they started wriggling as she walked down the corridor. She paused, putting a hand on the spot. 'I know, I know. Mama needs to have a talk with Daddy. I heard you; now, if you could stop kicking me in the ribs that would be great.' She rubbed her tummy till they stopped moving around.

The next day off, she told herself; the next time they had a day off together, she'd have a talk with him and tell him how she felt. She'd see where he was at, before she fell any deeper into this. Because one thing she knew for certain was that she was falling hard for Colton—had fallen. Waking up in his arms every morning, she felt complete, truly happy for the first time in years. She wanted those family days they'd talked about together. She'd don a soccer shirt and shout from the stands with her family; she'd do the family barbecues and nights watching movies. She'd be there when Colton took their children up in the air for the first time, and watch their faces light up when they saw their world from above.

She adored the father of her children, and that was that. She wanted him finally to take her again, to feel him inside her and show him how much she wanted and desired him. He was holding back that aspect of their relationship and, whatever he said to explain it, something in her did wonder whether he was hedging his bets. Whether he was starting to feel what Brett did—that in the end she wouldn't be worth sticking around for.

She only had a week left till her maternity leave started, and then she'd be a mum and too busy to deal with the additional emotional turmoil. For now, she had her patients to concentrate on, and that was something normally guaranteed to pull her out of her funk. But lately, hauling her huge baby bump around the clinic had been far more draining than she'd expected. Half the time when they got home after a shift, she ate with Colton and ended up passing out on the couch halfway through a show. Every morning, she'd wake up in bed in Colton's arms. Every night, he carried her up to bed and slipped under the covers with her. She'd never felt so looked after, so seen. The thought of not having that for ever was starting to depress her.

As much as she'd put the brakes on things before, his reluctance to take things further in bed was increasingly playing on her mind. He'd told her that he wanted to be careful because of the babies, that he didn't want to cause her discomfort, but every night she could tell he was finding it harder to hold back. She knew how he looked at her, how he tensed when she touched him. He was waiting until she was fully sure of them. She knew it. She knew him. He was being cautious, 'the hormones or me?' discussions they had getting more frequent. It was his way of checking in. She now hated that she had been the partial cause of his hesitance. Especially when all she wanted was him to finally take her again and to feel him right there, with her.

The next day off: she'd give it till then, and then she'd have the talk. Tell him how she was feeling, and hope that he still wanted the same things. Because she was fast realising that she was in this. She wanted to try. Work could be sorted. She'd be happy for him to keep his flying doctor job as long as he came home to them when he could. They could work things out so both of them were happy. He was the kind of man who was worth that. She just wanted him to be all for her, all in, because her heart was. Her doubts were soothed by him. He brought her out of her shell and made life fun. She was a home for him, something she knew he'd never really had in all his years travelling. She liked to care for him just as much as he did her but it wasn't a chore or a demand. They just did it naturally for the other; it was effortless.

She just didn't like the unknown, the fear it could end soon before they had ever really been together. If she could have the talk, then at least she could spend her maternity leave relaxing at home. If it went badly, then she'd have time to lick her wounds in private. Seeing him at work, knowing he'd rejected her, wasn't an option. Her heart wouldn't be able to take him being so close, yet so far away.

Deadline set, she got back to work with a sigh, wishing she could feel a little better about her situation. For now, her fatigue was enough to focus on. Staying on her feet was a mission today. Clinic days were always busy but today had been a lot.

Belinda's wasn't the only festive-preparation-related incident they'd had, or the worst. Old man Grissom had managed to slice half his thumb off with a saw blade when cutting down a Christmas tree. Another patient had fallen through his loft, landing in his bedroom and knocking himself unconscious. Colton had gone in the ambulance to bring him in. The patient was half an hour away, not worth scrambling the helicopter for, but urgent enough to need a doctor on the scene. They were expecting them back any minute, and she felt the familiar flutter when she thought of seeing Colton again.

He was never at his apartment these days. They not only worked together but spent all their spare time hanging out. He'd spent a lot of time finishing the nursery. Everything was ready for the babies—two of everything in white and neutral colours.

She had laughed so hard when she'd spotted two little soccer kits in their wardrobe. 'Sydney FC, really?' she'd asked him, laughing even more when he'd shot her a horrified look.

'Sydney FC all the way, baby!'

'And what if we're having girls?'

He shrugged. 'Girls like football too. Trust me, they

will learn to love their dad's favourite team. Wait for game days; it's going to be a family event.'

The next day, she'd ordered two soft footballs and placed them in the nursery. She wanted that—game days and zoo trips. It was getting easier and easier to see it. They snuggled in bed every night, him rubbing her feet and slathering her itching skin with lotion when he noticed her scratching.

She was eight months gone, and her midwife had said that getting to full term was unlikely. They'd discussed the possibility of a C-section but Neve had dismissed it. She was fully in support of that way of delivery, but being immobile with two tiny babies would make her feel out of control. Plus, in the back of her mind was the fact that Colton's contract would be up mere months after the birth. The twins wouldn't even be one year old. They would need a lot of care and attention. She wanted to be mobile and in her routine with the babies when he left.

Not that they ever spoke about him leaving, or their future. Colton spoke about things they were going to do as if they were together, but he hadn't discussed what they were to each other. With work, baby prep and the constant orgasms he gave her, she hadn't brought it up either. And here she was, letting her mind drift to him again. It was becoming a problem. *Focus, Neve. You're at work. Remember work?*

She got her head in the game and waddled to the clinic waiting area. She was just about to call for the next patient when a familiar voice saying her name stopped her in her tracks.

No. Please, no. Come on, world. Cut a tired mama a break.

Her breath caught in her throat when she spied a familiar figure she'd never thought she'd see again. Brett stood up from one of the waiting room chairs, his eyes widening as he took her in. She'd taken to wearing scrub top and trousers rather than the usual dress uniform she preferred. She felt more comfortable in the larger size trousers and, with how big she was now, comfort was needed. Everyone commented on how small and neat her bump was for twins, but she still felt like the side of a house most days. Which was unfortunate just now, because she wanted nothing more but to disappear.

Some of the other waiting patients were open-mouthed, watching the interaction. *Got to love small towns, right?*

'Brett? What are you doing here?'

He ignored her question, his expression cold. His whole demeanour was off. It made her spine stiffen. 'It's true, then.' He nodded to her bump. 'You look good, Neve.'

A couple more patients seated in the waiting room had noticed the visitor, and Neve saw them exchanging shocked looks. Nothing much passed by the residents, and Brett's return would no doubt be round the Falls by the end of the day. Just what she needed today. If he'd only come a week later, she wouldn't have even been here.

Why is he here? They didn't have anything left to say to each other. She didn't owe him a thing, least of all news about her life. Someone had obviously told him about her, though.

Colton. He was on his way back there now with a patient. She needed to get rid of her past before her present came striding in and all hell broke loose. The last time the two men had seen each other it had turned into a fist fight, and she didn't want that to happen in the clinic—or anywhere, for that matter. So much for a low-stress last week at work.

She needed to stay calm, or these babies of hers would be the second surprise appearance today. Brett was staring at her, his gaze drifting to her bump. She didn't like the tension she saw in him. Something was brewing, and she didn't want to burst the storm cloud hanging over her.

'I didn't expect to see you,' she told him, keeping her voice as normal as possible. 'I'm working, as you can see. Was there something you wanted?'

'To see you. I can wait, if you haven't got a minute now.'

Bronwyn came from the back to call her patient, and Neve clocked the moment she saw him. She came to stand at the side of Neve, leaning to whisper from the corner of her mouth.

'Did you know he was coming?'

'That would be a no,' Neve stage-whispered back. 'Cover for me...'

Bron took the clipboard from her. 'I'll get Liv on it. I have a feeling it will be better to keep her out of this.'

'Agreed.' Neve nodded, her heart thudding in her chest. Liv would take one look at him and probably show him the roundhouse kick she'd learned. She was still smarting from her almost relationship with Colton's predecessor, having broken things off when he left to work elsewhere. Since Dr Barnes had been away, he'd stayed in touch with Liv, trying to get her to talk to him, to win her round. In response, she'd started self-defence classes to get out her anger and frustration. Which, to be fair, had been welcomed by everyone around her—less chance of their little pocket rocket exploding.

Walking over to Brett, she'd never felt so pregnant. He couldn't seem to take his eyes off her bump, his face unreadable. 'Sorry,' she said for no reason she could decipher in her own head. 'Clinic day; busy. I don't think I can talk now. Shall I just call you later?'

He shook his head, finally looking her in the eye. 'This isn't exactly a phone conversation, Neve.' She flinched at his snooty tone. The way he spoke to her slammed her right back into the past, reminding her of the old Neve who would just have put up with it to keep the peace. As usual, he didn't even register her reaction. 'I heard you were expecting. I didn't realise you were so far along.'

'Heard from who?' She knew her friends wouldn't have told him. Then it clicked—it had probably been his biggest fan. She had always stuck her nose in. Getting divorced wouldn't have put her off. 'Let me guess—your mother?'

He had the decency to look sheepish. No doubt her nosy neighbour had gone running to his mother as soon as she'd come back from her extended cruise. They had got to know each other when his parents had visited the Falls. Obviously that relationship hadn't died off with the divorce. She would have seen Colton, too; his bike or car was always at Neve's house when they weren't at work. Brett already knew about the pregnancy, but he couldn't know Colton was the father. Her neighbour didn't know who he was, but this was a small town; his name wasn't exactly a common one.

She felt her defences clanging back up. 'You came here because your mother told you, right?'

'She might have said something.'

'Thought so. She was never happy with you moving here. Odd that she still keeps up with the town newsletter.'

'Neve.' His tone was full of warning.

'Don't "Neve" me, Brett. Tell your mother my life is not her concern any more next time she calls you to tattle on things that aren't any of your business. Is that why you're here, to see for yourself?'

'Well, I must admit I was a little surprised. It seemed a little fast. The divorce is still fresh and…'

She didn't hear what else Brett said, because the ambulance had just pulled up out the front. Her whole body tensed as she heard the familiar rumble of the engine. Her two worlds were about to collide, and the babies in her belly took that moment to give her a kick. *I know, little ones. Daddy's here. You might want to cover your ears for this one.*

Everything happened impossibly fast after that, but to Neve it felt like slow motion. The door opened and Colton strode in, eyes on his patient as they wheeled through the doors. His strong hands were on the gurney as he looked up towards them. The second he laid eyes on her, his serious expression shifted into something warmer. His eyes crinkled at the corners as his lips curved up into that smile she loved. It was tender, as if he was ecstatic to see her. Her own heart leapt too, but she tried not to show it on her face in front of their unwelcome visitor.

She could only stand there and watch as Colton entered the same space as Brett, her eyes on Colton and only him. She watched him get closer, his mouth opening to say something… And then his eyes slid to Brett, and his whole demeanour changed. Those gentle hands of his gripped the gurney tightly as the easy smile slid off his face. She was so busy watching Colton that she almost forgot Brett was standing there, glaring.

Till Colton addressed him on the way past. 'Brett,' he said coolly, his eyes sliding back to Neve and down to her belly before passing them and heading to the treatment room area. 'Neve, could you give me a hand? Treatment Room One.' He didn't pause or look back as the doors closed behind him, taking all the air in the room with him.

'I have to go,' she turned and told Brett, aware that all eyes were on them. She needed her ex-husband to leave. *Why is he even here?* She owed him nothing, least of all an explanation, but the look on his face was thunderous. Sure, Colton had been his best friend, but it wasn't as if they had sought each other out. Colton had initially come to the Falls for work. Yes, they had a history, but nothing had happened between them when she and Brett had been together. His friendship with Brett had been long over when Colton had crashed her divorce party. 'I can't talk to you right now. We have patients waiting.'

He ignored her attempt to get him to leave. He laughed, but it was hollow, mocking. 'I don't believe it.' He jabbed a finger towards the doors Colton had just gone through. 'You're having a baby with *him*?'

Well, that was a question she definitely didn't want to answer. Discussing Colton with Brett was not going to happen. She didn't wish to get into it, especially not here.

Thankfully, Bron came to the rescue. 'I'll cover the clinic; you deal with the new intake.' She was talking to Neve, but her eyes were on Brett, and the temperature had dropped a few degrees to say the least. 'Brett, not here. I think you should leave.'

Leaning fully into his arrogance now, Brett picked a piece of lint off his suit jacket as though he had all the time in the world. 'Fine.' The way he looked at Neve, she knew he wasn't done. Not by a long shot. 'I'll be at your house at eight tonight.' He didn't wait for an answer.

When the doors closed behind him, Neve felt Bronwyn's arm around her. She took her to the doors outside the treatment rooms, away from the waiting area. 'Are you okay? What the hell was he doing here?'

'His mother told him about the pregnancy, but he seemed surprised at how big I was.'

'Shoot.' Bron puffed. 'I'm guessing he doesn't know there's two in there.'

'Yeah, well, I'm not telling him. It's none of his damn business. I guess he's entitled to have some kind of reaction to it being with Colton, but they aren't friends any more.'

'You don't need his permission, Neve. He left you, remember? Long before you split up, he wasn't around. I just don't get why he's come back to chew you out now.'

'I guess I'll find out tonight. I better get back to work. Colton needs a hand, and half the clinic saw that little fiasco.'

'Okay.' Bron nodded, pulling her into a hug. 'Just stay calm, okay? We don't have capacity for a double birth today.'

'Cross your fingers.'

Bron winked. 'Cross your legs, sis. Keep those babies in. Catch me up later, and, if you need back-up tonight, me and the Karate Kid will be there.'

'Thanks, I love you.'

Bron blew her a kiss. 'We love you too, Neve. Here for you.'

CHAPTER NINE

THEY DIDN'T SPEAK about Brett for the rest of the shift. They fell into their team mode, working on the patient emergency and being professionals, putting everything to one side…until they left the clinic, and then all bets were off. Colton opened the car door for her and, once he was driving, he reached for her hand.

'Are you really okay? That must have been hard.'

'Yeah, well, my neighbour isn't getting a Christmas card this year. I would go over and give her a piece of my mind, but that would only show her that I am bothered.'

'We have nothing to hide. We are not cheaters, sweetheart. Your divorce was final when I came to the Falls.'

'I know, but perhaps Brett doesn't see it like that. He was just so angry. He said he was coming to mine tonight—'

'What? No way.'

'Colton, I have to talk to him and then he'll leave.'

'And where am I in all this? Do you want me there?'

'Do you want to be there?'

His jaw flexed. 'I am not leaving you alone with him. Not a chance in hell.'

'Colton, I know, but seeing you there…it's just going to make him worse. I am not ashamed about any of this, and it's nothing to do with him, but I don't want the stress of a massive row. Please?'

He pulled her hand to his mouth for a kiss. 'I'll go upstairs, but I hear one unpleasant word from him, one raised voice, and I am stepping in.'

'Okay, Batman. Good to know.'

His blue eyes blazed. 'I mean it, Neve. You do not owe that man anything, and I will not have him speak to you like that. He had his chance and he blew it. You and our family are my priority, and you always will be.'

She wanted to tell him right there and then that he had nothing to worry about. That seeing Brett had only reinforced in her mind that her ex-husband was not the one for her. She'd felt nothing but panic at seeing him, because he didn't belong there.

Colton did. Colt had made it feel as if the Falls was his home, as if he'd always been there. He'd made an effort with her friends; the patients all loved him. Abe treated him like a second son. When he spoke about the babies, it made her realise that Brett had never really been one hundred percent in it with her. They'd been a married couple, but a lot of their lives had been separate. Their big house had felt less of a home than hers did now, with Colton there. Brett had detached himself as soon as they had hit a hurdle starting their family. Colton had been surprised by the twins but he'd embraced every single moment. She loved him deeply and it wasn't the hormones. It was all him.

'I'm glad you're going to be there. I just don't want to have a big fight.'

'There won't be, not on my end. As long as he holds his tongue, we'll be fine.'

At eight o'clock on the dot, there was a knock on her door. Neve steeled herself, straightening her loose smock top over her maternity jeans and opening the door to her past.

'Come on in,' she invited Brett, standing back to admit him into the living room.

'Can I sit?' he asked, pointing to the sofa. She saw him scanning her space and her spine stiffened.

'I don't think that this is a sit-down conversation. I think it's better if you just say what you want to say and leave. It's been a long day and I'm tired.' She stood herself, not wanting to sit in the chair even though her whole body was exhausted and her muscles felt taut.

'Fair enough. A phone call could have avoided all of this. All you had to do was tell me, and I wouldn't have had to hear it from my mother. You owed me that, I thought.'

'Brett, my life has nothing to do with you. My pregnancy is none of your business either. Is this why you came, to see what I was up to? To give me your stamp of disapproval? I have no doubt that you will have been seeing other people since our divorce. Did you call me to let me know that? No, and I'm fine with that, because I don't care, Brett. Our life together is over. You left me, remember? Hot footed it back to Sydney the minute things got tough, and you know what? I'm glad you did. I'm happy.'

'Me seeing people is different from you being with Colton—worlds apart. We ended badly, sure, but I thought we had a mutual respect for each other.'

'Brett, I don't hate you, but I don't owe you an explanation either. We ended—badly. You made sure of that, but I have moved on. It's in the past.'

'You know it was more complicated than that between us. With the pressure of trying for a baby, we just weren't the same.'

'You checked out long before you left. I said we could pause on the baby thing, if you needed to. How did you think it made me feel when you pulled back after you got tested? I felt like a failure as a wife, as a woman. I was hurting and you weren't there for me. I thought it was my fault we couldn't conceive, and that hurt me. You didn't even see me through that.'

She shook her head, not wanting to dwell on something that was over. 'I don't want to get into it, because in the end it worked out for the best. Everything that came after the ink dried on our divorce papers is none of your concern. You have a cheek even being here.'

'Not when you're having a baby with my best friend.'

'Ex-best friend. Still none of your business.' She felt angrier by the second. He was practically sneering at her, and she felt her old frustrations rise.

'That's not the point, Neve!' He was shouting now. 'It's not even been a year since our divorce and you're having a baby with him! What was it, huh—get back at Brett time? I bet you two were laughing your heads off at me. It's disgusting, Neve. Not a good look. Frankly, you're embarrassing.'

Colton walked down the stairs barefoot, wearing a tank top and jeans, looking just as if he lived there. Brett's eyes turned black. Colton looked calm on the outside but, if looks could kill, Brett would be dead on the floor.

'Speak to her like that again and I will put you out of that door so fast, your feet won't touch the ground.'

'Oh really, big man?' Brett laughed. 'I should have known you'd be close by. Live here now, do you? Stepped right into the shoes I left, eh, Anderson?'

'We don't have to answer to you. Our business is ours alone. Did you really come here because you wanted to tell us you disapproved, or just to shout at a pregnant woman? Either way, you needn't have bothered. As for us being friends, that was done years ago.'

'Whose fault is that?'

'Careful,' Colton growled. 'You don't want to get into this with me.'

Brett snorted. 'Sure. I see you got what you always wanted. I should have known.'

'It wasn't like that!' Colton's fury was evident. 'And I don't like the way you've come here talking to Neve like this in her own house. She was a single woman when we got together. If you have a problem, it's with me.'

'Oh, really?' Brett's laugh was cold. 'You're having a baby with my ex-wife, and you don't think I'd have a problem with that? You've made me look like a laughing stock, and we both know you won't stay. Once the novelty of finally getting what you want wears off, you'll be flying off to the next thrill.'

Neve's heart fluttered at his words. She'd wondered about that herself, so many times over the last few months. They weren't properly together, but they weren't strangers either. He slept here most of the time; looked after her and tended to her every need. He'd done everything but claim her. The lines between them had blurred, but they hadn't spoken about the future past the birth of the babies.

'You don't know me as well as you think you do, Brett. What exactly did you want to achieve, coming here?' Colton made his way to her side, tucking her into him. She let him, her mind whirring.

'What did I want to achieve? What about you? Couldn't wait, could you? Waiting in the damn wings all this time. I should have known you'd come sniffing around.'

'She's not yours any more. What's happened between me and Neve is not your concern. You know how I felt, Brett. Did you forget our conversation?'

'Yeah, I bet that was great ammo for you, you player.'

'Just quit with the rubbish, Brett. We both know what went down. I stepped aside out of respect for you, but you messed it up all by yourself. What's wrong, regretting letting her go now she's moved on?'

'Moved on? My side of the bed wasn't even cold when you swooped in!'

Colton practically growled, and Neve went to step between them as Brett took a step closer. Colton stayed put, pulling her back to his side…or rather, behind him, as if he was shielding her. She listened to the two of them arguing, but something was missing. She didn't quite get what they were talking about. Brett made it sound as if Colton had been pining for her!

She nudged him. 'Colton, what do you mean, you stepped aside?'

He looked pained, and Brett's smug grin was back.

'Neve, we'll talk later, and I will explain everything.'

'Well, you'd better, because I don't understand.'

'Oh, he didn't tell you, Neve? He didn't tell you how I asked him to be my best man, and he told me he couldn't because he was in love with you?'

Neve froze. *Wait, what?* She remembered his words. *I came for you, sweetheart.* He took the job for her, just to be close to her… She didn't quite know how to feel about that, but it didn't change her feelings about him. Hell, it was she who had made the rules that first night, right?

'I told you the truth, unlike some. I stepped aside. I left you to live your lives, and I am not the one who didn't tell the truth, bud. You left and she moved on. So, yeah, I came to get what I wanted. Gave her what you couldn't—someone in her corner.'

'Yeah,' Brett boomed, fists clenched. 'And she just couldn't wait, could she?' He turned to Neve. 'Always wanted him, did you? Or was it just a case of taking any willing male to knock you up?'

'What do you mean, he didn't tell the truth?' Neve was trying to get answers but the two of them were too busy glaring at each other.

Brett looked at Neve and closed his mouth. 'Nothing; he's just talking rubbish,' he snapped.

'Am I? Seriously, you never told her? I told you to come clean, but no—good old Brett had to come off the hero, painting me as the ladies' man. You're a joke. I'm glad I punched you,' Colton said.

'Tell me what?' Neve interjected. Colton bit his lip but said nothing. Brett gave Colton a death stare so cold she could practically feel the icicles shooting across the living room. 'What am I missing here?'

'Nothing,' Colt murmured. 'It's okay, sweetheart.'

'Whatever,' Brett scoffed. 'I'm surprised you didn't talk just to get into her bed. Acting like Prince Charming; you were annoyed that I got the girl. She married me, Colt. You only knocked her up.'

'Leave,' Colton bellowed. 'Before I make you and, if you ever speak to her or about her like that again, I will end you. That's the mother of my children you're speaking to.'

Brett blanched. 'Children?' He looked at Neve's bump, as if seeing her for the first time, and noticing the size and shape of her changed body. 'What do you mean, children?'

Neve gathered the courage to speak, linking her fingers in Colton's hand. He squeezed her tighter, and she felt the warm strength coming from him in waves.

'I never so much as flirted with another man while we were together, and you know it.'

Brett's head drooped, but she kept going. She was going to say her piece this one time, and then she wanted him gone. She was exhausted, and being in his presence was so draining. 'I didn't even think I could have children. You left because you felt the same.' She rubbed her bump, cradling it protectively. 'Colton and I never planned our twins, but we are very happy about them. I'm sorry if my pregnancy upsets you, but you and I were over a long time before.'

'That's the thing,' Brett corrected. 'I didn't leave because I thought you couldn't have them, Neve. I left because I knew I could.'

Her head snapped back, and she felt Colton's body freeze.

'What?'

Brett's throat worked. 'When I had the tests, I found out it was wasn't me who couldn't have children, Neve. That's why I was so distant. We were already drifting apart, but after that I knew we would never work. I knew you wanted a family, and we were already struggling. Knowing that it was probably you that had the issues, I knew we were over. You would never have wanted to stay with me with no kid to hold us together. It's all we talked about, and without that… I didn't see things lasting.'

'I don't understand. Why would you not tell me that? You made me think it was my fault! I felt alone… You stopped talking about getting pregnant, you were distant. You could have just told me the truth. We could have…'

She almost said that they could have worked through it, but that was a lie. The truth was, the hope of a family had kept them together, but she just hadn't seen it at the time. But he'd come back from being tested and cut her out of the decision; made her feel as if she was defective, when they could have just gone through it together. Maybe if they had spoken back then, they could have saved a lot of pain. She wouldn't have felt like some defective wife either, unable to keep a husband because she was unable to give him a child. It was cruel, cold and so *Brett* she couldn't stand to look at him.

'Who are you?'

'I know I should have told you, but I knew how much you wanted a family. I couldn't handle it not happening for us, so I pushed you away—before you realised what was going on and it broke us anyway.' He glared at Colton. 'I wish to God I hadn't now. You wouldn't be in this sorry situation. When I found out you were pregnant, that was a shock, but this…?'

'I'm not in a *situation.* I'm incredibly happy. I'm sorry we didn't work out, but I know now that we weren't right for each other, family or no family.'

Being close to Colton had shown her what a true partner could be. Brett would never have been like this with her, so attentive and protective. They'd always been good friends, but they had led quite separate lives. Colton hadn't just made her part of his, he'd put the babies and her right at the centre. 'I'm sorry that you felt you couldn't tell me the truth; it might have saved a lot of pain for both of us, but it wouldn't have changed the outcome. Communication was never our strong point, was it? With children or without, we wouldn't have lasted.'

'Yeah? Well, you upped and had a baby with him the first chance you got.' Brett's pained expression turned into a sneer. 'Like this will last?' He jabbed a finger at

Colton. 'You really think he'll stick around once those babies are born and reality hits? Swallow Falls is not the place to keep his attention. I came here because I wanted to set the record straight—see if you were happy, tell you the truth.'

'Yeah, right,' Colton shot back. 'Because you are so good at telling the truth, aren't you? Anything else you want to tell her while you're at it? Other than the fact you left her because you knew not giving her a child wouldn't keep her tied to you?'

'I hate you,' Brett spat back. 'You never had my back.'

'Are you kidding me? You are the liar here. You couldn't tell the truth if your life depended on it. I think you should leave.'

'That's not your decision, or your business. Stay out of this. You've done enough. I can't believe I ever called you a friend.'

'You know exactly why we're not friends. I told you back then, and I kept to my word. I gave you the chance to be the kind of man she deserved and you failed.'

Neve looked between the two of them, trying to figure out yet again what they were talking about.

'Kept to your word? In what sense?' Her head was starting to swim. 'Will someone please tell me what the hell is going on?'

'Ask him,' Colton said sombrely, not taking his eyes off Brett. 'I told you back then I would never tell her, and I haven't. That was your crap to deal with.'

And she was back to wondering what the hell was going on. That out-of-control, panicky feeling was back, and she didn't like it one bit. Colton was acting strangely towards her, protective but with hesitation she hadn't sensed in him before. Was this all a game? It felt as if, whatever it was she didn't know, it wasn't good.

Brett snorted derisively. 'And I'm supposed to believe she just fell into your arms because of your charms? Bull.' Brett went to leave, turning back to give Neve one last piece of his mind. 'He'll never stay, Neve. Men like him never settle in one place for too long. I came because I wanted to see you were okay for myself.'

His lips thinned as his gaze drifted down to her rounded stomach. 'You will be a good mother, and I am pleased for you. I mean that, but you will be doing it alone. He'll get bored and then you won't see him for dust.'

Giving Colton one last death stare, he shook his head. 'Well, you got what you wanted. I just hope Neve isn't left to pick up the pieces when you leave for the next big adventure.'

'Leave, Brett, before I change my mind and open my damn mouth. You aren't the hero in this story.'

Brett scowled, and when Colton took a step forward he headed for the door. The slam of wood against wood rang in Neve's ears as the room descended into silence.

'Are you okay?' Colton ran his knuckles along her cheek. 'He never should have spoken to you like that, Neve. I wanted to deck him. Come and sit down. You look pale.'

She ignored his request, feeling sick to her stomach. She needed to know everything. 'No.' He reached for her and she stepped away from him. 'What did you mean, about keeping to your word? I felt like you were both speaking in code. What do I need to know?'

'Come and sit down,' he murmured again. 'Please, sweetheart. You've had a shock.'

'Fine,' she huffed, sitting down on the couch. He took the seat next to her. 'But I want the truth. He didn't just come about the pregnancy; you two looked like you had real unfinished business.'

Sighing deeply in his chest, Colton sat back against the couch cushions. 'He came because he wanted to protect his stupid reputation. See what you were doing without him, like he expected you to stay alone and pine for him. He's angry because I got you pregnant, because you're happy and getting everything you wanted without him. I know how he works. He wants to come off like the guy whose marriage failed because his wife moved on with his best friend. He hasn't changed a bit, even after all these years.'

'I get that. I know why he came, because it hurt his pride, but that doesn't explain everything.'

'It does, actually. It's about him not wanting his dirty laundry airing, but I never would have done it if he hadn't come here.' He reached for her hand, tentatively at first, but she let him take it. She felt so full of adrenaline, and her heart was racing. 'I need you to stay calm when I tell you this, okay?'

'Please, just tell me.'

He searched her face for a moment, dropping a kiss onto the back of her hand. 'All right. If you need me to stop, though, let me know.'

'Colt, I'm fine—tell me. You're freaking me out more by making such a big thing of it.'

'I just want you to understand that I did what I felt was the best thing for you at the time. I always want the best for you, Neve. When Brett and I fell out, it wasn't just a stupid disagreement. The day before he asked me to be his best man, I found out that Brett had cheated on you.'

Record-scratch... The whole room spun as she took in his words.

'It was a girl from college, a friend of one of our friends. I found out by accident, so when he came to see me that day I punched him. I told him that I was going to give him a day to tell you, or I was going to come to see you. He didn't deny it. He told me he was feeling under pressure with the wedding, that it was a one-night thing—an accident he truly regretted, but he wanted to put things right. He wanted to marry you.'

'I can't believe this. He never told me. Why didn't you?'

'Because he told me that you were pregnant, Neve. He lied to me to keep me quiet. I didn't want to be the one to ruin your chance of having the family you wanted, so I couldn't come to you and tell you everything I wanted to. I heard you back then, talking about home. How you wanted to set up your life back here, in the Falls—raise a family, build your career. He knew I liked you, Neve. I think he always knew, but a baby changed everything. I couldn't break up a family before it even started. I didn't want to hurt you.'

Neve couldn't speak. The last few years of her life

were running through her head. Brett had been stressed with the wedding stuff, but she'd never suspected that he'd been unfaithful. And faking a pregnancy to keep his secret… It was the worst thing he could have done. She couldn't stomach the betrayal roiling through her.

'Neve, say something. Please, baby. I am so sorry I never told you. I didn't find out till after the wedding that there was no pregnancy, and by then it was too late. You were married, and you were so happy. I figured he'd never told you, and I was right. If I could go back, I would do things so differently, but I couldn't bear to be the one to ruin your life. I wanted so much for you to be happy, even if that wasn't with me.'

She could barely speak through the lump in her throat. So many lies, so much confusion that could have been avoided. 'He let me walk down that aisle knowing that he'd cheated on me. He told you I was pregnant knowing that I wasn't.'

She choked down a sob, dropping Colt's hand and moving away. 'When he got his results, he was different. He could have just told me the truth, that he thought it was me. He wants a family too, and he knew we weren't happy. He let me believe that I couldn't have children by pulling away after, and he thought I would just stay. When things got too hard he left me, and then when I moved on he came back and tried to blow my life up. He's been controlling things all along, telling a story that fit his own narrative.'

'I know. This is the last thing I wanted to happen, believe me.'

'But you could have told me the truth. You let me

believe his lies for so long. We've spent months together—you could have told me this numerous times. You could have told me everything. I feel so stupid now, Colton. I was in the dark for years, and you had the chance to tell me back then, too, but you didn't take it. If you really cared for me so much, you wouldn't have let me go through that sham of a marriage with him.'

'I've been honest about us, Neve. That stuff was left back in the past, along with Brett. I know you don't like it, but I did it for the right reasons.'

'Which are?'

'That I wanted to make you happy. Have I not proved to you that I'm not that kind of selfish guy? I told you I came here for you! I am here for you, and our babies. I never lied to you about any of the things between us.'

'You didn't tell me that you liked me back then. You waited years to show me how you felt about me. I thought you came here for work, but you didn't tell me the full truth about that. Don't you get it? The trust is gone, Colton. That night, at the divorce party, you could have told me the truth then—let me know what the true reason for you coming here was.' The tears were flowing freely now. 'It's all just so messed up. This whole time you've been hesitant to talk about the future and I've been constantly expecting you to leave.'

His lips thinned. 'I can't believe we are still having this conversation. I've told you—repeatedly—that I was in this. All in, Robin.'

'Don't—' She hiccupped a sob. 'Don't be cute right now. I can't deal with this. I've spent the last year—

no, years—being lied to and having control of my life taken away from me. I would never have married Brett if I had known the truth!'

She wiped away some of the tears, cradling her bump as she desperately tried to hold everything together. 'If Brett hadn't just turned up I wouldn't ever have known, would I? Would you have told me? Tell me, Colt. When would you have been honest with me? I've been worried this whole time about being left again! Worried because you never chose to sleep with me again!'

'Neve, it's not like that, please! Don't let him destroy us.'

'It's not just him that did that. I am sick enough of worrying about people leaving me without them keeping things from me too. I'm so angry now. I think you should go.'

His face crumpled. 'No, Neve. I can't leave you like this. Please don't do this. We can work through this.'

'I'm too upset to do anything but cry,' she managed to choke out as her emotion spilled over. 'Please, just go.'

'Neve, I understand you're upset with me, but leaving you alone worries me. We can sort this out, I know we can. We've come so far. If you'll just let me explain, I'll tell you everything.'

'It's too late.' She sniffed, delving deep inside herself to steel her emotions. To get herself in check. 'I don't trust you, Colton. I don't trust anything in my life right now. Just leave.'

'Neve, I…'

She pushed herself off the couch and yanked open the front door. 'I don't want to hear it, Colton. I feel like some kind of pawn in everyone else's games, and I hate it. I hate you at the moment, too. Go. Now.'

He looked broken when he looked at her. He was crying, the tears running down his cheeks as he slowly got to his feet. When he got to the door, he stopped in front of her and dropped a kiss on her temple as his hand touched her bump, a feather-like touch that nearly broke her in half. It took everything in her not to hold him, to make him feel better, but she didn't.

He could have told her the truth about Brett's unfaithfulness. She would have preferred it that way. She wasn't a princess to be coddled; she was an independent forty-year-old woman who had just got her life back in order after something she could have run the heck away from. She would never have married Brett if she'd known, never have settled for what he'd given her. The man was a cad, pure and simple. Their vows had been spoken at an altar built of lies, and the jealous rat hadn't even told her that Colton liked her. She was spiralling, plain and simple, replaying every moment of her marriage and before in her mind. It was just too complicated to see straight at the moment. She felt as if everything was in tatters once again. She was mad at the world, at Brett, at Colton. At herself.

'I'm so sorry, Neve. It kills me that you don't trust me. I genuinely just wanted you to be happy, and I messed everything up. You know where I am. I will be waiting, when you're ready.'

After he left, she rang the girls. They were at her door within the hour, Liv armed with grape juice and wine,

Bronwyn with ice-cream and donuts. They took over instantly, washing her face, getting her to change into comfy pyjamas and swaddling her under a blanket on the couch. They listened as she told them the whole sorry story, and passed her tissues when she broke off into fresh sobs. Bron even checked her blood pressure while Liv rubbed her swollen feet. She was so grateful for them being there for her. She needed her girls more than ever, and as always they were there to catch her as she fell.

'Did you not ask Colton about what Brett said about him being in love with you back then? I mean, he punched the rat for cheating on you and broke off his friendship. That to me is a man in love.'

'Bron!' Liv piped up. 'Not helping! Down with men, remember?'

Bron crossed her eyes at her as they all sat snuggled together on the couch. 'Liv, come on. I know he messed up, but Brett is the dog here. We've all seen how Colton's been since he arrived. The man was reading a parenting book in the break room the other day. He's obviously still madly in love with her.'

'Not obviously,' Neve rebuffed, licking caramel-swirl ice-cream from her spoon. 'I mean, he never told me the whole truth about his feelings, and we haven't slept together properly since…well…this.' She pointed at the bowl balanced on her bump. 'He told me it was because he wanted to be careful with me. I thought he was holding back because he might still be thinking of leaving when his contract was up.'

'But he was keeping secrets, Neve, just like Brett. I

don't like it. You're so upset, and that's not good. You go on maternity leave in a week. It should be all foot rubs and daytime TV—nesting.'

'Yeah, about that…' She winced when she thought about the email she'd sent Abe. 'I kind of asked if I could start my leave early. Abe agreed; he's going to change the rota, so you might have an extra shift coming your way.'

'Whatever you need, darl'.' Bron smiled. 'But are you going to talk to Colton?'

'Make it quick.' Liv pouted. 'Because I'm planning to cut the brakes on his damn chopper when I get to work.'

'Liv!' Both women gasped before they all burst into laughter together.

'Don't try to maim the father of my children, please.'

'I'm making no promises.' Liv chuckled. 'But, seriously, what are you going to do? Is it over?'

'Over? Are you crazy? They are having a family; he loves her!' Bron objected.

'He lied—by omission, at least,' Liv countered. 'Brett lied too, and look what happened. They broke up, and she was left feeling like a failure or something. Have you forgotten how bad things were during the divorce? And now she is going to have two babies to raise with Colton. I can't, I just can't, see you unhappy like that again, Neve. I will chop his blades off.'

Neve laughed, but Bron looked thoughtful.

'What are you thinking, Bron? What's your take on this?'

Bron looked from friend to friend. 'I think if anyone

needs their parts trimming, it's Brett. Neve, I know it's hard, but Colton wouldn't have won either way—tell you, not tell you. Brett should have been the one to tell you the truth, not Colton. It's gaslighting rule one, for a start—faking a pregnancy to stop an infidelity coming to light! And he cheated, what, because wedding planning is stressful? He asked you to marry him, Neve. You didn't drag him up the aisle. I think we need to see Colton's point of view in all this. He fell in love with a woman he couldn't have, and he didn't come after you because he's an honourable man.'

Liv's expression turned slightly less murderous. 'Yeah, I suppose you have a point. I mean, we could all see how much he liked you, even from the divorce party. That must have been hard.'

'Exactly.' Bron nodded. 'He stayed away and then found out that Brett wasn't worthy of you, so he punched the guy. I mean, I'm sorry, but that's some knight-level honour right there.'

'Dark Knight,' Neve mumbled under her breath. Hearing it laid out like that, she did feel bad for Colton. It must have been hard. She'd been doing a bit of pining herself lately. She couldn't deny that she'd felt something for Colton back then either, however fleeting. It explained why he had stepped away, before leaving altogether.

'Oh wow.' Liv tutted. 'Brett is the villain, not Colton. He stayed away, knowing that he wanted you, for your sake. Then when you were single...'

'He took a job in the Falls, and walked into the Outback Bar seconds after hearing me telling Bron that I wanted a sexy adventure.'

'He heard that? Oh my Lord, that man is something else. He couldn't tell you, Neve! You would have run a mile if he'd walked in there and told you he was head over heels!'

'Aww.' Liv downed the rest of her wine. 'So he kept his feelings on the down low again. Jeez, I'm terrible.' She stuck her lip out theatrically. 'I miss Brian,' she admitted. 'He's never stopped trying to talk to me, and I keep shutting him down. I think my rage is a bit misplaced—like yours. When he took the job and wanted to do long distance, I should have considered it at least. Not having him here, it made me realise how much I felt for him. It's not like he wasn't coming back. I was just hurt, and feeling stubborn, but I let love leave without even trying to fight! You've let one little incident pull the pair of you apart when you were so close to finally getting it together!'

She refilled Bron's and her glasses. 'I'm sorry, but I think you need to talk to Colt. I promise not to kill him at work. Heck, after this I might even make him a coffee. I feel a little sorry for him, to be honest.'

Wow. That stung. Honesty was always Liv's strong point, and that one slapped hard. 'I kicked him out and told him I didn't trust him. I think it will take more than a coffee. I also dipped out of work like a drama queen. I don't really get my own reaction just now.'

'I do,' her friends said together.

Bron took up the mantle after a sip of Cabernet. 'Brett changed your outlook on love, and it was complicated—a friend of your ex… You like everything to be controlled, in order.'

'I get that.' Liv nodded. 'Colton frees you up, he pushes you out of your comfort zone. The guy has never put down roots before now, so it was only right that you had doubts he'd stick by you. He's the opposite of you. It makes a kind of sense, but we all know he's in love with you, and those babies. It also makes sense, all those years travelling around. He was looking for something to distract him from what he couldn't have. And, as the anti-romantic of our little group, I have to say—that's pretty hot. Like, *Notebook*-level yearning. He bought a car and car seats. He's reading pregnancy books! I mean, come on, Neve. Even with my cold, dead heart, I know that man is worth fighting for. Those books you lot read—he's straight out of the pages. Book boyfriend, husband material.'

Neve looked at her friends, replaying the argument she'd had with Colton with horrifying hindsight. She'd worried the whole time that he was going to break her heart, and all the time it was her doing the breaking—of his one-of-a-kind heart.

'Oh, God. Oh no, no, no… I'm a horrible person, aren't I? He's never mentioned leaving, not in any real way. He always told me he would be here, and I was too stubborn and jaded to hear it after everything. I think I'm his roots, even without the babies.'

'Agreed,' both women echoed.

'It's a good job I've got you two,' Neve said, misty-eyed.

Liv and Bron clinked glasses with her ice-cream tub.

'Back at ya, girl. Get some sleep, and then go get your man.'

After they had gone home, Neve tried to fall asleep in the bed that felt too large. Without Colton, the space felt huge. She could smell him all around her, and she just wished he was there now, to hold her like he had every night. Brett had come into town and left broken pieces in his wake, and the worst part was that she had let him. The whole time she'd known Colt, he'd never showed her anything but his care and devotion, and she'd pushed him away. Sure, he'd hidden the truth about Brett's cheating, but for her own good. Brett was at fault, and she'd lashed out at the wrong man.

Tomorrow, she was going to put things right. She was going to go and see Colton at work and ask him for a fresh start.

CHAPTER TEN

THE HEAT WAS already overbearing when Neve pulled up to work. She'd barely slept all night, tossing and turning to try and get comfortable. Every time she'd closed her eyes, all she'd seen was Colton's look of devastation when she'd told him to leave; the way his hand had shook as he'd touched her bump. Thank God for the girls coming over and making her see the truth. They knew what she was like when her shields came up. Her reaction was down to the woman that she used to be, not the expectant mother she was now.

Over the course of her pregnancy, she'd become so happy and hopeful, but now she felt that she'd broken Colton. She couldn't imagine how he'd felt, knowing that the woman he loved had been cheated on and not being able to tell her because of a baby that hadn't even existed in the first place. Brett had done what he always did: he'd manipulated the situation so that he didn't come off badly. He had pushed her away instead of having a real conversation. That was Brett—he always had to be the winner. She knew in her heart that, if she had been infertile, he wouldn't have been there for her. He'd already let her believe it, and she'd let him. She'd wasted so much time on him, and she was about ready to claim her future. Colton had waited for her for so long. If he still wanted her, she would be all in.

Her back screamed at her as she pulled herself out of the car. She'd woken up feeling all coiled up and she felt her lower back was on fire with these babies. One good thing to come out of last night was the fact that she'd started her maternity leave early. Working with her sore back in this heat would have been impossible.

She smoothed out her maternity dress, waving at Bron through the clinic window. 'Good luck!' Bron mouthed, and she gave her a shaky thumbs-up. She'd need more than luck; Colton could tell her where to go and she couldn't blame him. She'd overreacted and hurt the one man who had always put her first.

The walk to the hangar was torturously slow. She had to pause every few steps and stretch out her back. She felt as if her belly was hanging so heavy and low, her waddle was slower than usual. The heat was blazing, even this early in the morning, and she could feel the rivulets of sweat running down her back through the dress. The hangar came into view, and she held her breath while she scanned around for Colton. As she neared the doors, she spied him organising medical kit bags.

He looked up when he heard her footsteps. 'Neve?' He got to his feet, coming straight over. 'Are you okay? What are you doing here? Abe said you'd started your leave early.'

He stopped short of touching her, and she clocked his fists clenching.

'I came to see you.' She rubbed her back. The pain was getting worse now. She felt about ready to drop.

'I was going to call you after work and see if you wanted to talk.' He saw her rubbing her back. 'You don't look right. Want to sit in the office?'

'No.' She waved him off. 'I need to get this out.'

He bit his lip. 'Neve, are you in pain? Come sit, please.'

'No, Colt… I…'

'Just wait a second. You look like you're about to keel over. Let me get you a chair and some water. You need some water?'

Her back was killing her now, and his kind words broke the dam. The tears started to fall.

'Please, you don't have to take care of me now. It should be me doing that for you, after last night.'

'Shush,' he soothed, putting a high-backed chair down next to her. 'Please, just sit down. Let me get you some water.'

'Okay, but…ugh!' A sharp pain rippled across her belly. It felt as if a tight band had been lashed around her middle, and then there was an audible pop. Water cascaded down from between her legs, splashing on the concrete hangar floor.

'Neve!' Colton held her up as her knees buckled.

'Oh my God, Colt! My waters just broke. It hurts so much…argh!'

Colton lowered her down to the chair, running for the radio.

'Clinic, come in.'

Bron's voice crackled back a few seconds later.

'Go for clinic.'

'Neve is in labour. Waters have broken. We need the ambulance, stat.'

There was a second's pause down the open line before everyone sprang into action.

'Received. Ambulance en route now.'

Henry, their on-site ambulance EMT, came flying up to the hangar, sirens wailing, as Colton checked Neve over. Henry came rushing in with a wheelchair. Bron was on the radio, asking for updates. Colt picked up the radio, watching intently as Henry transferred her from chair to wheelchair.

'She's okay, Bron. I've got her. I'll update you all as soon as I can. Tell Abe to clock me out and divert any cases if necessary.'

'Received,' Bron replied, worry in her voice. 'Take care of our girl, okay?'

Colton looked a little surprised at her words, his lips quirking into a little smile. 'Always, Bron.'

He stayed by her side the whole way to the ambulance, taking over from Henry when it came time to get her into the back of the ambulance. Henry got to work, clipping the monitors onto her and checking her vitals. She'd just got settled onto the bed when another contraction ripped through her.

'Contractions are seven minutes apart,' he told Colton who checked his watch, nodding. 'Vitals are good.'

'Let's get to the hospital,' Colton said. 'These babies are in a hurry to get here.'

Henry closed the doors, leaving the two of them alone in the back. As Neve's contraction subsided, she sagged back against the pillows.

'You're doing so well, sweetheart.' Colton's hand

hovered over hers, and she reached for it. 'The babies are coming. It's my first day of maternity leave and they decide to come now?'

Colton laughed, and it was like a balm to her soul. 'Well, that's on brand for us, right?'

'Everything full-on? Yeah.' She laughed, wincing as her back sang. 'I have a feeling they are going to be trouble.'

'Double trouble.' He smiled, dropping a kiss on her palm. 'I'm here, okay? I want to be here for the whole thing.' His lips thinned, head dropping. 'I mean, if you want me to be.'

'Of course I do,' she said firmly, wanting those blue eyes back on her. 'Colton, I want you with me.'

His eyes glistened and he blinked a few times before swallowing. 'Then I will be—always.'

They got to the hospital in one piece, and things moved quickly. Neve was doing well, breathing through each contraction and keeping her cool. It was so hard to see her like that, going through so much pain to bring their children into the world. The feeling of helplessness was choking him. He didn't know what to do with himself, especially as the last time he'd seen her she'd asked him to leave her house.

Seeing her at the hangar that morning had surprised him, but he still couldn't read her at the moment. It wasn't the time or place, but he felt the gulf between them and hated every inch of it. If he ever saw Brett again, he would tell him how much damage he'd done to her, and him. He'd played with her ambitions to be a mother from the start, and even now it was as if he cast a shadow over the birth of their babies.

He tried to push that out of his mind. Neve needed him here, present. This was their moment, and he wanted to remember it for ever—if he could only quell the panic running through him.

She was early having these babies; it was safe enough, but his mind was still in overdrive, his medical training working against him. All he could think about was everything that could go wrong. Seeing Neve in pain was killing him, and all he wanted to do was hold her and tell her that everything was going to be okay. He couldn't take his eyes off the monitors. Everything he loved was in this room. He'd die if anything happened to his family. It was freaking him out, not being able to be there for her as he wanted to be.

He couldn't hold back another minute. When the next contraction ebbed, he seized the moment. 'I love you, Neve Truby.' Lying back on the pillows, she turned her head to his. Sitting on the edge of the bed, he took her hand in his and placed the other next to the monitor strapped to her belly. 'I know you think that I am not going to stay, but I could never leave you.'

'Colton, we shouldn't talk about this, not now.'

'This is exactly the time we should talk about it. I don't want to bring our children into a world where their parents are not together. I love you, Neve. When I first saw you on Brett's arm, I knew it. The second I saw you, it hit me like a damn lightning bolt.'

'Colton…' Neve's hand covered his, her eyes filling with tears.

'I wanted you then, and I want you now. I came here for you, nothing else. I should have told you the truth back then, but he promised to take care of you, and he did for a long time, so I kept quiet and tried to forget you. When I knew you were single, it became so clear to me. I had to see you, to find out once and for all if what I felt was just my feelings and mine alone. I had to know, sweetheart. I couldn't stay away a moment longer. I never told you how I felt when you were with Brett, and I had to live with the fact that I never spoke up. I never tried to stop you getting married, but after that night in the bar I came to your house to get you to date me.'

She smiled and a tear slid down her cheek. He wiped it away with his thumb, cradling her face and gripping her hand in his. *I am not letting you go now, not ever.*

'And you found the pregnancy test. Why didn't you say anything then?'

'Because you were in shock, and I felt like I had trapped you. Same as back then—I didn't want you to choose me by default. I didn't want to be selfish and blow your life up in the hope you would finally see me when the dust had settled. I believed his lies about the pregnancy, and I know you wanted a family. But the baby never came, and I knew in my bones he'd played me.'

'There was never a baby with Brett,' she confirmed. 'It was obviously never meant to be between us. I just wish I'd gone for tests, instead of thinking he was blaming me. I'm a nurse, for God's sake; I just thought with my irregular periods it had to be my issue. He walked away, and I didn't even think to question why. It was all to save face for him. To get the easy life.'

'He lied to us both. I could have told you the truth then, but you were newly married. From what I heard from friends, you were happy. So I stayed away.'

'I wish you had,' she said, and hearing her say that gave him so much hope. 'He never told me about the cheating. I had suspicions towards the end of our marriage that he was hiding things, but I guess I never really knew the real him.'

'That's down to him, not you. You deserved better.'

'So you came when you heard about my divorce.'

'I took the job just to be near you. I felt like it was fate, in a way. After our night together, I finally felt like things were going my way. That I might just have a chance to show you how good for you I could be. When I saw that test, I knew I'd messed it up again by waiting till the job started to come back. I was scared you'd reject me before I even started, I guess. I didn't want you to say yes because I had got you pregnant, but I was thrilled about it. It was so fast, but I want your babies, Neve. I love our children already—so much. I felt like I'd come and ruined your new life, and the only thing I wanted was to make you happy. To make you see that I was the man for you.'

'You did show me,' she half-whispered, her voice breaking. 'You took care of me from the start. I was just scared that I had trapped you into a boring, quiet life. We never said it was more than one night. Then Brett came and everything in me just wanted to run from all of the revelations. I was angry at the wrong person.'

Colton shook his head in disbelief to hear everything he'd longed for. 'It's all out in the open now. Done. He will never come back, and if he does we will be ready to show him the door. Just don't ask me to leave again, Neve, because you are my home. A lifetime with you isn't enough, sweetheart. You are my adventure—you and our babies.'

'So you're really staying?'

'I am where my family is. I don't want to be apart—ever. I just need you to trust me.'

'Colton, I…argh!' Her next contraction took over her body, and Jenny the midwife walked in.

'Right on time,' she quipped, coming to check the monitors throughout the contraction. 'Okay, so let's see where you are in terms of dilation. Heartbeats are strong. Baby A is engaged.'

Neve sucked on the gas and air till the pain subsided. The midwife examined her and smiled at them both. 'Well, you're fully dilated. It shouldn't be long now. How's your pain? Would you like some pethidine? I know you said you didn't want any earlier, but I can administer some if you need it.'

Neve waggled the gas and air nozzle in her direction. 'Nope, I'll stick with this. I'm good.'

'Are you sure?' Colton couldn't help but ask. 'It's a long time to be in pain.'

She fixed those beautiful green eyes on him. 'It will be worth it. I don't want to miss a thing. I'm only doing this once.'

'Okay, sweetheart.'

The contractions came thick and fast after that. Neve

was amazing, and Colton was in awe of how she handled everything. 'Keep going, sweetheart, you're doing great! I can see the head!'

'Colton!' Neve's head snapped up. 'Get up here, I don't want you to see that!'

Jenny laughed as Colton shook his head. 'Neve, I'm watching our child being born. Don't sweat it.' He flashed her a wink. 'You're always beautiful to me, sweetheart.'

Suddenly, the midwife's demeanour changed. Nudging Colton, she leaned in closer. 'Dr Anderson, I need you to listen to me and not react. The umbilical cord is currently wrapped around the baby's neck. I need to free it before she pushes again. Keep her calm.' Her eyes scanned the monitor.

Colton felt as if his world was on tilt as he came to Neve's head and held her hand while Jenny spoke. 'Neve. I need you to stop pushing for a moment and stay calm.'

'What's wrong? Colton?'

The midwife gave him a nod and he leaned in, dropping a kiss on her forehead. 'Everything's okay, sweetheart. Just hold still, okay?'

'Neve, don't push. Hold still. Everything's okay.'

Colton could see Jenny working to free the baby's neck, and he focused on Neve. 'Look at me, Neve.' Her eyes were full of fear, and it took everything in him to keep it together for her. He needed to be the strong one, the man she could depend on. 'We've got this. Just hold on, okay? Me and you, we've got this.'

Neve kept her eyes on him and then the midwife

spoke. 'Okay, Neve. Next contraction for the shoulders. Are you ready?'

Neve kept her eyes on his through every contraction that followed, gripping his hand tightly as she pushed.

'One more, Neve, and your first baby will be here. When that contraction comes, I want you to bear down and push as hard as you can for me. You ready?'

She locked eyes with Colton, her face flushed and sweaty. 'I'm ready.'

The contraction came, and Neve gripped Colton's hand tightly as she pushed with everything she had.

'Well done, Neve!' Jenny praised her as the baby slid free.

When they heard the healthy cry of their baby, Colton's eyes brimmed with tears. 'You did it.' He kissed her damp hair. 'Well done, gorgeous.'

Jenny placed the baby directly onto Neve's chest for skin-to-skin contact, and Colton watched as the little bundle made its presence known by bellowing at the top of its lungs.

'Look, our blond hair,' Neve half-sobbed, leaning close to kiss the top of the tiny curls. She looked to the midwife. 'Boy or a girl?'

'It's a boy.' Jenny grinned. 'Dad, do you want to cut the cord?'

Colton nodded, too dumbstruck to speak as he clipped through the spongy cord. Swaddling the baby up, Jenny called for a nurse and passed the bundle to Colton.

'He's perfect, Neve.' Coming to sit on the bed beside her, he placed the little boy between them and they both stared at him.

'I can't believe he's here… Are you happy?' Neve asked him, her face flushed and absolutely radiant. 'He looks like you.'

The little boy had stopped crying now, his tiny blue eyes opening for the first time to gaze at his mother. 'I hope he keeps his blue eyes.'

'I hope they turn green, like his mama's. Thank you,' he said, meaning every word.

'Well.' Jenny spoke. 'Don't thank her quite yet, because we still have another baby coming along any time now. We need to get the afterbirth out and get ready.'

The nurse appeared at their side. 'Is it okay if I take the baby now? I need to do the usual checks.'

Neve smiled, passing the baby over as Colton fluffed up her pillows. 'You need anything?'

'Water, please. I'm so dehydrated from the gas and air.'

'I'm not surprised, in this heat; I can't imagine how you're doing this.'

'Well, I'm thankful for the air con, put it that way.'

They laughed together as the two women worked around them. She felt another contraction coming and almost crushed the cup of water. Colton grabbed it, wiping sticky hair from her brow.

'Okay, Neve, this is the placenta. It's going to be pretty fast and furious from now. Once the first baby is out, things tend to speed up.'

'I'm ready.' She groaned and the pain took her over. Colton watched as Jenny worked and Neve pushed the placenta out of her body. The little baby boy screeched when the other nurse did the heel-prick test.

'Is he okay?' Colton asked her, trying to be there for everyone all at once.

'He's great. I'm just going to take him to one of the other nurses so I can assist Jenny with baby number two.' She wrapped the little boy up, putting a cute little blue hat on his head and an ID tag on his wrist before taking him out of the room.

There was little time to talk after that. The contractions took all of Neve's energy. She looked exhausted, lying back on the cushions and sipping water after each one.

'So, on the next one, I will need you to pant for the head. Don't push again till the next contraction hits, but wait for me to give you the okay. Neve, you understand me?' Jenny said.

Neve nodded, looking pale. 'I'm just so tired. I want the baby here now.'

'Soon, baby,' Colton soothed. 'Halfway there.'

'Yeah?' She shot him a half-lidded eye-roll. 'Well, if we ever do this again, you can give birth.'

'Deal.' He smirked, making her laugh. The next contraction ripped through her, and Colton could see her stomach tighten as she gripped his hand. 'Ow, Neve, baby—my fingers.'

'Screw your fingers,' she grunted, her face red. 'What about my lady parts? Oow, it hurts so much!' She sucked on the gas and air nozzle, the rhythmic suck-and-blow noise filling the room with her moans of pain.

'That's it, push! Push!'

'I'm pushing!' she bellowed, before returning her

mouth to the nozzle. *'Mmm!'* She groaned through it, crushing Colt's fingers to dust under her death grip. 'Colton, I can't do this! It hurts too much!'

'You can, baby, you are doing it.'

'Keep going, Neve!' Jenny said. 'The baby's head is coming!'

'Argh!' Neve pushed again, her face wet with sweat and tears.

'That's it! The baby's head is out! Well done, now rest. We need to wait for the next contraction. Keep breathing, that's it! Almost there.'

Colton kissed Neve over and over, before going to look. 'Oh baby, this one has hair too!'

'Blonde?' Neve panted.

'Yep.'

'Good,' she puffed. 'Can you tell him or her to hurry up?'

Jenny laughed but covered it with a cough.

'I can feel the next contraction coming,' Neve said after a moment. 'Colton…' She reached out a hand as she took in more gas and air.

'I'm right here. Baby number two's ready to meet his or her mum.'

'On the next contraction, Neve, I want you to push for the shoulders, okay? It's going to hurt but you're almost there.'

The next contraction came and the shoulders emerged. Neve was delirious by now, her face etched in pain as she rolled with each contraction and slowly brought their next child into the world.

Colton felt as if his heart was going to explode with

love for this woman. She was amazing, and he couldn't stop telling her how perfect she was, how well she was doing. For the first time since last night, he felt lighter. He'd said his piece, and they were here, doing this as a team, witnessing their children take their first breaths in the world.

On the next contraction, baby number two was born.

'You did it!' Colton laughed, looking at the naked little being Jenny was holding. 'Another boy!' he declared, feeling woozy with happiness. 'We have two sons!'

'He's not crying. Why isn't he crying?' Neve asked anxiously.

Jenny was working on him with the other nurse. They were turned away from them both, and Colton's heart turned to ice and splintered in his chest.

'Just give me a minute,' Jenny told them. 'I need to suction his nose and mouth. He has a bit of mucus in his airways.'

Colton stayed at Neve's side, watching the fear on her face as she waited.

'Neve,' he said softly. 'Eyes on me, honey. He's going to be fine.'

'How do you know?' She teared up. 'He's not crying. I can't… I can't…'

'He's going to be fine,' Colton said again, even though he wasn't sure himself. He just had a feeling, as if fate wouldn't be this cruel. 'He's going to be good, just like his brother.'

After the longest minute ever, the taut silence in the room was split by a lusty cry. Neve burst into tears as

Jenny brought over their son, a broad smile on her face. She placed the baby into Neve's waiting arms.

'Little guy just wanted to make a grand entrance,' she told them. 'He's fine, but we will keep a close eye on him. He swallowed some meconium during the delivery. We suctioned it out, but I do want to run some tests to check his lungs and make sure he didn't aspirate any. Signs are good so far, as once he was suctioned he started breathing well.'

'Will he need oxygen?' Colton asked.

'No, I don't think so, but if we do the tests or his breathing changes we will reassess. His breathing and heart rate are normal, and he pinked up nicely. Once we deliver the afterbirth, I'll give you a few minutes with him and bring his brother back in for you.'

'Thanks, Jenny, for everything,' Neve said and the two women embraced.

'It was a pleasure, Neve. I'm so happy for you both. The nurse will take this little one for now and do those tests.'

When the afterbirth had been delivered, Jenny got to work cleaning everything up. The nurse had taken the baby to be checked over and placed in a cot with his older brother, and Colton went outside the room to call the clinic. The girls had been blowing up the maternity ward phone all day, and he wanted to put them out of their misery.

He checked on the babies, who were both perfectly healthy and sleeping together in the same cot, like two little angels. He hit the canteen and the gift shop next, and he returned to the room laden down with balloons, baby gifts and lunch for them both. The staff practically swooned when he strode through the door, which made him blush. He was so happy, he damn near bought the place out.

Neve was sleeping. She looked exhausted and, as he sat there with all the gifts around him, he started to think about the night before—how stressed Neve had been, and how much hurt had happened between them. All of that had probably contributed to the stressed state she'd been in when she'd turned up at the hangar. If she turned him away again after this, he didn't want Brett to gloat.

Leaving the room again, he told the nurses he was making a phone call and headed out to the corridor, dialling a number he hadn't rung in years.

'Colton.' Brett's tone was cold when he answered. 'To what do I owe this pleasure? Are we doing pistols at dawn?'

'Neve had the babies today.'

'Oh.'

'Yes, oh.'

'Is she okay?'

'No thanks to you. She was beyond stressed last night, and today she went into labour right in front of me.'

'That's not my—'

'I am not getting into fault here, Brett. I told her everything after you left.'

'Like you hadn't already.'

'No, Brett, I hadn't. I thought of her, unlike you, but she knows the truth now. We have our children, and they are happy and healthy. That's all I care about, and I am telling you, here and now, this stuff ends here.'

'Are you threatening me?'

'No, Brett. You would know it if I was threatening you. I want an end to this. Neve doesn't deserve to be in the crossfire of our fight. She deserves better. I think we can both agree on that. She doesn't need your mother telling you all about her life. It's not fair. You coming here and attacking her like that was completely out of order.'

Colton heard Brett sigh down the line. 'It was a shock, hearing that she was having your child. I reacted.'

'I get that.' And he did. He'd had some pretty strong reactions to hearing their news over the years. He'd been waiting to hear that they were having a child, and when it hadn't come he'd still thought that it would eventually happen. 'We were friends once, you and I. I am not calling to fight with you. I'm asking you for a ceasefire. I want Neve to live her life and concentrate on being a mother.'

'She'll be a great mum,' Brett murmured. 'I am happy for her. Is she really okay?'

'She's sleeping now. The births took a lot out of her.'

'I'm glad to hear it. I can't believe you're a dad of two.'

'Neither can I, but I am happy about it. I just want the best for her.'

'I know you do.' Brett sighed. 'I messed up. Tell her I'm sorry. Please.'

'I will, when the dust has settled.'

'Thanks.'

'I'd better get back to her.'

'Are you together now, or did last night ruin everything?'

'I don't know,' Colton told him honestly. 'We still have some things to work out.'

'I get that. For what it's worth, I'm happy for you both. I hope you can succeed where I failed. Take care of them.'

'I will, always.'

'Then everything worked out. Maybe next time you're in Sydney, we can meet for a beer or something.'

'Yeah, sure. I'd like that. Goodbye, Brett.'

Both men knew that the beer wouldn't happen. Their friendship had been over for a long time, but something in Colton's heart mended all the same. Pocketing his phone, he pushed all thoughts of Brett out of his head and went back to be with his family.

CHAPTER ELEVEN

IF SOMEONE WERE to look up 'happiness' in the dictionary, thought Neve, their picture would be there next to it. They were cuddled together on the hospital bed, Colton's arms around Neve's as she cradled their sons in her arms. They both looked so much like Colton, it took her breath every time she looked at them: ten perfect fingers and toes, tiny blond tufts and a set of tiny fair eyebrows apiece. They were both staring up at their parents with matching bright-blue eyes. She'd dreamed of having a baby for so long, and now she had two sons. Two beautiful babies, and a man she adored.

'So, what do we call them? We never decided on any names.'

She saw them looking up into their father's eyes and she knew that he wouldn't leave. She would never let him go. If he wanted to travel the world, they would do it together. Her home was here in this room, with the three Anderson men.

'How about we each pick one? As long as it goes with Anderson.'

'You really want them to have my last name?'

'Of course. You're their father.'

‘And we’re a family now, right? I meant everything I said.’

‘I believe you, Colt. I know how you feel about me.’ She looked down at their babies and finally felt complete. ‘I came to the hangar to apologise to you. I should never have made you leave. I know you did everything with me in mind.’

‘We don’t need to go over that again. No stress today, sweetheart. Today is a happy day.’

‘I know, but I just want you to know. What you’re feeling, I feel the same. I really do. I think I’ve felt like that for a while, but after everything I didn’t trust it.’

‘I get that.’ He smiled. ‘You’re worth the wait. I love you, Neve Truby.’

‘I love you too.’

‘Don’t tease me, woman. I’ve been waiting to hear that for so long, I think I just hallucinated. You really love me?’

‘I do love you—so much. Not just for the babies you gave me. I love you for you.’

She felt his arms tighten around her and leaned into it. ‘Hormones or me?’

‘Definitely you.’ She laughed, stirring the babies. ‘I’ve been fighting it a long time.’

‘Because you’re annoyingly stubborn.’

‘In part,’ she teased. ‘I just didn’t want this to be something that either of us went along with because of these two.’

Colton’s gaze fell to his children, his face so full of love that she immediately fell in love with him that bit harder.

'I wanted you since I first set eyes on you, sweetheart. My only mistake was not stepping up in the first place. Now that I have you, I'm never letting go.' He kissed both babies. 'So, what are we going to call the Anderson twins? I like Henry for this one.' He ran a finger down Baby A's cheek.

Neve looked at his face, and it just fit. Looking at Baby B, who had scared them both with his arrival, an idea came to mind. 'How about Henry Colton for baby number one, and Hudson Abraham for this little daredevil?'

'After Abe?' Colton laughed, before his mouth came down to hers. 'Perfect.'

Their kiss was interrupted by a knock at the door before chaos swept in.

Liv and Bronwyn walked in, arms full of balloons and gifts. Liv held a bottle of champagne aloft.

'Congratulations!' Both women stopped short as Neve and Colton pulled apart.

'Sorry,' Bron winced. 'Bad time?'

Liv was not so subtle. She punched the air with the bottle. 'Finally! It's about time you two stopped messing around!'

'What she said.' Bron grinned.

Colton took it in his stride, ushering the women in and taking their gifts.

'Thanks, ladies. I couldn't agree more. Neve and I would like you to meet Henry and Hudson.'

'The newest members of the Anderson family,' Neve added, trying not to burst into tears of happiness.

'And not the last, if I get my way.'

There it was again, that look of determination that Colt sported when it came to her.

Even Liv swooned at that one.

The next day, Colton drove them home. Neve sat in between their car seats and laughed when the other drivers tooted at Colt for driving too slowly.

'You know, for a daredevil helicopter pilot and badass biker, you drive like my grandma.' She giggled when he pulled a face. 'In fact, if she was alive, then she'd have been the one doing the tooting.'

'Precious cargo.' He pouted, his face blanching. 'I think it will be a long time before I take them up in the air too.'

'Glad to hear it!'

Leaning over their matching cots in the living room later on, she felt that familiar rush of love envelop her. 'Gosh, they're just too cute. They even sleep in the same position.'

Colton's arms came around her as they watched over their babies. 'I'm pretty glad they're not identical. We would have had to tag them somehow; they're already so alike.' Neve's laugh made her wince, and Colton was right there, doing his 'protective bear' routine.

'Couch,' he commanded, tucking her under a blanket as soon as her backside touched the cushions. 'Do you need to eat? Want a drink? I could run and get you something.'

'Colt,' she chided, flashing him her best 'knock it off' look. 'I'm good.' When he raised a sceptical brow, she gave in entirely. 'Okay—turkey-salad sandwich, and maybe an iced tea? I could do with a nap too before they need to feed.' If she'd had to label his grin, she would have stuck 'triumphant' on it. 'Don't be smug about me letting you look after me.'

'Oh, sweetheart, I will never stop being smug about that.' He bit his lip. 'I had a phone call last night, after I left the hospital—from Abe.'

'Oh, did you tell him about the middle name?'

'No.' He came to sit next to her, taking her hand. 'I thought that honour should go to you. He called me to check on you, and to ask me to stay on at the medical centre.'

'Did he? Colton, that's great news! For how long?'

'For ever.' He looked happy, but she could see the hesitation rolling through him like an undercurrent. She wanted nothing more than for him to stay. There were no warning bells ringing in her heart. It was perfect timing, given that his contract would soon be over. 'Dr Barnes is coming back, and Abe has decided to take a step back, do less hours leading up to his retirement. He and Dr Barnes are going to run it together.'

His lips quirked. 'He didn't say as much, but I got the impression that Barnes is going to be taking over full-time, eventually. Abe seemed to think he wanted to make Swallow Falls a permanent thing. Like he had something—or someone—to come home for.'

'Liv!' Neve laughed. 'Oh man, that is going to be one rough ride. She is going to give him hell.'

Colton nestled her back against his chest. 'Yeah, well, the right woman is worth waiting for. I think we'll get along, he and I. Man after my own heart.' One of the babies snuffled in his sleep but settled back down.

'So, when do you have to make a decision by?'

'That depends on you,' he murmured, twining his fingers in hers. They were dwarfed in his grasp, but looked so right, as if she'd always held them. 'Do you want me to stay here? It would mean working and living together. You might get sick of me.' He chuckled at her eye-roll. 'I feel like this decision should be yours as much as mine, but I want to stay. I love the job, my family is here, I have friends… It fits.'

She turned to take his face in her hands. 'Then stay,' she said, pulling his lips to hers and pouring everything she felt into the touch of her mouth on his. 'We want you here, if you want to be here. And if you don't, that's okay too. We can make it work, although travelling might be out for the little ones for a couple of years.'

'I'm right where I want to be,' he told her, his eyes full of love and something else: contentment. 'I've been to a lot of places, sweetheart, but the only place I wanted to be was right here, next to you. You're my home.' He nodded to the cots. 'You and them.'

She sighed, feeling the last piece of the puzzle fit into place. 'Everyone has got what they want, then.'

'Maybe not Liv,' he said dryly. 'But I have a feeling she'll come round.'

'She has time to get her head round it before he gets back. She might rip his off, though, when they see each other in person. Abe will be pleased. He's a little match-maker at heart. He'll love this.'

'Oh, he does.' Colton grinned. 'I took the job the second he offered it.'

She pretended to be shocked, gasping and wriggling out of his grasp, but he held firm. 'And what if I had wanted you to go?'

'I'd have worn your stubborn ass down.' He laughed, which set her off. 'We've wasted enough time, Neve. Life starts now.'

The wail of two lusty cries stopped them from kissing to seal the deal. Colton brought one of the babies to her, returning to settle the other in his arms. 'You feed them, and I will feed you.'

As Henry suckled at her breast, Neve listened to the deep tones of Colton in the kitchen, talking to their other son as he made lunch. He'd bought a baby sling for the occasion, and she'd be damned if the sight of him carrying in lunch with his son strapped to him didn't set her ovaries afire all over again. She was going to be careful from now on, or they'd have a whole squadron of Anderson children on their hands.

Later, as he crawled into bed beside her, tucking her into him gently, she looked into those blue eyes once more, marvelling at how things had turned out. At how lucky she was that, every day onwards, she could be with this man and they could watch their children grow together.

'Move in with us tomorrow?' she asked in the dark, smiling as his face lit up once more. 'Your lease is up soon, and I would love nothing more than us all under one roof. No more wasted time.'

'Are you sure?' he checked, making her heart jump.

'Absolutely. My Batcave is your Batcave.'

Pulling her in for a kiss, he murmured the answer against her lips.

'I love you, Robin. When it comes to you, my answer is always yes.'

* * * * *

If you enjoyed this story, check out these other great reads from Rachel Dove

Faking It with the Firefighter
A Baby to Change Their Lives
How to Resist Your Rival
A Midwife, Her Best Friend, Their Family

All available now!

SNOWBOUND WITH THE SINGLE MUM

AMY RUTTAN

MILLS & BOON

This book is for all single parents out there, especially the ones I know, who are doing an amazing job.

CHAPTER ONE

PAULY GLANCED AT the arrival board at the Calgary International Airport.

Oh good. I'm not late.

Or at least she wasn't late to pick up Ares. Objectively, she was running behind and had been worried—what with the hour and twenty-minute drive from her place in Canmore to Calgary, on Halloween, with the first significant snowfall happening the night before, *plus* her son, Jeremy, being a-stick-in-the-mud about wearing his snow gear to school and almost missing his bus—that she was going to leave poor Ares standing out in the cold.

Literally.

It was one of the coldest and snowiest Halloweens she could ever remember since moving to Alberta, so *of course* it was the day she had to go to the airport. She didn't usually like to leave Jeremy alone. No, he wasn't alone, he was at school. But she never went this far from town without him.

She was trying hard not to think about it too much and instead focus on how excited he'd be when he came home and saw his godfather.

She also hated running late, which was just adding a whole other level of stress.

Thankfully, the fates were in her favor, and Ares's flight from Toronto to Calgary had been delayed. She just hoped

Ares was ready for snow, because she knew for a fact that Toronto was a lot warmer than Alberta at the moment.

Also, he had been traveling all over the world as a locum paramedic and first responder and his last job had been in the Caribbean, so she knew it was going to be a shock to his system. Pauly had only been in Canmore for three years and she still wasn't used to the dry cold of southern Alberta.

There were times, especially in the dead of winter, that she missed the milder climes of southern Ontario. She was sure Ontarians would disagree that it was more temperate there, but it was true. Still, she wouldn't trade her life here to move back. She loved being in Alberta and in the mountains, particularly.

Her late husband, Rex, had always dreamed about becoming a paramedic and first responder who worked in the mountains. He'd loved climbing. Pauly had too, once. That had been before she had Jeremy. Once she'd become a mom, she couldn't put her life on the line to scale mountains for fun. Rex had always loved the thrill far more than she did. She was glad, though, that they'd been able to make Rex's dream come true and move out here.

Only, it had been short-lived. Nearly two years ago, an accident had claimed Rex while he was at work on the mountain, leaving her and their then eight-year-old son all alone.

For the last two years Pauly been numb.

There had been moments she agonized over it, worried that maybe she could've protected Rex. Which was ridiculous. He'd died doing his job. Still, it ate away at her.

Family had come and helped her on and off over the last couple of years as she'd tentatively gotten back to work, but now she was facing the reality of maybe moving up from the desk job she'd taken at the paramedic station, and actually getting back out there in the field.

Part of her wanted it, badly. She was a field paramedic. The problem was Jeremy. There was a niggly little piece of her brain that was terrified of the idea that something could happen to her, and she'd leave Jeremy an orphan.

She wasn't sure how this was all going to work.

Since Rex had died, she'd made sure Jeremy had all the love and support he would've gotten had his dad still been there. She and Rex had always managed to balance everything. Now there was no time for anything else—her life revolved around her son.

Lately though, it felt like she was failing there too, and that scared her.

She didn't want Jeremy to ever be lonely, to feel the lack of a parent's attention. That was a feeling she knew all too well, and she swore she'd never put her kids through that. But the truth was, Jeremy was craving a father figure. It made Pauly feel so guilty that no matter what she did, she couldn't seem to fill that void for him.

So when, on one of their frequent virtual calls, Ares had said he was taking a sabbatical from his usual firm, and had offered to come and help her out, it had felt like a life line.

"You don't have to do that. I'll be fine."

She hoped that her voice didn't crack, because the truth was, she wasn't fine. She hadn't been fine since the accident. And she most definitely wasn't fine since all her extended family had returned back to their lives, leaving her and Jeremy alone.

Ares made a face. "You're lying to me."

Pauly chuckled. "How do you always know?"

He grinned, those dark eyes twinkling. "I think you said the same thing to me years ago, when I stopped going to classes after my parents' divorce. You called me out then and now I'm doing the same."

Pauly took a deep breath and relaxed. "I hate that you know me so well."

Ares shrugged. "That's what friends are for."

"You have a life to lead."

"So do you," he said, firmly. "Pauly, I love you and Jeremy. Let me come and help you out. My contract will be through in five days. I have to head back to Toronto and put in for my sabbatical, which I'm due, and then I can work and help you get back on your feet in Canmore. You know I love the mountains out there. Let me do this for you. Let me do this for Rex."

Pauly choked back tears. "I'm so glad to have you as a friend."

"Of course."

"And the guest room is open for you. I don't want to hear about you getting your own place in Canmore. Besides, it's a bit harder to come by accommodations when ski season starts."

"After all these years, I better be able to crash at your place," he teased. "Try not to worry. I'll see you in a week."

It had been the longest week of Pauly's life. Especially since Jeremy had found out that his godfather—or "Uncle Ari," as he liked to call him—would be coming to stay with them for the next year. There was an actual smile on Jeremy's face, real joy in his life, just at the thought. It had been so hard to find that little inkling of happiness since his father died.

When he'd gotten on the bus this morning, with his Halloween costume firmly packed in his rucksack, he'd been going over all the big plans to go trick-or-treating with Uncle Ari.

Ares has no idea what he's gotten himself into.

Just that thought brought a smile to Pauly's face and eased the anxiety she'd been feeling. She didn't want to rely on anyone, but she really could use Ares's help. Between her job and Jeremy, there was so much to juggle.

It was terrifying doing it all on her own. Lately, she felt like that lonely little girl she'd once been, left alone while her parents worked double shifts. The one who had spent her childhood raising herself and her little brother.

You're not alone anymore though.

There was a lot of chatter and the arrival doors opened up.

Pauly looked up to see a stream of people coming out the doors. She easily spotted Ares in the crowd. It was hard not to pick him out. A six-foot-three bronzed Greek god striding through the airport with a huge duffel bag slung over his shoulder. His dark brown hair was longer than she remembered, a bit flyaway. His skin was a deeper tan from the sun of the tropics. It really did look like he'd stepped off the beach. He was athletic and moved through the crowds quickly.

When his gaze landed on her, she waved frantically, smiling, and he grinned back.

When they were at college, every single girl she knew was in love with Ares Galanis. She may have been with Rex, but she could definitely see the appeal.

He opened his arms as he approached, dropping his huge duffel bag. "Pauly!"

"So glad to see you," she said, trying to hold back the rush of emotion she was feeling in that moment as his arms came around her and she snuggled against him for one of his warm hugs.

The last time she'd seen him in person had been at Rex's funeral. She didn't really remember that. Everything about that horrible day was a blur, but she had snippets of memories, of seeing Ares in her periphery taking care of Jeremy.

He had always been there for them, and she was glad he was here now. For the first time in a long time, she felt a bit of relief, some comfort and safety.

Instantly, the guilt hit her for feeling that with someone other than Rex, because Rex had been the first. The first to take care of her and comfort her.

Truly.

Ares has always made you feel that too.

Pauly stiffened and stepped out of Ares's embrace, wrapping her arms around her core to steady herself, otherwise she was going to get overly emotional and start blubbering.

One thing she'd learned as a child relying on herself—keep your emotions in check.

"You're a big girl." Her mother's words echoed in her head. Always the same reminder, whenever she broke down while her parents worked overtime.

She shook those horrible memories away.

"How are you feeling?" Ares asked.

"Today? Frazzled. I was worried I was going to miss your plane. I know you probably don't appreciate it, but I was very thankful for your flight delay."

Ares shrugged. "Flight delays are the norm in my line of work."

She glanced around him. "All you have is a duffel bag?"

"It's a large duffel. It's what hockey players use."

She cocked an eyebrow, fighting the smile that was tugging at the corner of her lips. "You can fit your whole life in there?"

He glanced down at the duffel. "Yes. This bag goes with me everywhere. Do you have a problem with it?"

"No. It just seems…you travel light."

"Well, I did ship out my rock climbing stuff. I didn't want to carry it on the plane, and I don't exactly trust airlines not to lose my luggage. So that will be coming in the next couple of days."

The moment he said the words "rock climbing stuff" she tried not to visibly wince. "That makes sense."

"I'm a nomad. I don't need much. This bag is my best friend." He winked, teasingly, knowing that she considered herself the deserving owner of that title.

"I hope you have winter gear in there," Pauly mused.

Ares frowned. "What? No."

"You climb mountains and you don't have winter gear?"

"It's bulky, so I shipped that too," he explained. "It's October. I didn't think I'd need it right away."

"Oh, you're in for a shock, my friend. We'll get you to a shop and get you some warmer gear. You'll need it for tonight."

Ares picked up his duffel as they headed out of the arrivals area and toward the parking garage where her truck was parked. "Tonight?" he asked, querulously.

"Trick-or-treating. Jeremy has elected you as his official trick-or-treat partner. He even has a rubber mask you can wear."

Ares rolled his eyes, but he was smiling. "I forgot today was Halloween."

"It's hard to forget when you have a kid."

A strange brief look fluttered on his face, which gave her pause, but only for a second.

"Well, yes. I suppose I don't really track the holidays much. The kiddie holidays, that is."

"Kiddie holidays?"

Ares grinned. "Carnival in Rio is something to experience."

"Oh, I'm sure." Pauly was a bit envious of his freedom. She'd gotten married straight out of college. She and Rex had immediately put down roots and made a life together.

As Ares had stated, he was a nomad. A traveler. Never staying still.

They stepped outside and he cursed under his breath as the wind howled down between the airport and the parking garage, whipping up the light dusting of the first snow. "You have snow?"

"It snowed in Ontario during some Halloweens."

Ares made a face. "I will admit it's hard to come from the tropics of my last job to…to this."

"You're regretting your decision, aren't you?" she teased.

"No. I'm looking forward to the mountains and the work. Also spending time with my godson. And you."

Her heart fluttered and she couldn't help but smile up at him. It was the way he said *you*, so softly and so tenderly. As their gazes locked, his dark eyes were twinkling at her and a strange feeling went through her.

You're just lonely. Lonely and tired. It's nothing.

Pauly tore her gaze away and tucked an errant strand of hair behind her ear. "Come on, we better get you some warmer clothes and then get back to Canmore before Jeremy gets home."

She was glad that Ares was here, but the other things she was feeling about him were strange. He was her friend, her best friend. It had only been two years since she lost Rex.

The only way she could rationalize it was that she had missed the intimacy, the companionship. But there was no way she was going to even entertain the idea of something more than that with Ares.

One, he loved his lifestyle. Two, he'd sworn off settling down years ago. Pauly knew that for a fact; she'd been there when that commitment was made. And three, there was no way she was going to ruin what she had with him.

She wasn't going to lose his friendship.

She's your friend and nothing more.

Ares had to keep reminding himself of that. It was clear from their previous calls and video chats that Pauly was struggling. Not that he blamed her in the least. His heart was still hurting after Rex's death. He couldn't even begin to imagine what Pauly and Jeremy were going through. Although Pauly would never admit it.

She was strong, something he'd always admired about her. While he and Rex were usually goofing off during college, she'd been looking after them. Making sure they ate right, attended classes. Pauly had always been responsible.

All he could offer her during that time immediately after Rex's death had been a shoulder to cry on. For the last two years, she had a lot of family helping her out, but now that was gone. Ares knew her family and Rex's had begged her to move back to Ontario, but Pauly had made it clear she loved it in Canmore, so did Jeremy. They had scattered Rex's remains amongst the Three Sisters and she had stated, in no uncertain terms to everyone, she wasn't dragging Jeremy away.

Ares was glad to be able to take this year, take a position in Canmore and try to help her as much as he could as she made this transition back. It was the least he could do. But he had to keep reminding himself that she was *just* a friend.

Of course, he'd been doing that since the day they met.

Her heart had always belonged to Rex, and Ares cared for Rex too.

Both Pauly and Rex had been there for him, supported him in times his family hadn't. They had been there in college when his whole world had fallen apart. When his parents, who he thought were the epitome of love and longevity in marriage, split.

And it had not been amicable.

Part of Ares blamed himself, because he and his father had had a blow-up argument six months before his parents' marriage ended. He hadn't even been on speaking terms with many of his family. But the final split had made Ares rethink his whole ideal of love and marriage.

Most importantly trust.

As the years went on, both his brothers' marriages had failed too, and his sister's was perpetually rocky. It was clear to Ares that marriage just didn't work.

It worked for Pauly and Rex.

Except "worked" was hard to quantify, in that case. Rex had died. If he hadn't, maybe even he and Pauly would've eventually split.

Ares hated the negative thoughts filling his mind. He pushed them away. Rex and Pauly had been his best friends. When he'd seen her at the funeral, she'd been hollow, a shell, and he knew her heart was shattered. As much as he wanted to be there for her, she had her family around her, so he'd kept his distance. Now was his chance, finally, to help her out.

Honestly, when he'd gotten off the plane in Calgary, he'd been pretty sure that this year would be easy. That he'd gotten over his tender, unwelcome romantic feelings about Pauly. And then he'd seen her standing in the arrivals area.

It was like she hadn't changed at all. She was the woman he remembered from college.

Her dark brown hair was longer than before, swept back in a side bun. Her long dark lashes hid stunning clear blue-gray eyes and her luscious red lips parted in a smile that completely lit up the room. The moment Ares saw her, his heart sped up with anticipation and he realized right then and there he'd been a fool to think he'd moved on.

He'd been in love with her for far too long.

It was bad enough that he was in love with someone he couldn't have, that no one he'd met since had held a candle to her. But, to top it all off, he wasn't even *looking* for someone to settle down with—ever.

He'd already irrevocably disappointed his parents when he hadn't followed in his father's business footsteps, so there was no point in trying to please them by marrying. It hadn't worked for them, and it probably wouldn't for him.

At least, that's what he kept telling himself. Because deep down there was a part of him that kind of envied what Rex and Pauly had had.

Now, as they traveled to a shop to buy him some better winter gear, Ares couldn't help but feel this sense of happiness to be with Pauly again. A joy that was conflicting with his own grief over the loss of Rex.

At least Pauly looked a bit better now. When they'd scattered Rex's ashes, she'd been lost. Pale, and just broken. Nothing like her usual self.

He wondered if she even really remembered him being at the funeral.

"Here we are," Pauly announced as she parked her big white truck in the parking lot of an oversized big-box outdoor supply store. She was smirking at him. "I still can't believe you packed so light for winter in Alberta."

"I've been spoiled in the tropical countries," he said.

"You really have," she teased.

They climbed out of the truck and hurried inside the store. There was a single second when he did regret his decision to come, with the cold biting at his skin. But it was only for a moment.

It's the jet lag. That's why I wasn't thinking straight about the weather. That's all any of this is.

Pauly would probably tease him about this for some time. Even though she was the responsible roommate, she'd always poked fun at the pair of them. That was okay. Ares liked their jokes, their ribbing. It had been a long time since she'd ragged on him. A little bit of the old Pauly was shining through.

The store was, thankfully, warm and it didn't take them very long to find Ares a thicker coat, a hat, gloves and boots. Once that was all purchased, they grabbed a quick bite to eat and got back out on the Trans-Canada Highway to head to Canmore.

The service for Rex and the spreading of his ashes had been in the summer, when they'd all been able to take the trail to the meadow, filled with wildflowers, which overlooked the mountains.

There were definitely no wildflowers out in the fields as they drove west now. There was snow, blowing snow, lots of it, and when they came to sections of the highway that were just open fields, the whiteness really did blind them.

It reminded Ares why he hated winter—why he always spent these months somewhere warmer.

"You're scowling," Pauly said, breaking the silence.

"Am I?"

"One thousand percent."

"Winter," he grunted.

She giggled softly. "I did warn you."

"I hope this subsides before tonight," he groused.

Pauly snort-laughed in that adorable way she always did. "Well, you won't get so much drifting in town, but it'll be cold."

"Great."

Pauly glanced at him briefly and they shared a smile. He loved seeing her smile again, but he could still see that sadness, that hesitation in her blue-gray eyes.

"Jeremy is going to be so excited to see you," she remarked, interrupting his thoughts.

"I'm excited to see him too." He loved his godson; he could endure winter for Jeremy. "What's he going to dress up as?"

"I can't tell you. He wants you to be surprised."

"Should I be worried?"

She grinned. "No, but I swore no hints."

"Fair enough."

He settled back to enjoy the drive into the mountains as they chatted about nothing in particular. It was just easy to talk to her—it always had been. Ares couldn't wait to spend some time climbing these peaks, all the ones he used to climb with Pauly and Rex a long time ago. It was just the cold bothering him. He'd have to build up an immunity to it again.

The mountains were hidden by clouds of flurries, but then they rose out of the clouds of snow, like great Goliaths of rock.

He was envious of Pauly being settled here, of getting to see this every day.

I could settle here myself.

He quickly ignored that little thought.

His life was too up in the air, too transient. He loved his work, and this placement wasn't permanent. He was only on a year sabbatical from his current job. There was an end date to his time here in Alberta.

Nothing could make him stay here permanently.

Really. Nothing?

CHAPTER TWO

PAULY WAS STILL inwardly chuckling that Ares had arrived in Alberta with no real winter wear. He was Canadian—he should know how the weather could be. But then again, he'd traveled so much the last fifteen years or so, that maybe he really had forgotten.

That was the way he always had been, ever since they were in college together. Always a little bit disorganized. When she, Rex and Ares had all shared an apartment together in Toronto, Ares's bedroom had generally been a catastrophe. So even though they weren't those carefree college kids anymore, it kind of made Pauly happy to know that not much had changed about him. Something was still the same in her life.

The drive back to Canmore was peaceful. They chatted about the flight and a bit about Ares's job in the Caribbean. Pauly was just forever grateful that he was willing to put his life on hold for this year while she properly got back to work and regained her footing after her world had been shattered.

Her world, and Jeremy's.

There were still times when Jeremy wasn't okay with Pauly leaving his sight, and she hated that for him. She hated that her child was feeling so anxious that he couldn't be a kid right now, that he felt like he had to protect his mom. All Pauly wanted for Jeremy was for him to enjoy his childhood and not worry about her, or anybody.

She didn't want Jeremy to go through what she had.

"Mommy," Pauly said over the phone. "When will you be home? It's dark and Sam is crying."

"You're a big girl of ten, Pauly. Keep the lights on and stay with Sam. You're his big sister and he needs you. Daddy and I both have to work late."

"Okay." She held back a sniffle.

"No crying, Pauly. Just take care of Sam. You're in charge."

She realized now that she shouldn't have been in charge at ten years old. Jeremy was ten and he needed her still. Just like she'd needed her parents.

Which made her transition back to work all the more difficult.

It was the reason why she'd been stuck at the station or in town for the past year, rather than out on the trails. Jeremy struggled with letting her go back out on the mountain, especially near the trail where Rex was killed. And as much as she liked being in the field, it didn't bother her to keep closer to town.

Eventually, though, it would mean a demotion and she didn't want that. She was a paramedic. Highly trained. She wasn't meant to sit behind a desk, even if it was the safest place.

Sometimes we have to do things, sacrifice things we love, to keep others safe.

She swallowed the lump in her throat as she turned off the Trans-Canada Highway and took the roundabout that whizzed them in the direction of Canmore. Her three-bedroom townhouse was on Benchlands Trail, a little bit away from the picturesque and touristy mountain downtown of Canmore. She was closer to the crowded bike trails, but it was so worth it because her back porch gave her an unobstructed view of the Three Sisters.

"This is perfect," Rex exclaimed enthusiastically as he walked around on the deck.

"Sh... Remember, we don't want to be too excited. We want to make a decent offer," Pauly teased.

Rex grinned and pulled her close. "I can't help it. This is like a dream. Jeremy will love it here when we move next month."

"I think so too." She drank in the mountain air. "It is beautiful."

"This will be our home. You and me. Forever."

"You okay?" Ares asked, interrupting her thoughts.

"What?" Pauly asked, hoping her voice didn't shake.

"You just zoned out there."

She could see the concern etched into his face. Ares knew her so well. "I'm fine. Really."

"Hmm. I'm not buying that."

"I figured you wouldn't," she mused, as she signaled and then pulled into the driveway of her wooden-sided townhouse. "Welcome to your new home for the next year."

"I appreciate you letting me crash at your place, but I really can get my own place in town if it it's too much hassle for you," Ares offered.

"No. No way am I having my bestie renting an overpriced apartment. It's winter, ski season is gearing up, so everything else is gearing up too, like prices for hotels, restaurants, short-term rentals…"

He smiled. "Well, I'm looking forward to helping you out and working here."

"Me too."

It was nice to have someone else around. Another adult.

Don't rely on him though. This is all short term. You're on your own.

They climbed out of her truck, and she unlocked the front door. They had about thirty minutes to get Ares settled before Jeremy's bus dropped him off and then Ares would be bombarded.

"The guest suite on the lower level is yours. You know your way around."

Ares nodded and made his way over to the large bedroom on the ground floor of the townhouse, just off the entranceway and the door to the garage. When he came to visit them, this was always where he stayed, except during Rex's funeral, when the house had been full of extended relatives, like Pauly's parents and Rex's family.

Pauly trailed after him.

"This is perfect, Pauly. Really." He set his duffel bag on the floor.

"Would you like a coffee? Or I can let you get sorted. I have to start dinner and get some stuff set up for trick-or-treaters."

"I can help." There was a twinkle in his eyes as he peeled off his coat and set it on the bed. "It's been forever since I participated in Halloween."

"Okay, but first I'll make you a coffee, so you can enjoy that while I roast a bunch of pumpkin seeds."

Ares made a face. "Yuck."

"What?" she asked, laughing as she left his room and climbed the stairs onto the main level of her house.

"I've never understood that," he stated. "Roasting pumpkin seeds. I hate them."

"Oh, come on, you've never tasted my pumpkin seeds. I season them with garlic and some with smoked paprika. I even do a maple sugar version."

"I just hate the outer shell. I think it's a sensory thing."

"So the world traveler is picky, eh?" she teased as they meandered into the kitchen.

Ares was grinning as he took a seat at the island. "I've tried my fair share of delicacies abroad and I'm not saying no to pumpkin seeds because I think they sound gross. I'm stating an actual fact—that I detest them."

"Well, I can't argue with that." Pauly turned on her coffee maker and then pulled out the pans she needed to lay out the seeds. "What's the weirdest cuisine you've tried on your travels? Like something you would've never eaten or even thought of eating before?"

"Probably a scorpion in Asia."

Now it was her turn to gag. "Bugs?"

"They're high in protein," he countered. "And sometimes, you're out in the wilds on a rescue mission or learning survival skills, and you have to eat bugs. Or prairie oysters."

"I've had those before."

He raised his eyebrows. "What?"

"I live in the west. Everyone has had them. Alberta has the best beef." She poured him a cup of coffee. "So you're telling me a bug is more desirable than a pumpkin seed?"

"Yes."

"You state that so firmly."

"Of course I do, because I'm completely right."

"I'm not buying it."

He grinned. "Well, the only way you could compare it is to eat a bug. A scorpion in fact."

She shuddered. "Well, you can't find that at the local co-op, so I'm going to say nope on that."

"Then concede I'm right. It's quite easy to admit it."

There was a twinkle in his eyes and a smirk on his handsome face.

"You're still absolutely hopeless." She shook her head and handed him his cup. As he reached out to take the mug from her, his fingers brushed hers and she felt this rush flow through her, sending a ripple of heat through her blood.

It completely caught her off guard. She almost dropped the mug, so shocked by that flood of sensation just from a simple touch. She wanted to pull away quickly, but she didn't want to burn Ares's fingers.

And there was a part of her that liked it. It felt intimate and she'd missed that. Like she'd missed the connection. The laughter.

Sure, she had family around on and off, but this one-on-one with Ares was different to in-laws and parents and siblings.

Then she reminded herself that Ares was her friend. And he was a risk-taker, to boot. There was no way she could fall for a friend, especially one who took risks like Rex had.

As soon as Ares had a firm grasp of the mug, she pulled back her hand quickly and ran it nervously over her thigh, like she was trying to rub off the feeling of his warm skin.

She shouldn't like the fact that she had touched another man. It was wrong.

No. It's not. It's okay.

She ignored that small voice. It was the same one that had been telling her lately that it might be okay to move on, that Rex would want her to be happy, but it was hard to believe it. What she'd had with Rex felt like a fairy tale. No one was lucky enough in life to have that twice, and she wasn't going to take the risk on dating again, looking for it, not when she had Jeremy to worry about.

Ares didn't seem to notice anything as he put a little shot of hazelnut flavoring into his coffee. He was completely oblivious, and she was relieved about that.

"Bugs truly aren't bad," he continued, interrupting her chain of thoughts and easing her nervous tension.

"Really?" she asked, hoping her voice didn't shake. "I find that hard to believe."

"No, they're good."

"Well, don't pay me back by roasting me some," she teased as she pulled out the various seasonings she needed for the pumpkin seeds. "Although, I wouldn't mind some of your mother's spanakopita."

When they'd all been rooming together, they'd shared cooking duties, but Ares was absolutely useless in the kitchen. Except for breakfast, he was good at that. Thankfully, his mother would often send him food and her Greek traditional dishes were some of Pauly's favorites.

"Oh, I'm sure she'll ship you a batch," Ares remarked. "She always did like you and Rex."

"That would be nice."

What Ares wanted to say was how much his mother liked *Pauly.*

"You need to find yourself a girl like Pauly and settle down."

It was the constant rhetoric that his mother nagged him with. That and the fact that his parents really didn't think he'd grown up all that much, because he hadn't done the right thing and settled down and had children.

Like they had? he scoffed under his breath.

They were so worried about him and his life, when they should've been working harder on their own, and with their relationships with their kids.

Especially his dad.

His father had been so disappointed that Ares hadn't gone into the family business and taken over the restaurant. His father had never really seemed proud of what he did. He just didn't seem to get that Ares loved saving lives.

"What about Nico and Stathis?" Ares argued.

"What about them?" his father asked.

"They can take over the restaurant."

"Nico is on his way to be a surgeon and Stathis just got called to the bar. Now, if you wanted to go to medical school... I can understand that."

"A paramedic is just as important as a doctor," Ares snapped.

"But not as important as the restaurant. As the legacy. You're the youngest, Ares. You have to take it over before it dies. If you don't, then we're done."

"Then I guess we're done. I guess it dies."

Ares hadn't talked to his father much after that. And then his parents' marriage ended and everything just fell apart.

Honestly, he did sometimes think about becoming a doctor like his brother Nico, but he liked the freedom of being a paramedic. Then there was the cost of getting any more qualifications.

After turning down his dad's legacy, Ares had kind of been on his own.

The only one who never nagged him about his choices and just listened to him had been Pauly.

It had always been Pauly, his go-to for everything. But pursuing that connection was out of the question. Pauly had belonged to Rex and vice versa. Ares would never have gotten in the way of their love, because if he had, he would've lost them both.

It had been hard watching them. He was happy for them, but he also longed for something that deep too.

"So, when I ask her to marry me you take the picture," Rex instructed.

"What if she says no?" Ares teased. Although, a secret part of him kind of wished for that outcome...

He instantly felt guilty, especially when Rex froze. "You think she might?"

Ares clapped his friend on the shoulder, hating himself. "No, man. She's going to say yes."

He had no doubt about that. Pauly and Rex loved each other. Rex was the luckiest man alive and Ares envied them.

Now, even though Rex was gone, he just couldn't do anything to risk his friendship with Pauly. She was too important to him.

There was a slam of the front door and Pauly smiled.

"We're in the kitchen, Jere!" she called out.

Ares set down his coffee and stood up as his godson came bounding up the stairs to the main level. When he was last here for Rex's memorial, Jeremy had clung to him. He'd been a rock to the young boy who had just lost his father.

And Ares was glad to do it. He was the godfather, after all, and that was something his family had always taken seriously. Even with all their issues.

Jeremy's face lit up at the sight of him. It made Ares's heart ache. He saw Rex there in that ginger hair and the smattering of freckles on Jeremy's nose, but the eyes were all Pauly.

"Uncle Ari! You came!" Jeremy shouted, dropping his backpack on the floor and running at him at full speed.

Ares laughed and knelt down to catch the boy in his arms, holding him close. "Did you think I wouldn't?"

Jeremy stepped back. “No. I guess I didn’t. You always keep your word.”

“Of course.” He tousled Jeremy’s hair. “You’ve grown.”

“He definitely has. I had to buy him new winter boots,” Pauly remarked, setting a pan of pumpkin seeds in the oven.

“You’re going to go trick-or-treating with me tonight, right?” Jeremey asked.

“Yes. I was told you had a secret costume and a mask for me.”

“More of a hat. I’ll go get it!” Jeremy raced off up the stairs to where his bedroom was, but not before stopping and leaning over the rail on the upstairs landing. “Mom, can we have pizza tonight?”

“Sure, buddy,” Pauly said. “I’ll order it now.”

“Awesome!” Jeremy disappeared again.

Ares chuckled to himself. He’d missed Jeremy and Pauly. And he still missed Rex—always would. But he was glad he could be here for his wife and son. Even though they weren’t blood, they were family all the same and Ares wanted to keep them safe.

“I think you’ll get a kick out of his costume.”

He turned to glance at Pauly who was holding back laughter and suddenly he was suspicious. “What is it?”

“I told you before, I am sworn to secrecy.” She giggled again. “I need to order the pizza from the local place before it gets too busy.”

“You’re purposefully evading me.”

There was a gleam in her eye. “I am.”

Jeremy came rushing down the stairs in the getup of a vintage video game character, with the fake moustache and everything. “See!”

“Oh, so I’m going to be your brother?” Ares asked.

"No way." Jeremy pulled out a dinosaur hat, and suddenly Ares knew that he was going as the little green dragon this character often rode. It was a ridiculous hat, with big googly eyes on the top and Pauly was already laughing quietly behind him.

It was absurd.

Ares took the hat from Jeremy and strapped it on. It was heavy and hot and he turned to look at Pauly, who was doubled over laughing behind the counter.

"It's perfect!" Jeremy announced. "Hey, can I hop on your back and you carry me around?"

"No. I love you, buddy, but no." That was where Ares drew the line.

Jeremy chuckled. "It was worth a try."

"Jeremy, go grab that big candy bowl out of the storage room while I go pick up the pizza," Pauly said.

"Okay, Mom."

Pauly continued giggling as she passed Ares. All he could do was cross his arms and glare at her.

"I feel like I was set up." He knew the crazy big eyes on top of his head were moving around, because he could feel them shaking.

"It's so funny."

He huffed and rolled his eyes, but was only teasing. He really didn't mind doing this for Jeremy. It was one night, and it was obviously bringing him joy.

Pauly came up to him. "You look adorable."

His heart skipped a beat as he looked down at her, her long thick lashes brushing the top of her white cheeks, her lips so close. He was fighting the urge to wrap his arms around her and kiss her on the tip of her nose.

He had to get control of himself.

She wasn't his.

She was just a friend.

"Thanks," he replied, gruffly.

"I'll be back in a few minutes. Keep an eye on the pumpkin seeds, they'll be done soon."

"Maybe I'll let them burn in revenge for making me dress up so ridiculous," he groused.

She laughed. "I guess that's fair."

"Go get the pizza."

She waved over her shoulder and headed down the stairs. Ares took a deep breath and wandered over to the living room with the vaulted ceiling and big picturesque window. The snow was dissipating and the sun was starting to get lower in the sky, but he could see the Three Sisters in the distance. The sun was causing the snow caps to glow, almost pink, and he couldn't help but smile.

He'd thought he could handle this year, helping out Pauly and Jeremy. He'd thought he'd buried those feelings he felt for her deep down. But just a couple of hours with her, and everything he thought he had locked tightly away was bubbling to the surface.

Part of him wanted to run away, to run from those feelings, because it would be easier. He'd been doing that for a long time, but he wasn't going to leave Pauly and Jeremy. Not when he'd made the promise.

He had to stick out the year, even though it was going to be the hardest year of his life.

CHAPTER THREE

PAULY COULD NOT stop chuckling every time she pictured Ares in that ridiculous hat that Jeremy made him wear. It was so endearing, because Ares did it solely to make Jeremy happy. Ares was never one to dress up and make a fool of himself. Not even at all the college parties they attended.

Sometimes, in big crowds, he was a little bit more reserved. Whereas Rex had always been the life of the party. She sometimes wondered how the three of them had become so close. Whatever the reason, she was glad Ares was here now, taking Jeremy out trick-or-treating.

It was something Jeremy and his father had done every year. The fact that Ares was willing to do it now meant the world to her.

Jeremy's first Halloween without Rex had been so heartbreaking and hard.

This helped to make up for all of that.

Ares may have looked ridiculous in that green dinosaur hat, but he was also so damn cute. And Pauly actually found it quite sexy, only because he was being such a good sport about it.

She paused, instantly feeling bad for thinking of Ares like that. To think of anyone like that. It was too soon.

I'm really hard up, she mused to herself as she finished off her glass of wine. She did miss physical touch and intimacy, but now was not the time and place to be dwelling on it. She'd had all that with Rex and now he was gone. Ares was just a friend with his own life to lead. If she ever did think about being with someone again, she needed someone grounded—not a self-proclaimed nomad.

There was a knock, and she headed to the door as she heard little voices on the other side calling out "Trick or treat!" She greeted the kids and parents, gave them their chocolate treats, then saw a very tired, tall dinosaur and her plumber son come walking up the driveway.

She laughed quietly behind her hand. It was too adorable.

"Hi, Mom!" Jeremy called out as he raced inside, leaving Ares behind. "We got a lot."

"Did you?" Pauly asked, smiling gently as Ares came in, shut the door, and took off the hat. His shoulder-length hair was a mess. Without thinking, she reached out and tenderly brushed some of it back.

Ares's gaze locked on her and her heart skipped a beat as she stared into his mesmerizing dark eyes.

What am I doing?

She pulled her hand away quickly. "Sorry."

"For what?" he asked, softly.

"For making you wear that ridiculous hat." It was a lie, but she didn't want to make things any more awkward and she certainly didn't want to chase him away by being all weird and clingy.

"Oh." He ran his hand through his hair. "It's fine. It was for Jeremy."

There was a knock at the door and she answered it.

"Trick or treat!" the little princess on the doorstep shouted.

"Why, Melissa, you look so cute!" Pauly gave her some candy, then looked up to greet Melissa's mom, Stacey, who was standing beside her daughter. She looked terribly pale. Instantly, Pauly had a feeling something was not right. "Stacey, you okay? You need to come in for a moment?"

"No…we're almost done," Stacey said, but it was breathy, like she was struggling for air. "I'm fine."

"I don't think you are," Ares said, from behind Pauly, and gently stepped past her, outside. "I'm Ares Galanis. Friend of Pauly and also a paramedic. You look exhausted."

Stacey looked him up and down, and wobbled a bit. "Maybe…maybe you're right."

"Come on, Melissa," Pauly said, holding out her hand to the girl. "Come see Jeremy. He'll put on some cartoons while we get your mom some water, okay?"

She tried not to show it, but panic was rising in her.

The last thing Melissa needed to see was her mom collapse. And Pauly could see all the signs of that happening soon—the gray pallor, the fine sheen of sweat, the way Stacey's eyes couldn't quite focus, making her appear a bit off balance.

"Okay, Mrs. Charpentier," Melissa said, taking Pauly's hand.

Pauly ushered her inside, and sent her bounding up the stairs to see Jeremy. Meanwhile, Ares helped Stacey in and escorted her to the small sitting room just off the ground-floor bedroom. Guests used it while staying, and sometimes Jeremy would come down and play video games there.

Ares got Stacey settled in a chair and helped her off with her coat while Pauly headed up to the kitchen to get a glass of water and an ice pack from the freezer.

When she came back down, Stacey had fainted and was now flat on the floor. Ares was gently calling to her and checking her pulse.

"What happened?" Pauly asked, kneeling down next to her neighbor. "How long has she been out?"

"I saw her fainting and I knew she would hurt herself if I didn't get her to the floor. She's been out for a minute. Her pulse is weak, but she's breathing. I've called an ambulance. Do you know if she has any medical conditions?"

"She's diabetic," Pauly stated. "She looked like she was going to faint."

"That might explain it. Still, she needs to get checked out at the hospital."

Stacey roused. "What…why?"

"It's okay, Stacey," Pauly said, gently placing the cool ice pack on her neck.

Ares pulled out a pack of candy Rockets from his pocket—little pressed discs of sugared candy. They were gross, as far as Pauly was concerned, but they were a great thing for a diabetic who might be having a bout of hypoglycemia. It was that or orange juice, and Pauly didn't have any of that in the house.

"Stacey, take some of this candy and that should help." Ares unwrapped it for her and handed it over. He was so gentle and kind with his patients, something that Pauly had always noticed when they worked together in the past. It was part of why she'd recommended him for the open position at the station. She knew Ares would be a good fit for the team.

"Thanks. What happened again?" Stacey asked, confused.

"You fainted. Melissa is safe. Do you want me to call your husband?" Pauly asked.

Stacey nodded and Pauly went to call her husband, Ryan. She was anxious to let him know what had happened to his wife and daughter, and to reassure him that Stacey was safe and would be okay, that the paramedics were on their way. It was a reassurance she hadn't gotten when Rex was first reported missing.

Ryan said he'd be right over. By the time that call was made, the paramedics had arrived. Thankfully most of the trick-or-treaters in the neighborhood were done for the night, and the roads had been clear. There wasn't a lot of time for chitchat as Pauly directed her teammates on where to find Stacey. She could hear Ares helping them to get her on the backboard, telling them information about when she passed out.

Ryan arrived, looking pale. Pauly called for Melissa, and her dad gathered her up into his arms.

"Is Mommy going to be okay?" Melissa asked Pauly.

Pauly's feet felt like lead as she walked stiffly from the viewing room where she'd identified Rex. Her brother, Sam, was with her, saying things to her, but she couldn't hear him. All she could think about in that moment was having to break the news to Jeremy and tell him that Daddy wasn't coming home.

When she got to the waiting room Jeremy was curled up in a chair next to her mother-in-law, whose face looked haggard. Pauly fought back the tears that she wanted to shed, all the screams and cursing she wanted to let out.

She'd just become a widow.

"Mommy?" Jeremy asked.

Pauly knelt down and wrapped him up in her arms. "I'm here. You're not alone."

"Is Daddy going to be okay?" Jeremy asked, in a small voice.

"Of course," Pauly replied, swallowing her emotions down, pushing away the memory. "You know she's a diabetic, right?"

Melissa nodded. “Yep.”

“It’s most likely her blood sugar got a little too low, but a doctor is going to check her out just to be on the safe side,” Pauly explained.

Melissa nodded.

“Thanks for helping,” Ryan said. “It’s good to have paramedic neighbors.”

Pauly smiled warmly. “Yes. It is a perk.”

Ryan followed the stretcher out and all Pauly could do was stand back and watch as they loaded Stacey into the back of the ambulance. Ares was standing next to her.

She was still lost in her own thoughts. All those memories haunting her.

“They seem like good guys,” Ares said.

“Who?” Pauly asked, absently trying to center herself.

Ares quirked his brow. “The paramedic team.”

“Oh. Yes.”

“You okay?”

“Fine.”

“Pauly…”

“You’ll be working with them tomorrow,” Pauly interrupted him to try and stop the barrage of questions, because she didn’t want to talk about this now. She plastered on a brave face as the ambulance finished loading and slowly made its way down her street. Big fat flakes of snow began to fall and the street was silent. Halloween was over.

They headed back inside. Pauly shut the door, taking a deep breath. Suddenly, she was just overwhelmed and exhausted.

“You really seemed out of it,” Ares stated.

“Every year I think Halloween will be easy, but every year it’s just a bit chaotic.” She smiled, but it was forced. “What did you think of trick-or-treating?”

She knew she was changing the subject, and she didn't care. She didn't want to talk about her feelings right now and she was surprised how tonight was stirring up all these emotions she thought she had carefully locked away.

"Well, besides the strange looks I got that centered around the weird dinosaur hat and probably the fact I'm a face they haven't seen before, surprisingly good."

She breathed a sighed a relief inwardly that Ares hadn't continued to press her on the matter. It was another good thing about him—he knew when not to pry and poke.

"Good thing you had that candy in your pocket," Paul remarked as they headed back up the stairs.

"It was my payment," Ares said. "From my godson. I'm worth one whole Rockets roll."

She chuckled. "That's a pretty sad fee for wearing that hat."

"I agree. I hate Rockets."

She laughed. "Me too. It's pure sugar."

"I can't even get a chocolate bar?" Ares grinned. "Oh well, I'm glad he had fun tonight. That's all that matters."

And she appreciated that about him. Ares was so easy-going—he just went with the flow. "How about a glass of wine and some bad Halloween specials?"

"That's a deal. But I do want to head to bed early tonight. I want to be my best when I'm formally introduced to my new colleagues tomorrow. I hear that the person in charge of training me the first week is brutal. Kind of a control freak."

"What?" Pauly shrieked, giving Ares a playful punch on the arm as he laughed. "Ha. Ha. Very amusing."

"I thought so."

Jeremy had dumped all his candy on the counter for Pauly to check through, but he was munching on a mini bag of potato chips and watching one of the old classic Halloween cartoons she used to watch when she was a kid. Her nerves might be a bit frazzled, but at least her son was happy this year, and safe. They all were and Stacey would be fine.

Pauly pulled out a bottle of red wine, poured her and Ares a glass and headed over to the couch to join Jeremy. Ares sat down next to Jeremy, who covered him with his fleece blanket. Pauly curled up at the other end of the couch.

She tried to focus on the television, but she couldn't help but watch Jeremy and Ares together. It hurt her heart a bit. This time last year had been hard. It had been the first Halloween without Rex. Jeremy hadn't wanted to do any of the old things and Pauly hadn't pushed him.

How could she?

All she'd been able to think about was the year before that, when they'd been whole as a family. There'd been laughter, candy, badly acted spooky movies. Then, when Jeremy went to bed, she and Rex had talked about trying to have another baby.

There'd been so much hope in that conversation. She'd been excited about the future, even if it meant going through the in vitro fertilization procedure again—she'd such a hard time conceiving Jeremy. They had decided to try, because it would be worth it. They wanted to bring another life into the world and just expand their love.

But then, three weeks later, Rex had been killed in that accident. And then there was no more thought to that.

She'd been so hopeful about the prospect of another baby, but instead she was left broken and grieving.

All she had was Jeremy and she was fine with that, but still tonight brought up a lot of memories, of the plans that were snatched away from her. She was overcome with emotion. She was so glad Ares was here and seeing him with Jeremy just warmed her heart completely.

This was the Jeremy she remembered. The laughter—that was the sound that had been missing in her house. It was all so natural and so right.

It made her melt and for the first time in a long time, it felt like she and Jeremy were a little bit more whole.

Ares finished his glass of wine around the time that Pauly and Jeremy were headed off to bed. He was more than ready for sleep, because it was already close to midnight in Eastern Standard Time and he was having a bit of jet lag.

He thought it would be simple to fall asleep and be ready for his first day of work the next day, but he was completely wrong.

He tossed and turned, a million thoughts racing through his mind. Mostly, they centred around Pauly. That moment she had looked up at him when he'd been wearing the silly mask, the way their fingers had brushed each other… And there'd been a few times he'd caught her looking at him, which had absolutely taken his breath away.

Tonight on the couch watching old cartoon Halloween specials, it had felt cozy and right, even if it was snowing outside in October. For the first time, in a long time, Ares had felt completely comfortable and at home.

It had been a long time since he had that. Not since he was a kid. Back when his parents had been happy and Ares believed in the perfect family, believed that he had one. But no one was perfect.

It reminded him not to get *too* comfortable.

This was a bad idea.

It was too tempting.

Finally, he'd had enough fretting, and wandered upstairs to make himself some warm milk with some cinnamon in it. It was something his *yiayia* had always done for him when he struggled to go to sleep on Christmas, when his excitement overtook him and he knew his parents just wanted him to go to bed.

Although right now, he could go for a shot of his parents' secret stash of ouzo too, but he doubted that Pauly had a bottle of that tucked away.

He grabbed a mug and poured himself a glass of milk, microwaving it. He found the cinnamon and then glared at the container of spiced roasted pumpkin seeds on the counter. He carefully picked one up to try it.

The seasoning was good, but, yeah, he still didn't like the texture at all. It was nasty. Still, he choked it down, because he couldn't find a paper towel to spit it out in.

"So?" Pauly asked, coming down the stairs bundled up in an oversized fuzzy bathrobe. It made her look so tiny. Her dark hair was braided and hung over her shoulder. "I saw you try one."

"You scared me half to death," he grumbled, pulling out his warmed cup of milk.

"You scared me! I was wondering who was lurking down here, took me a moment to realize it was you."

"I couldn't sleep."

"I thought you would be out like a light, what with the time change and all."

Ares shrugged. "This happens a lot. I get overtired and then I can't sleep."

"I should've told Jeremy you were too tired to take him out tonight."

"No," Ares said, quickly. "I was glad to do that with him. It made him happy."

Pauly smiled. "It did. Thank you. Last Halloween Rex's parents were here and we tried to get him to trick-or-treat, but he was so sullen, so not himself. It was good to see him smile with you. I appreciate it so much."

"He's my godson. I told you, we take that seriously in my family." Ares sprinkled some cinnamon in his warm milk.

"Warm milk?" Pauly asked, curious.

"Want some?"

She nodded. "Never thought of putting cinnamon in it."

"Something my grandmother would always do," he said, pouring another mug of milk and microwaving it. "Of course, when she made it, it was goat's milk and not two percent. So it was always so thick."

"Sorry, no goat's milk. I could put it on the grocery list."

Ares laughed softly. "Uh, no, that's okay. I'm fine with bovine dairy products."

"Are you worried about tomorrow?"

"No. Should I be?" He set the mug down in front of her. As he began to sip his own, he watched Pauly wrap her hands around the mug. Her delicate, soft hands.

"No. I was only teasing before. I think it will go smoothly. You're experienced, it's all just standard."

"I get it. Bureaucracy and all that."

"You've got it." She took a sip and made a *mmm* noise. When she set down her mug, there was a slight foamy moustache on the top of her lip. "So good."

He smiled at her. "You have a little something."

"What?" She stuck out her tongue, trying to lick it away, but she kept missing.

"No. Here let me." He gently touched her face, then ran his thumb across her lip. It was so soft and it made his blood hitch to touch her silken skin. Their gazes locked and his pulse thundered between his ears as he held her chin, staring at her.

What are you doing?

"Well..." He cleared his throat as he pulled away. "I think I should try and get some sleep. It'll be a long day tomorrow."

"Right. Yes." Pink tinged Pauly's cheeks. She set her empty mug on the counter by the sink. "Good night, Ares."

"Good night, Pauly."

He watched her scurry away, kicking himself inwardly for letting it slip again. For letting his emotions and feelings about her get the better of him.

He had to do better. She wasn't his and never would be.

CHAPTER FOUR

THE ALARM STARTED blasting music and Pauly bolted upright. She let the music play as the local news and weather reports started, but she was really only half listening to the reports that there was going to be snow and a low of minus twenty Celsius.

Typical.

She couldn't remember the last time she had slept so soundly. Well, it was probably two years ago, when Rex had been alive. Now sleep, if she did have it, was normally punctuated by many bouts of waking up, sometimes reaching out to see if Rex was there, though that hadn't happened in a while.

Her mind was usually a whirl of trying to keep track of everything so that nothing fell through the cracks, so she didn't make a mistake or miss something. So having a night where she didn't toss and turn was heaven. Apparently she'd needed it.

She had no clue that the simplicity of Ares's warm milk and cinnamon would do the trick. Or maybe it was the fact that there was someone else in the house.

Except, there had always been someone around, on and off.

She hadn't been left alone much. So what made Ares's presence so different?

She didn't know and she didn't have much time to sit

there and ponder over it. Today was Ares's first day at the station. As soon as Jeremy got off to school, she was going to introduce Ares to the rest of the team and get him set up with a partner. Then she'd go through all the proper training modules with him.

Not that Ares needed it.

He was qualified.

More than qualified.

So are you.

She was. And she missed the work out in the field so much. She would like to be his partner out there, just like old times. Except she couldn't. She had to be responsible for Jeremy's sake. She just couldn't be selfish and put her career before her child. Her parents had done that, and look how that had turned out.

Wiping the sleep from her eyes, Pauly reluctantly left her warm bed and padded across the hall to wake up Jeremy. But when she got to his room, his bed was empty. The scent of fresh-brewed coffee and eggs came wafting up the stairs, making her stomach growl in appreciation.

She crept close to the stairs and could hear Ares and Jeremy laughing. It made her heart skip a beat. Jeremy was not an early riser. She practically had to drag him from bed and get him ready for school, yet he had beat her downstairs? What kind of sorcery was this?

Pauly grabbed her robe from her bedroom, cleaned herself up a bit and headed down. Jeremy was sitting at the island on a stool. He had a plate with eggs and fruit, even toast. It looked like a healthy breakfast. Usually, he'd groan if she tried to get him to eat anything but cereal.

"Good morning," she said brightly.

"Mom, you slept in," Jeremy teased.

"Hey, Moms can sleep in too," Ares chided.

"Not my mom," Jeremy groused. "She's up at the crack of dawn!"

"Oh, really?" Pauly asked. "And how would you know? You never get up."

Jeremy laughed. "Okay, but you're always up before me and I think that's pretty close to dawn."

"That's cause she's a mom. Although, she's always gotten up really early. When we were in college, she'd force your dad and me to get up too." Ares winked at her and cracked another egg in the bowl to scramble.

Jeremy was still giggling. "Yeah, Dad liked to sleep in too. I'm like him."

"You definitely are," Ares said, grinning.

It melted her heart to see Jeremy so happy and ready for the day.

Pauly tousled his hair. "I'm proud you're up and you're eating breakfast and not just cereal. You're actually eating eggs!"

"Uncle Ari told me to have a good breakfast in the morning. He said I had to eat eggs or bugs."

Pauly shot him a look and Ares shrugged as he grabbed a plate and set it down in front of her.

"Bugs?" she queried.

"That cereal he was eating is full of sugar," Ares chided. "A bug would be better. Do you want coffee?"

"Please. I'll also take eggs over bugs." Pauly laughed quietly to herself as Ares poured her a cup of coffee.

"I figured as much."

"Uncle Ari said bugs have protein."

Pauly paused midway through taking a sip of coffee, trying not to imagine that taste. It was Ares's turn to chuckle.

"Did you pack your lunch?" Pauly asked Jeremy, changing the subject from bugs so she could eat breakfast.

Jeremy nodded. “Yep. I’m ready for school.”

“Wonders never cease,” she murmured taking another sip of her coffee.

“He’s ready,” Ares said, cracking a couple of eggs into the frying pan. “And tonight, after dinner, I told him we’d go sledding,”

“Yes! I’m going to take him down the biggest hill. It’s going to be awesome.” Jeremy continued eating and he was grinning to himself, no doubt picturing the ride.

“So you threaten my son with bugs and then bribe him with sledding?” Pauly teased.

“Well, it worked for me. I had to eat bugs though.” Ares slid the eggs on her plate. “Sorry, I should’ve asked how you wanted your eggs.”

“You’re making me breakfast,” Pauly stated. “I don’t care if you dyed them Easter egg colors, any way is awesome.”

Ares cocked an eyebrow. “Really? Well, maybe I’ll have to come up with some interesting concoctions, things I’ve had in other countries on my travels, and see what you think then.”

“You’re in for it now, Mom,” Jeremy chuckled. “Bugs!”

“No bugs. I swear,” Ares stated. “Jeremy, you done? Doesn’t your bus come soon?”

“Yep. Can you walk me to the bus stop?” Jeremy asked, sliding off the stool at the counter.

“I can.” Ares turned off the stove and followed Jeremy down the stairs to the front door, leaving Pauly alone to just enjoy a few moments to herself with the delicious breakfast and hot coffee.

She kind of felt bad that she hadn’t gotten up before Ares and made him breakfast, but it was nice to have it made for her.

When her family and Rex’s family had been there on

and off, they'd helped out as much as they could, pitching in so she could work and run errands, but she'd still tried to keep to a routine. She'd been the one getting Jeremy up and making sure his lunch was packed and he got on the bus. This simple act of Ares making her breakfast and coffee was so unexpected and very much appreciated. She couldn't remember the last time someone had done something like this for her.

Once she finished up breakfast, she cleaned up the kitchen, not that there was a huge mess. She then headed back upstairs to finish getting ready for the day. By the time she came down dressed in her uniform, Ares was back and had poured himself a coffee, reading something on his phone.

He didn't have his uniform yet, but that would change when they went to the station and got everything all set up.

"Thank you for cleaning up," Ares stated, as she came downstairs. "You didn't have to. I made the mess,"

"No, you cooked breakfast and got Jeremy out the door. That's kind of amazing!"

"Well, if I remember correctly Rex was never an early riser, unless food was involved. And Jeremy's a lot like his dad."

Pauly smiled. "I forgot you two were roommates before I moved in and straightened you both out."

Ares nodded. "He was also a terrible cook. The times he beat me to the kitchen…well, I'd rather eat bugs."

Pauly giggled. "He did get better."

Ares looked at her in disbelief. "Really?"

"Okay, fine. He never did. It was terrible. He tried though."

There were so many times when she'd been suffering from morning sickness and Rex had tried to cook her something, anything, to get her to eat, but it just turned out to be disastrous. She couldn't quite figure out how he always managed to make batches of brownies that were simultaneously burnt *and* raw in the center.

"I knew it," Ares stated, finishing his cup of coffee and then putting the mug in the dishwasher. "So, are we ready to do this orientation? Also, I'm going to have to rent a car."

"Why?" Pauly asked.

"I can't have you drive me everywhere," Ares said. "You don't need to manage me, Pauly."

It threw her off for a second. "I guess I'm used to it. Managing people."

He smiled at her warmly. "I know. I remember, but I'm here to help you out. Besides, I'm a world traveler, over thirty, I can take care of myself."

She laughed softly. "Yes. That's true."

"So I'll rent a car."

"I still have Rex's car. I take it out from time to time. You can use that. It's in the garage." She honestly had thought a lot about selling it, but she was glad that she hadn't, because Ares was right. Once this training week was over they'd most likely be on different schedules and she couldn't drive him everywhere.

Just because he was here to help her out and be there for Jeremy for the year didn't mean that he didn't have freedom to pursue his own life. Go on a date or something.

Just thinking about that actually made her stomach knot a bit.

An intrusive shred of jealousy niggled at the back of her mind, surprising her.

He's not yours. He's just a friend.

"If you don't mind me using Rex's car, that would be great. I don't want to be a burden to you."

"Ares, you're far from a burden. If anything…" but she stopped herself from ending that sentence. It would have been something about how *she* didn't want to burden him or tie him down, especially when he was so adamant about his wandering life.

She never wanted to be a burden. She couldn't be that. She was a good daughter, reliable, dependable. She'd proved she was strong enough to look after herself, even at a tender age.

Except, you weren't.

There was a touch to her chin. She looked up to see Ares standing in front of her. His dark eyes were soft, making her heart race just a little at the kindness and tenderness there. At the realization that she could easily melt in that caring gaze of his. That she could really use a pair of strong arms wrapped around her, to comfort her. She missed that.

Rex would want you to be happy.

That was true. He would. But she wasn't going to ruin her friendship with Ares because she was lonely. She wouldn't risk losing what she and Ares had. Besides, Ares had made it clear in college, after his parents split up, that he had no interest in ever getting married and settling down. It was clear that Ares loved his life of traveling the world and exploring.

There was no way she would ever dream of shackling him down, and she had to protect Jeremy. She didn't want him to be hurt, to have another fatherlike figure taken from him. Even though Ares would fit so easily into her and Jeremy's life…

And what about you? Falling for someone who could be snatched from you again by a simple twist of fate?

Yeah, she wasn't putting her heart through that again.

"Pauly, you're not a burden. I'm here because I care for you and Jeremy. You are my best friend, and this is what friends do."

Pauly swallowed the lump in her throat, and looked away. "Well, I appreciate it. We better get to the station house. It would look bad if you showed up to your first day late."

Ares nodded. "Lead on."

Pauly nervously tucked a strand of hair behind her ear and tried not to think about all those thoughts that had been running through her head. It was annoying that she was even giving them room in her mind. All she could do was chalk that up to loneliness.

But she was no stranger to isolation. She was used to it. So she was going to make sure she was more careful. The last thing she wanted to do was run Ares off early because he was scared of being tied down or couldn't handle her emotions.

She had to make sure he enjoyed his year here. He didn't need to shoulder anything. She could handle it.

If he left it would break Jeremy's heart and hers.

Ares was kicking himself for reaching out and touching her, just like he had last night, but when it came to Pauly he forgot himself. When Rex had been around it had been easier, because he'd never betray his best friend. He'd fought back the temptation.

He'd just felt so comfortable around her, he'd let down his guard. And now, as they drove to the station house, it was clear something had shifted. She had thrown up some kind of wall between them. He had to do better. Just because Rex was gone, there was no excuse. He still had no plans to ever marry or settle down, and Pauly deserved to be happy again with someone who wanted that.

Don't you deserve that too?

He shook that little thought from his mind.

He'd meant everything he'd just said to her.

She was his best friend. Rex had been too, but Rex was gone now, and Ares couldn't rely on his family much. There was too much turmoil there.

All he really had was Pauly and Jeremy, and there was no way that he was going to jeopardize it. Even if his heart was telling him otherwise.

"You okay?" he asked carefully, because he didn't want to make his first day working with her any weirder or more tense than it already would be after his slip at the house.

"Sure," Pauly said, glancing at him quickly.

"Hmm. Why don't I believe you?"

She smiled, her tense shoulders relaxing. "You know, I really hate you sometimes."

"I can read you quite clearly."

"You read me when it's convenient," she said, sardonically.

"How do you mean?"

"Like when I'd try and send you and Rex subliminal messages to study or clean up the apartment. You both seemed oblivious then."

"Okay, well, I've matured."

They both shared a look and laughed.

"It's training day and I guess I am worried about how you'll fit in."

Ares snorted. "You don't have to worry about me. I fit in anywhere. Anyway, I'm a big boy—I can take care of myself."

"Really?" she teased.

"What's that supposed to mean?"

"Well, there was that time you tried to clean the oven with dish detergent."

"It's soap!"

"You know if dish detergent burns, it releases toxins."

Ares groaned inwardly and scrubbed a hand over his face. "You would have to bring that up."

Pauly was still laughing as she pulled into the parking lot of the station house, a bright new building on the main road just outside of town. At least whatever tension was between them had melted away, and that was a very good thing indeed. He followed her out of her truck, and they headed in together. He wasn't nervous, but he was very aware that he was taking Rex's position. One that had been vacant since the accident two years ago.

Ares knew they were some pretty big shoes to fill.

"This is the best job I've ever had, Ares," Rex remarked as they enjoyed a couple of beers on the deck overlooking the Three Sisters peak.

"You seem to love it," Ares agreed, taking a sip from his bottle. "Can't beat that view."

"No. You can't. You should move out here too."

Ares shook his head. "Nope. I like my wandering ways."

"Well, I can't wait to spend my career here, saving lives up on these mountains."

Ares glanced over at his friend and his far-off expression. The one of hope and realized dreams. Rex had it all. Beautiful wife, a son, and now his dream job.

Ares wasn't even sure of his dreams.

"Now you've gone a bit quiet," Pauly said, holding open the door.

"Have I?" he asked.

She nodded. "It'll be okay."

"I know. Lead the way." And he followed Pauly into the

station house. There were a couple of ambulances in the bay as well as fire trucks. It was clean, well-kept and organized with their supplies.

So different from some of the places he worked. Towns and countries that had nothing. He was used to roughing it, so this would be like a vacation, sort of.

"What do you think?" Pauly asked.

"It's laid out well."

"We have a staff of fire, rescue, EMS and paramedics. Part-time, casual, full-time. We don't actually have any volunteers. We're fully trained." She spoke with pride and he didn't blame her. It was a beautiful town and an impressive facility.

"And what area do we cover?" he asked, following her as she made her way through the main bay to what looked like a bunch of training rooms and offices, just past a large kitchen.

"We serve Canmore, but we offer aid to Big Horn and Kananaskis."

He nodded. "I'm eager to get started."

In particular, he couldn't wait to climb, but he wouldn't tell Pauly that. Admitting that he was excited to get out there on the mountains would cause her some anxiety. He knew that. She didn't know that he saw her flinch when he first talked about his gear being sent out. And he couldn't blame her for the idea of it bothering her. Rex had died on the mountain.

It was sweet she cared for Ares too, in a way none of his family ever had. He was so used to being on his own, with no one looking out for him. It was kind of nice.

"We'll get you a uniform, fill out your paperwork with human resources and then we'll head out on the trails. It's a gorgeous day with fresh snow, we'll do a patrol of one of the more easily accessible trails."

As much as Ares just wanted to get out there and throw himself into his work, he knew this kind of bureaucracy was just part of working in a town like this. Pauly took him to the human resources department and introduced him to some of the team, then left. She didn't need to stick around while he filled out all the paperwork, signed his life away on a contract and got everything set up so that he could work.

He was assigned a uniform and found the dormitory that was used by crews on a long shift to rest. It was a nice enough setup.

This was going to be a good year—he had to keep telling himself that. He wasn't used to staying in one place for so long. Often, if he stayed still for too long, he became restless. Being on the move didn't give him much time to think of things, like past regrets. He was worried that a year in the same place would definitely test his strength, especially when it came to Pauly.

It would be hard fighting his attraction, but he'd done it before. And he was doing this for her, and Jeremy. And, in a way, Rex. It would be worth it.

Once he had changed and put his street clothes in his assigned locker, he went to find Pauly in the main bay where she was waiting beside a couple of snowmobiles. He smiled seeing her with a clipboard, going over everything. He'd forgotten how cute she looked in a uniform. When they were in school, he and Pauly had been assigned to the same placement and had to wear uniforms as they job shadowed a paramedic in Toronto.

He particularly loved the way she looked in this uniform. It was just work clothes, nothing special, but somehow she looked adorable in the big work boots, straight pants, the no-nonsense navy shirt with yellow EMS patches on the sleeve and her hair pulled back in a tight bun.

It was difficult being in love with your best friend for years and knowing you could never have her.

It was a special kind of torture.

You need to get a grip, Ares.

"Hey," he said, approaching her. "We're going out on a trail?"

Pauly looked him up and down, ignoring his question. "Well, that uniform suits you."

"I had to tie my hair back," he remarked.

"You don't have a man bun so it's all good." There was a secret smile. "To answer your previous question, yes, we're going on a trail close to town. Have you ridden a snowmobile before?"

"No. Actually, I haven't."

"Oh." She worried her bottom lip. "We'll have to share one. Then we'll get you set up with lessons, because they're a useful tool for some of the trails around here."

"No doubt. I can ride a horse."

Her eyes went wide. "Well, that's good. Not the right season for the horses on the mountain trails, but that is good to know. I can let other mountain rescue teams in the area know that."

"Good."

"Well, we have snowsuits and helmets. I've packed all the gear we need." She handed him a small binder. "This will have all the information about how the equipment is set up and what gear is recommended when out on the trails."

He flipped through it. "I'll study it."

"Yes. You can leave it on the bench there for when we get back."

"You're going to make me flash cards and quiz me, aren't you?" he mused sardonically.

"Maybe."

"You haven't changed a bit," he muttered as he followed her to grab the snowsuits and heavy boots. "So we're snowmobiling down the trail?"

"No. We have skis." Pauly pointed to what was strapped to the back in a little sledge that he hadn't noticed before. "We'll use the snowmobile to get to the trail head."

"Nordic skiing?"

She nodded. "Not many active snowmobile trails in Canmore, but out the back of this station is one that we can use as EMS. Then we'll ski through the groomed trail. It's a very popular sport."

Once they were suitably dressed, she opened the one back door. There was a trail from the back of the station house that led onto the main trail where they would be doing their training, so they didn't have to get the snowmobile onto a trailer and drag it somewhere, but Pauly explained that was what was usually done when they had to use the snowmobiles off trails when completing a search and rescue.

What was eating away at Ares right now was the fact that he was going to have to ride behind her. At least it was going to be a short ride. And he wouldn't have to wrap his arms around her. He could, but there was an option of handles on the back of the seat that he could grip.

And even though he wouldn't mind holding on to her, he really shouldn't tempt fate that way.

Pauly slipped on her helmet as the bay doors rose and started the engine. Ares climbed on behind her.

He wasn't exactly too thrilled about skiing either, but he understood he needed the training.

It had been a long time since he'd last skiied, and he hadn't started until he was an adult. There'd been a time in his travels that he went with some colleagues to Gstaad and did some downhill skiing for the first time.

Even though he was Canadian, his family, especially his parents, weren't big on the winter outdoor fun activities. The only thing he'd done as a child had been some tobogganing with his brothers. That had led to some fast rides down some very icy hills and a few broken bones. Still, it was always a fun time and he was eager to take Jeremy sledding later. He'd been so excited when Ares had suggested it, which made Ares happy. It had been so long since he'd gone sledding, so to be able to do that with his godson was something he was really looking forward to. It was something special he and Jeremy could share and he wanted that special bond between them.

He wanted to be just more than a godfather in name. Jeremy needed him right now.

What about you? Don't you need him too?

The thought caught him off guard.

There was a part of him, deep down, that always wanted the kind of family he'd thought he had when he was growing up, before things turned sour. A wife, children. But he just didn't see how that was possible. How could he be a good father or husband? He didn't have the most stellar examples from his past.

When he looked back, he realized he'd barely seen his parents as a kid. They'd always been at the restaurant.

At least Jeremy was getting the childhood he deserved. Pauly made sure of that. She was a good mother and the more Ares thought about it, the more he realized there was so much to adore about her.

She was doing it on her own, and yet Jeremy had all the love and attention he needed. Something countless couples didn't manage to give their children, even with two of them. Like his parents.

A niggling little thought crept into Ares's mind. If Pauly could make it work, why couldn't he?

"Hold on," Pauly shouted over the hum of the engine.

He gripped the handles on the back of the snowmobile tight as she navigated her way through the private trail, taking her time and slowing down at junctions where snowshoers and skiers might be crossing to connect to another trail. The sun was out and the mountains were glorious rising up into a clear blue sky. It was cold, and Ares was definitely missing the Caribbean and the warm sand, but there was beauty, even in a place where the air hurt your face.

Finally they got to the trail head and Pauly parked their machine. She took off her helmet and pulled her toque out of her pocket. "You ready?"

"To ski. Sure. To embrace this," he said, nodding at the snowmobile. "The jury is still out."

She smiled, but it was a sarcastic grin. There was a twinkle in her eyes.

Pauly deserved better than him. Someone who could give her the family life, grounded and rooted. Not somebody who was terrified of relationships because he really just couldn't let himself believe that they could work. And there was no way he ever wanted to be responsible for hurting her or Jeremy.

Focus on the work, he reminded himself.

He climbed off the snowmobile and they packed their helmets in the little hard-topped sledge. They pulled out their collapsible poles and goggles, then strapped on their skis.

Ares slid a bit, but he remembered the motion of gliding through the snow.

Maybe this will be okay.

"Come on. We'll do a run to the first junction and then back."

"Sure thing."

They set out on the trail. It was quiet. There were a few trees, but it was well groomed, with perfect grooves for the skis to slide through. Between the bright sun and the crisp white snow, he could see why so many people liked doing this. There was a connection to nature and even the mountain itself. It was quiet, just the sounds of the skis shushing through the snow.

He could get used to this.

It also gave him the perfect view of Pauly's backside.

Think about something else, Ares. Anything else.

Why did his brain keep betraying him? He was here to work, to help her out, not just lust over her. Again. She was off-limits.

"Help!" The shout echoed across the trail.

Pauly froze and he stopped to listen too.

"Help!" came the voice again.

Pauly pulled out her binoculars and scanned the area, but Ares saw it first—a tiny hand waving from beside the Bow River, well off the trail. The riverbank was particularly steep and it might be deceptive to a tourist who was skiing.

"There, Pauly!" Ares guided her, by pointing.

"I see them. They're on the riverbank." She put her binoculars away. "You have the EMS kit in your backpack, right?"

He nodded. "I do."

"Okay, let's go. Looks like you get a crash course on training day."

Ares followed Pauly off the groomed trail. The snow was deeper and harder to ski through, but this was what he was trained for.

To save lives.

CHAPTER FIVE

PAULY HADN'T BEEN in the field for so long, and now the rush she was feeling as she and Ares made their way over to where they heard the call for help was all adrenaline.

It reminded her of why she became a paramedic. One of the reasons.

"You're okay, sweetie," the woman paramedic said, gently wrapping her up in a blanket after the fireman had rescued her. "We're going to check you over now and make sure you're okay."

Pauly nodded, coughing. "I wasn't meant to start the stove. But my brother was hungry and Dad was late. I forgot to turn it off when they got home."

"It's all right. Your parents explained."

"I have to take care of Sam," Pauly explained.

"Your brother is fine." The paramedic set her down on the gurney, instantly calming her as they checked her over.

That paramedic had taken care of her. The early part of her childhood and adolescence, she'd taken care of her younger brother, Sam. After the fire, things changed with her family. Things had gotten better. Her parents didn't work so much. Her grandma took her and Sam for a while and then moved in with them when they went back to their parents. Pauly was no longer alone, though she'd still struggled with nightmares and panic attacks. But one good thing she'd gleaned from it all was that she knew without a doubt what she wanted to do. She wanted to help others.

Still, it was hard to be out here. What was supposed to be a simple training session was now something real and dangerous.

Pauly, they need you.

She locked away all the anxiety to focus on what she was trained to do. There was no way she was turning her back on people in need.

As they got closer she could see where the two skiers had become stuck. There wasn't usually this much snow by the beginning of November. It was still a little bit warmer compared to when he arrived and windy, and the snow had drifted in a false ledge over a steep bank of the Bow River, giving the false impression that it was solid, when actually it was hollow. As soon as the skiers had stepped on it, it must have caved in, dropping them down the bank, where they were precariously trying to stay out of the rushing, icy cold water below.

It wasn't a particularly long drop, but the frigid weather and cold water would mean that hypothermia would set in.

Fast.

"Be careful," Pauly shouted over her shoulder to Ares. "It's not as solid as it looks."

"Where's the riverbank?" Ares asked, coming up beside her.

"There are markers." Pauly pointed them out. "It's quite steep here."

"What're the coordinates?" Ares asked, pulling out the radio that connected to the fire station.

"Right here," she handed him the map of the trail. "Get them to send a rig to the Ascension Bridge."

Ares nodded and made the call while she dug through for a rope and some crampons.

“Help,” the person called again. “Not sure how long we can keep holding on!”

“Help is on the way,” Pauly responded. “Are you injured?”

“I think my friend is. They’re tied to me, but they’re unconscious and I’m worried about them falling into the river.”

Pauly found it interesting that the two skiers were tied together, but since they’d gone off trail and had the snow pack crumble beneath then, it was a blessing. The rope might’ve saved their lives. How could they have been so careless, putting their lives at risk?

That’s not important now.

She took her time to assess where the edge was and how she could approach a rescue without the snow giving way underneath her too. Her pulse was pounding in her ears and she couldn’t quite figure it all out. All she could think about was how dangerous it was.

“Let me go,” Ares said, after finishing his call to the station.

“You don’t know the river.”

“I don’t know a lot of rivers and I’ve still done fast water rescues before. And rescues in mudslides and avalanches. I can do this.” He pulled out the neoprene suit from the gear and started pulling it on over his winter gear.

“Okay,” Pauly agreed.

She didn’t argue with him. There wasn’t any time, and she was second-guessing herself a bit, which annoyed her. She hated that hesitation, but all she could think of in the moment was Rex and Jeremy. What if something happened to her? The idea of leaving Jeremy orphaned was something she couldn't contemplate.

This was what she'd trained for. This is what she dedicated her life to doing, saving others. She was good at it.

Everything will be fine.

It was hard to believe that when she assessed the precariousness of this whole situation. Her pulse was pounding between her ears, her throat dry as she just ran through all the most terrible scenarios in her head.

You have to stop.

She trusted Ares, but if anything happened to him under her watch… Well, her stomach knotted just picturing it. All she could think about was how she couldn't save Rex, how crushed Jeremy would be if something happened to Ares or her.

How devastating it would be to lose Ares.

Her body trembled.

She thought she was ready to go back in the field. Maybe she'd been wrong.

Breathe. This will all be okay.

She took a deep calming breath to ground herself back in the present, and shook those niggling thoughts of self-doubt from her mind. There was no place for them here as she continued to help Ares get ready, so they could start the rescue before the rig arrived. She knew it wouldn't take long for the rest of the team to get there; she just wasn't sure if these two skiers had that long in them.

Ares hadn't been lying—he seemed to know exactly what he was doing as he approached the riverbank cautiously from the side, making sure to break a path so that he didn't lose his footing with the crumbling snow.

Thankfully, the whole riverbank wasn't as precarious. The two they were trying to rescue had just been unfortunate. Watching Ares work was awe-inspiring, but it also called up a flash of panic.

It hit her so hard.

Please. Keep him safe.

Rex had *died*, doing this job, up the mountain.

She tried to focus on her own work, forcing an anchored post through the snow into the not-quite-frozen ground, something they could use to help them hoist the skiers to safety. But she couldn't stop turning to watch Ares as he threw out a line to the conscious skier, then made his way slowly to cut the tie between the two and secure the unconscious patient., All she could think back to was that moment she heard what had happened to her husband. It played over and over again in her mind.

Her stomach was in knots as she paced the station house. At least Jeremy was safe with the sitter, but she'd heard the rumbles and she knew Rex and the team were on the mountain when the avalanche hit.

So many avalanches for December.

As she waited to hear about the team, the chief motioned for her to join him in his office.

"Have a seat, Pauly," Pierre said, gently.

Her insides churned, her whole world dropping out beneath her like she was free-falling without a parachute. It was Pierre's tone, his sympathetic expression. As she sat down numbly in the chair, she knew, her husband was gone.

But this wasn't Rex. This wasn't the mountain. It was all right.

She took another deep breath to steady her shaking hands, waiting in anticipation for Ares to give her the all clear.

"Okay, Pauly. I've secured the second patient, pull the other up," he called out.

"All right," she acknowledged. She secured the rope around the anchored post, then used her body weight, sitting back into the snow bank and digging her heels in so that she could help the first skier up.

The rope just guided the conscious victim and gave him a little extra push as Pauly verbally encouraged him to crawl up the bank to safety. Once he was up on the solid bank and out of harm's way, Pauly helped him stand. She could feel him trembling and knew he was cold—he'd been hanging on for some time.

"It's okay," Pauly reassured him. "I've got you."

The man didn't respond with words, just an exhausted nod of acknowledgement. The rest of the team had arrived as she'd been hoisting, and they rushed over with a stretcher, ready to assist. Pauly was so focused on her patient, that it was a moment before she remembered Ares, still helping the unconscious skier back up the bank of the river.

"Ares?" she called out. Her pulse was thundering between her ears because she couldn't see him. She'd lost track of him.

All these horrible thoughts ran through her head. What if he slipped? What if he was in the river?

Picturing him hurt or injured made it a bit harder to breathe.

Just calm down. It'll be okay.

Only she didn't know that.

The idea of losing her best friend was too much to bear. Worst-case scenarios circled around and around in her head.

That had never happened before, back when she started her career. She and Ares had done a lot of their co-op and placements together in school, and not once had she worried about him. But now she had this existential dread filling her mind, her chest, and all she could do was hold her breath, placing her hands over her heart, waiting.

Then she saw an arm wrap around the rope at the bank, and Ares came up, the unconscious skier tied to his waist. The breath Pauly hadn't known she was holding released as relief washed through her. She carefully approached the edge and helped Ares as they got the other skier onto solid snow and another stretcher was brought over.

"Unconscious female. Appears to have hit her head on a rock," Ares rattled off as the rest of the team worked over the woman. "There was blood. One pupil is dilated, but the patient is still breathing. Their lower extremities were in the water, so I suspect hypothermia as well as a concussion."

Pauly threw herself into the work, but it was easier now. She felt better knowing that they had saved the two stranded skiers and both she and Ares were okay. All that worry was melting away.

They got the two patients loaded while an RCMP officer came to get their statement. Unfortunately, the two victims of this accident had been skiing off the groomed trail where there was clearly posted signs and they would face some fines.

Once that was all done, they loaded up their equipment in the back of the patrol car and the RCMP officer got Ares and Pauly back to the snowmobile so they could return to the station house.

Neither of them really said anything, which was kind of a relief because Pauly was still so confused about her reaction out there in the field. She was mad at herself for letting those worries creep through her mind, immobilize her.

Maybe this going back to work in the field wasn't going to be as easy as she thought.

That worried her, because she loved her job. It was the one thing she had left, but she couldn't do her job effectively if she was terrified. And today watching Ares put his life on the line had scared her.

And then there was Jeremy. The thought of leaving him alone cut her to the quick. She knew all too well what that was like. And suddenly she felt like that little girl version of herself. The child who had to grow up far too quickly.

That wasn't what she wanted for Jeremy.

Ever.

That was the thought playing over and over in her mind as they rode the snowmobile the short way back to the station house.

"You look worried," Ares said, a question in his voice, as they took off their winter gear to be dried.

"Do I?" she asked absently.

He gave her a look of disbelief. "Really? Come on, Pauly how long have we known each other?"

A wry laugh escaped her. "True. Okay, I was a bit worried."

"About?"

She sighed and sat down on the bench as she finished removing her winter boots. "I had a moment of panic, when I couldn't see you."

His brow furrowed. "What?"

"I know. It was my first day back out in the field and… I don't know what came over me. I just kept thinking about…" She sighed again and wrapped her arms around herself. "I kept thinking about Rex and Jeremy. It's been two years and it's still affecting me. It's silly."

"No. It's not. Those feelings are valid."

She shook her head. "How can I do my job if I'm worrying like this?"

Ares squatted down in her front of her. His warm eyes stared up at her and he placed his hands on her arms. It was comforting, it was nice and it grounded her instantly.

"You will get there. Of course you're going to have anxiety after what happened to Rex. Give yourself some grace in this situation." His words were soft and tender. They were exactly what she needed in that moment. Something she had been missing for some time.

Rex had known about her childhood, but Ares didn't. Anxiety was something she'd worked hard to manage her whole life. It was hard to do that when your rock was gone. She hadn't had that security in a long time now and all the while she had to be that safe harbor for Jeremy. She appreciated Ares being there for her. For understanding.

"Thanks."

"It'll be okay. I promise you. You better not give up because of one moment of uncertainty."

"I won't." Her voice shook, but all that worry and tension she had been feeling because of that rush of anxiety in the field was beginning to melt away. She was so glad Ares was here. She wanted to get back to work. She wanted to find a sense of normalcy again, her confidence. She wanted to feel something other than grief and this survival mentality that she had been operating in the past two years.

She wanted to live again.

"Good." Ares stood and then held out his hand to help her up.

She slipped her hand in his and he helped her to her feet. They were close together and she looked up at him. Suddenly her heart was racing again, but now it was with something different.

Quickly, Pauly took a step back. As much as she wanted to get back to a normal life, she wasn't quite sure that she wanted *that* much normalcy, no matter how lonely she was or how much Ares meant to her.

There was no way she was going to jeopardize their friendship.

Not for anything.

"Well," she said, clearing her throat. "You have some more training modules to complete and I have some paperwork to file thanks to the impromptu rescue operation that happened today during your training, which we didn't really get to complete."

Ares nodded. "Right."

"I'll be heading back home about five. Jeremy is staying with his sitter until then, so after our shift we have to pick him up."

"Sounds good. How about we have dinner somewhere tonight?" he asked. "Grab Jeremy and just celebrate our first day of working together. Which I think was definitely calmer than the first time."

"What do you mean?" she asked, crossing her arms.

He laughed. "You were ready to murder me after our first job placement together. You said I kept getting in the way."

"Why are you mad, Paul?" Ares asked.

"Ugh, because you were constantly doing everything."

Ares looked confused. "What?"

"I'm learning too. I can do stuff too. You don't have to do everything." Pauly took a deep breath. "Sorry, I'm frustrated. It seemed like the paramedics were ready to trust you, but overlooked me. Sorry I blamed you there."

"Ah," Ares said, then he smiled warmly. "You're too quiet, Paul. Not with me, but with them. You have to speak up. Fight for it, for the opportunity."

"Even if it means fighting you?" she questioned in a half tease.

"Especially me." He winked at her.

Pauly laughed. "I'd forgotten that."

"Figures," he grunted. "Remember how Rex made us all go out to dinner and settle the differences with a game of pool?"

"Well, we could go bowling tonight," Pauly suggested. "Jeremy would love that. I wouldn't mind skipping tobogganing."

"Ditto. I've had enough snow and cold today. Will Jeremy mind?" Ares asked.

"Nope."

Ares nodded. "That sounds like fun. And I think you need some fun tonight."

"You're right. I do."

"Good. I'll see you later, boss." Ares saluted and left the ambulance bay.

Pauly sighed nervously and finished cleaning up her gear. It was nice to have Ares around, but she was surprised at how much emotion he was stirring up, how many forgotten memories.

But they were all *good* memories.

And she had to remember that it was only temporary.

After the excitement down by the river the rest of Ares's day was boring. He hated paperwork and all the human resource stuff that he had to go through. This was the reason he liked traveling all over the world and working in places that a lot of others in his line of work didn't get to. His whole reason for becoming a paramedic was to help people, *that* was what he liked. This morning, he'd really enjoyed being able to help those two stranded skiers.

Sitting in a meeting room and going through the endless new-hire stuff, on the other hand, was putting him to sleep and making him a bit squirrelly. What he had to remind himself of was that he was doing this to help Pauly and Jeremy.

He was doing this for Rex.

Honestly, he'd always envied Rex for what he had, even if Ares had spent most of their college lives telling everyone who would listen that, with his messed-up family, he *never* wanted to settle down He'd had multiple girlfriends over the years… Well, he couldn't even really call them that—they were more like one-night stands. His longest-lasting relationship was maybe a week.

None of those times had made him truly happy.

The truth was, there was a part of him that wanted something more. Something real, but he was terrified of what could happen if it didn't work out. He didn't want to have kids involved in the breakup of a marriage. He knew what that was like. Even though he'd been in college when his parents had split, able to look out for himself, he'd seen how his brothers' failed marriages had hurt his nieces and nephews.

Clearly, his family was cursed or something.

Yet, when he saw Pauly, Rex and Jeremy, he knew it could work out, for some people. There was happiness there. There was love and he wanted that. Secretly, he wanted all of it, but there was no way he was going to jeopardize anything to achieve that.

It was better to just stay Pauly's friend and be there for Jeremy, because if something went wrong and he lost them, it would devastate him. He didn't want to lose more of his family.

Only, it was hard to keep reminding himself of that promise he had made to himself. Especially, when he was working alongside Pauly again.

It felt like it did all those years ago.

And as he stared at the module on the computer screen, another silly test that the station's HR department was making him take, his mind wandered to all the fun times that Pauly and he shared when they had been doing the portion of their schooling working on the job as students. All the nutty things they'd seen. All the jokes they'd shared.

She belonged to Rex though.

That niggly little voice was back again, reminding him that no matter how much fun they had together, when it was just the two of them, she always went back home to Rex. Always was in Rex's arms in their shared apartment.

Pauly had never been his. And she wasn't his now.

Ares groaned and scrubbed his hands over his face as he glanced at the clock. It was ten to five and he was just thankful that this day was almost over. When he sat idly or sat and did paperwork his mind would always dwell on things that he really didn't want to contemplate, like Pauly.

At least tonight Jeremy would be there, and Ares could focus on his godson. It was good to spend time with him, see him smiling again, though he knew Jeremy was still grieving his father.

Ares still remembered the day of the memorial every time he looked at him.

He found Jeremy sitting alone while Pauly greeted guest after guest. They had just come back from spreading Rex's ashes on the mountain.

Jeremy had slipped out of the house and was idly swinging on his tire swing, his feet trailing slowly through the dirt.

"Hey," Ares said, gently.

"Hi, Uncle Ari," Jeremy responded half-heartedly.

"How are you?"

Jeremy shrugged. "Dunno."

"Can I sit with you awhile?"

Jeremy nodded and looked up at him. "It hurts."

"Yes. It will."

"You were his best friend right, Uncle Ari?"

"I am. Always will be. I'd like to be yours too."

Jeremy smiled. "Me too."

"Hey," Pauly said, interrupting his thoughts.

"Yeah?"

"You ready to go?" she asked.

"Sure," he responded, shutting down the module. "I can finish the rest later at home."

"You don't sound too sure," she teased.

"I loathe paperwork," he grumbled.

"Right. All part of the job. And here I thought you were thinking about how I'm going to kick your butt at bowling." There was a glint in her eye as she said it. He'd forgotten that Pauly was slightly competitive.

Actually, that was a complete understatement.

She was really competitive, bordering on the annoying side.

For someone so sweet, she was kind of ruthless.

"Seriously? Kick my butt? You're a mother, you should know better," he teased.

Pauly rolled her eyes. "Come on, really? A mother? That's a pathetic attempt to curtail my awesomeness."

"It wasn't an attempt to curtail anything. You're super competitive and you know it," he countered.

"Like when?"

"Oh, like when you threw darts at my head because I beat your score."

She opened her mouth to say something else. "Fine. I promise I'll behave because Jere will be there."

"Hmm, why don't I believe you?" Ares followed her out of the boardroom. He grabbed his stuff from his locker. They were going to go home and change, then pick up Jeremy to have dinner at this restaurant that also had a bowling alley. It was a place to get a good meal and have fun bowling—or glow bowling, as Pauly had called it. It sounded very different from the bowling allies he used to frequent in his hometown of Whitby, where there were a lot of middle-aged men, tacky eighties decor and the lingering smell of smoke and feet in the air.

The place they were going definitely sounded more upscale. He had no doubt that Pauly still was going to be completely obnoxious about winning or losing, but that was fine by him, because for all her goodness, that one flaw she had made her even more endearing.

I have got to stop thinking about her this way.

They were friends and nothing more.

CHAPTER SIX

ARES HAD BEEN bowling as a kid, but he couldn't remember *ever* bowling with his family. His dad had always been so focused on work, not his home life, which in retrospect might've been the problem between him and his mother all along.

The more Ares thought about it over the years, the more he saw of his brothers, the more he realized how similar they were to their dad. They worked too much and didn't spend time with their families, their kids. And Ares knew he was so dedicated to work, as well. Just another reason not to settle down.

Except…he liked spending time with Pauly and Jeremy. They'd had to drive over an hour to reach the alley. Pauly had acknowledged that it was a trek just for bowling, but there just wasn't a place like this in Canmore.

Canmore had a lot, but not this retro-inspired, neon-fueled, glow-in-the-dark bowling alley that he had been dragged to. As soon as they'd stepped inside, Jeremy had completely forgotten about tobogganing and Ares was more than okay with that. As much as he loved the mountains, and even though he wanted to share the experience of sledding with Jeremy, he didn't really feel like frolicking in the snow tonight. Not after the freezing river rescue earlier.

Jeremy was practically bouncing-off-the-walls excited

by the time they were assigned their lane, which had a vinyl booth and a place for them to have their wood oven pizza while playing their game. It looked like a fifties diner, but with bad shoes and the crash of pins echoing.

"This is great!" Jeremy announced, lacing up his ugly bowling shoes. "I'm going to pick out a neon green ball."

"Why neon green?" Ares asked, curious only because it was so specific.

"'Cause it's cool," Jeremy responded in a tone like Ares was clueless or something.

"Well, I guess it sounds cooler than puce," Ares teased.

Jeremy's use wrinkled. "Puke?"

"Puce," Pauly corrected, laughing softly.

"Don't you think neon green is kind of…snot-colored?" Ares asked, knowing it would bug Pauly. But who else was going to teach Jeremy all the immature, gross stuff, all the laughs that he knew Rex would have shared with his son.

"Gross, guys," Pauly said while Jeremy chuckled wildly.

"No, Uncle Ari! It's *not* booger-colored. Neon is cool. I'm going to go get it." Jeremy leaped up.

"Nothing too heavy!" Pauly called after Jeremy as he went to pick out his ball from the rack. "Thanks for the booger talk, Ares," she groused, but he could see the twinkle in her eyes.

"I'd say I'm sorry, but I'm not."

"I know you're not. Put your shoes on." She handed him the bowling shoes.

"You'd think a place like this would have better-looking shoes," Ares grumbled tying his bowling shoes.

"I think it's sort of part of the experience of bowling," Pauly remarked. "You have to have ugly shoes."

Ares grunted, but they shared a smile which made his pulse race. "I suppose so."

"Just think about it this way, you're not throwing yourself down an icy hill in bitter cold weather."

"That's the bonus." He stood up. "Though I am looking forward to doing that with Jeremy. I loved it as a kid."

"Yeah, but now you're over thirty. It's not the same as when we were kids."

"I'm not decrepit."

She laughed. "I know, I'm just saying it's a bit…tiring."

"That I will agree with you on. Now, do you want me to grab some balls?"

Pauly's eyes went wide and her lips trembled with a badly contained smile. "Pardon?"

Ares realized what he'd said, and how it could be completely misconstrued. "I mean bowling balls. Jeez, Pauly, are you twelve or something?"

She laughed. "Okay, but come on! That is not something I ever thought you would say."

"Not usually." He couldn't help but think about what he'd rather get his hands on, but he kept that thought to himself, much like he'd always done when it came to Pauly.

"Sure, you can pick out a bowling ball for me," she teased. "Pink, definitely not blue."

He groaned and rolled his eyes. "Pink it is."

He walked over to the rack, passing Jeremy as he clutched his green bowling ball to his chest and walked back to their lane. Ares chuckled to himself, then picked out a pink ball and a yellow one for himself. He wanted to pick the blue ball, because then maybe Pauly would be too busy laughing at her immature little joke and choke on the game, but he decided to be nice.

He took the balls back to the lane and set them on the ball return next to Jeremy's neon-colored one, which was, thankfully, a better green than he'd been anticipating. Not a booger in sight.

Jeremy was back in the booth bouncing up and down as Pauly was ordering pizza from the waitress that had come to the lane. When he made his way back, the young woman smiled at him and batted her eyelashes. It was an obvious invitation to flirt—Ares was more than used to that.

He smiled back politely and nodded. It wasn't that she wasn't perfectly nice-looking, but she wasn't Pauly. Which had also been the problem for most of his adult life.

No one ever held a candle to her.

Pauly had a strange look on her face, like she was biting back a mischievous grin.

Oh. Great.

Ares knew what that look meant. She was going to try and set him up, just like she had in the past.

"Um, what do you want to drink, *Uncle* Ari?" It was pointed, the way she said *uncle*. He didn't like that she was calling him that, not in this instance anyway. She might as well have said *unattached*.

"I'm getting a chocolate milk," Jeremy exclaimed.

"I'll have an iced tea," Ares answered. "Thank you."

"Sure," the waitress said. "I'll be back in a few with your order."

Ares was not here to date and Alberta wasn't his home. In fact, he didn't have much of a home. There really wasn't time to even entertain a fling here. He was here for his best friend.

"She was cute," Pauly hinted. "She was totally blushing when you walked over."

Ares shrugged. "I suppose."

Jeremy was coloring on the kids paper place mat, completely oblivious to them.

"You know," Pauly said, "we never talked about your social life while you're here for the year."

"Pauly, I'm not interested in dating. You know that," he replied, flatly.

"But…"

"No," Ares stopped her quickly. "I don't have plans to settle down. My job takes me all over the world. Actually, this is the longest I'm staying still in one place, ever."

"Fine," she said, quietly. There was a strange expression on her face, but only for a moment, then it was gone. "I just don't want you to feel like you're stuck."

"I'm not stuck. Far from it. I want to be here with you and Jeremy." He reached across the table and took her hand, giving it a squeeze as their eyes locked. Her hand was so soft and tiny in his and he held on to it for longer than he should.

Sure, he'd dated in the past, but it was only ever casual because he never wanted to settle down. He liked his freedom.

Do you? How much?

"Can we play a game before the pizza comes?" Jeremy asked.

Ares let go of Pauly's hand, quickly. "Sure, buddy. You going to go first?"

"Yep."

Ares slid out of the booth so Jeremy could get out, then followed him to the lane, watching over his godson as he picked up the ball, slipping his little fingers into the three holes and walking up to the painted line. He looked like some kind of professional.

"You know how to throw?" Ares asked, impressed.

"Yeah, Mom taught me." Jeremy let the ball go. Ares stood back, watching that neon green ball roll painfully slowly down the polished wooden lane, before it finally took one pin out at the end.

Well, so much for the pro bowler theory, Ares mused.

He glanced over his shoulder at Pauly who was clapping and cheering her son on. It warmed his heart to be here with her and Jeremy. He kept telling himself over and over again that he never wanted to commit to anyone or plant roots, but when he was here with them he forgot all that.

His parents had been in love once before it all went wrong and yeah, Ares had already spent a lot of years putting his career first, just like his dad. What if his life was destined to go the same way? He just couldn't take that risk with Pauly or with Jeremy. They didn't need heartbreak. They deserved better.

Better than him.

He didn't want Jeremy to ever experience that kind of pain that he went through, that his family continued to go through. The estrangement from his father hurt him to his very core. His family was broken.

So even if he secretly wanted all of this—family, togetherness, happiness, love—he just couldn't have it. He couldn't risk it, because he just didn't know what the future would bring and he really didn't believe in a fairy-tale happy ending, because most fairy tales he knew hadn't ended so happy.

Pauly wasn't sure why she'd suggested that Ares could date. It was obvious that the waitress found Ares attractive. In fact, most women did, and Pauly definitely didn't dispute that fact. The first time Rex had introduced her to Ares, she'd been kind of taken aback at how handsome he was, but he'd made it clear time and time again that he wasn't interested in anything long-term.

He liked his life.

Ares was carefree and had a wandering soul. There were times she envied his freedom and how much he traveled. She was glad he was here with her this year.

So she didn't understand the sudden drive to push him to date. Maybe, deep down, she wanted to protect herself and keep the temptation of falling for him at an arm's length, because it would be easier to put the idea out of her head if he was with someone else.

Would it, though?

She'd been relieved when he told her he wasn't interested in dating anyone, when it really shouldn't matter to her at all.

"Pauly, you're up," Ares called out, waving her over.

"Right." She put all those thoughts about Ares, dating, everything out of her mind. She was hating the idea that it kept popping up time and time again. The most important thing right now was to focus on having fun with her family.

But that thought also gave her pause, because they weren't a family.

Not really.

Ares is family, though, in a way. He always has been.

She picked up her bright pink ball. As she got under the black light of the lane, Ares smiled at her. His teeth were so extra white that she couldn't help snort-laughing a bit. Jeremy scampered off to watch his ball return up the shoot.

"What?" Ares asked, glancing over his shoulder.

"Your teeth are so white in this light. It's hard to concentrate. It's blinding."

He crossed his arms. "So are yours. They're glowing."

She quickly shut her mouth, pressing her lips together tightly. "You're just trying to sabotage me."

"Ha!" he barked with laughter. "Always so suspicious. There's a reason for that!"

"Oh?" she asked.

"Only competitive cheaters think everyone is out to get them."

"Cheaters?" she asked in mock outrage. "I can beat you with my eyes closed."

He cocked an eyebrow. "Oh, really? Show me then. Walk up to the line and close your eyes."

"Don't you think that's dangerous?"

"How? You roll it down the lane."

"What if I throw it at someone?"

Ares glanced around. "No one is next to us on either side. Are you telling me you're so strong you're going to shot put it at someone's head?"

"Maybe," she teased.

He rolled his eyes. "I'll guide you. Get up to the line and I'll make sure you don't take someone's head off."

Pauly went to the line at the start of the lane and closed her eyes. She could feel Ares come up behind her, his arms slip over hers as she held the ball up. His breath was hot on her neck and her body trembled a bit.

This was a mistake.

Only she didn't pull away. It felt so good.

"You ready?" he asked softly against her ear. The fan of his hot breath against her neck sent a rush of heat through her, making every nerve in her body light up in anticipation.

For what? A part of her wanted to ask, only she kept that to herself. His strong hands slid over her arms, leaving a trail of gooseflesh under his fingertips. Honestly, it was nice to have the arms of someone she trusted around her again. It was comforting.

In this moment she felt safe again and it hit her she hadn't felt like this in a long time.

"You ready?" he asked again, shifting his weight, her back pressed against his hard chest.

"Yep," she managed to squeak out.

"Okay. It's safe, let it go."

Pauly pushed back and he stepped away as she let the ball go down the lane. She could hear the rumble of it against the wooden floor and she opened her eyes as the pink ball headed straight down the lane, dead center, to the first pin—knocking them all down with a loud crash.

"Wahoo! A strike." She threw a fist in the air and spun around, but as she did the spin her bowling shoes slipped on the polished floor and she fell forward. Ares reached out, catching her and steadying her, just as her hands, bracing for the impact of the fall, hit him in the chest. She could feel his heart racing under the palms of her hands as he righted her, and she gazed up at him. Her breath caught in her throat, her body thrumming.

"You okay?" he asked.

"Fine," she said quickly, but she didn't step out of his embrace. She didn't want to, so she lingered, enjoying the moment.

"Well," he said. "I guess you've proven me wrong."

She laughed. "I guess so."

They just stood there for a few moments, staring at each other. Her pulse thundered between her ears as she got lost in his dark eyes. It was taking everything in her not to reach out and run her fingers through his hair.

Get a grip on yourself, girl.

"John!" someone screamed.

Pauly jumped back and they both looked down the bowling alley to the people three lanes from theirs.

There was a man lying on the floor, having what looked like a seizure. Instantly, Ares took off like a shot and Pauly went to be with Jeremy who looked scared.

"Mom, you have to go help," Jeremy said, clinging to her.

"You going to be okay?" Pauly asked, not wanting to leave him by himself.

"I will, Mom. I'll stay in the next lane. I can see you from there."

Pauly kissed the top of Jeremy's head and ran off with Ares. She looked back to see Jeremy climbing into the booth of the lane next to the man on the ground.

Ares was talking to the woman who had called out the man's name, telling her that they were paramedics and that she needed to call emergency services. Pauly did an assessment of John's airway and breathing. He was coming out of his seizure, his movements were relaxing, but Pauly could see that his fingernails were slightly blue and his body was still rigid.

"Help me get him on his side, Pauly," Ares instructed.

She nodded and scooted over, helping Ares to gently roll him on his side. There was a contusion on the back of John's head from where he had fallen, and it was bleeding steadily.

"I need some napkins," Pauly called out. She was handed a stack of napkins so she could apply pressure to the head wound.

Ares was busy loosening the buttoned collar of the man's shirt and checking his breathing again.

"John," Ares called softly. "John, let us know you're okay."

Only John wasn't waking, which wasn't surprising after a seizure. It took a lot out of a person.

"How is his breathing?" Pauly asked.

"Still good. And his head?" he asked.

"It's deep and he needs to get a CT scan. It seems he hit his head hard on this floor."

It wasn't long before the Calgary paramedics came in and they got John loaded up onto the gurney to head to the hospital. Pauly went to wash her hands as Ares spoke with the paramedics. When she came back John's party was breaking up and Ares was standing with Jeremy. The waitress who had been openly flirting with Ares was standing at their booth waiting patiently.

"I think our pizza is ready," Pauly said, her voice shaking as the adrenaline was running out. "You guys hungry?"

Jeremy nodded. "Yep. You both did awesome."

Ares smiled down at Jeremy and tousled his head. "You're a good kid."

Jeremy shrugged. "I know."

Pauly shook her head in mirth and walked back to their lane and sat down. Although suddenly she wasn't very hungry. Just exhausted as her body came down off that high of helping another. And she was proud of how Jeremy handled himself, especially in that tense situation.

"Every time we're together something seems to happen," Ares remarked.

"What do you mean?" she asked.

"Halloween, training…now this." He gestured where John had been. "Like I'm being tested."

"Maybe, but I'm glad we were here to help him."

Ares nodded. "Me too."

They finished their pizza, their game and then headed back to the truck. It was a clear night, and they got a very tired Jeremy loaded and buckled up. As soon as they hit the Trans-Canada Highway to head back to Canmore, Jeremy was asleep in the back.

"He's out like a light," Ares remarked.

"I could easily nap too."

"It's been a lot of excitement," Ares said as they drove west out of the city and into the foothills toward the mountains.

"It has," she said, quietly. "He's so happy you're here."

"I'm happy to be here," Ares replied. "How about you?"

"What do you mean?"

"Are you happy I'm here?"

"Why wouldn't I be?"

Ares shrugged. "I don't want to step on your toes and invade your space."

"You're not. I want you here, Ares. I'm so glad you're here." And she quickly glanced at him. "I just don't want to hold you back from your life."

"Is that why you brought up me dating while I'm here."

"I suppose so."

"Well, you're not holding me back. Besides, what life do I have?"

"Traveling?"

He scoffed. "I mean it's fun, but… I don't have a wife or kids. I don't have family that misses me. I have no roots or connection."

"Isn't that what you always wanted since your parents' split?"

"Yes," he responded, quietly. "Still, I get…lonely. It's weird not having family."

"Do you not talk to your parents, your siblings?"

He shrugged. "My mom, yes, but my brothers and my sister are busy with their lives and their work and Dad and I…we haven't spoken in years."

Pauly sighed. She knew it had been hard for Ares when his parents split up and that he didn't like to talk about it much, but she thought by now that he and his father would've patched things up. She and Ares shared so much, but there were still things she really didn't know about him. Things he kept close to his chest. Just like she did. It was like he didn't trust the world around him.

Do you?

It was hard for her to trust the world, because she wasn't sure that she was back in it. She was still kind of mad over losing Rex. Life was cruel sometimes, infinitely so. Fate too.

It hurt, a raw pain, even after all this time.

"Wow," Ares gasped, breaking her silent rumination.

"What?" she asked, looking out ahead of her.

"Pull over at the rest stop," Ares instructed.

She didn't question and pulled over on the small turnoff that was used mainly by long-haul truckers on the highway to rest. It was basically a parking lot, with endless open fields on either side and a couple of port-a-potties. She parked her truck.

"What're we doing?" she asked.

"Turn off the car and then step out."

Pauly gave him a quizzical look, but did what he asked. Ares climbed out and then Pauly slid out of the truck, locking it and coming to stand beside him. He was staring up at the dark clear sky to the north.

"You know, this is how those old urban legends about men with hook hands start," she teased.

"Just look and let your eyes adjust," he said, impatiently.

"Fine." She crossed her arms and gazed where he was looking. As her eyes adjusted to the darkness a ribbon of brilliant color erupted across the sky. It was brilliant reds and pinks that shimmered and danced across the sky.

"Oh," she gasped, surprised as it took her breath away.

"It's the northern lights," Ares exclaimed. "I've never seen them before."

"Never?" she asked.

He shook his head. "Nope. Spent my whole childhood in Toronto and most of my work is down south. Never got to see them. Too much light pollution."

"I love them. They're calming." Actually, she couldn't remember the last time she'd seen them. She really didn't pay attention to them anymore. Usually, they were faint and green, but these were strong and brilliant. She closed her eyes. "Maybe we can hear them."

"Hear them?" Ares questioned.

She nodded, keeping her eyes closed. "I've heard them hum. Once, when I was up in Yellowknife for work."

There was something about the lights tonight that grounded her and made her feel connected, brought her peace. Ares slipped an arm around her and pulled her into a side hug, like he always did. She rested her head against his shoulder and just stood there for a few moments, enjoying the lights.

Enjoying the moment.

Something she hadn't done in a long, long time.

CHAPTER SEVEN

IT HAD BEEN two weeks since they'd gone bowling and shared that moment on the turnoff of the highway with the northern lights. Pauly could have stayed there forever, wrapped up in Ares's arms, but Jeremy had woken up and it was getting late so they'd driven back to Canmore.

It had been a stolen moment, but it had been peaceful. There had been no other thoughts in her mind. It was empty and she'd felt grounded. Ares, in that moment, had completely centered her. It was more than just support and she couldn't let herself explore it further.

Pauly was trying not to think about it and instead just focus on the routine they were building both at work and with Jeremy.

Focusing on building that foundation for the year was a way to keep her mind completely occupied, or so she thought.

But it was the moments when they were at home, all together, that kept triggering those little thoughts. Dangerous thoughts, that made her want to think about Ares in a new light. Not just as a friend, but something more.

Thoughts she couldn't let herself entertain. She didn't want to ruin what they had, because she didn't want to lose someone else from her life and that was what she had to keep reminding herself of. The loneliness, the abandonment she kept locked away, seemed to be creeping out the more she thought about Ares. But it was a good reminder not to mess with what they had right now, because it worked. His presence made her feel not so alone anymore. Like she could be happy again.

Maybe life didn't have to be so hard.

Ares was getting along well with others at the station. Especially, the chief, who Pauly knew shared the love of mountain climbing. It was why Rex and Pierre had gotten along so well.

Still, anytime she turned her thoughts to Ares going up the mountain, into the most treacherous passes, she began to panic inside. The idea actually filled her with dread, which was silly because she'd used to love climbing. And it wasn't as though she could stop Ares from doing it. But every time she pictured him up there, all she could think about was him dying. Like Rex.

He's not Rex. But that thought didn't quell the anxiety. She wished she could tell him no.

But all he was, was her friend. She had no say over what he did.

There was a knock on her office door and she glanced up to see Ares standing there. He looked so good in the dark navy uniform, with his shoulder-length hair tied back. For a moment, seeing him standing there, it was like no time had passed. She was transported back to when they were in college and working together. And how all the women who saw him in his uniform used to swoon.

"I don't know how you do it, Paul," Angela said, sighing.

"Do what?" Pauly asked.

"Work with that hunk," Angela stated. "That uniform looks so good on him. He's so dreamy."

Pauly glanced over at Ares and her cheeks heated. "He's handsome."

"Gorgeous," Angela corrected. "Is he single?"

"I think so."

"Isn't he your roommate?" Angela asked.

"Yeah, Rex and I room with him. I don't talk to Ares about his sex life though."

Ares looked at her and winked from across the classroom and she blushed again, but Angela was oblivious.

"He's cute." Angela sighed again.

"Ugh, stop objectifying my roommate and focus on the work," Pauly groaned. Although she couldn't blame Angela. Ares was very easy on the eyes.

"Hey," Ares said, waving a hand in front of your face. "You there? You zoned out."

"Yes," she cleared her throat. "Sorry. What's up?"

"My usual partner is out sick and there's a call about a trapped hiker on one of the trails. The hiker called in their coordinates and I have a track so we can follow the avalanche beacon. The hiker states they have a suspected sprained ankle and can't get out. Chief said we need to take the snowmobiles out and retrieve the hiker. The ambulance can't get to him where he is now, but we can bring him down to one of the junctions so they can pick him up."

Out on the mountain. Dread knotted in Pauly's stomach and she clenched her fists, digging her fingernails into her palms. She wanted to say no, but there was no one else. She had to do it, even though she was dreading it.

Just the thought of a beacon made her queasy, because she knew that sound well. She'd been in the office, listening to the sound of the beacons over the transceiver. The faint beating, almost like a heart rate monitor. Only Rex's heart had no longer been beating by the time they were able to track him.

Pull yourself together, Pauly.

"Sure. Let's go." She only hoped her voice didn't break as she said it.

It might do her some good to get some fresh air and get out there and work again. When she was with Ares on that trail for his training two weeks ago, it had been such a rush to be out in the field again. At first.

It was this or desk work, she told herself sternly. That wasn't what she'd been hired for, or what she'd thought she'd be doing as a paramedic. It was only fear holding her back.

They got their gear ready, everything they might need, including a portable stretcher that she and Ares might have to use to carry out the hiker, especially if the trail was too deep or too steep or too narrow for the snowmobiles, and had to go on foot with snowshoes or crampons.

That was something else that had been happening the last two weeks, so much snow. It was a deep layer of fluffy powder on top of hard-packed snow and ice, and it could look deceptively shallow.

Ares had managed to get his snowmobile safety registration; he was officially competent enough to ride his own machine. That meant they could take more gear and be extra safe.

As they headed out onto their access trail behind the station house, the snow was coming down in thick big fat fluffy flakes. The mountains weren't visible, but they could still see a good distance in front of them. They took their time, Pauly following Ares, who had the GPS coordinates mapped out on the navigation device.

The trail the hiker was on climbed up the mountain a

bit and the snow got deeper. It was making Pauly more anxious. If they went up too much farther, there *could* be a threat of an avalanche, even though they weren't in an area that was prone to slide.

Her heart was pounding between her ears.

Don't have a panic attack, Pauly.

Ares came to a stop and she pulled up beside him.

"How much farther?" she asked, stiffly.

"Not much, just around that ridge. But I think we're going to have to take it on foot. It's so deep. I don't think the machines can get up there."

"Agreed."

They dismounted and collected their gear, strapping on their snowshoes and making their way along the trail. Even though it was still steadily snowing, Pauly could make out the trail that the hiker had taken. Every step farther up the mountain, her pulse quickened. It was like a dull roar, throbbing between her eardrums.

Breathe. You're safe.

It wasn't long before they saw the brightly colored snowsuit of the hiker in question One look at him, slumped over in the snow, made Pauly think that this injury was more than just a sprain. As they got closer, she could see he was partially buried in the snow. She could hear the familiar sound of a rescue beacon through the transceiver Ares held. It was a useful tool, one that was used by skiers when in the mountains, just on the off chance there was an avalanche and they were trapped.

Just hearing that familiar sound made her stomach knot.

Rex had a beacon. It was how they eventually found him, but in the end it had been too late. The beacon was to guide rescuers—it couldn't actually save a life.

"He's barely conscious," Ares remarked.

The man groaned. “Here. My name is… Chris.”

“I’m Ares and this is Pauly—we’re paramedics and rescue from Canmore. Thank you for being smart enough to provide coordinates,” Ares said, sitting down next to the patient.

“I was walking and I misjudged the depth of the snow,” Chris said, breathlessly. “Got my leg caught on a buried rock. There was a twist and a pop in my knee. Blinding pain. I can’t feel it any longer.”

Not feeling the extremity was not a good sign. Pauly exchanged a worried look with Ares. She took off her snowshoes to kneel down in the packed snow.

“It’s not trapped anymore,” she stated as she carefully removed the snow covering the leg. The moment she did so, she could see blood and bone poking through Chris’s thin ski pants. “It’s a fracture. We need a splint.”

“My wife…” Chris said. “She’ll be worried. And my kids.”

“We’ll call your wife as soon as we take care of you,” Pauly stated.

“She’s the one who called it in,” Ares mentioned. “She had his last-known coordinates.”

Pauly pursed her lips together. There was so much blood. The fracture looked worse than she’d initially thought as she gently palpated it, and she was starting to worry that Chris might have severed an artery. “We need a tourniquet.”

Ares got one prepped and they placed it above Chris’s knee. Chris slipped back into unconsciousness again as they splinted him.

“We have to get him to a hospital,” Pauly murmured. “Fast.”

What if they couldn’t get him down quick enough? It was just the two of them.

"Agreed. We'll have to put him on the sled."

"I can carry the gear. No problem."

Working alongside Ares she managed to stabilize Chris and get him bundled up and secure on the small sled Ares had pulled up there. Ares was stronger so it made sense for him to pull it back down to the snowmobile.

Pauly took the bag that Ares had carried along with her own, and went ahead of them to try and pack down the trail even more so the sled could slide smoothly. It was a longer walk back down, because Ares was pulling Chris's weight, but they got him down without incident, and secured him on the bigger sled behind the snowmobile. Then they hurriedly packed their gear, called in to the ambulance about their meeting spot and Chris's status. Then, slowly, they began to head back down the trail.

Each step down to the snowmobiles had felt like an eternity, but the trip on the machines felt just as long. They had to get Chris to a hospital. All Pauly could think of was his poor wife and the agonizing torment she much be going through, wondering and waiting for word on her husband.

And she was a bit angry at Chris for coming up on this trail. Alone. It was a completely irrational anger, but it kept her focus sharp, helped her concentrate on getting him down to safety.

When they got to the junction, the ambulance was waiting there. Pauly filled Sean and Casey in on Chris's injuries, while Ares helped get him on the gurney. Once Chris was loaded, Sean and Casey drove the ambulance away and left the pair of them to take the machines back to the station.

"This feels slightly repetitive," Ares joked.

"Being left behind?"

He nodded. “Doing the hard work and letting Sean and Casey do the easy part.”

Ares was only kidding—there wasn’t anything easy about transferring a patient to the hospital. Sean and Casey could be stuck there for a while if the emergency room was busy. They wouldn’t be able to leave their patient.

Pauly knew Chris would be a priority triage with such a bad break and extensive bleeding, but all she could think about was his wife. She’d been in those shoes before.

“Well, it’s almost five,” Ares stated. “We better go.”

She glanced at her watch. “Shoot. Yes, Jeremy will be waiting. We better get back to the station house, file our reports…” She trailed off as she tried to start her machine, but the engine wouldn’t turn over. It just kept sputtering. Had she got snow in the system?

She pulled the starter cord again, but it was loose.

Great. Just great.

She let out a few choice cuss words. If she was late, Jeremy would worry.

“What’s wrong?” Ares asked.

“I think I might’ve got snow in the exhaust,” she muttered as she pulled off her gloves and opened the hood to take a look at the motor.

“Should we call someone?”

“No. I know how to deal with this.”

Ares’s eyes widened. “You do?”

“Why are you so shocked by that?” she questioned. “I think I should be highly offended by your surprise. I’ve changed multiple tires on the 401 in Toronto, during rush hour I might add, and I know how to put chains on my tires.”

“Chains?”

Pauly huffed. “You need them to navigate mountain roads up here.”

She took a deep breath, rubbing her temples. She had to concentrate, fix the problem so she could get home to Jeremy. And it was her responsibility to return the machines to the station.

Only, she couldn't get that sound of the beacon out of her head.

How worried she'd been listening to the beacons after the avalanche that had killed Rex. Listening to his particular beacon and hoping she'd see her husband again.

Focus.

"What can I do to help?"

"Grab me the tool box. It should have everything I need."

Ares handed her the tool box and she went to work. She pulled out the spark plugs and made sure there was no snow in the manifold, then sprayed some lubricant down into the holes. It was then she noticed the pull cord to start the engine wasn't working, so she pulled the plugs again and began slowly rotating the motor backward, until she had the right resistance on the pull cord.

Ares handed her tools as she needed. She was focused on the work, but she could sense it was growing darker. They either needed to get this fixed, or leave the machine there and call for a tow. She was about ready to do just that. All she could think about was getting home to Jeremy.

He'd be so worried, and she just wanted to let him know she was okay. He didn't even need to worry about her. She was *fine*. It was frustrating beyond belief.

"Blast this thing," she shouted, wanting to kick it.

"It's okay," Ares replied.

"No. It's not," she snapped, then she felt bad. "Sorry."

"No need to apologize. I get it."

She nodded. "We'll try this again."

"Deal."

"Okay," she replaced the plugs one more time. "Pull the cord for me now."

Ares pulled the cord, and the snowmobile revved to life.

Yes.

It was something Pauly had taught herself. She'd always been interested in how engines worked and liked to tinker. Rex knew nothing, but she didn't like being stuck anywhere. Sometimes, Rex had been a bit helpless. He always liked to joke how she took care of him. She was the adult. Something she was very used to.

Who takes care of me?

The thought caught her off guard, because she'd never even considered it before. Rex cared for her, but she'd always been more grounded than him. There had been times she wished she could be free, not be responsible for everything, but she wasn't even sure she knew what that was really like.

"That's impressive," Ares remarked.

"Thanks." She closed the hood and then packed up the tools. She wiped her hands and sat down on the seat for a moment, taking a breather. She was still shaking over the whole ordeal. Panic was still rising up in her, like the swell of a tide, even though the crisis had passed, and she didn't know how to control it. It was hard to breathe. All she needed right now was to be held, but she couldn't ask Ares to do that, so she wrapped her arms around herself, trying to get her nervous system to calm down and ground herself back into the present.

Ares stood in front of her and then knelt down. He reached out and touched her cheek, running the pad of his thumb across her skin. It felt good, comforting and she wanted a bit more. Only, she couldn't have more.

Could she?

"What're you doing?" she asked, her voice catching in her throat.

"You have a little smudge of something."

"Oh," she said, breathlessly. Her heart was racing. Then she placed her hand over his and closed her eyes, reveling in the warmth, the closeness. Even though she knew she shouldn't, she just wanted to hold on to this moment. This contact. This connection. It was calming.

"You okay?" he asked, moving closer.

She wanted to tell him no, she wasn't. She was lonely, she was numb and she just wanted to feel something—a tie to someone. She was also scared. Scared of the mountain, of leaving Jeremy. And then, the thought of almost losing Ares. Not that the hike had been risky, but what if she hadn't been here to help fix the snowmobile? What if he'd ended up trapped overnight and she hadn't known where he was?

It was all so overwhelming. All these feelings rushing through her. It was like she was spinning out of control today. What she needed was a moment of clarity through connection. Scooting forward she brushed a strand of Ares's hair away, running her fingers over his face as she leaned closer and pressed her lips against his.

It was only supposed to be a light kiss, but the moment their lips touched, a jolt of heat rushed through Pauly and the kiss deepened. She wanted more.

Ares wrapped his arms around her, pulling her flush against him. His tongue pushed past her lips and she melted against him, never wanting this rush, this flood of heat and desire to end. In his arms, she felt safe.

A crackle came over the radio. "Team 671 are you there, over?"

They both jumped back. Ares grabbed the radio. "Team 671 here."

“You’re an hour late. You require assistance?” Erickson at the station house asked.

“Not required. Slight mechanical issue that’s resolved. We’ll be there shortly,” Ares responded.

“Ten four.” The radio went dead.

“What time is it?” Pauly asked.

“Six.”

“Oh, my gosh. Jeremy will be super worried now. I lost track of time trying to fix the engine. I should’ve just called for a tow, but…my responsibility…” She was free-falling.

“It’s fine, Pauly.”

“No. It’s not.” She stood up. “About the kiss… I didn’t mean to…”

“It’s okay,” he said, quickly.

“I hope this doesn’t mean things will be weird.”

Ares grinned. “No. Scout’s honor.”

Pauly nodded, but she was still kicking herself inwardly for letting her guard down, for falling for temptation. She could’ve ruined everything.

“Let’s go.” She put on her helmet.

The kiss had been amazing, but it was definitely a mistake she wasn’t going to repeat again. She wouldn’t ruin things. And she hated how she’d forgotten about everything else for a moment, including Jeremy. She was mad at herself for that.

They would be two hours late picking Jeremy up from the sitter and she had no doubt that he would be worried.

As much as she wanted to savour the kiss and talk about what happened, this wasn’t the time and the place for it. She had to get to Jeremy and let him know that she was okay.

They got back onto their snowmobiles and headed to the station house. As soon as Pauly got back she made a call to the sitter.

"Hi, Britt. It's Pauly."

"Hey, Pauly. You okay?"

"Yeah, we got stuck on a call," she replied. "Sorry I'm late."

"Oh, I don't mind. Do you want to talk to Jeremy?" Britt asked, quietly. Pauly could tell from her tone that Jeremy wasn't doing well. It made her heart sink. She just wished she could be beside him right now, to embrace him.

"Yes. Put him on."

"Hold on."

Paul could hear Britt calling for Jeremy.

"Mom?" Jeremy choked on the other end. She could tell he had been crying, which broke her heart even more.

"I'm here, Jere. I'm okay," she said, gently. "I'm really all right and I'll be home soon."

"You and Uncle Ari?" Jeremy's voice was still a bit wobbly.

"Yes."

"He's okay too?" Jeremy asked.

"We're both okay. We helped a man get to the hospital. A snowmobile broke down," Pauly explained. "I had to fix it."

She was trying to make light of it so Jeremy would cheer up.

"Oh, you fixed it?"

"Yep."

"Good," he said. "Are you coming to pick me up soon? I really want to see you."

"I am, with Uncle Ari. We'll be there as soon as we can, but don't worry, we're safe. I love you."

"Love you, Mom."

It was a hard phone call. It tore at Pauly's heart.

She couldn't do this anymore, field work, not until Jeremy was grown up. It wasn't fair to him.

She rushed through the motions to get the paperwork filed so they could leave and she could just hold Jeremy. She was still kicking herself for going out on the snowmobile in the first place.

"I have my report," Ares stated, walking into her office. "Just sent it to your inbox."

"Great," she answered, quickly logging back onto her email.

"Jeremy okay?" he asked.

"No. It's…it's the worry he's always had since Rex died. I haven't seen it in some time, since you came to stay with us. I guess I was foolish to think that he would be okay if I took more jobs out in the field." She dropped her head into her hands. This was not how she planned her life. There were a lot of things she was regretting right now.

Even the kiss.

Right now, she was regretting that too. Not because it had been unwelcome—she'd wanted it badly—but she couldn't be selfish. She didn't have time to focus on pursuing anything romantic with anyone. Especially not with a friend, not with Ares. He wasn't even meant to be here for long.

She was going to ruin everything. She was going to make things awkward, be a burden to Ares. And he would leave, breaking Jeremy's heart even more.

And what about your heart?

She ignored that thought, because her heart didn't matter in all of this. Jeremy needed Ares, his uncle—what she needed didn't factor into this equation. She was fine.

Are you?

She had to hold tight to her decision. Ares was a wanderer. He'd be leaving in a year. She didn't need to complicate their lives further and push him away sooner.

Jeremy needed him.

What about you? that little voice insisted, but she ignored it. All that mattered was Jeremy and it was clear what her path was. She couldn't be heading out into the field, not with the uncertainty of it all. It would be too much for Jeremy.

Ares took a seat on the other side of her desk. "What're you thinking?"

"I'm thinking about taking a permanent administrative job. That way, Jeremy won't ever have to worry about me going out in the field again."

Ares's eyes widened. He couldn't really believe what he was hearing. Pauly sitting behind a desk, instead of doing what she loved? It didn't sit right, and he knew without a shadow of a doubt that she loved her career. He'd been there, right at the start. She loved her work.

"How can you think about walking away from your career?" he asked.

Her blue-gray eyes latched onto his and he knew instantly that he was treading on dangerous grounds. Pauly was stubborn and strong-willed.

"How could I not?" she asked. "I have to think about Jeremy."

"Jeremy will be fine," Ares stated, gently. "In time. Yes, he has trauma from what happened to his father and that's understandable, but you can't coddle him."

She sat up straighter, her eyes narrowed. "You don't know what you're talking about."

"I think I do," he replied. "Pauly, I know you want to protect him and if taking that desk job is how you think you can, then I can't stop you. But there are other ways accidents can happen. A desk job doesn't mean you're immune."

"It's the safer option."

"Is it?"

"It has regular hours."

"Yeah, and you know how many accidents happen just driving home from work?" The idea of her being hurt in a car crash filled him with horror, but he wanted her to see what she was saying made no sense. She was too good of a paramedic to give up so quickly.

Especially when she didn't *want* to give up.

She took a deep breath. "You're right. There are so many unknowns, but I know what's best for Jeremy."

"You can't sit around and wait for the bad to happen, because then you've wasted your life just sitting around and waiting. The best thing you can do for Jeremy is show him how strong you are and how you're not afraid to live out your dreams."

Pauly reached out and took his hand. "Thanks for always sticking by my side, but I know what's best."

He wanted to ask her if she really did, because to him it seemed like the wrong decision. Then again, he didn't have children, so maybe he was talking out of turn.

All he could do in this moment was support her, even though he thought what she was thinking about was a huge mistake. He'd just have to work hard and show her the job was worth it, even if it scared her. That it could work out.

"Of course, we promised. No weirdness between us, right?"

Although, he wanted just a little bit more of that weirdness. When they had shared that tender kiss up on the trail, it was like all his secret dreams were coming true. He'd been so shocked when she'd kissed him. The moment her soft luscious lips touched his, he was lost. His blood ignited, his senses reeled and all he wanted to do was drink in her sweetness.

In a way he was glad for the radio call from the station house, because he didn't want that kiss to escalate further. Well, part of him did. But he didn't want what they currently had to change.

He didn't want to lose what he had with Pauly.

There were a lot of estranged relationships in his life, and he wasn't going to risk letting this one with Pauly and Jeremy go, even if his heart wanted something completely different.

Pink tinged Pauly's cheeks and she took her hand back. "Right. No weirdness. Friends."

"Friends." The word was hard to say, it stuck thick in his throat, because that's not what he wanted. It just had to be that way.

"Okay, let's go get Jeremy and we'll have a cozy evening at home watching movies, or maybe playing some video games."

"That sounds like a plan." He stood and she came up to him and he pulled her close, hugging her like he always did, drinking in the scent of her, wanting so much more than just friendship.

Longing for another kiss, especially now.

But he'd made her a promise, one that he really didn't want to keep.

CHAPTER EIGHT

THIS WAS A side of Jeremy that Ares had never seen. He was almost unreasonable and just terrified. Back when he'd been out here that summer they spread Rex's ashes in the mountains, Jeremy had been withdrawn and grieving, but this anxious side of him was something new. It broke Ares's heart to see someone so young struggling so much, all because they had been a couple hours late.

Jeremy clung to Pauly when they picked him up. Pauly held on to him as they walked back to their house from the sitter's, just hugging him and stroking his back. Once they were home they made Jeremy's favorite food of hotdogs with macaroni, cheese and ketchup, which Ares did have a hard time stomaching, but it was all to cheer Jeremy up. He tried to make some jokes, but Jeremy wasn't interested.

Then they went to the couch and curled up on their big sectional, under fuzzy blankets. It took a while before Jeremy started to relax. Then he was begging to play video games with Uncle Ari and Ares was only happy to oblige.

After an hour of old-school gaming, Jeremy started yawning and fell asleep on the couch, exhausted. Ares just tucked him in and let him lie there.

"He's pretty good," Ares remarked as he got up. "I think I'm definitely too old and out of practice. My hand-eye coordination sucks."

"Same," Pauly mused, curled up in the corner and looking a bit worn-out herself.

It had been a long day. Ares still hadn't processed it all, including Pauly's admission she wanted to take a desk job. It was so not like her.

"Do you want some tea?" he asked.

"I would love some with honey in it."

"Done." He got up and put the kettle on.

"You got a package, by the way," Pauly said, offhandedly. "It's on the kitchen table there. It was delivered this morning."

Ares spun around and saw the box sitting there, wrapped in brown paper. Instantly, he recognized the writing. "It's from my mom."

"Well, open it. It might be some of her spanakopita."

"Uh, spanakopita wouldn't ship well. It's egg," he reminded her.

"Right. Oh, maybe it's her baklava. I could use some of that."

Ares chuckled. "You're probably right—it's probably treats."

Although, it had been some time since his mother had sent him anything. It was kind of out of the blue.

He undid the box. Pauly was right—it was several containers of his mother's baked treats. Pauly got up and scurried over to steal a piece of baklava as he poured the boiling water in the cups to let the tea steep. There was also a letter. Ares wasn't sure if he wanted to open it, but he'd have to eventually. There was no time like the present.

Dearest Ares,

I hope you are doing well in Canmore. I'm so glad you are there with your godson and Pauly. I like Pauly. You should settle down with her. I've called you a few times and got voicemail. Your father won't tell you, but the restaurant has closed and he has been diagnosed with pancreatic cancer. It's time you speak with him. I tried to get him to call, but you know your father. Stubborn. Please reach out, Ares, and visit soon.

Mom.

Ares's world dropped out beneath his feet.

Pancreatic cancer?

He was furious his father had forced his mother to tell him. His father was too hardheaded to call and tell him personally.

Would I even have picked up the phone if he called?

He cursed under his breath.

"What's wrong?" Pauly asked.

"My dad has cancer." The words seemed a bit dry as they came out of his mouth.

"Oh no," she said, quietly. "I'm so sorry. Do you have to head back to Toronto?"

"No." He folded the letter and put it in his pocket. "What's the point? He couldn't bother to tell me himself. He made my mom do it."

"You still haven't talked to your father since the divorce?" she asked.

"He didn't want to see me. Last time we talked I basically told him I didn't care if his family business failed. Well, the restaurant closed. I wasn't aware of that either until now."

Why couldn't his father tell him that? Although, what would Ares have really done about it? He hadn't wanted to run it, so he understood why he wasn't told. It stung all the same. He was angry at his father for divorcing his mother, for ending their happy family and for trying to put so much on his son's shoulders without ever seeing the value in what he did choose to do. But on the flip side Ares also missed him.

Deeply.

And now his dad was dying, and he was so angry at Ares for choosing his own path he hadn't even wanted to reach out.

If this was what family was all about, it was better that he remained single.

Is it?

When he looked at Pauly and Jeremy, he saw a different side. One he wouldn't mind being a part of.

"That is rough," Pauly agreed. "I had my own issues with my family, but it's better now. It got better."

"You had issues with your family?" he asked, curious. He hadn't realized that Pauly had any problems with her parents. The few times he'd met them, they'd seemed like nice, supportive people. He particularly liked her brother, Sam, who absolutely adored his big sister.

Most of all they were all still together. She had an intact family. He saw how they'd helped Pauly after Rex died. He saw the closeness and he'd often wondered how his family would react in that situation. Usually when he entertained those thoughts, it never turned out quite good.

"My family was never perfect when I was growing up," she sighed and fiddled with the string of the tea bag in her mug. "I grew up poor and I was left alone a lot taking care of Sam. I was about Jeremy's age when I accidentally turned on the stove and caused a fire. There was… we spent some time at my grandmother's house after that. There were some court cases and Sam and I were almost taken away. I almost caused the breakup of my family because I was supposed to know better."

Ares was floored. "You blame yourself for that? You were just a child."

"I had responsibilities. My parents worked and…"

"Again, you were just a child. You amaze me."

She looked shocked. "What do you mean?"

"You have your own amazing career, and still you've never been that kind of parent to Jeremy. I'm surprised you still talk to your parents."

She shrugged. "I'm working through it, but I guess I blame myself for it as much as you blame yourself for the distance with your father. The thing is, we talked as a family, we worked it all out. Maybe you should call your dad?"

Ares scrubbed a hand over his face. "I doubt he'd want to hear from me. My mother had to tell me everything. My father is very stubborn and set in his ways."

"Oh, really? I wonder who that's like." There was a little smile that played on her supple pink lips and a little twinkle in her eye as she teased him gently.

This was the kind of moment that made him want to take her in his arms. Their shared kiss played out in his mind again.

Teasing him.

Taunting him. The sweet taste of her was still burned on his lips, the softness of her body etched into his skin.

"I am not like my father," he grunted.

"I think you are. Just a bit. You're both very invested in your work."

"True." Ares couldn't argue with that logic. "I just don't know if he would want to hear from me."

Pauly blew across the top of her mug. "You'll never know unless you reach out."

"Why do you have to be so logical?" he asked, teasing slightly.

"Something you pick up when you're used to taking care of everyone for most of your life I suppose."

"And what about you?"

"What about me?"

"What about taking care of what you want?"

The question caught her off guard. She thought they were talking about Ares, and not her. She had her life figured out, for the most part.

Do you really?

The truth of the matter was, no she didn't. She just liked to think that she did. She'd had a clearer vision of what she wanted in life when Rex was still alive, but since his death, she wasn't sure where she was going.

She was free-falling and nervous about taking chances, like stepping down from the job she loved to work on the administrative side. And then there was that kiss, that connection she felt with Ares on the mountain. It had been so amazing to be held, to be intimate with someone again. Especially someone she trusted. She had initiated the kiss; she'd wanted it. In that moment she'd forgotten herself.

There was a part of her that could easily fall in love with Ares.

It could be so simple. She knew him; he loved Jeremy and Jeremy loved him. They were best friends and… Her thoughts trailed off because she just couldn't let herself think of Ares as more than just a friend.

I wouldn't be alone then.

Just that thought completely grounded her, because that was no basis to start a relationship with someone. She didn't want that insecurity to cloud her judgment, because she didn't want to hurt Ares and she didn't want to lose him.

Yet, she recalled the way she felt in his arms and the

way his lips had fired her senses. She'd almost melted up there. It had been so long since she had that touch, that warmth. It made her feel alive again, when she'd been feeling numb for so long.

"I guess I do prioritize others first. I always have," she agreed.

"Exactly."

"I feel kind of embarrassed."

"Why?" he asked.

"I've never told anyone, except Rex, about what happened when I was kid. It was just easier to bury that side of myself."

"Thank you for sharing it with me. For what it's worth, you're the first I've told about my family too."

Her heart skipped a beat. "I guess that means we trust each other?"

"I suppose so." Ares came around the counter and stood in front of her; he reached out and touched her chin, tilting her head so she'd look at him. Her heart was beating so fast, her body reacting to the gentle touch of his strong hands.

What she wouldn't give to just let all her insecurities go and kiss him again and continue what they started. But the logical side of her brain was too loud. She couldn't give in, no matter how tempting Ares was.

She reached up and touched his hand. "Thanks for being my friend, Ares. Jeremy and I would be so lost without you."

"Anything for you…for you both." His voice was deep, husky and it made her body ache with need. He was so close. What harm would it do to just give in, for one night?

"Mom?" Jeremy called from the couch, groggy. As much as she didn't want to break this connection with Ares, she was glad for it.

Ares stepped back and Pauly headed over to the couch where Jeremy was rubbing his eyes.

"Right here, buddy," Pauly answered. "You fell asleep on the couch. You ready for bed?"

"Yep."

"I'll carry him," Ares offered.

And before she could argue Ares had scooped up Jeremy in his arms. Jeremy curled up against Ares and rested his head on his shoulder. Her heart melted watching him carry her son up the stairs. A sob welled up in her throat and tears stung her eyes as she bit back the rush of emotion.

Jeremy needed Ares in his life and there was no way she could let her own emotions jeopardize that. She didn't want to ruin things by driving Ares away.

They needed him.

Ares tossed and turned most of the night. He was going over the kiss, the conversation with Pauly over her giving up work in the field, but also Jeremy's reaction when they picked him up. Seeing his godson suffer tugged at the fibers of his soul. He understood now why Pauly thought going to a desk job would be better. He still didn't agree, but he sympathized.

Pauly was doing all she could to shield Jeremy from pain. It was admirable, but Jeremy was old enough to understand more than she realised. What he needed was a man-to-man talk. And who better to give him that than his godfather?

So Ares made sure he was up bright and early, hoping Jeremy came down first. He did, looking tired, like he hadn't slept much. It hurt to see a kid struggling so much at such a young age.

"Morning, buddy," Ares greeted.

"Can I have cereal?" Jeremy asked, sullenly. He was

completely not his usual happy-go-lucky self. It reminded Ares of the sad, heartbroken boy from a couple years ago.

"Sure. It's Saturday. I'll have some too. I would ask you if you slept okay, but it looks like you were wrestling gators all night."

A minuscule smile crept on Jeremy's face. "No gators in Canmore."

"Probably it's too cold."

Jeremy nodded. "Yeah."

"You okay?" It was a silly question. Ares knew he wasn't, but he didn't want to bombard Jeremy right away.

Jeremy climbed up on a stool, rubbing his eyes. "I was scared yesterday."

"I know," Ares replied, calmly, as he pulled cereal out of the pantry cupboard. "But you don't have to be scared whenever your mom is late. It's not always a bad sign. My parents were late all the time, working, and they were fine."

Jeremy sighed. "Yeah, I can't help it though."

"I get it, pal, I know it's hard. But what happened to your dad… That was an unusual accident. It doesn't happen often. And, remember, your mom can handle a lot. She's awesome."

"Yeah, I guess…"

"I mean, she saves lives. Like at the bowling alley. You remember that, right?" Ares asked, softly, glad Jeremy was opening up instead of shutting down.

Jeremy looked at him in disbelief. "Of course."

"Yesterday, she did the same."

Jeremy rested his head against his fist. "She did?"

Ares nodded. "We were out helping a man who'd gotten hurt on the trail. She saved his life. He had kids. Like you."

Jeremy didn't say much, just nodded, but then looked up. "So why was she late?"

"Snowmobile problems. Remember? We weren't in any danger, except of getting cold. And not for long. It's pretty neat that your mom can fix them, huh?"

Jeremy smiled. "Yeah."

"Your mom loves her job, but not as much as she loves you. She's good at it, but she might give it up."

"Why?"

"She doesn't want you to worry, pal. Neither do I." Ares felt a lump in his throat. He loved Jeremy so much. It killed him to see him suffering. "But maybe you don't have to worry quite so much. What do you think?"

Jeremy looked thoughtful. "I don't want her to quit. It's cool what she does. Maybe… I think I can be brave."

"I know you can." Ares tousled his hair. "I'm glad you think your mom is cool. Guess that means you think *I'm* cool too, huh?"

Jeremy smiled, just a little. "Of course. You're the coolest. You save lives too. Just like Mom."

It made Ares's chest tight with emotion to see that hint of a smile back on his face. And even though he'd been the one to say the words first, hearing them reflected back to him in Jeremy's sincere voice made him glow with pride. "Wish everyone saw it that way, buddy."

Jeremy looked confused. "Who wouldn't?"

Ares sighed. "My dad," he said, thinking again of the letter, all the feelings it had stirred up. He pushed the thoughts away. "That's not the point."

"Well, that's silly." Jeremy's nose was wrinkled. "Maybe he just worries like I worry."

"Maybe." Ares didn't want to take the conversation down that road, not when Jeremy was finally looking happier. "But, hey, I might not be a mechanical genius like your mom, but I can look after myself too. Did you know I climbed Everest?"

Jeremy's eyes widened. "You did? Weren't you scared?"

"A bit. It's the tallest in the world and a dangerous climb, but I'm here still. Sometimes, you just have to decide to experience something amazing. You can't let worry and fear control your life."

Jeremy nodded. "Mom used to climb mountains with Dad. I saw pictures. Wonder why she stopped?"

Ares was pretty sure he knew why. "I wonder about that too. You know, she worries about you a lot too."

"She doesn't need to. I can be brave for her."

"You sure can," Ares said, proudly pouring him cereal.

Jeremy was clearly still thinking as he poured in the milk. "She's good at taking care of people. Like the bowling alley guy."

"Exactly. Sometimes, she'll get delayed. You've got to be brave for her and only think of how she's safe, because she's trained."

"Yeah, you're right. I do." Jeremy took a bite of cereal. "She's a cool mom. She needs to do her work. Help others."

"Most definitely," Ares agreed.

"I'll be brave."

"I know, buddy. You'll worry, I get that, but you're strong. Like your mom. And like your dad. You know, he wanted to climb Everest too? He would've gone to the top with me."

"Why didn't he?"

Ares grinned and poked Jeremy's nose. "He was here. You were born that same day."

Jeremy laughed. "I think I can be strong for Mom. I'll make her proud."

"Of course you will, buddy. You're an awesome dude."

Jeremy was his bubbly self again, and Ares could see the pride in his face. Admiration for his mom and some for Ares too. That felt surprisingly good.

Maybe Jeremy was right, and his dad did worry about him. Ares wanted to believe that, but it was hard to ignore years of frosty silence.

Still, it got him thinking about things he never thought before. About family. He remembered what Pauly had told him last night. He'd been running from something he thought could never work because of his own parents, but she'd had a rough childhood too. She hadn't run from marriage or a child—she'd embraced it. And made it work.

Maybe he didn't have to be so scared about settling down. He was trying to convince Pauly not to give up on something good because of fear. Maybe he should learn to take his own advice?

There was something to be said for Saturday morning cereal talks.

CHAPTER NINE

AFTER HE AND Pauly had shared that moment over tea a week ago, Ares had thought something more might've happened. But nothing much had changed. Except, his talk with Jeremy had gone well, and that pleased him. Everything else just sort of went back to normal, even though it didn't feel normal.

It had felt like a huge burden had been lifted off his shoulders when he told her about his estrangement from his father. It had always been this secret shame he carried around with him. Basically, he was unloved. Talking with Pauly that night was the first time he'd really opened up about his family and what had happened between them, since telling her about the divorce so long ago in college. No one in his family ever talked about it; they always put on a brave face. It was a shameful failure, not to be discussed.

It was almost like his parents were trying to hide it or something, which was silly given how his father moved out. But his father liked perfection. Ares could see that now. Successful business, children who had admirable careers.

Except Ares.

Since college, Ares had kept it all locked inside too, eating away at him. All these years he'd been living his life in defiance of his father's disappointment, thinking that he was out of his control, but maybe in a way his dad had been influencing his choices after all.

Either way, it had been good to finally share that truth with someone.

And now that Pauly had opened up about her childhood, about her fears, he understood her better. He was touched she'd felt so comfortable sharing that vulnerability.

He'd never felt as connected to anyone as he did in that moment. He'd thought he really knew Pauly, but he hadn't known this side of her. So she'd been hiding something secret away all these years too, and the fact that he was the first person she'd shared it with meant so much. Neither of them was alone. Their friendship had become deeper than he'd thought possible.

Except, now he wanted more.

I can't have more.

Something it was getting harder and harder to convince himself of as he spent more time with Pauly and Jeremy. Even though he lived his life on his terms and the way he wanted, nothing had ever compared to the last few weeks in Canmore. This was exactly what family should be.

Yet, this was temporary, because there was an end date. His contract here was only for ,a year.

He'd have to move on next fall.

Who says?

The idea of leaving his work, his traveling to take this job here permanently was terrifying. It was something he never contemplated before.

"Hey, Galanis, there's a meeting with the chief in boardroom three," Erikson said sticking his head into the locker room where Ares had just finished putting his stuff away.

"Thanks," Ares acknowledged, waving to him.

He had to put everything out of his mind and concentrate on work. Usually when thoughts were plaguing him all he had to do was just focus on the job and it would be easy to clear his mind. The problem now was the main thing he was ruminating on was Pauly and he couldn't escape that.

She was everywhere.

Ares found boardroom three easily enough. Everyone was taking seats. Pauly was at the front and he sat down next to her.

"Any idea what this is about?" he whispered.

"No idea," Pauly responded. "I wonder if he's going to address the influx of snow we've been having steadily since the end of October? It's a bit early for this amount, so they might be closing some of the trails and passes."

"That would make sense." Ares sat back and crossed his arms. "But would that require a meeting?"

"It could. We'd have to go over protocol on rescues. Some of those trails and passes are treacherous."

The chief, Pierre Lloyd came into the room and took to the podium at the front.

"Good morning, everyone," Lloyd addressed the crowd.

There was a murmur of "morning" returned.

"I've called you all here because we're getting reports of serious avalanches."

The moment the chief mentioned the word *avalanche* Pauly's spine straightened and Ares saw her hands ball up into tight fists. He wanted to reach out and comfort her, but he knew she'd hate that.

Chief Lloyd continued. "I've been conferring with the station houses in Banff, Kananaskis about the amount of snow and the temperature. Environment Canada has also confirmed with us about the extreme fluctuations. With the up and down temperatures there have been a lot of avalanches, more than we usually get for this time of year. Highway 93 headed north from Banff to Jasper has been closed. Also with this amount of snow, the influx of tourists and skiers has increased exponentially. And with the increase in tourists, signs of closed trails and dangerous ski hills are often ignored. We all know Russ is once again operating that foolish helicopter ride where skiers are dropped and then ski down; and with the way the snow packs are, it's a great danger. What I need is rescuers who are skilled mountain climbers to join a joint rescue team, that, when called, will traverse in the high mountain passes to perform rescue operations of possible trapped people."

There were a few questions and Ares leaned over to Pauly.

"Russ does what?" Ares asked, under his breath.

Pauly rolled her eyes and nodded. "I don't think it's smart, but Russ is a licensed pilot and the skiers do have insurance and take classes. They like the extreme ski from high in the mountains."

"I guess I can't really complain… I climb them, they just hurtle themselves down them?" He was trying to make light of it, because he could sense Pauly was anxious and he wanted to diffuse the situation.

Pauly sniggered. "Yeah, you could put it like that."

"Any more questions? And not about Russ and his black diamond helicopter rides," Lloyd asked, with a tone of weariness.

There were a few laughs in the crowd.

Ares put up his hand. "I have mountain climbing experience. I would like to volunteer."

The moment the words came out of his mouth he heard Pauly's head whoosh to look at him and he could feel her eyes boring into the side of his face. But she shouldn't be surprised that he was volunteering. Part of the reason he took this job in Canmore for the year was because he had mountain climbing skills. He might as well put them to work. He knew she would be worried and he felt bad, but he was experienced and they needed him.

He'd climbed Everest and some of the other biggest peaks in the world. This is what he wanted to do.

"I was hoping you would step up, Galanis," Lloyd stated, smiling. "Just need you to sign these forms and then we're going to join in on a virtual meeting with the other station houses and go over protocols this afternoon."

Ares nodded and got up to sign the forms with Lloyd. He glanced back once, but Pauly was no longer staring at him. She was staring down at her hands and looked upset. He felt bad, but this was what he loved to do.

And this is why you can't be tied down, a little thought reminded him.

Only, he wasn't sure if that was really the problem. He knew that Pauly was thinking about Rex and about how he died, but Rex had died doing what he loved and saving lives. That's what Ares was here for. If saving lives didn't matter to him, he would've never become a paramedic. He would've done just what his father wanted and taken over the family restaurant.

And been completely miserable.

As much as it pained him to turn his back on Pauly and leave that room with the chief, this was his career. He had the skills and he needed to be there to help.

Pauly didn't see Ares for the rest of the day and she wasn't surprised by that. He was going through some training about the protocols for avalanches and rescue operations on high mountain passes. Meanwhile, she went out on a few local calls with Erickson, in the ambulance.

Though she tried to completely focus on her work, she couldn't help but think about Ares up there on the mountains and the danger he was putting his life in.

It made her sick to her stomach when she thought about it. All the anxiety possible poured through her over the thought of something happening to him. She cared for Ares, and it terrified her to think of losing him.

Every possible worst-case scenario ran through her mind and she tried to strategize a solution. Only she couldn't. All she could come up with was fear, fear of something she couldn't control.

I'm only thinking like that because of what happened to Rex.

Which was completely true.

When Rex had been out on the perilous mountains, she'd been a bit concerned, but she'd never really worried about it, not until he died on the job and left her alone. It was then that she'd become angry at herself for not stopping him from taking those dangerous rescue operations. Logically, she knew he'd died doing what he loved, saving others, but she was still angry he'd left her.

Now the thought of losing Ares up there as well? It was too much for her to handle. Her heart couldn't survive that.

Her stomach twisted and a stress headache was starting to pound behind her eyes.

This is why he agreed to come and work with fire and rescue services. He wanted to be out on the mountain.

In theory it had all sounded good, but now faced with reality, she wasn't handling it very well. It wasn't like she had a real say over the jobs he took either. She wasn't his significant other, she was just his friend.

That thought cut her to the quick, because there was a part of her that wanted to be more than just a friend. A part she was trying hard to ignore.

But she was finding herself entertaining the idea of more with him and that was a scary prospect indeed, because she knew how he felt about marriage and what a transient life he led. Would he really want to be tied down in Canmore to a widow with a young child? That wasn't just a step to settling down, that was *really* settling down. And if things didn't work out, then Jeremy would lose his beloved Uncle Ari and she'd lose her best friend.

It just wasn't worth the risk, no matter what her heart was telling her in this moment.

As she finished up her final report and sent it off, Ares came back into the station house and looked a bit exhausted as he approached her, his knapsack over his shoulder.

"Hey," she greeted, trying to sound all bubbly and cheery instead of letting her voice shake with the existential dread that was screaming deep inside her. "How was your day?"

"Long, but I'm excited about being part of the team." There was a twinkle in his eyes as he started to tell her about everything that happened during the day. She could see the fire and passion in his face and hear it in his voice. All the while her leg began to bounce with nervousness. She had to place a hand on her knee to stop it.

There was no way she could ask him to not do it. She didn't have that right.

"I'm glad." Which was a complete lie.

He cocked an eyebrow and stared down at her. "Uh-huh. Sure."

"What?" she asked.

"I know this is hard."

She shook her head vehemently. "It's fine. This is what you came to Canmore to do. You brought your own equipment here, for heaven's sake. I get it, Ares. Am I worried? Sure, but I know that you're a skilled climber."

Although, Rex had been a skilled climber too. Didn't

matter how good or careful you were, Mother Nature was always more powerful in the end.

His eyes narrowed and he looked at her uncertainly, like he didn't quite believe her. "I don't think it's fine."

She let out a long sigh. "I guess there's no hiding it."

"No." He ran his hands through his hair. "It'll be okay, Pauly."

"You can't be certain of that," she snapped.

"No. I know I can't." He frowned. "I have to do it though."

Pauly felt guilt for making him feel this way. That was not her intention. "Look, I'll worry, but I swear I'll be fine, Ares."

Ares didn't look convinced. He let out a sigh. "We should do something fun tonight. It's Friday and it's snowing… Maybe tonight is the night we take Jeremy tobogganing?"

"You say that with such enthusiasm," she teased, forcing herself to lighten up.

"I promised him, and I liked it as a kid. I'm just tired."

"You don't have to do it."

He groaned and then grinned. "I know, but it'll take your mind off everything right? You can't really think when you're freezing cold and throwing yourself down an icy hill on a piece of plastic."

Pauly laughed. "No. I suppose not, but you have a shift tomorrow. Are you sure you want to do this?"

He waffled. "No, but let's do it anyway."

"Okay." Pauly was still concerned, but her anxiety was melting away as she tried to focus on how happy Jeremy would be tonight. "You know, I was hoping you'd put up more of a fight about sledding."

His laugh was loud and joyous, like his old self. "Yeah, I know. I'm surprised at myself."

"You'll forever be Jeremy's favorite uncle."

“Good. You almost ready to go?”

“Yep. All done.”

“Let’s go then.” Ares held out his hand and she took it. It felt so right to slip her hand in his and she did feel slightly better, but she was going to continue to fret about it. She couldn’t help it.

She was waiting for the unknown and that was never a good thing.

Why did I suggest this?

This was the question that Ares kept asking himself every time he got to the bottom of the steep sledding hill and had to climb his way back up. Pauly was right. Definitely a different experience as an adult versus being a kid. Especially after a long work day.

He had to admit it was kind of fun to toboggan in the dark though. The sledding hill was lit up and there were big fat flakes falling. When you got to the top of the hill you could see the town of Canmore’s lights twinkling. It was the middle of November and people were starting to put up their holiday lights in preparation for Christmas. With the snow and the colorful lights it was cozy. In the daylight, it looked like a cute mountain village, which it was. At night, with this weather and at this time of year it was almost magical.

Rocketing down the hill was a blast, even though the snow stung his face as he slid, but the hard part came at the bottom, when he had to get off the sled with Jeremy and climb back up the hill in his snow gear. After a long day of just sitting and going through rescue and emergency protocols, his body was stiff and the climb got a little tedious.

“Come on, slow poke,” Pauly teased as she grabbed the

toboggan from him and raced up the hill after Jeremy. Ares grumbled and trudged after them.

He may have grown up in Canada, but he really didn't like the cold and snow. Unless he was climbing a mountain, and even then it was hit or miss. When he'd been up on Everest it had been so cold and snowy, but the difference there was the warmth that came from the accomplishment.

An accomplishment I celebrated alone.

No one had been with him on that climb. When he'd called his mother on his satellite phone from the summit, all she had said to him was, *"That's nice."*

His father didn't even know about it.

That summit, that climb, had made him realize how utterly alone he was, but that was the life he'd chosen for himself.

Now, spending time here on this ridiculous hill, in the snow, hurtling himself down on a sled, he wondered again if he was making the right decisions in his life. Maybe, just maybe, he didn't want to be alone after all?

But his work was perilous. Traveling to some countries was dangerous and now mountain rescue... He was always going to be putting his life on the line. How could he even think about putting Pauly and Jeremy in that situation, afraid of losing someone, again? Would she want to open her heart to another dare devil?

Ares seriously doubted it. The last thing he ever wanted to do was hurt her. And it was clear she was already struggling with it all.

"Let's all go down together," Jeremy shouted, his eyes sparkling in the dark and his cheeks bright red. "On the same sled."

"Can we all fit?" Ares asked, puzzled.

"Sure we can," Pauly said. "Jeremy in the front, then me and then you and you can push us off."

Jeremy got into the front of the sled and then Pauly sat behind her son, her legs straddling him. Ares's pulse began to race as he thought about coming up behind Pauly, once again, just like on the snowmobile that first day of training.

Get a grip on yourself.

He slid up behind her, her body pressed against his chest. His legs were so long that, stretched out, they went down the length of the toboggan.

"Let's go!" Jeremy squealed, holding the rope at the front of the curled sled.

"Okay, hold on." Ares used his hands to push off and then wrapped his arms around Pauly as they shot down the steep incline. Jeremy was shouting and so was Pauly. Ares just reveled in having Pauly in his arms and spending time with her and Jeremy.

It was like a picture-perfect moment of domesticity.

And he loved it.

Every second of it, even in the cold.

As they came to the bottom of the hill, he let go of Pauly's waist and slowed their descent so they didn't take out one of the dozen other people at the bottom of the hill. A fast-moving sled could knock someone straight into the air.

"That was so much fun!" Jeremy shouted.

"It was," Pauly agreed breathlessly. "How about we go and get some hot chocolate now at the coffee shop?"

"And a donut?" Jeremy asked, excitedly.

"Sure," Pauly agreed. "I'd usually say no to sugar, but you're already pretty hyper from all this sledding."

Ares stood up and stretched. "Hot chocolate and donuts sound great, but after that will have to hit the hay early tonight. I have work tomorrow."

Jeremy paused. "Don't you work with Mom?"

"Sometimes," Ares said, picking up the sled. "And sometimes our shifts will be different."

Jeremy nodded, but went a little quiet. "You'll be okay though, right? We were going to play video games tomorrow night."

Ares put his arm around his godson, pulling him into a reassuring side hug. It wasn't like he could promise him that nothing would happen, but he didn't want Jeremy to worry either. "Remember about Everest."

Jeremy nodded. "Right!"

"I'll be back to whip your butt at that racing game," Ares teased.

"Cool." Jeremy broke away and ran toward the truck.

Pauly was worrying her bottom lip. "I'm sorry about that."

"It's okay. He needs to heal just as much as you."

"What did you mean about Everest?" she asked.

"I told him about doing that climb. The one Rex and I planned to do together until *someone* got pregnant."

Pauly laughed. "It wasn't all my fault."

"I know, but Jeremy was pretty impressed."

"No doubt! Thanks for being his pal."

"I'll always be that," Ares stated.

She nodded and he pulled her into a quick hug with his free arm. She wrapped her arms around him and it felt so good to have her snuggled against him, even with all the layers. He could stay like this forever.

He could be with both of them forever. He wanted to tell Pauly how much he loved her. Only he couldn't form the words. He couldn't be selfish.

Instead, she pulled away.

"Hot chocolate is on me," she said.

"Deal."

CHAPTER TEN

"THERE'S A BAD snowstorm coming. I can see it brewing on the horizon," Pauly remarked on Tuesday, when she came back to work. She'd been off for the last couple of days, but now they were back on the same shift.

Ares had been working solidly. His next day off was on Thursday. He'd kind of missed working alongside Pauly, but partnering with Erikson the last few days hadn't been so bad. Even though he saw her at night, when he was on the job, he could finally put some distance between them. At least that was his theory.

Honestly, he'd *tried* to throw himself into his work to forget about her, but he couldn't. All he could think about was being together on the sledding hill, all the tender moments they shared and how much he was enjoying this life, pretending to be a family. He thought he would miss his work traveling to different exotic locations, but he didn't.

In Canmore he felt a bit more grounded, like it could be home for him too.

"I saw there was a bad storm. They're even calling it a blizzard," he said. He sat down at her desk, trying to ignore all the possibilities raging in his mind. "Think we'll get a lot of calls?"

It was a joke—he knew they would—but she gave him

some serious side-eye. "Of course we will. It's going to be a busy day and night."

"Is Jeremy at the sitters?" Ares asked.

She nodded. "Britt knows I might be late. It's happened before in the past, when Rex and I both worked long hours during a storm or even forest fires. Jeremy loves her boys, so he's in good hands. He's not alone, so that's the main thing."

"And how did Jeremy take it?" Ares asked, curious.

"Well, actually," Pauly admitted. "He took the news well. I'm glad."

Ares could sense the hesitation in her voice as she said those words and now he understood that trepidation a bit better. The pain of feeling abandoned. He understood that, as well.

"You never wanted to move back to Toronto?" he asked.

"No." She smiled. "I do love it here. I have friends here."

"Yes, but more family out there. More help."

"I get that. Rex's family have been trying to talk me into moving back forever, but this is where I made my life with Rex and he's up there in the mountains. I don't want to leave him there. I want to stay here."

"I get that."

"Do you? You don't seem to want to settle."

"I like exploring..." he trailed off, because he really didn't want to admit right now that he'd been thinking a lot lately about maybe planting his own roots. It felt too scary an endeavor to even admit. There was all the uncertainty. All the unknowns.

As he was sitting there pondering, not filling out some crucial paperwork he needed to fill out, the small office where Pauly worked became darker. The room had huge glass windows overlooking Canmore, and it was as though night was creeping up on them outside. It was only ten in the morning. Then there was a blast of wind, howling and whistling fiercely.

It startled Pauly and she looked up from her computer, staring out the window. “Wow.”

Ares followed the direction of her gaze. He couldn’t see Canmore, except for some streetlights barely shining through the snow. There was a loud rumble, and he knew it was the wind hitting the side of the station house. He’d never seen anything like this before. Toronto rarely got such intense weather—all the tall buildings downtown acted like a natural windbreak. He’d never really experienced a true whiteout.

This was like something out of a movie.

He got up and wandered to the window. “This is wild.”

“This is definitely intense. I mean, Canmore gets snow, it’s why people come here to ski in the Rockies, but since I’ve been living here I’ve never seen an actual blizzard.”

An alarm went off. An emergency call.

There was no more time to talk about it. Now was the time to get to work and save lives.

When he’d started his shift, Ares had had a feeling in the pit of his stomach that this was going to be a long, gruelling day, and it looked like he was being proven right.

There was really no pause as they attended call after call. There were accidents on the highway, because the snow was causing whiteout conditions. It wasn’t long before the RCMP put up barricades and started shutting down roads to motorists. The snow was falling so rapidly that snowplows were trying to keep the roads clear, just so that emergency services could still get through. The wind was blowing the fresh powder that accumulated across every open area. Cars were being buried, making the snowplows work even harder as they had to stop and tow out people who'd been stranded.

The hospital was becoming overloaded with patients in the ER and it was only three in the afternoon. Ares and Pauly were finishing a drop-off there when they got another call.

"Calling 671," the switchboard operator said. "We have reports of a stranded hiker on Spruce Ridge Pass. Please respond."

"Copy that. We're on our way," Pauly responded as she carefully pulled out on the snow-covered roads. As they made their way to the hiking trail, it wasn't so much the snow that was hard, but the ice hidden under the layers of powder. The drive became more and more treacherous, especially as they drove a little bit out of town to where some of the steeper trails were.

The ambulance was equipped with chains on the tires for situations like this.

"Who would hike in a blizzard?" Ares asked as Pauly navigated the winding road to the parking lot at the head of the Spruce Ridge Pass trail.

"Lots of people. This trail is usually shut for winter, though," she said, through gritted teeth. And he knew she was struggling with her fear of going up the mountain again. "It's a summer trail for backcountry camping. But we get the odd daredevil who ignores the signs and goes out on the trails in the winter anyway."

Ares saw the flashing lights and flares of the RCMP in the parking lot. Not only was it dark from the onslaught of snow and howling winds, but night was coming. Daylight Savings Time had passed, so darkness came earlier and would continue to come earlier until they reached the winter solstice in December, a month away.

They got out of the ambulance and began to pack the gear they'd need.

The RCMP constable came over to them. "Glad you could make it. I'm Constable Greer. My team have located the hiker, but we're having a hard time traveling down the slope. I heard one of you was adept at climbing?"

"I am," Ares stated. He grabbed the gear bag that had all the equipment needed for a mountain rescue. The trail was higher in elevation than the town of Canmore, but he wouldn't really call this "up the mountain." Still, Constable Greer had mentioned that the injured hiker had slipped down a slope, and they wouldn't have the equipment to attempt a rescue. And because of the weather, they couldn't airlift the hiker out. He'd need to be carried.

"Great," Constable Greer stated. "The hiker is injured, fairly bad."

"Lead the way, Constable." There was a definite nervous edge to Pauly's voice. Ares wished that he could comfort her and tell her it was going to be okay, but this wasn't the time or place for that. As they were heading up the trail another paramedic team joined them, which he was glad for.

Ares was the only one with experience climbing mountains and scaling cliffs, so it became quickly apparent that he would be the one leading this rescue. He'd done rescues on cliffs before, just not in the snow. They packed as much emergency gear as they could. Their packs were big. At least with a large team they would be able to carry the rescue toboggan together, as well as the litter. It would be sent down a guideline, then the patient would be strapped down and lifted off the side of the cliff.

All Ares could think about was the sled they had used with Jeremy a few days ago, the happiness he had felt going down that hill.

This bright orange rescue toboggan was a bit more sophisticated than Jeremy's sled. They'd be able to secure the litter carrying the trapped hiker inside and transport him out. It even had handles to allow them to pull or push the toboggan down the trail.

It was at least a twenty-minute hike to the site of the accident, a narrow trail leading to a steep drop-off. There were markers to indicate the slope, but it was hard to see in the snow. It hadn't been a smart idea on the part of the hiker, taking a mountain trail in a blizzard, but that was an opinion Ares would keep to himself and let the RCMP figure it all out after.

All he had to do was rescue the trapped man.

At least the blizzard was dying down for now, but the darkness was coming in quickly. Pairs were tethered together to keep each other safe, just on the off chance of an avalanche.

Ares hoped that didn't happen, but it was better to be safe than sorry in this kind of situation. Pauly was tied to him, so he was able to keep his eye on her.

Constable Greer, who was leading the pack, put up his arm. "Here!"

Ares and Pauly made their way to the side. He unhooked Pauly in case he slid down the slope and because he needed to be able to move to get in his harness.

Flares were set so he could see where the hiker had fallen. He was against a tree that jutted out the side of the rock face. Underneath was a hundred foot drop to the forest below.

The rest of the slope had a gentle incline down. Of course the unfortunate hiker had to fall in the one spot that was steep.

Ares was working to calculate his artificial high direction so that he could tell the team where to anchor the guidelines in order to allow the litter the smoothest transition back up the side of the cliff.

"Tell me what to do," Pauly said.

He could hear the fear in his voice, and he could see it in the way her lips were pressed together in a tight line. But he admired her dedication and commitment to the work. She was willing to swallow her trepidation down. Which was good, because he needed her right now. He needed his partner, someone he trusted, to do this risky rescue.

Ares hoped, if they succeeded here, she'd change her mind about giving up her career to sit behind a desk.

As he got hooked into his harness and put on the rest of his safety gear, he instructed the rescuers. "We need to anchor the tracking line system here and here."

Once everything was secure, he started his descent, gently rappelling on the cliff, trying not to stir up too much snow. It was hard going; the storm had begun to intensify again.

There was a creak. Ares's first thought was *avalanche.* But nothing shifted.

Once he had made it to the hiker, Ares saw he was unconscious, just like the skier from the riverbank. He could tell that the man's arm was dislocated or possibly fractured because it was at an odd angle. There was also a definite contusion on his head and some bleeding, but it was hard to see more than that in the dark, even using the headlamp on his helmet.

"Send down the rescue litter," he called up.

"Okay," Pauly shouted.

Ares waited as the litter was lowered and grabbed it. Then he focused on getting the injured hiker safely strapped on. Once he had everything secure, he gave a tug on the guideline. "Pull him up!"

The litter began to rise and Ares followed, climbing

slowly beside it and making sure that it didn't get bumped or jostled or caught in a tree branch. Finally, it disappeared over the top of the cliff, and Ares climbed after it. He got unhooked, then they loaded the patient onto the toboggan.

"Head contusion, left pupil dilated. Possible fracture or dislocation of the left arm," Ares informed the other paramedics.

The four of them worked together to secure the man. Then the two other paramedics headed straight back down the trail, pulling the rescue toboggan. Pauly hooked herself back up to Ares and they packed up the gear.

There was a crack, and they all stopped to listen.

"We better get down off this trail," Constable Greer stated.

"We're good to go," Pauly said, but Ares could hear the gut-wrenching fear in her voice.

He knew she was thinking what he was thinking. It had been snowing steadily for hours and there was at least thirty centimeters in the pack above them.

Greer and his officers led the way, Pauly just behind them. They took their time, carefully making their way down. But then there was a large snap and a *wumpf* sound.

"Avalanche!" Greer shouted from up ahead.

The snow was going to cut them off from the RCMP. It was headed straight for him and Pauly.

"Swim, Pauly," Ares shouted over the roar. "Swim to the side, back toward me."

Don't let me lose her.

It was his last thought as the snow poured like a river from above them.

Pauly spun around and did what Ares said—she swam back the way she came, trying to keep as close to him as she could, fighting the current of snow. She held her hand in front of her face so in case she was buried, there would be a pocket around her mouth and nose to breath. At least she'd remembered that from her avalanche training.

The snow had hit her hard. It was cold and moved like heavy, wet cement around her. It went through her snow gear and her legs grew wobbly.

Oh god. Please. I can't leave Jeremy. I can't lose Ares.

She stayed focused on Ares and fought, but her legs gave way.

"No!" Ares shouted and she felt his hands grip her and hold her as they came out of the flow.

She clung to him as they stood back, watching in horror as the snow rushed down the side of the trail, effectively washing the trail away. Finally, it slowed, but they were completely cut off from everyone else and judging by the size of the snow wall in front of them, they were going to be there for a while.

"Pauly, Ares, are you okay?" Greer called over the radio.

"We're good," Ares answered.

"We're calling a snow removal team, but it'll take some time in this weather. There's a cabin, half a kilometer up the trail. It's stocked with wood and you can shelter there."

"We'll do that," Ares replied.

"Keep your radio on."

"Constable, please call the station and have them inform my son we're okay. They know how to find him," Pauly pleaded.

"Copy that," Greer said.

Pauly's body felt like jelly as she tried to catch her breath and process everything that had just happened. Despite how hard it had been, despite the fact that she felt almost like she was going to pass out, being in the field today had felt like she was where she belonged. When she'd gotten into the work, she'd forgotten everything else. It had reminded her of why she loved her job. Though she was worried during that cliff rescue, Ares had it all under control. When the avalanche hit, she'd just focused on Jeremy and Ares and she was here still.

Even though they were trapped that hiker would live. Today, no one was lost in the avalanche and that rush she got from doing the job she loved the most washed through her.

She hated being cut off from Jeremy, but at least she was with Ares. She was safe.

They were alive.

What she tried not to do was focus on Rex and what he might've felt when he was caught in that avalanche. Had he felt the way she had? As soon as she'd thought of it, try as she might, she couldn't get that terror out of her head.

"I've got you," Ares said, reassuringly. He still had his arms wrapped around her.

It eased her mind. Just for a moment as the adrenaline wore off. All she could do was cling to him as she tried to catch her breath.

"Pauly, let's get to the shelter. We need to get warm. Think you can make it?"

"Yeah," she responded and they began the walk up the trail.

The cabin was usually used by backpackers or as an emergency shelter. It had a wood stove and a good supply of firewood, everything to keep warm. It wasn't much, but it was someplace where they could stay out of the storm, which was beginning to worsen, and wait to be dug out.

The main thing was, they were safe.

Albeit cold and tired.

Pauly had never been so terrified in her life as when the snow had come rushing down off the steep rock face. She'd seen avalanches from a distance and she'd been stuck in traffic along a road for hours after one had swept across the highway, but she'd never been in one before today. And all she could think about in that moment was where Ares was and how she didn't want to lose him. How she didn't want to leave Jeremy. So she'd fought with all her might.

Now all she wanted to do was hold on to Ares and have him hold her. She wanted to chase away the terror that her body was letting her feel.

"You stay here and I'll get wood," Ares stated.

She nodded, her teeth chattering. Her boots were full of snow and they had to get some heat going before they succumbed to hyperthermia. Maybe it was just because she was so cold, but she felt like Ares was gone for an eternity. Finally, he came back with an armload of wood. He knelt down in front of the wood stove and piled in the wood. Then he opened his backpack and pulled out a tiny hatchet.

It was an emergency survival kit that he had to carry working with the mountain rescue team. Pauly had never been so glad to see it in her life. He quickly split some of the smaller pieces of wood into kindling and then struck a match and got the fire started.

"I'm going to get another couple loads of wood from the lean-to. I don't think we're going to make it out of here until morning."

Pauly nodded and scooted close to the fire. "You're right."

Ares brought in the wood and then latched the door. The little cabin was basically no bigger than a shed. There was a covered latrine just outside the door, a small bunk and the wood stove. It was meant for roughing it.

Ares dug in his bag and pulled out a couple of vacuum-packed emergency blankets and a sleeping bag.

"You need to get your clothes off," he stated.

"What?" she asked, through chattering teeth.

"Pauly, first rule of hypothermia. Get out of the wet clothes and we'll huddle close for body heat."

"Right." But her heart was racing at the suggestion. It made logical sense, she knew that. The snow had gotten through down to her uniform. Still, the idea of being naked with Ares was making her body thrum with excitement—and a little bit of fear.

He tossed her a blanket then began to peel off his winter clothes as the cabin started to heat up. He had his back to her, but she couldn't help but watch him out of the corner of her eye. She'd seen him with his shirt off, long ago at the beach while they were in college, but this was something different.

She quickly glanced away and tried to get her own clothes off as fast as she could. Once she did that, she wrapped her blanket around herself and scooted to the sleeping bag to sit down on it.

Everything of hers had been wet.

Ares had wrapped his blanket around his waist. His shoulder-length hair was tied back, but she could still see the broad, muscular expanse of his bronzed chest. He picked up the clothes and laid them all out, hanging them up so they could dry by the wood stove.

"That should work. Once they're dry, we can get dressed again and try to get some sleep," he remarked.

"Sounds good," she managed to squeak out, but her mouth had gone dry. All she could do was stare at the way the light from the wood stove played across his chest. There was no other light in the cabin. It wasn't hooked up for electricity, so it was just them, sitting in the darkness, naked and huddled in front of a wood stove.

Ares sat down next to her.

"You need to climb inside this sleeping bag. We need to be close together for…warmth."

Their gazes locked and her breath caught in her throat. She was so close to him, it was intoxicating. All she could think about was being in his arms, the way his lips felt on hers. It had been so long since she felt that intimate connection with someone. Right now, she wanted to be held and comforted.

Why not let it be Ares, her best friend, a man she trusted and loved?

She wanted Ares.

"Are you okay, Pauly?" he asked, his voice trembling slightly.

"I think so."

"What're you thinking about?"

"How much I'd like you to kiss me."

CHAPTER ELEVEN

SHOCK RAN THROUGH ARES, but only for a brief moment, because he wasn't completely certain he'd heard her correctly. And he wanted to make sure it was real.

"You're sure?" he asked.

"Very sure," she said, her voice trembling.

How many times had he wished for this? Longed for this? Too many. It was a dream come true, but he didn't want to take advantage of this situation.

He cleared his throat. "I'd like that too."

Pauly was so close. Her dark hair hung loose, brushing over her soft creamy shoulders and he was well aware that only a blanket separated them. He was so very tempted.

But there was their friendship. He didn't want to hurt her, and he never wanted her to regret this. If they were going to share this moment together, she deserved something special and meaningful. Just like he did. So he hesitated, not wanting to rush her or push her.

Right now, he hated his conscience just a little bit.

"Do you not want to kiss me? You seem hesitant," she questioned.

"It's not that. Not at all. Trust me. I want to kiss you again."

She moved and sat up on her knees, reached out to touch his face. Her soft fingers fired his senses, because her touch was so light, yet it made him want more. It made him burn with need.

"Then what is it?" she asked.

"We're friends."

"Yes."

"It's complicated. I don't want to ruin things, but to tell you the truth… I've always wanted you. I've always been attracted to you." He held back telling her how he also had been in love with her for years. How he'd always dreamed of this moment, even when she belonged to another.

"I want you too, Ares. You're my best friend, I trust you and I want this. I want to share this with you."

He swallowed hard, staring down into her beautiful blue-gray eyes, her body so close to his. He wanted to give her forever in this moment, but he couldn't because he wasn't sure about forever himself. He didn't want to make a promise only to break it later. "I can't promise you anything."

"I understand. I can't promise you anything either, but tonight, I just want to be held again. And I want you to be the one. I just want… I want you."

"I want you too." And before he could overthink anything, he captured her lips in the kiss that he'd burning to taste once more. The one he couldn't stop thinking about.

For years he'd been fighting his attraction to her, but now, he couldn't hold it back any longer. Pauly wanted him and the need overtook him as he ran his hands over her body, kissing her deeply and fiercely. It was as though all other kisses he'd ever experienced in his life didn't exist.

Only this one.

As much as he wanted to continue, he stopped himself.

"What's wrong?" Pauly asked.

"I don't have protection," he murmured. "Not something I carry around in my emergency kit."

She laughed softly. "I can't get pregnant the usual way."

"What?"

"Blocked fallopian tubes. Rex and I had Jeremy through IVF."

"I didn't know," he replied, softly.

She shrugged. "We didn't share it with many people."

"Are you sure you want to do this?"

She grinned, letting the blanket fall away so he could drink in the sight of her naked body. "Positive."

She pulled him down and he kissed her again, brushing his lips over her soft mouth, over her collarbone, anywhere that he could. He ran his hands across her body, luxuriating in the feel of the silkiness of her skin. It heated his blood to touch her, to be with her here, that she trusted him this much. He wanted her so badly, but he had to pace himself and take his time.

If this was to be his only moment of bliss, a dream come true, he wanted to savor it for as long as possible.

"You make me feel…" he trailed off.

"What?" she asked.

"Alive."

"Same," Pauly said. Her heart was racing. Each kiss, each press of his lips against her skin sent a jolt of pleasure through her. His body was close against hers. They were skin to skin, nothing between them and it felt so right. She'd never really thought she could feel this way again, but she was glad it was with Ares. She trusted him and knew he would never willingly hurt her. He made her feel safe and protected again, which was what she needed more than anything. She opened her legs, arching her hips, wanting him to claim her, take her.

"Pauly, I want you so much," he groaned.

"I'm yours," she panted.

He silenced her words with a deep kiss, their tongues entwining and she wrapped her legs around his waist. Ares slid his hand between her thighs, stroking her. She cried out as pleasure washed through her. At that moment it felt like the haze that had been controlling her life lifted. She was alive again, she was getting lost in the sensations coursing through her.

"Please," she begged.

"What?" he teased, sliding his tongue around her sensitive nipples.

"I want you."

He groaned and moved his hand. His cock pressed against her entrance and he slowly thrust into her, filling her.

It was overwhelming.

"Damn," he moaned. "You feel so good."

Pauly moved her hips, urging him to move, but he wouldn't. Ares just held her still, buried deep inside her.

"You're a tease," she said.

Ares just chuckled and then he moved, slowly at first, taking his time. Pauly wanted him hard and fast. She wanted to feel all of him. It didn't take long before he quickened his pace, thrusting in and out of her. She met each thrust with her hips, faster and faster and until she could feel her body succumbing to the sweet release she yearned for.

Pleasure overtook her and she cried out his name. Ares's thrusts became shallow until his own release came a moment later.

He rolled off her and she curled up against him, listening to his breathing. It calmed her. This connection was what she'd been craving, for so long.

"Thank you," she whispered, tears stinging her eyes.

"Pauly, are you crying?"

She added. "I'm glad it was you. I needed the comfort after…my life flashed before my eyes out there. Thank you for being here for me."

Ares just wrapped her up in his strong arms. "You're safe. Everything will be okay."

Pauly nodded, closing her eyes and listening to the reassuring beat of his heart. She wanted to believe everything would be okay and stay the same, but she doubted it ever would.

Everything in that moment had changed.

Pauly fell fast asleep in the safety of Ares's arms and slept just as soundly as she did that first night he'd come to live with them. At about seven in the morning, they got a call on the radio that the storm was over and the rescue crew were almost done clearing the path. As much as she didn't want to leave the comfort of this moment with Ares, she had to get dressed and get back to Jeremy. Although he knew they were safe, she was desperate to see him and hold him.

It had been so close a call. Despite her thoughts from the previous night, despite the fact it would kill her to give up field work, she knew it would be better if she stayed behind the desk or the switchboard.

It made her sad, but it was the right thing. The responsible thing. That way she wouldn't have to take any more risks. She'd almost died up there, and the thought of leaving Jeremy alone… Well, it was heartbreaking. She wouldn't let that happen.

She pulled on her warm clothes as Ares roused and got dressed too.

They weren't saying much, but they both had agreed that last night was a onetime thing. They couldn't make any promises to each other. But she couldn't help but wonder what this all meant for their future.

She felt like Ares might be avoiding eye contact, and she hated it. But then their gazes locked and he smiled at her, just like he always did.

Maybe everything would be okay. They might not have forever, but things weren't weird or ruined between them.

Still, she worried about what he would say when she shared her decision about the desk job, because she knew he was against it.

She only hoped he'd still support her and understand her reasons why.

Once they had made sure the fire was out and the cabin was secured, they hiked back down the trail and were met by rescuers and cheers. She'd never been so relieved to see other members of the station house there.

Chief Lloyd was there, smiling. "Of course my best mountain rescuer gets trapped on a simple trail."

Ares chuckled. "Well, it could've been worse."

"We were lucky." Pauly shivered just thinking about that avalanche and the rush of snow that surrounded her. But she only let that thought intrude for a moment. Last night with Ares had helped her chase all that away. Being wrapped up in his warm arms had been so reassuring. It completely grounded her, and reminded her she had survived. She was alive.

"We're going to take you both to the hospital to get you checked out. It's standard protocol, so don't even try to complain," Lloyd stated firmly.

Pauly nodded in agreement, but she really didn't want to go to the emergency room and get checked out. All she wanted to do was get back home and comfort Jeremy. And she wanted to talk to Ares about her decision.

He wasn't going to talk her out of it. That avalanche just firmed her resolve.

Ares sat in a trauma pod in the emergency room. He'd had his evaluation. Now he was just waiting for a doctor's decision, and the all-clear to leave.

He and Pauly had been separated, which was probably for the best at this moment. Things had changed up on that mountain.

It had been amazing having her in his arms all night. Finally, he'd felt peace. And in the morning, everything was different. When they'd woken up, he'd changed his mind about the promises he said he couldn't make, about how he would never settle down,

Having her, holding her after the avalanche, knowing she was safe when he could've lost her and then making love to her, he'd known for sure what was missing in his life.

Her.

It had always been her. When he watched her almost get swept away by that wall of snow, he'd thought all his dreams were being washed away. It was like everything slowed down and he couldn't move quick enough to save her.

He'd almost lost her and that made him sick to his stomach.

He hadn't been sure what he wanted at first, but now he was certain. If Pauly wanted him, he'd give it all up to be here for her and Jeremy. He was all in.

What if she didn't want it though? It was a terrifying thought.

"Mr. Galanis?" A doctor entered the trauma pod where Ares was waiting.

"Yes."

The doctor looked up from his chart. "Everything is good. I'm discharging you."

"And my partner?" Ares asked.

"Yes. About to do the discharge now."

"Thank you, Doctor." Ares stood up and took the slip of paper from the physician. He walked out of the trauma bay and met Pauly on the way out of the hospital. "All good?"

"Yep," she said. "I'm going to pick Jeremy up now. Do you think you can handle the report?"

"I can do that." His heart was racing and he couldn't get the words out.

"Okay. Well, we'll talk later, right?"

Ares nodded. "Yes. I think we need to."

Pauly left the hospital and Ares scrubbed a hand over his face. He'd done a lot of scary things in his life, but this prospect of declaring his love, changing his life plans, it was probably the most frightening thing of all.

Pauly headed straight for home and then walked to Britt's to pick up Jeremy. It had been hard leaving Ares behind, because she didn't want to let him go, but she knew that she had to. He was safe, as was she.

But in a way it was a relief to have space to figure stuff out. Ares hadn't exactly been chatty since they were rescued, and she was so conflicted about the feelings he was stirring deep inside her.

Right now she didn't want to talk about it. All she wanted to do was be with Jeremy.

"Mom!" Jeremy yelled and came running out to her, throwing his arms around her. "You okay?" He was excited, but not crying.

"I am. You're not as upset as you were the other day?" Pauly wondered, pleasantly surprised.

"Britt told me you were just snowed in a cabin with Uncle Ari. Where is he?"

"He had to file a report and drop off gear, he told me to come here and pick you up." She swallowed the lump in her throat. She was glad Jeremy didn't know about the avalanche.

Jeremy nodded. "It was such a big storm. I was sort of worried."

Pauly smiled and they walked hand in hand back home. "I'm glad you weren't *too* worried."

"Uncle Ari and I had a talk about it all."

"I didn't know that. Was this that Everest talk?"

Jeremy shrugged. "We talk about a lot of things. You should talk to him more often. He's cool."

"He definitely is. So tell me about this talk."

"Well, Uncle Ari made me realize how important it is for you to save lives. He told me to be brave because you and Dad were. Mom, you're awesome and I want to do what you do when I grow up. I want to save lives too. Also, I want to climb Everest."

Pauly's heart swelled. "Wow. I'm so proud of you, buddy."

"I'm proud of you too, Mom." Jeremy hugged her tight. "I was scared, but you're okay and it's okay to be scared."

"I am indeed okay and yes, it's okay to be scared of things."

"Right. It's just how you handle it. Face your fears!" Jeremy said, enthusiastically.

Pauly smiled to herself. Ares had said all that to Jeremy? It meant so much that he talked to him, that he was acting as a strong male role model for him. More than a godfather, but as a friend. As a father.

And, yes, she definitely needed to talk to him, especially about what happened between them last night and what it meant for the future.

He might be stepping up for Jeremy while he was here, but she knew that Ares wasn't ever planning on settling down permanently. If she ever thought about getting into a relationship again, it had to be with someone that was willing to live in Canmore, because she wasn't going to move Jeremy away from where he was happy. From where his last memories of his father were spent. And just as she couldn't risk her heart on someone who wasn't going to stick around, she couldn't put Jeremy at risk of losing another father figure.

Jeremy ran up the stairs and Pauly followed slowly after she took off her coat and kicked off her boots. She had to have a shower and a big cup of coffee. Jeremy had disappeared to his room and she flicked on the coffee maker.

As the coffee percolated, she heard the front door open.

"Ares?" she called out.

"Yeah. It's me." He came up the stairs. "I dropped off the gear and then I picked up some donuts."

"Yum. Want coffee?"

He nodded. "Please."

There was still that awkward tension between them since this morning. Yep, things had definitely gotten weird, but she didn't regret what happened last night. She'd wanted it and she was glad it happened. Now, she could see, it had been building for a while.

"So," Ares said, breaking the silence. "Should we talk?"

She nodded and poured him a cup of coffee. "Yes. I think we better."

"Pauly, I think you know that I care about you deeply..."

"Ares, you don't have to explain anything. I meant what

I said, I don't need a promise, so you don't have to make an excuse."

Ares's eyes widened. "I understand that, but…"

"I'm okay." She wrapped her arms around her.

"I know you're okay. Pauly, I'm in love with you."

The words came out so fast and it was unexpected. She almost dropped her mug. "What?"

"I'm in love with you, Pauly. I always have been."

She carefully set her mug down, because she couldn't quite believe what she was hearing. There was a part of her that was thrilled with his admission, and another that was terrified. She just didn't know how to take it.

"You…love me?"

Ares nodded, his expression pained. "For years. Do you know what it's like to fall in love with your best friend who happens to be married to your other best friend?"

"No," she replied, quietly.

"Pauly, I love you. There's been no other for me."

She worried her bottom lip. She wasn't sure *what* she was feeling. She was so scared of loving again, especially someone she might lose to the mountains like she lost Rex. So scared of being left alone once more. It was too much to handle.

And what terrified her most was that she was falling for him too.

"Ares, I don't know what to say." She could see the disappointment in his face.

Tell him how you feel.

Only, she couldn't get the words out.

"It's okay," he said, quietly. "It's a lot. A lot of things changed, but I wanted you to know how I felt."

"I appreciate that." She tried to muster a brave face.

"It's so overwhelming. I've made some decisions of my own too."

He cocked an eyebrow. "Oh?"

Her pulse was thundering in her head. "I'm taking that desk job."

"Why?"

"We could've died up there," she countered.

"But we didn't."

"This time."

"Pauly, every job has risks," he stated.

Pauly shook her head. "I've made up my mind."

"Is it what you want?" he asked.

She paused. No, it really wasn't. She loved being out there in the field, but nothing was going to change her mind. "I won't leave Jeremy alone."

"But he's not. He has us."

"Us?" she asked. "He has me."

"I'm here too."

"For now, but you leave in a year. Or have you decided to actually stay put somewhere?"

Her words stung, but she wasn't completely wrong. There was a time limit to his stay in Canmore. He'd been thinking a lot since they made love and it had taken every ounce of courage he had to tell her how he really felt about her, but she'd responded the way he'd feared she would.

Could he give up his life, his career, for someone who didn't share his feelings? He'd give it all up if she wanted him, but if she didn't feel the same he'd have to move on.

He couldn't stay here and watch her settle down with someone else.

There really wasn't any point in trying. And she wasn't returning the affection. It was clear she wasn't ready to move on. She was scared still. That was okay, but he wasn't sure he could put his life on hold forever on the off chance that one day she'd fall for him too.

Maybe it was just better to stay friends. But right now he wasn't sure their friendship could survive this.

"You're right. I am here temporarily." He got up. "Maybe it's best I go now."

"No," she said, quickly. "Don't do that."

"Why? Because you're afraid to be alone?" Instantly he regretted the words as he said them. Her spine stiffened.

"Why are you running away?" she asked.

"Why are you?"

"I'm not. I'm here. This is my home."

He shook his head. "You're running away from your career, because you're scared about what happened to you as a kid."

"I lost Rex."

"We all did, but at least he died doing what he loved. He didn't let fear rule him."

"You're one to talk," she snapped.

"What do you mean?"

"You're afraid to face your family. You're afraid to live your life because you don't want to be like your father. Why are you so stubborn? Are you so afraid of settling down because of what happened with your parents?"

He opened his mouth to say more, but he heard a shout and saw Jeremy running down the stairs.

"Uncle Ari, I'm glad you're okay!"

Ares plastered a smile on. "Why aren't you in school?"

"Snow day. Want to play a game?" Jeremy asked.

"Sure, pal. I'll be right up there."

Jeremy dashed back upstairs and he turned to look at

Pauly. She was looking away, her lips pressed together firmly.

“I’m not the only one scared of change, Pauly.” And he left to go upstairs. Their conversation was unfinished, but she was right, he was stubborn and he was scared of making a mistake or driving away the woman he loved. The woman he’d always loved.

And yet, he realized he already done just that. With his confession, he’d driven her away. She wasn’t ready and now maybe she’d never be ready.

He’d ruined it all. Just like his father had done to his mother.

CHAPTER TWELVE

ARES COULD SENSE there was some awkwardness between them when they had dinner that night. Thankfully, Jeremy was completely oblivious.

It didn't feel like the blow-out fights that his parents used to have, but he also felt there was a heaviness, a finality in their silence.

There was a part of him that was mad that Pauly was going to take the desk job, that she was too scared to do what she loved, but he also saw her side of it. She was so terrified of leaving Jeremy and he couldn't blame her for that.

And he was thinking about everything else she'd said too. How he was stubborn. He was and he knew it, but what had stung him the most was when she said that he was similar to his father. That was something he had been fighting his whole life, being like his dad or his brothers. Settling down, marrying, and then divorcing.

He'd still turned out exactly like all of them.

Stubborn like a mule, as his *yiayia* would say.

He finished washing up the dishes and Pauly came back down the stairs, slowly, like she was trying to walk on eggshells. He didn't want her to feel like this in her own home. He didn't want their relationship or friendship to end because of this silly fight. The only thing he could think of that might help was to put some distance between the two of them.

"Is he asleep?" he asked.

"He is. Thanks for doing the dishes."

He shrugged. "I don't mind. You made dinner."

She took a seat at the counter. "Should we finish our conversation?"

He nodded. "I think so. I'm… I'm going to find my own place and then hand in my notice. I could easily hop back into the agency and be sent somewhere else."

Her face was a bit unreadable. "You don't have to do that."

"Well, you won't need me around if you're taking that desk job, and I think some distance would be good."

Pauly frowned. "Look, I know you don't agree with it, but it's the best thing. Rex and I actually talked about it…"

He cocked his head to one side. "Did you really? It just doesn't seem like something Rex would agree to. He knew how much you loved your work, how you liked being out there on the front lines saving lives. Don't deny it."

"I won't be selfish," she snapped. "I have a son I have to take care of. I won't abandon him, but you wouldn't understand that because you're never going to settle down. You're never going to take on that level of responsibility."

Her words stung, but there was so much truth laid out in those words. He didn't know what it was like. He didn't have a family or kids, because he was terrified of ruining it all.

"No, I guess I'm not," he said, quietly. "Pauly, I don't want to fight."

"I don't want to fight either," she said, her voice breaking. "I don't want to lose you."

"Is it because you love me? Or is it because you don't want to be alone? Really, you can be honest."

"I don't know. Everything has happened so fast…but how can I change everything for someone who can't promise me anything? And I don't expect you to do that, give it all up for me."

It hurt what she said, especially after he'd put himself out there. Ares walked around the counter. He wanted to pull her in his arms and comfort her, but he couldn't.

"I'll see you in the morning, for work."

He had to walk away from her, when all he wanted to do was offer her everything. But she hadn't said that she loved him.

Did she have to? Couldn't he give her time?

When he'd seen her almost be washed away in that avalanche, his life, her life, Jeremy—it had all flashed in front of his eyes. That was what he wanted.

So why couldn't he just let go of this stupid fear of commitment, so that he could have it? Why did she have to reciprocate it right away for him to say he'd stay? What if she needed to hear that first?

Once he was in his room, he saw the letter from his mother.

The letter telling him about his father. The letter that accused him of not answering his phone and it was true, he screened his calls, but his father never called him. Why should he be the one to make amends?

Because you are the bigger person. You're not your father.

That thought smacked him right in his face. And he put himself in his father's shoes. No, he and his father had never really seen eye to eye ever and Ares always felt like a disappointment to him, but he'd never told his father how he felt.

He just walked away because it was easier.

At least, if he reached out now before it was too late, before his father died, he would have that peace of mind knowing that he was the one that had bridged the gap. If his father didn't want to talk, then Ares would know definitively where he stood.

His hands were shaking as he picked up the phone and punched in his father's number. The phone rang.

"Hello?" his father answered on the other end.

"Dad, it's Ares."

There was a moment of silence on the other end. "Aristotle, it's you? Truly?"

Ares rolled his eyes at his father using his full Greek name. Aristotle was such a mouthful; it was why he went by Ares, or Ari to Jeremy. Only his dad would ever use his full name.

"Yes, Dad. It's me. Ares."

"I'm glad you've called me. It's been…a long time."

"It has. I got Mom's letter."

"Ah." His dad sighed on the other end. "I suppose you're going to yell at me about not telling you. Your mother certainly did."

"No. I'm not going to lecture you about it."

"You're not?" his father asked, stunned.

"I'm worried about you," Ares stated, trying to fight the flood of emotion raging through him.

"There's no need to be worried, son. I am glad you called. I wanted to apologize for the way I behaved when you were in college. I was a… I was a fool. It's not easy for me to admit that, but I was foolish. Prideful and stubborn."

Ares laughed softly. "I do understand the stubbornness part. I have been accused of being that too."

His father chuckled. “I think we are more alike than either one of us wants to admit.”

“I agree. And I’m sorry for what I said about the business you built up. I’m sorry I didn’t want to take it on, and I’m sorry it’s closed.”

“It’s okay, son. It is in the past. What I’d like is to see you happy. Are you happy with your life, Aristotle—I mean, Ares?”

The question caught Ares off guard. Everything that had happened since college played through his mind. There were moments where he had felt happy and proud, but they were few and far between. His life was lonely. He’d tried to fill that void, that hole in his heart with other things, but… No, he wasn’t particularly happy.

There was more that he wanted. Most of all, he wanted to be with Pauly and Jeremy. He’d always miss Rex, but he wanted to take care of them. He wanted a family with them, here in Alberta. He just had to fight to get it.

“I think I will be,” he said.

“Good. That is all I ever wanted for my children and my grandchildren.”

“I’ll fly out and visit you as soon as I get some time off. Things are a bit busy with all the snow and avalanches.”

“Avalanches? Are you being careful?” his father asked.

“I am. I’m part of a mountain rescue team.”

“Well, they certainly should have you on that team. You scaled Everest.”

“How…how did you know that?” Ares asked, stunned.

“Your mother showed me a picture.”

Emotion flooded through him and he fought back tears. “You and Mom talk?”

“A lot has changed in the last decade or so,” his father said, gently. “We still care for each other—we just don't want to be married anymore. Though, the amount she comes around and pesters me it's like she is still married to me. She's my best friend."

Ares swallowed the hard lump in his throat. "I have to go. But I'll call you again, Dad. I love you."

"I love you too, son." His father's voice broke. "Thank you for calling me. We'll talk again soon."

Ares ended the call and ran his hand over his face. He had a sense of loss, of grief for the years they'd both managed to waste. But with what time his father had left he was going to make sure it counted. And he was going to fight for a life with Pauly.

This time he wasn't going to run away.

Pauly was his best friend and he wasn't going to let that go. Even if she didn't want to have a romantic relationship with him right now, he was still going to be here for her. He wasn't going to let his pride stand in the way.

He wasn't going to abandon her.

He couldn't, because he loved her and that's what counted. If he had to wait for her, he would. He just wanted her in his life.

Why didn't I tell him I loved him back?

Pauly was wrestling with that little voice in her head. Right now it was berating her for not telling Ares how she felt. Instead, she'd just come up with excuses. But when he said he was going to leave, it had scared her. She didn't want him to go.

But it was hard to even contemplate moving on with someone else, someone she cared for deeply.

When Rex had died it had crushed her to her very core. And, since then, she'd just existed, numb.

When it came to Jeremy, she put on a brave face for him,

because she had to. She wanted his life to be as normal as possible, but in the process of trying to keep things that way, she'd been burying her own emotions.

Grief. Anger. Loneliness.

And then Ares had come into her and Jeremy's life and there was happiness and laugher again. She didn't know what it was that sent Ares to her when she needed him the most, but she was thankful.

The problem was now she was worried that she'd ruined it all. That she'd driven him away, because she was so scared of telling him how she felt. Telling him that she loved him too. That she was terrified to act on it, because what if she lost him?

What if she lost her best friend?

I'd be alone again.

It didn't have to do with the guilt of moving on. She and Rex had even talked about that once. They'd both agreed that, if either of them died young, they'd be happier knowing the one left behind might find love again. It was about making space in your heart to allow that to happen.

She would always love Rex. He was her first love, her first everything. But now she was in love with Ares too.

She just wasn't sure if he would stick around long-term.

"What do I do?" she wondered out loud, staring at her bedroom window. She could see a ski hill all lit up and little black dots whizzing down the hill in the distance. People. It always gave her some comfort to watch them.

It was the mountain where she spread Rex's ashes. The mountain where he lost his life doing what he loved.

Is Ares right? Can I really give up the job I love?

"Rex, what do I do?" she asked again, dropping her head into her hand. In this moment, she felt like that lost little girl again. She and her parents might have worked that all out years ago, but there were still times when she felt so alone.

"Mom?"

Pauly spun around, wiping the tears from her eyes to see Jeremy standing in the doorway. "What're you doing awake?"

"You were talking to Daddy." Jeremy came into the room and climbed up on her bed so he could see out the window. "I talk to him too."

She smiled and took a seat next to him. "I'm glad that you do."

"I also like talking to Ari," Jeremy stated. "He loves us. Both of us."

"I know he does," she replied softly.

"I want him to stay. Forever."

"You do?"

Jeremy nodded. "At Daddy's funeral, he talked to me. He told me that Daddy was one of his best friends, you were his other best friend and that I could be his best friend too. Best friends should stick together."

She wiped away another tear. "You're right. They should."

"You love him too. Don't you?" Jeremy asked. "Uncle Ari, I mean."

Her heart began to race. "I think I do. Would it make you angry if Ares did stick around forever and lived with us? If we maybe become a family?"

"No!" Jeremy said, smiling. "I think that's what Daddy would want."

"And you'd like that?"

"Mommy, you're sad. Uncle Ari makes you happy. We're family and don't families stay together?"

Pauly pulled him into a hug. "They do. But you know

we do the same kind of job, right? Are you really okay with that? Are you okay with Mommy *and* Uncle Ari out there together?"

"Yep. He told me. You, him and Daddy all save lives. That's cool. You have to help people who are injured or stuck. You can't give that up. If you do, then who will help those people who need you?"

"Good point." Pauly kissed the top of his head. "You're smart."

"I know," Jeremy stated.

Just then there was a rumble. It shook the whole house. Holding Jeremy close, Pauly turned to see the mountain, where the little skiers had been moments ago, had been eclipsed by a torrent of white, rushing down the hill like a tsunami.

Her stomach sank and her heart began to race. She couldn't believe what she was seeing and for a moment she felt the bite of the cold snow against her skin, the force of it trying to drag her down.

You're okay.

"Mommy!" Jeremy whispered.

"I know, buddy. I know." Her world was spinning out of control.

Ares came rushing upstairs and into the room, obviously hearing the roar. "What… Oh my god."

He came to stare out the window at the snow tumbling down.

Pauly pursed her lips together and they watched as the snow covered the ski lodge and all those skiers. It finally ended and as soon as it did her work phone rang, as did Ares's. Ares stepped out in the hall to answer.

Pauly picked hers up, her hands shaking. "Pauly speaking."

"It's Lloyd. We're calling everyone in."

"I figured so. I'll be there as soon as I get Jeremy off to the sitter."

"Thanks, Pauly."

Pauly ended the call and turned to Jeremy. "I have to go. I'm going to take you to Britt."

Jeremy nodded. "I'll go pack and change. You go help those people, Mommy."

He ran off and Pauly texted Britt. Britt would understand—her husband was Fire. He'd be called in too, along with all emergency service people in the area. Everyone would be needed on that mountain.

Ares came back in the room and for a minute her pulse began to race, thinking of the decision she'd just made. Everything she wanted with him.

Then she saw his face and worry blotted all of that out. "So, I guess we're both back on duty."

He'd be doing some of the riskier rescues. The thought filled her with dread, especially now that she knew how she felt. She might lose him today, right when she'd decided she couldn't live without him.

If she dwelled on the fear, she wouldn't be able to save lives.

"Yep. It's all hands on deck."

"Okay. Get changed and we'll go after we drop off Jeremy."

Ares nodded and then left.

Pauly took a deep breath and looked at the mountain. It was going to be hard working up there, but she had to put all her fear, all her anxiety aside and do her job.

And she knew one thing for certain—this wouldn't be the last time.

She'd tell Ares about it all later, but she wasn't walking away from the job she loved because of fear. And she wasn't walking away from him either.

When the time was right, she'd tell him how she felt and how she wasn't going to let him go. She wanted a second chance at life and she wanted it with him.

They were risking their lives tonight, but it was worth it. She just hoped that at the end of this tragedy, there'd be happiness for them all.

CHAPTER THIRTEEN

PAULY GOT JEREMY to Britt's house then she and Ares traveled to the station house. So much for their day off to recuperate from their own avalanche experience. But when it was an emergency situation like this, everyone was needed. Every hand counted. And although Pauly was wrestling with her feelings, her new realization, now was not the time and place to discuss it. They had to stay focused and stay collected to do their jobs.

The moment they got to the station house the chief, Lloyd was there.

"Pack all your emergency gear. Teams from Banff, Kannaskis and Calgary are en route. The Canadian Armed Forces have been called in. There is a triage center being erected on site. You will be picking up teams of trauma doctors from the Canmore hospital to take up to the site and they will direct you on which patients to bring back down the mountain. We're preparing for the worst. One ski lodge was buried. Those with mountain experience, you will be headed out onto the snow pack to listen for avalanche beacons. Stick together and stay safe."

Pauly and Ares didn't say much to each other as they loaded the back of the ambulance with the equipment he would need to traverse up the snowpack. Just the thought of him being up there made Pauly's fingers tremble, but he was one of the qualified candidates to do that job. The uncertainty of it all filled her with dread, but much like he'd told Jeremy, she had to be brave so he could do his work and save as many lives as possible.

Still, it was hard not to think about the dangers. Even after an avalanche settled, if the angle of the slope was right, it could give way again, or the snow pack could be deceptive and rescuers could be buried themselves.

But there were lives that needed saving out on that hill. This was why they became paramedics.

"You ready?" Ares asked, breaking the silence.

"As ready as I'll ever be." She offered him a brave smile. "Let's get this done."

He nodded.

They climbed into their rig and headed straight for the hospital. The first team of doctors were ready with their gear and dressed for outside. Once they'd piled into the rig, they made their way to the barricaded road outside of town.

Fire and the RCMP had blocked the road leading to the mountain.

As they approached the barricade and were let through, navigating drifts of snow, Pauly held her breath, her pulse hammering between her ears. It was like nothing she'd ever seen in Canmore.

This road led to one of the more elite ski lodges in the Canmore area, and it was usually plowed and lined by beautiful trees. In the summer, when they offered up tree-top trekking and obstacle course types of events, the road-side would be bursting with flowers.

Now trees were knocked over, snapped like twigs, their branches stripped bare by the first of the snow.

Other emergency crews were plowing out the snow that had partially covered the road.

"This is awful," Pauly murmured, gripping the wheel tighter.

"This will be bad," Ares said.

"Have you ever worked a natural disaster before?" she asked.

"Yep. Hurricanes." He sighed. "Have you?"

"Forest fires, but nothing quite like this." She craned her head to look at a dangerously low-hanging power line, but the top of the rig wasn't going to catch it.

When they reached what used to be the main parking lot of the ski lodge, they were stopped by a member of the military.

"You have doctors?" The corporal asked when Pauly rolled down her window.

"Yep."

"We're having all ambulances park over there by the tent we set up. We have crews excavating the buried ski lodge and bringing out the wounded. Back in so that you're able to leave quickly and we'll make sure you're not boxed in," the corporal stated, gesturing to where the makeshift hospital was set.

"Thank you," Pauly replied.

She drove over to where she was told to park and backed in. After she parked, they opened up the rear doors and let the medical team out. Ares grabbed his gear from the back.

All Pauly could do was watch. Her stomach was in knots and she wanted to stop him, to keep him safe.

There was so much she wanted to do or say, but this wasn't the time or the place.

The corporal who had directed them came over to them now. "I was told one of you is experienced with mountain climbing?"

"I am part of that team," Ares said. "I'm ready, just tell me where to go."

"I'll take you there right now," the corporal said. "We're only having experienced climbers traverse the snow pack."

Ares nodded. "Lead the way, Corporal."

As he turned to walk away, Pauly grabbed his arm, not wanting to let go. She wanted to keep him safe. Ares paused and looked down at her.

"Be careful," she said, hoping her voice didn't break. And then she completely broke work protocol and kissed him, telling him how she felt in that kiss. All the words she wanted to say, but couldn't. "Be safe."

Ares touched her face gently, his expression soft. Something had changed and she hoped he knew how she felt in that moment. Maybe, just maybe he felt what she was feeling. "I will come back to you. I promise."

"You will."

He smiled, his eyes twinkling with warmth. "Yes. Always."

Pauly nodded and watched him disappear.

It was breaking her heart that he was leaving her, but she knew that he would come back. She had to keep focused on that. She couldn't have it any other way. She couldn't lose him. She couldn't save Rex, but he'd died doing what he loved. He never gave up and Pauly couldn't control everything. Uncertainty was a part of life.

She couldn't even control her feelings for Ares. But she could control how she acted.

She loved him and when he came back down, after all this was over, she was going to tell him how she felt. That even if he wanted to continue his work traveling the world, she didn't care. They could still be together. That was all she cared about in this moment.

That they were together.

Forever.

* * *

The imprint of Pauly's lips were still burned on his, her taste still lingering on his tongue. Although she didn't say it, everything was in that kiss and he knew how she felt. When he made her that promise that he'd come back to her, he meant it.

Right now, he had to push those thoughts aside to work with the rescue team. When they got to the main site Ares was in awe, but also horrified at the size of the snow pack. What was left of the ski hill, everything that wasn't buried under the snow, was a mess. The ski lift was a tangled heap and the big lights that lit up the hill were on their sides.

There were electrical crews out there, trying to make sure the downed wires were safe.

"Do we know how many are unaccounted for?" Ares asked, as they were gearing up to head out there and search for beacons.

"Fifteen are missing out of the list of those who were on the hill tonight," the head of mountain rescue stated. "The resort requires all skiers to carry an avalanche beacon. You have your probes. Once you locate a beacon with the transceiver, use the probe to search for the victim. When they have been located leave the probe in the snow and shovel downward."

Ares headed out carefully on the pack.

Only fifteen people unaccounted for. The mountain rescue team was at least twenty-five strong. They had to work quickly.

As Ares started his search all he could think about was Rex. He'd been doing a rescue just like this when a second avalanche had hit and even though he'd pulled his beacon, he had hit his head on a rock and died. It hurt to know that

Rex had done everything right, but a twist of fate, a rock in the wrong spot, had ended his life.

But as Ares worked, he also thought of Rex by his side. Rex lived, loved and worked in these mountains and he'd wanted Ares to be there too. Although this wasn't the mountain where Rex had died, Ares felt his spirit was tied to the Rockies.

He'd always felt like that, even before Rex died. Even though Ares wandered, Rex and the Rockies had always been a beacon, calling him back. And Pauly had always been a safe harbor.

Now it was like Rex was here beside him, guiding him as he worked, just like always. Like he'd been by Ares's side when they had been climbing.

"Do you think we'll ever tire of this, Rex?" Ares asked as they sat on a cliff after finally getting to the top of the summit. They had just finished their climb of Mount Edith Cavill together.

"Nah," Rex responded, smiling. "I hope to bring Jeremy out here one day. Pauly too. I'll never get sick of it." He glanced at Ares. "I'm going to die on these mountains."

"Why would you say that?"

Rex shrugged. "It's something I've known for a long time. I want to to die on the mountain. I belong here. I don't want to die in a hospital bed or my sleep. I want to die doing what I love."

"I don't think Pauly would appreciate that much," Ares teased.

Rex laughed softly. "Well, I don't plan on it happening anytime soon. But, when it does, my ashes need to be spread on a mountain, okay?"

"Okay, fair enough."

"Don't get me wrong, I'm not ready to go yet. I love my

life, my family, and I love mountain rescue. I'm telling you, you need to come here and do this with me. We could be unstoppable, eh?" Rex grinned. "Saving lives. Together."

"I love my freedom to travel too much."

"I get that." Rex sighed. "Still, when I'm out here I think about all three of us. You, me, Pauly doing what we love on the mountain. That would be a dream."

Now Rex was gone and even though he'd gone out the way that he wanted, there were times that Ares regretted not coming here sooner and working with him. But as he worked here now, he could feel his late friend.

He could feel the very essence of him in this place, the place he loved most of all.

And it was almost like he could hear his voice saying, *"I'm right here, buddy. Always by your side. I got your back."*

Now, Ares would have his, and take care of Rex's family.

Ares moved his probe over the snow. It wasn't long before he got a hit on his transceiver. Using his probe, he searched in the standard radius pattern from the lowest point, probing the snow until he found who he was looking for. Ares signaled to his partner that he had a positive hit for a beacon. He pulled out his shovel and began digging, under the probe, working carefully so he didn't injure whoever was buried under the pack.

There was a little pocket of air and the person rolled out, unconscious, but breathing.

Ares knelt down in the snow and checked for vitals. "You're okay. We'll get you down."

The woman groaned.

"I need a stretcher," Ares called out, and his partner waved to signal to members of the team who weren't sweeping the pack that they had someone who needed to be taken to triage.

Ares helped load the woman up and they got her off the snow pack and down to the triage area. As he removed his probe from the snow pack, he looked around and saw more people being pulled out. Some hadn't been completely buried in a depression.

One down. Fourteen to go.

Pauly worked with the doctors in the triage area. While the doctors focused on the more seriously injured, Pauly was able to triage and treat those that were being brought down from the buried ski lodge and from the snow pack. Thankfully, a lot of them had minor injuries and those with serious injuries were being sent to the hospital, by air lift.

The Armed Forces had brought one of their helicopters and there was a clear pad to airlift the really injured victims to Calgary, because most of Canmore's medical team was up on the mountain currently.

Pauly was able to wrap up minor cuts and bruises and there were enough paramedics on the scene to shuttle doctors back to the hospital and some of the patients back down the mountain. One of the head doctors in the makeshift triage area wanted Pauly there to direct patients and she was only too glad to stay and assist.

She had no problem driving a patient to the hospital if it was needed, but really she wanted to stay up on the mountain until she was sure that Ares had gotten down okay. She could see the rescuers out on the snow pack, from a distance; she was impressed by how efficiently they were working and the fact that they were finding so many people.

The first woman to be brought into triage only had a

minor concussion and they got her off in an ambulance straight away. However, some of the people they were pulling from the ski lodge weren't so lucky.

While her body moved quickly and efficiently, handling patients, all she could think of was Ares. When he came down, she was going to do more than kiss him. She was going to make up for her hesitation and tell him she loved him and wanted a life with him. No more wasting time.

She heard crying and turned to see a little girl, standing by herself, wrapped in a blanket.

"Are you okay?" she asked, kneeling in front of the little girl.

"I was screaming outside. Mommy said don't yell, I could cause an avalanche and then…and now… My mommy is missing!"

Pauly wrapped the blanket around the little girl tighter. "I've got you. My name is Pauly and I'm a paramedic. Can I check to see if you have any cuts or scrapes?"

The little girl nodded.

Pauly picked her up and carried her to her rig, where it was warm and bright and she had a gurney. She set the little girl down.

"What's your name?" Pauly asked.

"Mary."

"Mary is a nice name. Does anywhere hurt?"

"My leg," Mary responded.

"Can I look?"

Mary nodded. Pauly examined her leg and saw some bruising and a deep cut that would need stitching. "Ouch, we're going to get some antibiotics on it and bandage it, then we're going to get you to the hospital."

"I can't leave without my mommy," Mary sobbed.

"What's your mommy's name?"

"Heather," Mary responded.

"Okay, we're going to bandage you up, then see if we can find her and then we'll get both of you to the hospital."

"Okay," Mary responded. "I don't want to be alone. I'm scared."

Pauly felt her heart break, just for a moment, because right then she was transported back to when she was a child. When she had been the one standing, all alone, crying. And all the times she felt that loneliness over the years.

Every time she felt that, she was that same lost little girl, like Mary.

But not anymore.

Ever since Ares had come into her life, she hadn't been alone. She no longer had to shoulder all the burden and take care of everything. He'd been so good to Jeremy, talking to him, supporting him and her. They were partners in every sense of the word.

In that moment, she realized she could make anything work as long as Ares was in her life. She could see it all now with crystal clarity.

"You're not alone," she told Mary, and for once she believed it for herself too. "I'm here and there are so many people out there helping."

Mary nodded. "Did I do this?"

"No," Pauly responded quickly. "Avalanches happen because of snow. Too much snow. It's been snowing a lot. Are you from Canmore?"

"No. I'm from Victoria."

"British Columbia?" Pauly asked, trying to distract the girl.

"Yep."

"So you have mountains, maybe not the snowfall like we get. Well, you have to have a lot of snow and then the temperatures have to be just right. It gets to a point that the mountain just can't hold all that snow any longer and it breaks away."

"Oh."

"So you see, your little scream didn't cause this."

Mary smiled tearfully. "Oh good. I'm glad."

"Mary?" a woman called out, frantically. "Mary? Answer me!"

"That's my mom. Mom!" Mary shouted.

Mary's mother spun around and came rushing to the ambulance, the relief palpable on her face. "Oh my god, Mary. You're okay?"

Mary wrapped her chubby arms around her mom. "I'm okay, Mom."

"She has a deep laceration," Pauly responded. "I stopped the bleeding, but she's going to need stitches and possibly a tetanus booster or antibiotics. I cleaned it and bandaged it, but she might need to be checked out for a break. She's not walking very well. I would like to take you both to the hospital."

Heather nodded. "It's just us two on vacation here. I was terrified when that..."

"I didn't cause it, Mom," Mary said proudly.

Heather kissed Mary on the top of her head. "I'm sorry I yelled at you."

"Can we go now?" Mary asked, Pauly. "Mommy is here and I don't feel so good."

"Sure thing," Pauly said. She got Heather and Mary secured and then let the corporal in charge of the triage area know she was transporting a patient and her daughter to the Canmore hospital.

Once everything was ready to go she left the accident site and did the patient transfer down to the Canmore hospital by herself. Alone, but not lonely. And though it bothered her to leave Ares up there on the mountain, she knew he could handle himself. He'd promised he'd come back and she believed him.

"This is our last shift together," Ares stated.

"What?" Pauly asked, distracted.

"We graduate in a couple of weeks."

"Right." She worried her bottom lip. "It's going to be weird."

"What is?" Ares asked, finishing up some paperwork.

"Us. All going our separate ways." She glanced down at the engagement ring on her hand, thinking about the life she and Rex were going to lead. "It'll be weird not having you as my partner."

Ares smiled and he nodded. "We make a good team."

"We do. And it'll be weird we won't all be living together anymore."

A strange expression flashed across his face. "I know, but you and Rex are getting married. You don't need me as a third wheel."

"Ares, you're one of my best friends."

Ares stood up and pulled her into a hug. "I'll always be that, Pauly. I won't abandon you or Rex."

"Promise?" she asked, holding tight to her partner, to her friend. Wondering where this next chapter would take him.

"Always."

Just thinking back to that caused Pauly's eyes to fill with tears. He'd always been there for her, just like he promised. She couldn't let him walk out of her life. So when he came down off that mountain she was going to make everything right.

She was tired of being too scared, of worrying about

everything that she couldn't control. All she could do was take life one day at a time and she wanted Ares by her side when she did that.

It was a long wait at the hospital, but she got Mary and Heather transferred and then she went back up to the mountain. She did a few more transfers, then, when it was almost midnight and she was on yet another trip back up to the hill, she learned that the last of the missing people had been found and retrieved. All the rescuers were coming down off the mountain.

Everyone had been extracted from the ski lodge, as well. Soon they would be able to start transporting the doctors and the remaining patients back down the hill.

It would take days for the cleanup to happen, but as far as Pauly heard, no one had died, which was kind of a miracle.

She waited, somewhat impatiently, for Ares to return. She wanted to set everything right. Even though there was no guarantee it would work out forever, she knew there would be no hope unless she took the chance. It was risky, but she was ready.

When she finally saw him walk through the tent, she was ecstatic. Her heart began to race in anticipation. Their eyes locked across the tent and it took everything in her not to run up to him and throw her arms around him, but they had doctors to transport back to town.

This wasn't the time and place.

"Hi," he said, his eyes shining and his smile so warm.

"You came back." Her voice broke.

"Just like I promised."

She nodded. "We have to take the team of doctors back to the hospital and then go to the station house."

"Let's go then."

Her pulse was racing and relief washed through her. Somehow she knew it would all be okay.

They didn't say too much more to each other. They got the doctors settled and then Pauly drove the rig back into town. Once the doctors had been dropped off at the hospital, they headed straight for the station where they offloaded their gear and made their reports.

Separately.

It was two in the morning by the time they were done and able to head back home.

"You going to pick up Jeremy?" Ares asked.

"No, I think I'll let him sleep. I let Britt know, and that her husband, Ernie, is okay and still up there."

"It's going to take a long time to clean up."

She nodded and parked the truck. "It will indeed."

They headed back into her house and Ares went to go in his bedroom, but Pauly grabbed his arm.

"I think we need to talk," she said, hoping her voice didn't tremble. "There's a lot to say."

"Sure. I want to talk too, but I thought you might be tired."

"I think I have a bit too much adrenaline after the last couple of days."

They headed up into the kitchen and Pauly put the kettle on and set out two mugs. It was out of habit, because her heart was racing thinking about what she wanted to talk to him about.

"So, you kissed me," Ares started. "I wasn't expecting that, but…it meant a lot."

"I did, because I wanted to tell you I love you, and it was hard around everyone and with the work we had to do. I just couldn't let you go without letting you know, some way, how I feel."

Ares eyes widened. "You…you love me?"

She nodded again. The kettle whistled and she quickly shut it off, turning her back to him and taking a deep breath. As she stood there, Ares came up behind her and placed his hand on the small of her back; she turned back around to face him.

"You know how I feel."

"I do." She swallowed. "And I know how much you love your life, your freedom. I know that you always swore off getting married since your parents divorced."

"I know I did, but here's the thing, Pauly. I've been in love with you for a long time, but you loved Rex and I cared for both of you. I never wanted to come between you and…it was hard for me to tell you how I felt, especially with Rex gone."

"I understand. It was hard for me to admit it too. I've always cared for you. I've always been close to you and it was hard for me to even think about opening my heart again, but there's room for you both and I can't think of a better man, than you. I do love you and I'm willing to give this a try, even if you continue your work and travel."

"But, you don't like to be alone."

"I'm not alone though," she said, quickly. "Not if I have you."

Ares couldn't believe what she was saying. He was thrilled, because this was everything he'd hoped for. Pauly was in love with him, she didn't care if he wanted to keep wandering, they could be together.

The only thing was, he didn't *want* to continue to live his transient life.

Not anymore.

"I don't expect marriage or for you to settle down with me. I know it's a lot with Jeremy and…"

Ares silenced her speaking with a tender kiss. "I want that."

"What?" she whispered.

"I want a life with you and Jeremy. I want to be settled down. I loved what I did, but I want to plant roots. And, when you're ready, I want to be married to you. I want to take care of you and Jeremy."

"You do?" she asked, softly.

"Yes."

"What happened to change your mind?"

"I called my father," he said.

"You did? How did that go?"

Ares smiled. "Good. I apologized to him and he apologized to me and I think… I think things are going to work out. I took my anger out on him by swearing off everything he thought a good life stood for—the career he wanted for me, settling down. I was scared, too, about marriage because my parents did love each other at one time and seeing that turn to hate and animosity…it was too much to bear. Then my brothers both had failed marriages, and my sister's started disintegrating too. I didn't want that. And I didn't want that for us, but I can't live without you, Pauly."

A tear slid down her face and he brushed it away with the pad of his thumb.

"I want to marry you, Pauly. And I want to stay here in Canmore with you and Jeremy. If you'll have me."

She nodded, smiling. "I would like that too. I never thought that I would fall in love again. I wasn't expecting to, but you made me see there is more to life than grief, worry and sadness. I love you so very much, Ares."

Cupping her face, he bent down and captured her lips in a kiss. He was still shaking, because he didn't know what the future was going to hold, but he was glad that he was going to be able to do it with Pauly.

The woman he'd always loved.

"Jeremy is going to be thrilled," she murmured, leaning her head against his chest as he held her, stroking his back.

"I hope so."

"Of course he will. He adores you."

"He can still call me Uncle Ari if he wants too. I don't expect anything else. I wonder if I'm still a godparent if I'm a stepparent?"

"I think both," Pauly laughed. "How about we go to bed?"

Ares cocked an eyebrow. "Your place or mine?"

Pauly kissed him again. "How about ours?"

EPILOGUE

Summer, Calgary

ARES WAS ANXIOUSLY waiting at the airport. At least it wasn't as cold as the first day that he arrived. Pauly and Jeremy were with him, for moral support, but he was still nervous about this incoming flight.

Although Pauly had met his mother, she hadn't met his father. Only Rex had met both of his parents. They'd really liked Rex and had mourned his loss, just as Ares had. So they couldn't wait to meet Jeremy.

And now both of them were coming in from Toronto.

Together.

And, honestly, he felt bad for the flight attendants.

"They'll be fine," Pauly said, reassuringly rubbing his arm.

"I know they'll be fine. It's everyone else on the plane. I was surprised that they both wanted to travel to our wedding together."

"I think it's nice."

Ares widened his eyes. "Be prepared for some loudness in your house for the next couple of days."

"I'm definitely prepared for that," Pauly teased. "Between you and Jeremy, I think I can handle my new in-laws."

"You might change your mind about marrying me." He was half teasing.

"Doubtful."

Jeremy came running over. "What do I call your parents, Ari?"

"I don't know, pal. Knowing my mom she might want to be called *yiayia*," Ares replied.

"*Yiayia*," Jeremy repeated slowly. "That means grandma, right?"

Ares nodded. "You got it, pal."

"Cool."

The arrival doors opened and instantly Ares could hear his parents through the din of other people coming off the plane. Pauly was silently laughing behind her hand as Ares walked forward to find his parents waving their arms around and talking very loudly and quickly.

As soon as his mother saw him, she called out his name and wrapped her arms around him, kissing him.

"You're finally getting married. Where's Pauly? I told you she was a good girl!" His mother moved on and saw Pauly and went to hug her and kiss her.

Ares went to his father. He looked a little more frail, but overall he wasn't in too bad of shape for someone who was battling cancer. Ares was just thankful that he was here and able to celebrate his wedding to Pauly.

"You're looking good, son." His father hugged him. "I'm glad you're getting married to the right woman."

"I am too. I'm glad you're here."

"So am I. Now, apparently I have a new grandson?" his father asked.

Ares turned and saw that Jeremy was being accosted by his mother. She had a hold of his cheeks and was kissing him and rubbing Jeremy's red head. "Uh, that's Jeremy."

His father chuckled. “It looks like Yiayia got a hold of him. He does look like Rex.”

“He does, but he’s got a lot of his mother in him too.”

“So do you. So like your mother.” His father clapped him on his back and went over to meet Jeremy. Ares heard his father say, “I’m your *papou*!”

Then his father turned to Pauly and gave her a hug and a kiss on the cheek.

As his parents fussed over Jeremy, Pauly and Ares grabbed their luggage and then they all walked out of the airport toward the parking garage.

“Yiayia and Papou. Grandma and Grandpa, right?” Pauly asked.

Ares nodded. “Yep.”

“Good. I’m going to have to get used to that, especially when our baby starts talking.” She walked ahead and Ares froze, not sure if he heard her correctly, but hoping he did.

“Our what?” he asked.

Pauly turned around and smiled at him. “Our baby. I found out this morning. My doctor called.”

“I thought…blocked fallopian tubes.”

She nodded. “I know. I guess one got through. I made sure that it wasn’t ectopic. I wanted to be certain that everything was okay before I told you, but everything is good and in eight months or so we’re going to have a baby. Now I’ll really have to take a desk job, but only for a short time. I’m not giving up completely.”

“I never expected you would.”

“So,” she asked, her voice filled with a bit of trepidation. “How do you feel about it?”

Ares let go of the luggage and picked her up in his arms, kissing her and laughing. “Are you serious?”

“Very serious.”

Ares kissed her again, slowly, just overcome with complete joy. "I love it. I love you and our new baby. I can't wait."

"What's going on you two?" his mother asked. "Can't you wait until the wedding?"

"Shall we tell them?" Pauly asked.

Ares nodded and set her down, putting his arm around her. "Pauly just told me, she's pregnant. So I guess we couldn't wait for the wedding."

"I'm going to be a big brother?" Jeremy asked. "Awesome." He ran up to hug them.

"A baby?" his mother shrieked. "I'm so happy!"

His father was grinning and then said. "Maria, let's celebrate at a restaurant. I'm starving."

"Yes, let's go have something to eat," Ares agreed.

"Let's go to the bowling alley! They have great pizza," Jeremy stated.

"Maybe some other time," Ares said, laughing. "Take your *yiayia*'s suitcase."

Jeremy nodded and took over the suitcase, rolling it, following behind his new grandparents. Ares slung his arm around Pauly.

"You happy?" she asked.

"Yes. I have everything I've ever wanted."

She cocked an eyebrow. "That's not what you said in college."

"Well, I was a fool then."

"And now?" she teased.

"I'm just a fool for you."

* * * * *

FESTIVE REUNION WITH THE DOCTOR
Deanne Anders

Anna had changed in many ways since the last time he'd seen her.

There was a maturity in her emerald eyes and a confidence in her walk that even in medical school she'd lacked. But one thing hadn't changed. She still had a stubborn streak a mile long.

'Come on in,' he said, giving up. He'd might as well get this over with so that he could get back to his patient.

Walking around to his desk, he motioned her to join him.

'Whose X-ray is this?' Anna asked as she bent over him, her hair brushing against his shoulder, the fragrance hitting him hard.

Memories of their time together poured through him. He remembered the feel of her hair as he'd run his hands through it. He remembered the smell that had lingered on his pillow long after she had left him.

And he remembered the letter she'd left behind, the one that tore him apart until he'd wrapped his mind around the fact that what she'd done, though hurtful, had been the right thing for both of them.

COMING SOON!

We really hope you enjoyed reading this book.
If you're looking for more romance
be sure to head to the shops when
new books are available on

Thursday 20th November

To see which titles are coming soon, please visit

millsandboon.co.uk/nextmonth

MILLS & BOON